All Blogged Up

S. R. Joyce

Strategic Book Publishing and Rights Co.

Strategic Book Publishing and Rights Co.
12620 FM 1960, Suite A4-507
Houston, TX 77065
www.sbpra.com

ISBN: 978-1-61204-908-3

Interior Book Design: Judy Maenle

To all who have helped me in creating this book
and supporting me to bring it to life,
my most sincere thank you.

To Charlie and Keyha

One of the very first
editions of my first book

Steve Joyce.

....

31ˢᵗ December 1998

Kevin woke up well into the latter part of the afternoon. What the hell happened? He'd missed the first half of the last day of the year. He switched his computer on to update his blog. New Years Eve 1998, where to start? Now seemed as good a time as any . . .

> Hi Peeps
> I've only just got up. Yes I am very lazy, yous lot all know this already though. Still I am alert and ready now. Yes, I am happy, it's New Years Eve for God's sake! I've showered and checked my pits, and they smell ok. I've shaved and washed all over and of course my entire not to mention bits.
> Today is a party day, God it's the penultimate New Years Eve, the one before the world blows up. That's what the experts say anyway! I'm going to party tonight. Like its 1999, ha, ha, I really wanted to get that in! Well, I have to get ready, I'm on an all dayer today. If I bump into to any of yous today or tonight, party on dudes! Love and peace to the world, and to me if you meet me! We'll catch each other soon, all of us, when we've seen the year in.

He closed his blog page and opened his private file, the one he didn't post for everyone else to read.

> One hundred and sixty five days, the sack's fuller than it's ever been. Twenty days fuller to be exact. Tonight, all the babes will have their defenses down a bit. You just need to find the right one at the right time. Tonight is your night, I can feel it in my bones. Of course I want to feel it in my loins. Here's wishing me luck. 'Good luck Kevin!'

Today was to be pleasurable and relaxed and Kevin got ready at a leisurely pace. He was meeting Alexis and Jane at seven-thirty in the Red Lion, then going to their party. Alexis was his closest friend and had been since childhood. Her partner of five years, Jane, had become a surrogate best friend since she'd been with Alexis.

Alexis had promised Kevin there would be quite a few single ladies at the party. She had been keeping a calendar on Kevin's lack of female attention. She even told him in front of Jane if he went three hundred and sixty six days, she'd jump him herself. This made Jane's eyebrows rise into a bit of a frown.

They left the pub at twenty to nine, it was usually only a twenty minute walk however they all arrived back to Alexis's and Jane's building at twenty to ten to find all the guests were waiting outside! Alexis sobered up first and apologized.

He had been getting on really well with Jo and he was making her laugh with his jokes. They were both throwing rum punch down their necks and smoking each other's cigarettes and he had sat next to her when Jane served the chili. Like the klutz he was he somehow emptied his plate all over Jo's yellow dress. He tried to wipe it off, making sure he didn't touch her boobs, he didn't think this would go down too well at this early stage of their relationship. He thought he'd rescued the situation, which was until he spread the greasy tomato mixture even further into her dress. She looked down and screamed.

Alexis jumped in and took Jo away, returning ten minutes later with Jo dressed in a pair of jeans and a nice white tee-shirt. Jo walked past Kevin and whispered 'clumsy idiot.' Oh shit he thought to himself, eleven o' clock and his first chance of emptying his sack gone, at least for tonight. He would try to win her over by the end of the night for another attempt in the future, she was hot!

Trying to hedge his bets and have a contingency he then started to flirt with Anne, Anne however wasn't that drunk and realized she was the fall back so was as frosty as the weather. Midnight came and they all went to the street for the Auld Lang Syne rendition. Kevin did manage to hold Anne's hand and they shared a brief kiss.

He couldn't remember much after that. He woke up in the early hours finding himself in bed with a naked Jane and Alexis. He often slept there and they always went to bed naked, Jane often told him they did this to wind him up.

He got up and had a glass of water and a cigarette. He looked at the time, five past six in the morning. He grabbed his clothes and got dressed, leaving Alexis and Jane a note thanking them for the night and that he had gone home to sleep and probably play with himself. They would laugh at that.

As he got undressed for bed he pulled two pieces of paper from his front pocket. One had a telephone number for Jo and one for Anne, perhaps not a completely wasted effort?

03rd January 1999

Even after the whole day and night of the second day of the year in bed, he woke up late again. The shower beckoned so he obeyed and cleaned his bits, you never knew! He met Dave in the Bells at four-thirty. They both left the Bells at nine-fifty, Dave slurring that Joanne would be after his blood with Kevin saying his missus would be after his blood if he had one!

Dave just looked at him giggling like a stupid teenager. He somehow wobbled his way home and got there ten to eleven. Kevin fumbled and opened the door to his apartment; it was work already tomorrow, where had the days gone?

04th January 1999

He managed to get up by twelve and was in the office for a respectable quarter to one. He'd told his assistant Mary he'd been ill during the morning. She'd completed a disciplinary interview, interviewed the potential new Health and Safety Manager, and hadn't even had chance for a pee. As the manager of the department Kevin wanted a full de brief on his arrival.

Mary told him she needed a break. Kevin told her she could have one later, when she had updated him on the morning's activities. Mary screamed at him she would pee herself. He didn't like to pull rank but did advise her to wait until she had finished updating him. He was the boss after all.

Mary updated him in about twenty two seconds and ran, in Kevin's opinion a little too fast for Health and Safety requirements, to the ladies' room. After she had gone he noticed there was a pool of what looked like water under her desk. He would have to have a word with her about being careless with refreshments at the desk. There were separate on site facilities after all.

He was home for five o'clock, ready for the very important task in mind ring Anne and or Jo. He decided to call Anne first. He wasn't going to make the same mistake again and wanted her to know this. He dialed the number, it went straight to the answer phone. Kevin decided to leave a power message. He dialed the other number for Jo, again another bloody answer phone. He left another message. He knew he had sown the seeds, he now needed them to grow. Perhaps some watering was required but that would be later in the week.

Kevin thought about updating his Blogs but cracked open a bottle of red, sinking the lot, then opened another, before eating his food, cheese on toast with Worcestershire Sauce. The wine really complimented this food. He was a master of taste he told himself.

....

08th January 1999

After most of the week, trying to get into work early, today he pulled out all the stops and was in for nine-thirty. He greeted Mary and wished her a good morning and asked her if she'd completed all the objectives he'd set her.

She told him she was on it and by Monday would be there. Great, he had replied, telling her she could join him for a drink after work one night soon, and also told her it would be his treat. He was always good to Mary, it paid to have a good assistant you could trust.

He left at three. He told Mary he had a tribunal to attend, it was a bizarre case and he wanted to see how the panel reacted. It was always good to be right on the pulse he had told her. Kevin actually went home for a power sleep, he was absolutely exhausted. He needed an hour before pursuing Anne and Jo again. He slept from four to five-fifteen and awoke fully alert. Watch out babes he had told himself, the Kevster is on the prowl!

He rang Jo first this time. He thought the change of approach might net better results. 'Hi, is that Jo?' 'Yes, who's that?' 'It's Kevin Julie Jo, we met New Years Eve' 'Hi Kevin, how are you?' 'Not bad, the first week back in work is always a hard task, same for everyone.' 'Yeah, I know what you mean, I'm exhausted already.' 'I'm with you there Jo, God I hate the first week back.' 'Me too Kevin' 'Did you enjoy yourself New Years Eve, apart from me being an idiot and spilling food over you?' 'Yes Kevin, at least now I can see the funny side of it' 'That's good, I was such a klutz, I wouldn't have been surprised if you blanked my calls' 'Don't worry about it, it's all water under the bridge, or chili washed out of the dress' 'Thanks Jo, I appreciate that' 'No problem Kevin' 'Jo, I was wondering if we could meet up, you know, perhaps give me the chance to make things up to you?' 'Ok Kevin, how about Saturday?'

Finishing the call he skipped around the room like an excited teenager, he had a date, she was coming to his place, all he had to do was nail the meal and he had a chance of nailing Jo! As the ever astute lonely male he still wanted to pursue the Anne opportunity so dialed her number. This time he was out of luck, it clicked to answer phone. Kevin left another brief message.

He was happy with his day's work so far. He needed to update his blogs and start thinking about planning for Saturday with Jo. Perhaps his goal was in sight. Just maybe, with a little luck, the glands would finally be released! Panic then set in. He knew what he wanted to cook but didn't know how to bloody well cook it!

Just as he was getting really stressed an idea hit him like bolt of lightning. Mary could work Saturday, get his list of ingredients and he would pay her overtime. Another brainwave hit him. What if he paid Mary to stay all night and secretly cook his food? He was the master of planning he told himself. He smiled at his own cleverness.

He rang Mary at the office. 'Mary, will you work tomorrow?' 'Yeah, I suppose so, if I'm coming in I want eight hours pay mind' 'Ok but I need to meet you for a drink now to go through the task details.' He met her at Gio's, a nice jaunt, at seven. He wanted to impress her, get her into the sprit or more importantly get spirits into her. He needed her at her least argumentative.

After several cocktails Mary protested she needed to go home if she was going to work in the morning. 'Ah,' Kevin said. 'I was really wondering if you could work all day and probably all night tomorrow.' She looked at him with a very funny expression. 'What are you suggesting?'

Kevin looked directly at her, deep into her blue eyes, which he noticed were fluttering. 'Mary, I have a knock out date tomorrow night, but I can't cook!' He explained looking really worried.

'I thought initially you could pick up my shopping list, but then thought a bit more and wondered, sort of thought really and then sort of wanted to know if you would cook the meal for me at my place.'

She looked back at him with fire in her eyes. He quickly added 'I'll pay you for the whole weekend, I don't know who else I can ask. Will you help me Mary?' Kevin added with a desperate look in his eyes. Mary stayed silent for five full long minutes, looking at him and looking up at the ceiling before she eventually blurted out 'Get me another cocktail!' And slumped back in her seat. Following two more drinks Mary eventually agreed but was shaking her head as she did so. Still agreement was agreement, Kevin did wonder if she had a bit of a drink problem though.

He sorted all the receipts out to reclaim from his Company expenses and grabbed Mary supportively to leave the bar. He put her in a taxi and told her to be at his house with the list of ingredients at three o' clock on Saturday afternoon. He got home and warmed his PC up.

> Yo Peeps
> What a week, I can't believe it's already over. Shagged up all my resolutions and will have to tackle them all again next year. Work has been a bitch all week, I haven't stopped. I can't remember a start of year I've worked more hours. Still I've kept my staff in line and managed to ensure they have met my strict objectives. It's a hard task keeping on top of them but I'm sure yous lot all know what I mean. I've got a great weekend planned and am cooking for a lovely lady, Jo. Will let you all know how it went early next week. Remember all, be good to each other, love each other and be cool.

....

09th January 1999

He was a little bit confused. He never set the alarm clock for a Saturday. He always used the weekend to catch up on sleep after his tough Monday to Friday job. The alarm today though seemed to be going on and on, he got up and switched the clock off at the wall. He could still hear it though. He shook his head and then realized it wasn't the alarm but the bloody doorbell. Who on earth was trying to wake him at such an ungodly hour on a Saturday?

He got out of bed and opened the door in his half woken up state, naked apart from his silkiest Y fronts. Mary was stood at the door, her hands full of shopping bags. The realization eventually hit him. 'Sorry Mary, I overslept.' 'Evidently' she said with a grin. 'Nice pants Kevin' Kevin looked down and shrieked.

Mary was already unpacking and bending down when he entered the kitchen. Kevin couldn't help thinking how pert her rear was. If she wasn't so bloody frigid he would have definitely had a go at Mary a long time ago.

'How's it going?' He asked brightly. 'Fine, it will take me about an hour to prep and then I'll set the table.' Kevin was looking directly at her chest, he hadn't noticed how great it was before. She obviously dressed more conservatively in work. Mary already had the steaks out and was taking the packaging off them. 'Great breasts' Kevin said brightly. 'I'm sorry Kevin!' Mary said a little loudly.

'Oh God, sorry Mary, I meant great steaks, I didn't mean to offend you, not that I don't think you do have great boobs of course but I was talking about the steaks, I don't want you to think I was making a play, not that you don't warrant a play for you, I mean you are really pretty and a great ass, God Mary, I didn't mean to say that either, I mean your ass is great but I didn't mean to say that.' Kevin spluttered out in rapid fire.

She just looked at him, 'Kevin, you are a dick sometimes, just leave it there and shut up.' She said smiling. He managed through a red face to tell her he was going for a shower, handing her a chilled bottle of white. He needed some horny time, if he pulled Jo he couldn't afford to be two pumps and a squirt, especially after letching over Mary!

Checking his watch, it was seven o' clock, an hour to go before Jo arrived. He asked Mary if she was on target. She told him not to worry, everything was under control. Kevin topped them both up with the chilled Chablis and opened another bottle.

At ten to eight he put a fresh bottle of white in the cooler on the table and opened another bottle in the kitchen for Mary to sip whilst she cooked and topped both of them up again. His door bell went at five past eight. Jo had arrived and looked good enough to eat. 'Hi' he said welcoming her in. 'Hi Kevin, wow something smells good.' 'Yes, that's me' Kevin replied with a wink. Jo smiled.

He asked her to sit and poured her a glass of the cold Chablis. 'Your meal is a surprise Jo' he said with an air of confidence, 'I've got everything under control. I just need five to check the starters, have a look at the selection if you want to change the music.'

He went back in to the kitchen. Mary greeted him by asking if she could have a fresh bottle of the Chablis. Kevin opened another cold one and filled her glass. 'Can I take the appetizers?' He asked eagerly. 'Yes, all ready.' Mary replied and showed him two great looking plates on the warm oven hob. 'Careful, the plates are hot.' She told him.

They chinked glasses and Kevin asked Jo to eat. Jo was giving him come on eyes, somehow he was pulling this off. By the time the main course came they might not even make dessert! They finished the beautiful starter in ten minutes, Jo moved closer to Kevin and kissed him on the cheek, 'that was really nice Kevin, I really am impressed.' 'Wait until you taste my meat babe' Kevin said with a huge wink. Jo giggled and winked back saying 'Can't wait Kevin!'

Kevin swaggered back to the kitchen carrying their plates and winking at Jo as he entered the kitchen. Mary looked at him with tears in her eyes, 'I'm sorry Kevin I've only bloody ruined the sauce.' 'How?' He asked sounding really worried. 'I'm drunk Kevin, I've been sick and it went in the red wine sauce.' Mary sobbed pointing at the lumpy effort.

'Let me see,' he said looking at the sauce. 'You can't see it, it's mixed up with the carrot and leek, but I know it's in there.' Mary sobbed further. Kevin was horrified, he couldn't think what to do then asked 'is everything else perfect Mary?' 'Yes' she replied still upset. 'Sieve it Mary, we won't know the difference, sieve it and serve it, I'll be back in five to collect the plates.' As he returned for the plates Mary told him she was desperate for a pee. He told her she needed to hold it, just for a bit longer. He thanked her and took the food into an expectant looking Jo.

He put the plates down gently and poured them each a glass of red he'd opened in the last hour. Jo started to eat and was commenting on how good the food was. She said the sauce was wonderful. Kevin had scraped his from his steak. Jo giggled 'I was sucking the juices off your meat Kevin and it tastes wonderful.' Kevin felt himself rise out of control in his pants.

Jo moved close to him and kissed him really passionately this time, tongue as well! 'I want you Kevin, but I need some dessert first' she said looking deeply into his eyes. 'Let me get the dessert then' he said running back to the kitchen.

He opened and closed the door quickly and asked Mary if the dessert was ready. 'Yes' she said jumping up and down. 'What's the matter?' He asked a little bit frustratingly. 'I'm dying for a pee' she replied quite aggressively. 'Mary, here's a mixing bowl, try and hold it in until I get Jo into bed or pee in that if you can't wait.'

He grabbed the perfect Crème Brule's and went back to Jo. He presented her with the dessert. She was all eyes for him, he had cracked it, and he was going to have his brains shagged out.

They finished the desserts in less than two minutes and embraced each other. Jo said in a sexy voice 'I want your real meat now Kevin' Inside two minutes he had her top and bra off and was having his own dessert. He took her jeans off and she had him completely naked making efforts to keep her promise to him when there was an almighty crash. As he turned to look horror had struck. Mary had fallen through the kitchen door with her pants around her ankles trying to pull them up in mid fall, with a mixing bowl by her side leaking liquid all over the floor.

As he gasped Jo pulled away from him, quickly got dressed and shouted 'What the hell do you think I was up for Kevin? I don't do threesomes you pervert!' Before he had chance to catch his breath or try to explain she had left. He stood up aghast and then and saw Mary knelt in front of him. She looked at him and slurred 'You've got a hard on Kevin' and fell back over.

....
10th January 1999

Kevin woke up about eleven o clock. Walking into the bathroom in his naked state with his morning rise pointing upwards, there was a little bit of an issue. In the bathroom was an equally naked and very non hairy, good looking Mary. Kevin looked at her smooth shaven bits. He saw her look at his boner. There was a moment of stalemate before he retreated to his bedroom. After he did have his shower Kevin went into the kitchen and found a note.

> Dear Kevin
> I had to go, I'm sure we are both really embarrassed about this morning. I hate to say I can't remember last night either. Please can I ask you that you don't mention this weekend again, especially in work. Have a nice rest of the weekend. See you Monday.
> Mary

Kevin reread the note. He could bloody well remember this morning and the fiasco last night. She'd cocked it up for him. He had had Jo in the bag or sack if it hadn't been for Mary. What was she on about, not to mention it? He'd bloody well paid her overtime!

He turned his computer on feeling frustrated and decided to update his blog in a sober state. He didn't trust himself to write to the Peeps after a few beers following last night's disaster.

> My Peeps, friends and acquaintances
> Last night was a blast. I cooked the most spectacular meal. God the night was going good, yous lot knows, Kevster good. The young lady I had for dinner was so impressed. The Kevster was in the groove. By the time we got to dessert though all yous Dudes and Dudesses we almost had to skip it for bed. I was the man last night Peeps, everything under super Kevster control.
> There was a bit of a commotion, I won't go into the details Peeps but the beautiful lady that started the night didn't end up being the one I met naked in the bathroom this morning! Catch that guys and gals! Well somehow I've got to decipher the real meaning of that and the rest of the day is set entirely for that purpose. Jus remember all yous lot, now yous can add great cook to my repertoire if you ever want to join me for top nosh.

Kevin was pleased with his blog entry. He added his personal update immediately.

Dear Kevin

Well you completely balls'd that up didn't you? Jo was putty in your hands and you still cocked it up. One note to mention and store though is that Mary's cute and grooms downstairs, a sign of a less frigid person. She'd also seen the boner! Well we're at day one hundred and seventy four now Dude. How, with all the naked bodies is that? Still, right hand strong and work tomorrow. I don't think we can consider Jo for a week or two, she'll need some time. We need to go after Anne in the next two weeks or look at other opportunities, Mary maybe? Good luck Kevin.

....

11th January 1999

As he walked into the office he saw Mary working hard at her desk station. 'Hi Mary, would you like a coffee?' 'Yes please, that would be lovely, thank you Kevin.' Returning ten minutes later with a coffee for Mary and a tea for him, he spluttered out 'Nice weekend?' Mary stared at him. Shit he thought I am the world's biggest klutz!

After a few agonizing hours Kevin eventually told her to finish up at ten to three. He was taking her to Gio's. Mary scowled and followed him out of the building at three o' clock. Mary spoke first. 'Kevin, we're not going to go through all the details of the weekend are we?' 'No Mary, we going to get smashed, what happened Saturday happened and I want us still to be real good friends and colleagues?'

Mary's mother Suzanne arrived later to pick Mary up. She took all of two seconds to look at Kevin and say 'Nice. I'll be having a bit of you big boy and soon'. Kevin nearly choked. Suzanne was hot, now he knew where Mary got her looks from. Before he could make any kind of a fool of himself Suzanne had whisked Mary away.

....

14th January 1999

After working from home the past two days with a cricked neck he strolled into the office around five to twelve. Kevin had a scarf on telling Mary it helped with the pain. She jumped up and fussed all over him and rushed to make him coffee.

The next hour he spent on the net. He needed to learn to cook something as he was on the Anne chase from tonight and couldn't try the Mary trick again, even though it had so bloody well nearly worked. 'Shit, shit and more shit' he shouted out to the wall. Jo was there for the taking, his bloody sack was going to explode!

He found the recipe he was going to try. He left work, threw the scarf into the bin in the car park and headed to the supermarket. He was making prawns on a bed of lettuce with sweet chili and tomato sauce. Arriving, he went straight to the fish counter. There was a young girl behind the counter, quite cute actually. Her name badge said Mel. Behind the counter was a sign saying the fishmongers were all highly trained and customers could draw on their expertise if they wanted to know how to cook fish.

This was like Christmas for Kevin. 'Hi Mel, I'm Kevin, I'm a bit of a novice cooking and am trying out a new starter, and I've got a lady coming' he said in a whisper and with a wink. 'Ok' Mel said, 'What are you going to cook?' 'Well Mel, I was thinking prawns for the starter with a sweet chili and tomato sauce, sounds cool doesn't it?' Kevin said looking smug.

Mel looked at him and said 'I thought you said you couldn't cook.' 'Ah, that's where your expertise comes in my pretty little fish filleter. I was hoping you'd tell me how?' She looked at his droopy silly eyes, giggled loudly and said with a double wink. 'Yes, I'll tell you how. I would suggest you buy the chili jam we do though, far easier than trying to make your own sauce, no matter how tasty it is.' Kevin smiled and said 'Hit me with it then babe.' He left the shop with raw king prawns, some shop bought chili jam and a phone number for Mel, a really successful grocery trip.

He cracked open a beer and hit the shower. When he was presentable for the world he got his notes from Mel and set about cooking. Firstly he tore the lettuce and put it onto the plate. Then he opened the chili jam and arranged some like a chef would (so Mel had told him anyway) on the side, with a little swirl.

Next he shredded some lemon zest and grated some garlic. He oiled the hot frying pan and mixed the prawns with the lemon and garlic. He hit the pan with them. They sizzled, just like Mel said they would. He then stirred them frantically for three minutes and removed them from the heat, just like Mel had told him.

Next he added the gorgeous smelling prawns onto the top of the lettuce and took the plate to his table. He opened his bottle of Chablis, sipped it and picked up his knife and fork. The food looked like restaurant quality, he was pleased with himself. Mel was a real good chick, one he would add to the list of possibilities. Kevin tasted the lettuce with the chili jam and smiled inwardly.

He cut into his first prawn, it looked delicious. He put it into his mouth, tasted the divine flavor and then nearly choked. The bloody things had bones in them or something; there were hard things like finger nails in his mouth, he was nearly sick. Mel was in big trouble! He would be going to see her tomorrow . . .

....

15th January 1999

He had promised to be more supportive with Mary so arrived at work early at eight-fifteen. She was already in and busy as normal, Kevin was finding himself looking at her rear and imagining her shaven bits. He had to stop this. His boner was evident, even through his work pants.

Finishing at three he went straight to the grocery store, Mel was on the fish counter. She greeted him smiling. 'Hi Kevin, how'd it go, with the prawns?' 'Well my darling, that's why I'm here. You didn't tell me the things had bloody bones in them, I nearly choked.'

Mel looked at him strangely 'Kevin, what are you talking about, prawns don't have bones.' 'These bloody ones did Mel, they were like finger nails' 'Kevin you fool, you didn't peel them did you?' Mel said now struggling to hold her laughter. 'What do you mean peel them, I cooked them as you said and ate them.' He said defensively.

'They've got shells you fool, you cook them in their shells and take the shell off to eat them. The shells are for presentation.' Mel said still giggling. 'That wasn't on your instructions' he said now feeling really foolish. 'Oh Kevin, what are you doing later?' 'Nothing, why?' Mel handed him a piece of paper saying, 'I'll see you later' rushing off to serve the waiting customers. He read the note, it had an address on it and a time, seven-thirty, with a little x. Kevin left the shop happy, he had somehow managed to bag himself a date!

Rushing home he did the Kevin version of a makeover; he called it the crack, back and cock wash. He made sure he had relieved himself, just in case, he didn't want to be wham, bang, thank you mam and all over in seconds, if he had the opportunity. He also shaved and put his coolest clothes on. He was ready for seven so ordered a taxi immediately.

He arrived at the address Mel had written on the note at twenty-past seven. Mel ushered him in. She already had a bottle of white wine on the table and glasses ready. Kevin sat and she poured them both a large glass each.

'Right then, come to the kitchen with me.' Mel told him whilst leading him by the hand. 'This is a raw prawn, this is its shell, watch how I cook it and then watch how to eat it.' Mel said looking at him really seductively.

Mel marinated the prawn in lemon, garlic and a few chopped chilies'. She heated her pan and then oiled it, she dropped the single whole prawn into the pan and they both watched it sizzle. Mel stir fried it and took it off the heat. She let it rest, staring deeply into his eyes. Kevin was already out of control. His boner wouldn't go down, no matter what he thought about. Mel seemed to notice and smiled brightly at him.

After five minutes Mel took the rested prawn and ripped its head off, she then carefully peeled the shell off and hand fed Kevin half of the moist pink prawn. He was losing all will. He was so hard he nearly fell over. He ate the moist, hot, fragrant prawn and saw Mel eat the other half. 'How was that?' She said looking right at the bulge in his pants. 'Mesmerizing' was all he could respond.

Mel looked directly into his eyes and said softly. 'Kevin, I'm going to get you in the sack tonight, but we eat first, is that ok with you?' Kevin managed to blubber some kind of a yes response.

She took him to the kitchen after this and showed him how to make a red wine sauce, potato rosti's and a medium rare fillet steak. Listening to her talk he didn't want to eat anything but her. Still, he was learning new skills. They sat at the table at eight-fifty with the main course. Mel insisted they fed each other. This was driving Kevin wild with sexual tension.

Mel went to finish the dessert off when the doorbell went. 'Can you get that Kevin?' 'No probs.' Kevin went to the door and opened it. In front of him was a rather large man. 'Who the hell are you?' The man said aggressively, 'I'm Kevin, who are you?' He replied. 'I'm Andy, what are you doing in my apartment?' The guy said even more angrily.

He left Mel's after Andy had been pacified that he was a colleague who Mel was teaching to cook cursing his luck. He got home and sorted out his uncontrollable rise before feeling really ill.

....

20th January 1999

Kevin had had four days in bed, struck down by flu. Today he felt better. Mary had told him to stay off so he didn't spread germs into work. He decided to phone Alexis, Jane answered. 'Hi Jane, its Kevin, any chance I can come round to you guys tonight, I've had a bad couple of days with this flu.' He grabbed an overnight bag. Jane arrived in fifteen minutes and drove them back to her and Alexis's place.

Jane looked at him and told him to lie on his front on the floor, on the rug. Kevin looked at her funnily and said 'Why?' 'I'm going to give you a massage Kevin.' He did as he was told. Jane disappeared and returned with some oil. She then straddled Kevin and pulled his tee-shirt off. She poured some oil onto his back, it was freezing but also relieving. She massaged his back for well over half an hour, it really was helping.

She told him she was doing his legs next and pulled his jeans down. Jane greased his legs and massaged them. Kevin could feel all his aches and pain disappearing. Jane then put her hand inside his pants and felt his boner. 'Sorry' she said 'I just wanted to check if I made you rise like Alexis does.' Kevin sighed, 'Jane you both do, how many times do I have to tell you?' 'Just checking babe, if you get to three hundred and sixty six days I might just beat Alexis to trying a man!'

They cooked him Lasagna served with salad followed by ice cream, and got him totally smashed. They all went to bed at about two o' clock in the morning all naked as normal. Kevin was however being checked over by both girls throughout the night, both were checking if he had a boner, no shocks there, he always had a boner in their bed. Alexis wrapped her legs around Kevin and he fell asleep happy, she was like his security blanket.

....

23ʳᵈ January 1999

Saturday arrived and Kevin decided he was going to start to learn to cook properly. After showering he left for the grocery store, though he wasn't going to his local one today. He went to one further away and bought everything fresh. He was definitely turning over a new leaf.

He ate the steak meal, sipped his wine and burst into song. 'I'm going to get laid I'm afraid, I'm going to get laid, when I cook for Anne . . .' This was followed by a dance around the apartment he would never tell anyone else about. It was time to speak to his Peeps.

> Yo Dudes and Dudesses
> Sorry for the lack of news the last few days, flu I'm afraid and yes man flu at that. On the cooking front Peeps I have continued in a big way. Just watch the TV for a new chef superstar.
>
> Not much other news really, it's been a tough couple of days. One note is I've had some luck with a couple of ladies and my new skills will be tested fully in the next couple of weeks. Hope yous lot are on top form too. Crack open an egg.

....

25ᵗʰ January 1999

The flu still hadn't gone, that's what he told Mary. He told her he'd work from home as he had done Friday. At least for a couple of hours anyway. He thought about a planning a party for New Years Eve and also came up with a training plan for the company, something that just hit him as he was perusing the Net. Following all this effort he decided to try the Anne trail again.

As it happened Anne was unable to talk, she was at the vets with her cat Edge. He liked the cat thing, he'd always liked cats. Perhaps he would eventually get one, he'd been thinking about it for some time now. The fact the time had been ten years didn't worry him in the slightest.

Anne rang him back at seven and apologized for taking so long, she'd got Edge home and then sorted Flick and Ripple out, her other cats. Kevin went straight for it and asked Anne to come for dinner, he told her he'd been practicing especially so he could cook something nice. They arranged for her to come to his place on Friday at seven o'clock.

He updated his personal blog.

> Yo Kevster
> Buy a cat! It's got to be a sure thing if you have a cat. Too many days now and the sack's filling up at a scale you will never be able to empty. Two hundred days isn't a mile away, buy a cat and you'll be in there. Good hunting Dude.

27th January 1999

He was at the cat centre before nine. It was really cold, Jack Frost had done his stuff. The gardens looked really pretty. At ten to ten a young man approached. 'Hello I'm Ed, you look freezing' 'Yes, bloody freezing' Kevin replied, thinking internally that Ed could win competitions for being so astute!

He walked up and down with Ed for over an hour, he couldn't really choose. He asked how people did choose. 'Different ways really Kevin, but you have to be sure, these little guys and girls need a home for ever, not just for a couple of weeks.' Kevin nodded.

Another hour later he had picked his cat, she had climbed the cage and licked his hand. This was the one, she obviously connected with Kevin. The little cat was between one and two years old and as black as soot. Kevin immediately picked out the name Snowy. Ed agreed it was cute. With the added fees for all the injections, cat box, bed, litter tray and all the food he left Ed two hundred pounds lighter. Still he had the cat. The cat to catch the pussy he laughed to himself.

He got Snowy home and set her free. This was a longer exercise than planned. She wouldn't come out of the cat carrier. The more he tried the more she refused. After twenty fruitless minutes he left her in the box, in the middle of the room. He set her litter tray up, her food and water bowls, filling them both and opened her toys and put them in close proximity.

It was now two in the afternoon, he decided he'd pop out for a beer, buy some ingredients to practice his meal and let Snowy have some personal time to adapt to her new home. He got back at nine-twenty after picking up a takeaway. He opened the door quietly, hoping Snowy would be there waiting for him. No luck, just a dark silence. He went the kitchen, tipped his food onto his plate and went into the lounge. He turned the light on.

He nearly dropped his plate. His cushions were all over the floor and his sofa was scratched to pieces. The curtains had been climbed and had some new design pattern into the raw silk finish. The cat litter tray was empty but a turd and a pool sat nicely beside it. All the cat food had gone and Snowy was sleeping in the cat carrier!

He sat at the table and started sipping his wine talking all the time to Snowy. After two bottles of Chablis, twenty cigarettes and talking himself hoarse he gave up. The stupid animal wasn't coming out of the carrier. Kevin told her she was being stubborn as he staggered to bed.

....

29th January 1999

He'd spent the whole of yesterday training Snowy, making slow progress. As he woke, Kevin got up and looked at Snowy's soft cozy bed, it had two dumps in it, she'd had three if you counted the one now stuck between his toes. He looked at her as she purred at him from his bed. Hopping to the bathroom he ran his foot under the tap.

He sat on the sofa and called her. Snowy jumped straight onto his lap. Kevin told her in a sermon lasting twenty five minutes about the new house rules. Snowy purred and bit his finger, he was sure she hadn't meant to draw blood.

He told her he was off out, he needed supplies and was going to practice his meal again tonight. He got back about three o' clock. He had seven bags in his hands as he opened the door to go in. Snowy was waiting for him and made him drop the shopping down so she could be picked up for a cuddle. He was winning the battle. Man versus cat and man winning hands down!

He unpacked the shopping, filled her food bowl and changed her water. She was straight at her food, this cat could sure eat! He walked into the bedroom tentatively. He checked her litter box, one large dump and evidence of a pee or two, an absolute resounding success! He changed the litter, moving the box a foot to the right of its original position.

Next was his dress rehearsal on the food for tomorrow night. Even if he said it himself it was top nosh. He sat at his computer with Snowy on his lap and started to update his blog.

> My beautiful Peeps
>
> Sorry I have been a bit elusive for the last few days. I'm fully on the road to recovery now. Had an addition to the clan, a little black cat, she's gorgeous with a capital G. She took a few days to settle but I've got her number now, perhaps I should change careers and be to cats what Barbara Woodhouse was to dogs!
>
> I'm also becoming the new Keith Floyd as the days go by, my hot date tomorrow won't know what's hit her, it will be as good as any of the top restaurants. I guess you know that means I'm in for lazy weekend after the meal tomorrow, know what I mean?

....

30ᵗʰ January 1999

Today was the day, he was sure of it. Getting to his bedside table to grab his pants he felt yet another warm sensation on his foot followed by gooey stuff squelching through his toes. Snowy was purring on the bed. Kevin gave her a stern talking to for fifteen minutes. He told her the cat box had a new home and she had to use it. As a safety measure he put newspaper down in front of his bedside cabinet.

At twenty to eight his door bell went, Anne had arrived early! He was about to offer her a wine when Anne said 'Where is she then Kevin?' 'Who' he replied a little confused, thinking she might have spoken to Jo. 'Snowy, where's Snowy, I can't wait to meet her.'

Anne spent the next ten minutes talking to the cat. Kevin handed her a glass of wine and returned to the kitchen to check the food. She'd arrived early to see the cat! The new best friends were still in deep conversation in-between purrs, meows and coos. Kevin tried to join in but Anne said 'Not now Kevin we're still bonding.'

He sat there until nine o clock and then asked 'Shall I put the food on now Anne?' 'Not yet thanks.' She replied talking some language to the cat Kevin didn't understand. 'Ok, would you like another drink Anne?' 'Yes please Kevin.'

At ten o' clock he was now extremely pissed. Anne was still talking Cat and Snowy seemed to understand her every word. 'Anne, I've just got to pop out for some cigarettes, is that ok with you? I shouldn't be too long.' 'Fine Kevin, can you top my glass up before you go please?'

He went straight to the pub and ordered a pint of cider. He sat at the bar talking to Sam, he bought Sam a pint of bitter and had another cider. Along with everyone else he got kicked out of the pub at eleven-thirty. He grabbed a sausage in batter on the way home and got back at ten to twelve. He walked in and looked down at the cat box, a damp patch and two turds!

Anne said she really should be making tracks. 'Oh, one thing I forgot to tell you Kevin, I taught Snowy how to use her cat box for you.' 'Thanks Anne, that's great, I'll ring the taxi for you now.' 'Oh you're such a sweetie.' Anne replied smiling and kissed him hard. 'Next time I might stay the night.'

....

31st January 1999

He was up early and rang Alexis and told her all about his failure with Anne. She sympathized as a good friend should. Kevin then told her about his dilemma. He had prepared food which would have to be eaten by tonight. He could freeze some of the steak but asked if she and Jane wanted food at his tonight. Jane was out with her friends but Alexis said she would come over and was looking forward to sampling his new skills.

He had all the food prepared. All he had left to do was cut the fillet in to steaks. He cut two huge ones, cut off all the sinew and made some steak nuggets as he called them to boil for Snowy. Snowy thought she had the cream when he gave her an additional dish and repaid him by crapping in her box.

Alexis turned up at quarter to five and asked what he was cooking and if she could have a peek. He told her to keep her sweet rear out of it and would serve by six, giving her a bottle of Chablis.

They had a cigarette and Alexis asked him how he had felt about last night with Anne. 'Truth told babe, really frustrated, that was until she left, snogged me and said she may stay next time. What the hell was that all about?' He replied like the confused male he felt like. 'Don't worry babe, she wants you, she was just setting a scene, a scene she will return to.' Alexis said in an all knowing voice. Kevin looked at her and said 'You women are something. I'll live to two hundred and never get it.'

He served the food and they ate without talking. Kevin looked at her and his empty plates and said 'And . . . ?' Alexis said calmly 'I'd marry you for that.' 'You liked it then, really?' He gasped. 'Kev, that was just gorgeous.'

As they stripped for bed Alexis said 'You know I promised I'd shag you if you went over a year?' 'Yes' Kevin replied. 'Well I meant it babe, I just wanted you to know.' She said getting into his bed. Kevin got in and kissed her as normal but she grabbed him back and kissed him passionately. She then added quickly that she wanted to give him a blow job as long as he reciprocated. Kevin somehow found his voice. 'Great idea babe, are you going first or second?'

....

01st February 1999

He'd told Mary he was working from home for the next couple of days and did spend some of the day on his training plan before firing the blog page up.

> Hi Peeps
> The Kevster has had a roller coaster of a ride the last few days. To say it's been a chore is a huge understatement. I've bought a cat, been outwitted by the cat, and out dated by the cat but love the stupid thing to bits. How the hell did that happen?
> I had such great weekend planned, it almost went to Kevster's expectations but not quite, as you guys and gals know I roll with the punches and did this to great effect this weekend. It's been entertaining to say the least and I've learned some good lessons. Hope yous lot did too. Peace, love and harmony to the world.

04th February 1999

Kevin had really spent some time on his training plan the last few days and was in for eight o'clock this morning. He went through his training proposal with Mary. She was gob smacked. 'You think all the days I was late I never worked?' He said to her looking a bit hurt. 'Kevin, well of course not.' Mary managed to splutter but looking embarrassed.

Getting home at five, he rang Alexis first, she answered immediately. 'You ok honey?' 'Great, can I come round on Saturday night?' 'Of course Babe, we'd love to have you. 'Can I cook for both of you, my treat?' 'Babe, you need to ask?' He showered and changed and grabbed a beer and set about writing his menu for dinner with Alexis and Jane. Three beers later he had it sussed.

He was really quite pleased with his recipe and would try it out tomorrow. He wanted to impress them both with his new talent for cooking. Five beers in he was ready for updating his blog, it had been a few days, and his flock would be missing him.

> Yo my special Peepsters
> Sorry for the delay in saying hello, a mad, mad few days. Not got loads to update yous all on really apart from a busy schedule. I'm still on the cooking trail and also deep into a big project in work. My cat's been a great addition to the household and makes the place feel more like home. Wish me luck as I wish all yous lot luck in everything yous do.

He switched the file an updated his personal blog

> One hundred and pigging ninety five days dude. When are you going to sort it out? You're walking around like John Wayne after he's got off his horse. Anne is a possibility in a few weeks, Mary is looking hot but it's not quite happening. Alexis and Jane, Dude keep that thought away, the blow job was a one off. Why not give Jo another call, see if she'll forgive the last debacle? That's a good idea Bro, speak to Alexis and Jane about it on Saturday, perhaps they can put in a good word.

05ᵗʰ February 1999

Today was a big day in work. He had a review with the MD. His proposal had been reviewed by the Board and he had a feedback meeting at ten o' clock. He was expecting rejection but at least it showed his worth in his current position.

Kevin went up to the MD's office at ten to ten, at least the day would be shorter with this meeting. Two and a half hours later he returned to the office and looked directly into Mary's eyes. 'He bought it, lock stock and two smoking big ones!' Mary ran at him and hugged him. 'Well done Kevin, well done.'

He looked at her 'That's the good news' he said and left it lie. 'What's the bad news Kevin, what, tell me' Mary said in a high pitched voice. 'Well the bad news my sweet is we have to go to Germany next week, we've got to present it to the European Board and provide an implementation plan!'

Getting home not quite believing how today had gone he set about preparing his food for his trial run. Snowy had been fed and was keeping the bed warm. After showering he set about cooking his dish. By eight he'd nailed the scallops. Perfect. He brought the lamb and sauce together by nine, it was on the money. He didn't practice the dessert, this was an M & S cheat. He was happy. He needed an early night.

06ᵗʰ February 1999

Jumping and screaming at the same time, he checked the clock again and screamed even more loudly. 'Snowy, you cow, why didn't you wake me up earlier?' He had a shower, quickly sorted Snowy out and raced to the shops.

He changed Snowy's food, water and cat box and got ready to leave. He opened a bottle of Chablis and ordered the taxi. The taxi came bang on time at seven o' clock. He kissed Snowy goodbye telling her he'd see her in the morning. He left her an extra bowl of food and water.

He carried his box up to Alexis's and Jane's apartment. He rang the bell. Jane answered and Kevin nearly choked. Jane had the shortest skirt on that he'd ever seen. She smiled brightly at him. 'Come in darling, God I'm looking forward to you cooking, you're a right little surprise lately.' Jane said enthusiastically but giving him a funny wink.

The phone went at ten to eight, Jane answered. 'Uh hum, no, is she ok? Are you sure Alexis? Do you want me to come over? Well say hello for me. That was Alexis Kevin, she's popped round to her aunt's, and she's not very well. Just you and me babe, we'll have to eat for three.' 'Yup, you and me babe, I'm going to blow your socks off.'

He served the scallops at quarter to nine. Jane ate and stayed silent. When she finished she looked at him with serious eyes. 'Kevin, that was lovely, they say the way to a man's heart is through his stomach. I think it must be the same for women.'

They sank two bottles of red before Kevin served the main meal. She finished her plate and said 'Kevin, I've just come, I want to suck your dick, and I don't want any silly rejection. You won't be shagging me but I want your dick, I really need a dick, I really need to know.'

Kevin looked at her and managed 'Before dessert?' 'Of course before dessert Kevin, drop your pants!' He dropped his pants as instructed with a shocked look on his face.

....

07ᵗʰ February 1999

As he arrived home Snowy was around his feet meowing loudly. Taking the hint he fed her, changed her water and changed the smelly cat box, at least she was pooing and peeing in the thing now.

He spent the rest of the day getting ready for his trip to Germany. His mate Steve was coming around to look after Snowy. Kevin had apologized for not catching up with him before asking for a favor. Steve was as accommodating as ever and they said they'd catch up for a beer on the Friday night. He'd already agreed to cook a meal with Alexis and Jane on the Saturday and Alexis said she was bringing a mystery guest.

He went to bed at nine after getting everything ready. He needed to be up at two-fifteen in the morning, in his opinion an ungodly time of the night; who in their right mind had decided that time was morning? Kevin wished he knew so he could curse the bastard!

08th February 1999

They arrived in Berlin at nine-thirty local time and were met in arrivals by a company representative holding a sign up saying Julie Nevins. Mary laughed out loud.

The driver took them to the company building. They were there by ten-thirty. The day mainly consisted of meetings and greetings, the presentations would be on Tuesday. The same driver collected them and dropped them off at the Company apartment. He gave them school boy looks as he carried the bags up and said in broken English, 'Are the bags for the same bedroom sir?' Kevin scowled at him and asked him to leave the bags in the dining area.

Kevin playing the gentleman asked Mary which room she wanted. Mary looked at him and picked the largest bedroom, the one with the en-suite. He took his stuff to his bedroom and was happy enough. He unpacked and then shouted to Mary that they should get ready, have an early dinner and spend the rest of the night checking their presentation.

09th February 1999

Kevin woke and walked naked to the bathroom. His normal morning rise was activated and he thought he'd use it in the shower. As he walked into the bathroom he was greeted by an equally naked Mary. 'Shit Mary, I didn't expect to see you in there, you've got an en-suite.' Kevin gasped at her. 'Kevin, I'm sorry, I wanted a bath so got up early.' Mary responded with bright red cheeks.

Whilst making tea all his thoughts were on Mary, huge horny thoughts at that. He bloody well needed to control this he told himself off sternly. He showered then joined Mary for a working breakfast. Between them they'd nailed the presentation Kevin was somehow confident. Mary had been a rock.

The driver dropped them at the office at just before nine o' clock, the traffic had been dreadful. Daniellie was first to arrive, he saw Kevin and asked him if he was ready. Kevin nodded and said that he was all prepared. The rest of the Board arrived, six members, seven including Daniellie. Kevin started bang on time.

The question session only lasted forty minutes. Daniellie asked that Kevin and Mary retire for lunch and rejoin them at four o' clock. They both went to the cafeteria and had a sandwich and coke which they finished by two.

What seemed like five hours later they were both stood back in front of the Board, Kevin feeling a little sick with nerves. Daniellie stood up and looked at both of them with a very serious face. 'Kevin, Mary, that was very enlightening, myself and the rest of the Board wish to back your proposal.' He said now smiling broadly.

They had a quick bite to eat and prepared to deliver the presentation a little differently to the managers and staff tomorrow. They both retired absolutely spent, Kevin did however manage a quick bit of horny time fantasizing about Mary.

....
10th February 1999

Kevin walked into the bathroom. Bloody Mary was in there again naked, drying herself. 'Sorry Kevin' he heard her say as he retreated to his bedroom with another boner.

He walked into the kitchen. Mary was now fully clothed, 'Sorry Kevin, I wanted a bath again. I thought as we'd gone to bed so late you wouldn't be up so early.' She said looking really embarrassed. 'Don't worry Mary we had a really late night. It's been really tough.' He said, thinking she had nothing to be embarrassed about, from what he saw she had things to shout about!

They spent the day convincing the managers of their proposal. Following lunch and the completion of the question and answer session the management team endorsed the proposal, agreeing with the Board without exception.

The rest of the sessions with the staff were completed, in Kevin's opinion, successfully. They received unanimous support and by five o'clock had wrapped up the presentations. They changed and went to the restaurant recommended by Daniellie.

Kevin and Mary arrived in Franco's, apparently the top city restaurant and Kevin told the Matradee who they were. 'Ah, guests of Daniellie, you have the pick of the house Sir and Madam.' Kevin looked at the menu as they were sat at their table and saw a few choices of starter, mains and deserts.

The Head chef, Carlos Perez actually arrived at their table and introduced himself. 'Kevin and Mary, welcome to my restaurant, I have picked out my favorites and will cook your choices personally.' He said with a bow.

Kevin said he was choosing the Chicken, Turbot and Peaches. Mary decided on the White Truffle Salad, the Turbot and the Chocolate Fondant. They swapped parts of their starters by fork feeding each other.

The rest of the meal was just as exquisite and Kevin called their driver who arrived fifteen minutes later. As they got into the apartment Mary kissed Kevin and said very seriously 'I want you Kevin Julie, I want all of you and I want it now!'

Their kisses intensified and they were ripping each other's clothes off. They didn't mess around and explored each part of each other's bodies. Mary said to Kevin, 'Take me to the bedroom, I want you Kevin.' Kevin spluttered back 'I need to go to my room Mary, you know, to get, well you know. I'll be two minutes.'

Could he find the bloody condoms, could he hell as like, and cursed loudly to no-one. He emptied his bags all over the room and after ten minutes found the packet. He rushed back to Mary's room with the boner of all boners!

'I've got them' he shouted as he barged into the room. Mary was lying on the bed, completely naked and snoring like a pig. He covered her over with the duvet and went back to his own bedroom.

....

12th February 1999

Kevin woke at about eleven. He dressed in a pair of joggers and a tee-shirt walked into the kitchen area. Mary was cooking bacon on the hob. They ate breakfast and then decided on the bath and shower schedule. Their flight was at two-thirty and they needed to be at the airport at one-thirty. They were being picked up at quarter to one by their driver.

They left the apartment bang on time and were in the airport in time for their check in. As a bonus they had been upgraded to Business Class, a note from Daniellie handed to Kevin by the check-in Clerk. Kevin got home at just before quarter to five.

Snowy ran to him as he entered and jumped into his arms for a cuddle. At least this pussy wanted him he thought to himself!

He reflected on the night that could have been with Mary and decided the trip had been a success on the work front and not a total disaster with Mary. What she didn't remember wouldn't embarrass her on Monday. He cuddled up to Snowy and told her he needed half an hour to update his blogs and he'd be all hers for nice warm sleep. She meowed back at him.

The Kevster's back Peeps

Kevin Julie has just developed. Yous maybe asking what's he rattling on about but stay with me my worldwide acquaintances, I shall reveal all very soon. Before I do tell yous lot about my week, and boy was it a week, I wanted to ask yous lot about your weeks. Were they successful, did you realize your personal ambitions? Ask yourself honestly and if you did, my glass is raised to you as I write.

Me, for once have surpassed any ambitions I might have had, I was jet setting across Europe this week and if it went well have the opportunity to expand to the worldwide audience. Well let me tell you the Kevster did succeed, beyond even my confident expectations. The Kevster has been released to the world to ply his trade!

Not only did I seal the deal, tipped the top, and impressed the unimpressed, I sealed a personal deal with a very nice lady. Beat that my beloved friends. Peeps this is the new me, the one to meet and greet the world's expectations. All I can say to those who haven't had the Kevster pleasure yet is hello world, the Kevster is coming.

Personal page:

What the hell went wrong, on a plate and you still don't eat! Two hundred and four days, two hundred and four days dude! If Alexis and Jane don't bring Jo tomorrow or anyone else, you really need to consider other options. Alexis, Jane, or if really pushed, paid for services. Pecker up Kevin.

13th February 1999

Seven-thirty the door bell went. He walked coolly to open the door. Alexis, Jane and to his pleasant surprise, Jo were stood there each holding two bottles of wine each. Kevin smiled at them and hugged each of them as they came in. Snowy quickly got in on the act and expected the same from the new guests.

Jo looked nervously and whispered to Kevin 'I don't need to worry about a half naked lady falling through the kitchen door tonight do I.' He gave her his best how you could think such a thing stare and replied by shaking his head. Jo smiled brightly back at him.

Kevin needed to finish and serve the main course. Jo asked if she could help him. 'You trust coming into my kitchen?' Kevin replied sniggering. 'No one would do that twice Kevin, I'm pretty sure of that.' Jo replied giggling too.

They got into the kitchen and Jo closed the door. She grabbed Kevin and started to get frisky with him. 'Tonight Kevin I'm going to shag your brains out.' 'That would be nice and very desirable' He somehow stuttered back.

Kevin said they really needed to keep control if they were going to eat tonight. Jo asked him what they were having. When he replied Turbot, she beamed, 'Wow Kevin, that's serious fish cooking.'

Kevin placed their Turbot dishes in front of them in his sauce with the sautéed vegetables. They all cooed and clapped as he sat down with them. They were all eating and chatting and Alexis actually said it was the best meal she'd had. Jane echoed this and as Jo opened her mouth nodding her head she started to choke!

They all reacted instinctively. Jo was really struggling. After twenty minutes panic Jo said she had a bone stuck in her throat. She was breathing normally now but was still in distress. Kevin offered to take her to the hospital but Jane took over. 'Kevin, I'll take her, don't worry.'

Kevin and Alexis both sat wordlessly for a while before Kevin managed to speak. 'Babe, another night I've cocked up again. Am I destined to be a new age virgin?' 'Don't be silly Hon, you had tonight nailed, and you can't be responsible for a rogue bone.' Alexis said hugging him.

Kevin hugged her back 'Can we just get hammered Babe?' They both finished the remaining wine and by two in the morning were completely out of it. 'Bed Hon' Alexis slurred to him.

....

14ᵗʰ February 1999

He woke up at what he thought was early morning. He had a rise as normal, there was nothing strange about this, a normal morning activity. What wasn't normal was the mouth around his boner. Alexis was giving him another bloody blow job. He tried to say something but before he could she had moved and was on top of him.

Despite his desperation for sex, this was something else. He had always loved Alexis; these feelings came to the fore and he made love to her for hours. They didn't speak the whole time but got twenty five years of longing, frustration and desire out of both their systems.

By eleven he was tidying up the apartment and feeling good but bad. Alexis was his best friend, he'd shagged her, crossed the dreaded line, and he'd allowed her partner to give him a blow job as well, what the hell was he doing?

He wanted to ring Alexis but knew he had to wait for her call. He brooded around for the rest of the day and by eight o' clock was ready for bed. He updated his blog first over a few wines. He lit a Benson and sipped his wine as he wrote.

Yo Peeps
What a weekend, I'll be getting a restaurant if I carry on with the grub I'm putting on plates lately. If I do, yous lot is all invited. It would be called Julie's. Well my lady and lad friends a really busy one this weekend. The effort on learning to cook has definitely netted results.

February is flying peeps and the Kevster is thinking of ideas for the party of parties for the Millennium Dudesters. What I need from yous lot now is your thoughts Peeps. I can't believe its work tomorrow, already. God who decided to make the weekends go so quickly recently. Well as home next week I will be on line regularly so expect a bit more from yous lot this week. Enjoy the rest of what's left of the weekend and catch yous all again tomorrow.

....

15ᵗʰ February 1999

Mary came into his office with the tea at ten and looked deeply into Kevin's eyes. 'Kevin, will you come around to mine for Sunday lunch?' 'Mary, I'd love to.' He got home and Snowy was waiting, she wanted food and she wanted a cuddle. Kevin obliged with both then jumped in the shower. He got out and really wanted to ring Alexis, but didn't. She called however and said she'd be around tomorrow and wanted feeding.

He started on a Bolognese sauce. He wouldn't eat this tonight as it took three hours to cook; instead he would binge on red wine. He ate a few snacks and blasted the music out loud. Tonight he wanted oblivion!

He checked his watch as he opened his second bottle of red it was only ten past seven. He surged on with his drinking. By nine he was pole-axed and the Bolognese sauce was ready. He pulled it off the heat and put it safely to cool. He didn't want to Blog tonight, he was still really confused.

....

16ᵗʰ February 1999

He rang Mary and said he had severe migraine and would work from home the rest of the week. Alexis arrived at ten past four 'Hi Hon, I finished early, crap day, dying for wine and a cig, hope you've got some food as well babe, I'm starving.' Alexis said in one breath. 'Slow down Babe, what's first, wine?' 'Yes please Kevin, sorry my head's in a bit of a fizz today.'

He looked straight into her eyes and said softly 'Alexis are you ok, I mean ok with what we did?' 'Yes Kevin, I'm fine with it, before you ask for any deep meaningful reasoning, don't. Just ride with it for now, please?' Alexis said looking slightly upset. 'Of course I will Alexis, but you know we crossed a line Babe?'

'I know we crossed a line Kevin, we actually bulldozered our way over the line. But don't ask me to go into detail yet, I'm still confused and I want to stay here with you tonight and cross the bloody line again, that ok for now?'

He put the lasagna on at just gone seven. He poured them each a large red and cuddled into Alexis. 'I don't want details Babe, or understanding or anything deep, but what about Jane? She's your partner and my friend too.' 'Kev, we're just having a bit of a struggle, we've decided on a trial separation and to see other people for a month.' Alexis replied with a tear trickling down the side of her cheek.

She told Kevin his food was getting better and better, 'If you carry on like this Hon I'll be investing in you to set up on your own.' Kevin beamed at her 'Keep talking Babe, you know how to get me like putty in your hands.' They retired for a fairly sleepless night.

....

19th February 1999

He got ready. He was meeting Steve at six in the Red Lion and then they were off into town. When he got to the Lion just before six, Steve was already there. Steve bought Kevin a pint and they sat at a table. 'Alright mate, you look lost?' 'Just a bit of girl worry, I'm not really sure but it's been some strange days and I'm a little lost by it all.'

'Wait a minute, this from a bloke whose two best friends are probably the best looking girls I've ever seen, who shag each other senseless all the time and let you sleep naked with them in their bed when you stay over!' Steve said winking.

'It's a bit more than that at the minute Steve, look I've been shagging Alexis for the last week or so. Twenty five years we've been friends and we've never done anything before.' 'You're shagging someone who'd beat any page three girls for looks and you're sighing? You need your head testing.' Steve said seriously.

'Come on Steve, you know how long we've been friends, we've crossed the line and I feel I've betrayed Jane. I think I love Alexis, I'm trying to get it on with Anne and Jo and am not at all sure about Mary, and by the way, her mother Suzanne wants a piece of me and well to be honest mate she's bloody hot.' Kevin said in one breath.

Steve sighed too and told Kevin they were going to Nero's, a cool small club that had a good buzz about the place. As they hit the shorts an older woman was trying to make an impression on the dance floor. Kevin remembered seeing her before. She was only bloody Mary's mother Suzanne!

Suzanne saw Kevin and made a beeline straight to him. 'Hello gorgeous' she said fluttering her eye lashes. 'Hi Suzanne, how are you, you look . . . great' Kevin replied realizing his mistake a little too late. 'Glad you think so hunk, buy me a drink and then we'll have a dance and I'll let you feel how great I look.'

Don't shag Mary's mother he kept on repeating inside his head as Suzanne went to the ladies. She came back carrying three drinks telling Kevin she was going back to her friends but was having a slow dance with him when one came on.

By half-one Kevin and Steve were like giggling teenagers. Suzanne came back as the slow records came on and grabbed Kevin and took him to the floor. Steve watched from the side still laughing loudly.

After the first dance Suzanne pulled him back to Steve. 'We're going now Steve, are you ok to get home on your own?' She said to him with eyes daring him to disagree. 'I'm fine Suzanne, you two go and enjoy yourselves.' Before he got dragged somewhere he shouldn't go Kevin apologized and said he needed to go, he couldn't do anything, and he was going to be sick.

....

20th February 1999

He woke up with a bad head and a void for a memory. His head still hurt, he needed some air so went out for a walk. He got back and went straight back to bed, Snowy joining him for a cuddle.

....

21st February 1999

Kevin arrived at Mary's at two. She looked stunning, there was no other word for it. She'd had a haircut and had on a skirt so short his eyes nearly popped out. They were hugging when he heard a voice that made his spine tingle with fear. 'Well, well, well. Forty-eight hours after agreeing to shag me, you're having a go at my daughter!' Kevin looked up and saw Suzanne stood in front of them.

Mary screamed 'Mum! What are you here for, what are you saying?' 'Sweetie, I saw Mr Golden Balls Friday night, if he hadn't puked he would have been in my bed shagging my brains out darling.' Suzanne said in a matter of fact tone. 'Kevin, is this true?' Mary asked him desperately. 'I don't know Mary, I really don't know. I know I was drunk, I think I met your mother but as for the rest I honestly don't know.'

'Get out! Get out now Kevin, just go!' Mary screamed and launched an ash tray at him. Kevin just managed to duck under the ash tray and ran out. He left and walked in a daze to a taxi rank, what on earth had just happened; this was a mess, a real mess.

Getting home at six o' clock Snowy welcomed him lovingly. He was all over the place. He cracked open a bottle of Chablis and tried to reflect. He rang Steve, bloody answer machine. There was something about being kicked out for something you knew you did, but he didn't have a clue what he had or hadn't done.

The door went at eight-thirty, Kevin went and expected to see Mary but to his horror it was Suzanne. 'Can I come in Kevin?' She asked looking seriously at him. 'I suppose, I mean yes, come in Suzanne.' She sat down, lit one his Bensons and asked him if she could have strong vodka. Kevin agreed, he always bloody well agreed and where the hell was it getting him he asked himself.

Suzanne sighed and looked right at him 'Kevin do you remember the other night?' 'To be honest Suzanne no, not really.' 'Well baby boy, we got it on, on the dance floor. I was taking you home and you got ill. If you hadn't been ill you would have woken up with me in my bed stud.' He just looked and didn't say anything but gulped his wine. 'Thing is Kevin, Mary thinks you did, so therefore I thought I'd come over and make you do the crime you're paying the time for.' Suzanne said looking deep into his eyes.

'What? I mean Suzanne I'm confused, what do you mean?' Kevin managed as some sort of a reply. 'Kevin, shut up' Suzanne said as she stripped off in front of him. As he looked he realized she was fitter than he'd given her credit for.

Suzanne led him to the bedroom and said softly 'Kevin, I don't want to hear you talk, I just want you to do what I tell you, nod if you understand.' Kevin was so shell-shocked he nodded.

....

22nd February 1999

He was in by seven o' clock. What was going to happen today he didn't know? To his surprise Mary was in by seven-thirty. 'Would you like a tea Kevin?' She asked softly. 'Yes please Mary' Kevin replied. Mary came back with the teas five minutes later. 'Kevin I came in early to talk.' Mary said handing him his tea.

'Right, let's start by saying I don't blame you. She's always been the same my mother, always trying to shag the blokes I get close to. If you met her when you were out, she will have exaggerated the story, the likelihood is she did all the chasing and you did all the running away.' He tried to respond but she held a finger to her lips.

They left at five and went their separate ways. Kevin was all over the place, he needed to see Suzanne and it had to be tonight. He rang her as soon as he separated from Mary and went to the Black Cock. He ordered them both a drink and she arrived five minutes later. 'Hi babe' she said as she strolled in. Kevin kissed her softly on the lips and asked her to sit down.

'Suzanne, what we did last night was mind-blowing, something I'll never forget.' He said looking at her. 'Kevin, it was the same for me, I want to do it again tonight.' 'No, listen to me Suzanne, what we did was a one off.' 'Tell me what you mean Kevin?' Suzanne said looking a little annoyed. 'What I mean and I really mean is what we had together is over Suzanne, it can't continue. For Mary's sake it can't continue.' 'Kevin, I'll cut you some slack.' Suzanne said winking. 'What the hell does that mean?' 'Take me home tonight. Spend the night making me feel special and then, God forbid if I have to be your future mother in law, then so be it!'

....

24th February 1999

He phoned Mary at eight-fifteen to tell her he would work from home again today. She told him Daniellie had arranged for him to go to the States but would have more info in the coming days.

He still cringed as spoke to her and couldn't believe what a selfish cock he was. He was also really worried about Alexis, she hadn't phoned in days.

He put lots of work in today, especially after finding out he was off to America. Alexis rang at four and arranged to come over. She arrived at ten to five, she flung her arms around him as she came in and kissed him deeply. 'Hi' 'Hi Babe, I've got a promotion, Worldwide Security Manager, my Head Office is going to be Chicago for the next six months, then I revert back to the UK and travel between sites, me Kevin, a Jetsetter!' Alexis blurted out.

Now more shocked than ever all Kevin could do was hug her as she led him to the bedroom. She made love to him like never before. Kevin also showed her a few of his new tricks, courtesy of Suzanne.

'Kevin Julie, well I never, when did you go down that route?' Alexis said but was grinning. 'You know me, always unpredictable Honey.' Kevin said holding her tight. 'Kevin, you know I love you don't you?' 'I love you too but Jane . . .' 'We've agreed to be separated whilst I'm away and I have to soul search. I told her I wanted these few days with you though.' 'You told her about us?' Kevin gasped. 'Yes Kevin, I couldn't go away without telling her the truth' 'What did she say?' Kevin gasped. 'That she was going to shag you when I've gone basically.'

'We've agreed a pact, I won't go with anyone else and get a few great days with you and Jane, if she wants to and you're ok with it gets to shag you whilst I'm away. When I get back, well, we'll see!' Alexis said as if she was offering Kevin a contract.

....

27th February 1999

Following a day and night in bed they awoke and made love again. Alexis sat back smoking and said softly 'Well Hon, I've come up with the perfect plan for you.' 'Come on then, hit me with it.' 'Well babe, I leave for the airport at one o' clock Sunday afternoon. At four o' clock Jane's moving in with you for four weeks. One week to get to know you, you know what I mean, two weeks looking after Snowy whilst you're away and a week to reflect on something new.' Alexis said beaming at him.

01st March 1999

At ten past-ten his door bell rang. Jane was stood there with a huge suitcase and greeted him with a kiss. He invited her in and as she walked passed him noticed how short a skirt she had on. Jane dumped her bag and said 'Coffee please Babe, I've rushed my nuts off.'

He stared at her again, again noticing how short her skirt was and how hot she looked. Kevin tried to refocus. This was mad, absolutely off the scale mad. Jane helped a little by saying 'Kevin, this is crazy, I know, but for now can we be like we've always been? I'm here for a month.'

By the time they got to five o' clock, it was almost like it had always been. Kevin was warming to having Jane so close to him. The situation they were in though was not describable. Here he was pining for the love of his life with the woman who was feeling probably worse and they were supposed to get it on!

He served his take on Chinese food at seven-thirty and they were already on their third bottle of wine. He wasn't sure who mentioned physical contact first but by eight-thirty they were both naked and had engaged in sex.

It was good without being spectacular and there wasn't the love he had with Alexis. Jane was a perfect specimen of a beautiful woman but definitely held something back. Kevin felt the same, other than he wasn't exactly a perfect specimen of a hunk of a male!

02nd March 1999

He was working from home again so set everything up and addressed his recent silence on blogging.

> Howdy Partners
>
> The Kevster's on an AA flight to the land of plenty in five days time. I've got to apologize to yous lot for the break in communication, God it's been a roller coaster of a ride the last week or so. Suffice to say the Kevster's not really on top of the lady front, I'm somewhat behind, it's been like a rodeo the

last week Pals and Gals, a physical and emotional challenge let me tell yous.

Well I'll be gone for a fortnight and not able to speak to yous beautiful Peeps whilst I'm away. Keep thinking of me though out in the big bad world caus I'll be thinking of yous lot. Bring peace to the world, love to those who desire it and kindness to all!

He really needed to update his own blog if only to record the madness of the current situation he found himself in.

Dear Kevin

Where the hell are we? You love Alexis, but will she choose Jane? Jane is now getting into man woman sex, where the hell will that lead? Anne is a few weeks away from being back on the scene, Mary's gorgeous and definitely wants to go further (shagging her mother's going to be a bit of a stumbling block) Jo's not out of the question and that's all before the States visit. You need to write notes and analyze in the two weeks you're in America. God the head currently hurts. For the next week though its head down, cock up and banging Jane, good plan Dude.

Jane got back from work at three-forty. She told Kevin she was giving him the works tonight. 'What's that Babe?' He asked looking intrigued. 'You'll find out' Jane said with a wicked grin, adding she was waxing and shaving him all over.

Kevin gulped and said 'I need more to drink first Jane.' 'You carry on Babe, I need to be sober so I don't cut you.' Jane said telling him to strip naked. He poured a vodka so strong the orange juice tried to object, sank half of it and stripped for Jane.

Jane went to town, under his arm pits, his legs, his forearms an then, for God's sake his down below hairs. He felt bald but then looked in horror as she got the wax strips out. She pulled the first strip off. 'Shit, ow, cow, bitch, shit' screamed out of Kevin's mouth. Jane gave him more vodka, this time omitting the orange juice altogether. Some fifty minutes later a bald Kevin was in position, washed, dried and moisturized. He was too hammered by now to care.

03rd March 1999

He worked hard all day, well until two o' clock anyway. He had an attempt at a shower and saw all his shaved hairs protesting to the world and trying to get out again without any success. He also itched like he'd never itched before and spent the next hour having relaxing scratches.

Jane was home by four and tried to entice him with a black rubber outfit and whip. Kevin politely declined, not his scene at all. He'd tried to connect with her, it had always been so easy but now . . . Jane eventually spoke 'Kevin, Alexis is gone, she told me she might love you, I'm trying to make you love me so I get to call the shots.' 'Look Honey, what happens will happen, we both love Alexis, this isn't easy for either of us. We can wallow in self pity or see if this changes anything.' He said leading her to the bedroom.

05th March 1999

He checked his hair growth, nothing happening but the itch, he was still as smooth as a snooker ball. Kevin needed to pop into work, realizing something huge during the night and wanted to talk to Mary about it. He got to work by nine o' clock, Mary was already there. He held her hand and asked really sincerely 'Mary, when I get back from the States, can we have a go at being together?' 'You mean me and you, boyfriend and girlfriend?' She said still looking really embarrassed. 'Yes Mary, lock stock and two smoking.'

He needed a real serious chat with Jane tonight. He got home late and Jane acted like a bloody wife, moaning he was late and dinner was ruined. Kevin tried to fight back but no sense came from his mouth. He sat there thinking and Jane somehow managed the next really sensible comment. 'Oh Kevin, I'm sorry, you know the sex we've had has been fun but it's just not us, not really, is it?' 'No, well it's been really physical but no, not really, it's not really us I agree.'

'Oh Kevin, hug me please, I wanted to tell you but was worried I'd upset you, I'm not a guy girl, I'm a girl's girl. I thought if I tried hard enough I might change my mind. I can't though Kev, I can't, I tried and I can't.' Jane said tears now streaming down her face.

Kevin sort of hugged her and patted her on the back. Snowy jumped up between them both and licking Jane's face. Kevin was sure she gave him a dirty look as if to say how dare you upset her? Jane went to bed with Snowy leaving him to think. His vodka friend was company until a time he couldn't see, never mind remember.

....

06th March 1999

Kevin scrambled out of bed in some state at eleven. Almost falling into the kitchen he saw a note. Jane had said she felt they weren't relationship material but tonight he was hers for what she wanted, no arguments.

He reread the note and wondered what she meant; the bloody woman had shaved him bald for God's sake, what more could he do? Secretly he wondered if his hairs would ever grow back and if he had to scratch forever.

He started packing and then had a sit down with Snowy. 'Right darling, after tomorrow night I will be away for two weeks, Jane will look after you, are you ok with that?' He said as he smoothed her on the sofa. Snowy agreed by purring. 'When I get back my baby, you've got to learn to go out, I'm going to teach you and put you a cat flap in, is that ok?' He asked her again. She purred her agreement. 'Darling I'm also going to get a puppy, ok?' He was really going to miss her, even though she bit him, following the puppy comment.

He tried Alexis's mobile number, no answer. He left a message and had a shower. He came out of the shower and nearly jumped out of his skin. Jane was stood outside the door as he came through it. 'Jesus Jane, you scared the crap out of me!' He said alarmed. 'Sorry Hon. Just got back and went looking for you. Tonight's going to be a blast Babe, a real blast. I'm cooking, scheming and beaming. You are having it all tonight Babe, all!'

Jane was preparing something and told him to keep his nose out. Kevin did as he was told as she gave him, God forbid one of her special vodka's where the first sip nearly knocked him out. He sat on the sofa cuddling Snowy and smoking.

Jane came in and joined them on the sofa. 'Food's ready at seven Hon, but I want you drunk as a skunk first. You've got to do something tonight you may not yet agree with.' 'What the hell does that mean?' 'You'll have to wait and you'll have to be drunk that's all I'm telling you Mr Julie!'

He was now on the way to cuckoo land and feeling warm and fuzzy when she came back with a ladies clothes bag. She looked at him and said assertively 'Kevin, now for my surprise. Strip Baby, completely naked please.' Even as drunk as he was he sensed something weird but went along and stripped naked. Jane complimented him on his smooth body telling him it was as smooth as a woman's. 'Yeah, apart from the meat and veg' Kevin said in a boyish giggle.

Jane ignored this and told him to stand up straight. Jane put a pair of silky black panties on him as well as some stockings and suspenders; she then put something over his head telling him all the time to just go with it.

Jane spent the next twenty minutes playing with his hair and messing with his face. She led him to the full length mirror in his bedroom and switched on the light. Kevin looked in the mirror but didn't see himself, he saw a woman in his body, he had a dress on, full make up and a bloody wig, he looked like a chick!

'Jane, what the bloody hell are you doing?' He managed to splutter out. 'Darling, sweet Alexis, I'm going to make love to you.' She replied in a trance like voice. 'Wait, Jane, for one you're Jane and for two I'm Kevin, Kevin with a cock!' 'Not tonight you're not, tonight you're Alexis, the most beautiful girl in the world and you're going to make love to me darling.' Jane finished with him and told him lovingly 'Alexis I love you' as she fell straight into a deep sleep. Kevin got out of the bed and discarded the dress, pants and stockings. Tonight had been the most bizarre night of his life to date.

....
07ᵗʰ March 1999

Kevin woke with a vague recollection of panties, dress and a wig. He was naked however and sighed, perhaps the dress and pants had been a dream.

Jane came bounding in with eggs and toast on a tray. 'Last night Babe, well it was amazing, I know we said it'd be our last but can we have a goodbye shag, you know, one for the road and all that?' She said jumping back into bed with him. 'Jane, can

I ask you something first? Last night, I mean you and me last night, I think I remember I was dressed as a woman.' Kevin said confusedly. 'Babe, you had too much vodka, don't worry about it and make my goodbye special.'

Jane left by eleven, promising to be back on Monday for Snowy and wishing Kevin a good trip. He finalized his packing and was going to update his blog but decided against it, the dress and pants thing still too fresh in his cringe bank to write. He had an early night and fell asleep as soon as his head hit the pillow. He had dreams of the dress, panties and wig all night.

08th March 1999

'Well baby cat, this is it, the day I'm off to the USA. I'll miss you sweetie but Jane will look after you. You two girls will have a really nice time together' he told her giving her lots of hugs.

His flight was non-descript and he fell into a deep sleep. He awoke as he heard the pilot's voice saying they were starting their descent and would be landing in thirty five minutes. He stretched and sat up picking up his magazine, before he knew it they touched down in JFK.

He breezed through customs and was in arrivals at two o' clock. He had been told by the Worldwide HR Director, Thomas Bronter, a driver would collect him. True to his word the driver at the front had a card out with Mr Kevin Julie written in bold on it.

He checked in and went to his room. It was more like a suite. There was a letter from Thomas. The letter had an itinerary for the next three days and a kind gesture advising Kevin to sample New York's finest food and wine, all on the Company. Kevin was apparently not to hold back. His kind of an invite! Still tonight he was too tired to do anything other than a burger in his room. The night was only marred by one dress dream!

18th March 1999

Kevin was sat on the chair in his hotel room ready to pass out. All he'd seen for the whole ten days was offices, hotel rooms and the bloody car. No wonder Daniellie had told him he'd get a bonus after the trip.

Knowing he had a day off he ordered the vodka without the food tonight. Four huge glasses and six Bensons later he was comatose in bed. He slept right up to the time he was collected him some thirty four hours later.

··

20ᵗʰ March 1999

He'd slept all the way home on the plane and was still sleeping as the taxi driver got him back to his apartment. He walked in to his home and shouted for his cat. Snowy gave him the cold shoulder, he promised he'd make it up to her. Tonight though he needed to catch up, what the hell had happened to the last two weeks?

He rang Jane first. She gave him the mother of all bollockings for not keeping in touch. He apologized and told her of his schedule. Jane relented and said she'd be round to cook for him and give him a massage. Before he could object she put the phone down and was there an hour later.

Jane was true to her word, she cooked, ate with him and gave him a massage. She left at nine, kissing him on the cheek. At ten he phoned Mary, he didn't want to get into anything but told her he'd be off for a few days and was jet lagged but asked her to come around to his on Monday night.

With Mary pacified he turned his attention to Snowy. 'Darling, I am sorry I've been gone so long, believe me it was no blast, I'm sure Jane looked after you whilst I was gone and I'm taking the next week off, balls to the lot of them. The USA office experience, you can keep it sweetheart. It was dark the whole time I was there, I'm not even sure if I saw the sun. Thomas Bloody Bronter and his you can have what you want whilst you're here Kevin bullshitter' he told her sincerely.

Snowy listed intently and accepted his explanation; she purred and cuddled into him. As he was about to fall asleep Kevin realized he hadn't dreamt about the dress thing lately. Some progress he thought as he drifted off into a deep sleep.

··

21ˢᵗ March 1999

Getting up he jumped in the shower. The hot water felt good and he noticed hairs coming back. Liking the feeling he had had for weeks he decided he'd used the strips Jane had left in the bathroom cabinet.

To his surprise the pain was nothing like the first time and he was as smooth as a snooker ball again. Why he liked it he didn't know but knew he did. He wondered what Mary would think. God tomorrow they might get some frustration out of their systems?

He spent most of the afternoon, fitting the bloody cat flap and wondering who on earth's idea it had been! Eventually he showed his work to Snowy. She looked at him blankly, something they had to deal with this week.

He cracked open a bottle of red, sank back, lit a Benson and chilled for ten minutes. He phoned Mary, confirmed tomorrow and was jumping like a school boy when she asked if she should bring her toothbrush. He turned his PC on and set it up to update his blog page.

> Howdy Partners
> The Kevster is back from the trip of a lifetime to the US of bloody A. Man that place is cool. The Pals and Gals out there are top notch, let me tell yous all. The weeks were hard work man, the company needed the Kevster to sort out the Yanks and the Kevster delivered.
> I saw a lot of the US of A and met some really cool Peeps, lots of party ideas Dudes and Dudesses. Back on home soil now though and still need all yous lots ideas, when I've got those I can really put a proposal together friends, the best millennium party ever, just for us lot. Still a little bit lagged though yous lot (jet) so need to get back to my pussy and bed for nows but will catch yous lot again tomorrow. Worldwide Loving

....

22nd March 1999

'Right honey, today is the first training day' he told Snowy seriously. She looked at him interestedly. He started by explaining the principal of the cat flap to her. She purred so he knew she'd understood. He then continued to explain about the magnetic safety system. Snowy was still following him, so far so good!

He then explained about the collar, she raised her eyes. Kevin continued and showed the pink designer piece that came with the flap. She wasn't having it and bit him for good measure. Cow, he thought silently. Three hours later and he was no closer to putting the collar on her. He tried a new approach, turned off the magnetic protection and showed her how the flap opened to let her out and opened the other way to let her back in.

She got this inside of one minute, jumping out, back in, back out and back in again as if she'd always known what it was there for. After her showing off she jumped out and disappeared.

Kevin opened the door and went out after her, forty minutes later he gave up looking. He was really fretting and wondering how he'd cocked it up so badly. He got back into the apartment and Snowy greeted him with a nuzzle and a purr. He relented and trashed the collar, this cat was far too clever for him but he was happy she'd sussed out the flap.

Mary arrived bang on five o' clock, she looked gorgeous. He prepared the food and let Mary put the music on. She chose The Jam, one of his favorite bands ever. They were on the white at the moment and Mary was loosening nicely.

At seven there was an unexpected knock at the door. Kevin went to answer and Jane jumped in, holding a bottle of red and shouting 'Hi Babe, no shagging tonight, as we agreed but I thought you'd enjoy the company' as she walked straight into the living room, Snowy ran to her on hearing her voice.

Sensing the atmosphere he jumped in. 'Jane, sit down, I'll get the drinks.' He lit a Benson and wondered what the hell to say next but was interrupted by the door going again. Anne was stood there holding a bottle of champagne and shouting 'Hi Kev, I wanted to call round to make it up to you for not giving you the attention you needed the last time I was here.' Snowy, hearing Anne's voice jumped off Jane's lap and ran to Anne.

Anne joined the strange party and Kevin poured her a large glass, topped up Jane's and Mary's and poured himself a vodka strong enough to kill the orange. This was going badly wrong with a capital W. Kevin stood up to refill their glasses when to his astonishment the door went again. He opened it thinking it couldn't get any worse than it already was. He was so wrong. Suzanne pushed through with a bottle of vodka saying 'Hi big boy, thought you might be bored so popped round on the off chance!'

Mary got up and stormed out. Kevin tried to stop her unsuccessfully. Anne got up, apologized for intruding and left. Jane was eying Suzanne up. 'Right, that's it, I've bloody well had it. Jane, you stay, do whatever you want with Suzanne but stay and look after Snowy, I'm off after Mary.'

He left them to it and ran out after Mary and caught up with her at the bus stop. Trying to get oxygen into his system managed 'Mary, wait.' 'How Kevin, how did all that just happen?' 'I don't know, I really don't, please don't blame me, I planned for me and you Mary, I really did.' He said desperately and still out of breath.

They got back to Mary's at just before nine-thirty. 'Kevin, tonight I'm getting as drunk as I ever have been you're sleeping on the sofa, I'm taking a sick day off work tomorrow and if I haven't killed you in the night we might discuss us in the morning!'

....

23rd March 1999

Weeks of frustration took several hours to get out of their system. Mary purred for the whole morning and well into the afternoon. They got out of bed at three o' clock. Mary made them breakfast or whatever it was called at this time of day.

They ate without talking, there was no need. When they finished Mary demanded something more from him. 'Kevin, I'm going sick for the rest of the week, you're staying here. Get Jane to look after Snowy. For tonight I just want you and tomorrow we'll talk seriously about what we're going to do long term. I don't want excuses, I just want agreement.'

He called home, Suzanne answered. He eventually got Jane to the phone and she agreed to look after Snowy. Kevin asked her about Suzanne and Jane just replied 'Sex on legs Kevin, sex on legs.'

'Are you ok to stay Kevin?' 'Yeah, all sorted, Jane will look after Snowy for the next few days.' 'And my mother?' 'No idea Babe.' He lied through his teeth.

She told him to sit at the table thirty minutes later. Kevin sat back smoking and sipping his wine with a huge smile on his face. 'What is it?' He asked when Mary returned with two plates. 'This is our meal Honey, an appetizer I've developed into a main meal. It's Scallops in a wine, cream and saffron sauce and with seared asparagus.' Mary said looking at him for a reaction.

'Wow!' From the look on her face this was the response she had been hoping for. They finished the food and he held her hands softly but firmly. 'Mary, that was out of this world, no bullshit, it was stunning, absolutely gorgeous.' She nodded and let him lead her into her bedroom.

....

24th March 1999

Mary was full of beans this morning. She asked if they could go out together. Kevin agreed on the proviso they went via a clothes shop. They jumped on the bus into town and got there just before one o' clock. He headed straight for Checkman, his favorite store. They were only in there thirty minutes, he was nine hundred and ten pounds worse off but walked out in a new pair of Armani Jeans, a Replay top, a pair of Timberland's and a Boss jacket. He'd also bought Mary a designer dress for three hundred and fifty notes and said he needed a drink as he felt dizzy from his spending spree.

They went to the Glasshouse for lunch, Mary insisting on paying. Kevin sighed with relief as they walked through the door. They had a liquid and solid lunch and left there at four, both three sheets to the wind. They got a taxi back, hit the vodka's and were both in bed snoring by eight o'clock.

....

25th March 1999

Kevin woke and mentioned his plan to get a puppy. Mary lost the plot. 'Kevin, can we look today, can I help you choose? It's so exciting!' She said jumping up and down like a teenager. He tried to explain it was just an idea but she wasn't having any of it. He eventually agreed to go to the pound with her.

They went to the Bridges Sanctuary at eleven o' clock. By five-past four, after seventeen viewings and an intense interview Kevin had in principal agreed to take on an eight month old white golden Labrador who he named Sooty.

The Labrador had been mistreated and left in squalid conditions and needed a loving home. His only solace in his old home was the female cat he doted on. Kevin had made the decision to pick this dog purely based on his cat friendliness.

They got back to Mary's and Kevin phoned Jane. He told her about the dog and said he wanted to bring him home tomorrow and she had to tell Snowy. Jane agreed and they also agreed Kevin would bring Mary back and they'd all have a meal together and all stay the night at his. Suzanne wanted to tell Mary Jane was her new partner. He was dreading this and knew he had to speak to Mary tonight.

'Mary darling, tomorrow when we take Sooty home to mine Jane is going to be there to help with Snowy.' Mary's eyebrows raised but she gave him a 'go on' stare. 'Well darling she's going to stay as well, in the spare bedroom of course.' She still looked at him in suspicion. 'Well honey, that's not all, um, I mean, your mother is also staying.' He managed to splutter out nervously.

Mary didn't respond immediately and finished her glass, Kevin topping her up quickly. Mary, seeming to consider something, finished her wine, asked for a strong vodka before saying. 'What I think you're telling me Kevin is my mother, who you've already shagged is now together with Jane, who you've also shagged and both are staying with us tomorrow night in your apartment and are seemingly now an item.' 'Yes Mary, that's about the sum of it.' He replied expecting a slap.

Mary drained her vodka, asked for another and lit one of his cigarettes. Kevin knew this was a bad sign. Mary again sank half of her next vodka in one gulp before adding 'That's fine then darling. If they're shagging each other they won't be trying to shag you will they?' He managed to nod and took her to bed wondering how the hell he got into the shit he got into. Mary was wrecked and Kevin lay there excited, he was getting a dog tomorrow and wanted Snowy to agree and love him too.

···

26th March 1999

They arrived at Bridges just before quarter to nine. At eleven o' clock they went for a meeting with Sooty. He was so nervous but warmed to Kevin inside of fifteen minutes. Kevin had told him all about Snowy and this seemed to seal the deal with Sooty.

They had to have an hours break and then go for their second meeting with Sooty, this time he went to Kevin inside of a minute and they had their first cuddle, a bonding session. Kevin was asked to leave and Sooty tried to follow him. The handler agreed it was time. Kevin was taking his dog home.

They got back to his apartment just after four. Jane answered the door. Mary gave her an awkward stare as they entered. Snowy had come out to have a look, saw the puppy, bit Kevin and scratched Sooty inside of thirty seconds.

Suzanne came into the lounge and hugged Mary. She then hugged Kevin and kissed him far too hard and sensually on the lips. Mary tutted and Jane stared at Suzanne. Jane then managed a blinder. 'Mary, this must be shit for you, I'm sorry. I know we could probably get on but tonight's not the ideal time or situation. Can we tolerate each other tonight and build from there? It would really help with stress for the animals, never mind ours.' She said holding out her hand to Mary.

Mary sighed with a smile and seemed to have realized Jane made sense and shook her hand and gave her a hug. Suzanne beamed and grabbed Kevin for a hug, grabbing his bum in the process. Jane said she was going to prepare the food.

Kevin said he was going to check on the animals. He went to Snowy first. He needed to show her she was still his number one. She was on his bed and meowed as he entered the room. He sat with her and explained about Sooty. She was pissed right until the part when he told her he'd been mistreated and his only friend had been a cat.

He went into the spare bedroom. He couldn't see Sooty at first, what he could see made him giggle. There were toys on the bed and sexy panties. These two had been going at it hammer and tong. He eventually found his new boy, he was behind the curtains chewing on his new rubber toy. Kevin trying not to laugh smoothed Sooty as he chomped on the black dildo. He'd gone straight through it and he was thankful it wasn't a battery operated one, Sooty might have been electrocuted.

As Kevin finally led Mary to bed he turned on the light and tears of joy streamed down the side of his face. Snowy and Sooty were on the bed together cuddled up with Sooty snoring peacefully.

27th March 1999

Kevin's morning rise woke up far too early to a lovely wet blow job. Mary was also kissing him hard on the mouth. In his just woken status he was wondering how Mary had two mouths!

Sooty was inside the covers and had been giving Kevin a friendly lick. Kevin called him quietly. 'Baby boy me and you need a chat about the birds and the bees.' Sooty was like a lunatic, the shy boy of yesterday was now running around like a headless chicken.

Mary left at an hour after Jane and Suzanne at ten. Kevin told Snowy he was going to take Sooty out for his first walk at eleven. Snowy gave him a worried stare. He got ready and told Sooty they were going walkies. Snowy pricked her ears up as well. Kevin put the lead on Sooty and took him through the door. As they got to the street he heard a meow and saw to his amazement Snowy was alongside them.

He walked around for an hour, keeping Sooty on the lead, Snowy staying right by them. Towards the end of the walk a little Border-Terrier took a fancy to Snowy. She stood her ground but to Kevin's further amazement Sooty pulled away from his lead and told the Border-Terrier in no uncertain terms to stay away from Snowy. Snowy licked him in appreciation.

Later, after Kevin returned from buying some cigarettes, he approached his door . . . He heard the most amazing noise. Sooty was howling and Snowy was meowing. Snowy was outside his front door and Sooty half way through it stuck in the cat flap! He managed to free Sooty before opening the door. Snowy ran in to check on Sooty. He decided on ten minutes of madness to celebrate his freedom. Two broken vases later Sooty calmed down and went to lie on his bed.

Kevin spent the rest of the evening explaining the house rules to his dog as his cat sat alongside him making sure he listened.

29th March 1999

Kevin woke up and went to open his bedside drawers. The little pine handles were no longer there, all three were missing, he checked the other side, and they were all gone too. The chewed handles were all over the floor and two in Sooty's bed. Sooty had found a new game. He grabbed his lead and told him he thought he'd understood last night's chat and he'd have to tell Snowy on him. Sooty's head drooped.

Kevin was having a lazy afternoon on the sofa with his animals. He fell asleep watching some film he couldn't remember with the dog and cat cuddled into him. When he woke he opened a bottle of white and set his PC up.

> My most beautiful and wonderful Peeps of the world
>
> Days again I'm afraid, mad doesn't describe them but in the land of the Kevster they're real and full on Dudes and Dudesses. Still on with new love of my life and my animals have bonded big style man. My pussy and pooch are new best friends. Not much more to say at the mo but stay sharp Peeps, April's not far from us now, closer in fact than it was last time, ha, ha. I'll be in regular contact the next fortnight Peeps so keep those party ideas coming. Love to all the small people of the world

He sipped his wine, smoked a new Benson and thought nothing could stop him now. He was on the upside of life and loving every second. He tried Alexis's mobile again and left another message. The cow hadn't responded to one.

Wanting an early night he headed to bed just before nine. A noise woke him up soon afterwards, he checked his clock. It was only ten to ten. His door was being banged so loudly it would either collapse inwards or the bloody neighbors would wake up.

He went to the door and opened it. Suzanne was standing there tears streaming down her face shouting 'Bitch, cheating bitch' Kevin told her to come inside. After some persuasion she followed him in. Snowy and Sooty had also got up and came to have a look. Suzanne was plastered. He boiled the kettle and made two black coffees. Suzanne drank her cup amidst some foul mouthed dissing Kevin couldn't get the gist of, before saying she needed to go to bed. He showed her the spare room and left as she started to strip off. Snowy and Sooty followed him back into his room.

30th March 1999

He made himself a cup of tea and a naked Suzanne walked into the kitchen. 'Headache babe' she said holding her hands on her head. 'Clothes babe'. 'Oh yeah, sorry, back now' she spluttered. Suzanne came back in a decent state and Kevin sighed with relief. 'Suzanne, why did you come here, of all places?' He said a little bit pissed.

'Kevin, I am truly sorry, I didn't have an agenda. Jane and I had a huge fight and you were the nearest. I didn't mean to put on you Kevin but I knew you'd be there for me.' 'Suzanne, I know I'm a bit of a pushover but now I'm seeing your daughter, seriously seeing your daughter, doesn't that count for some decorum?' He said still pissed with her and still hating himself for wanting to take her straight to his bedroom.

'I know Kevin, don't tell her please? I'll shower and sort myself out and leave, thanks again honey.' She said looking so lost he had to smile. 'Go on then but don't ask me to scrub your back' he replied. 'Spoilsport' she said winking back at him. Suzanne left at ten o' clock. Kevin rang Jane straight away. He told her what had happened and said it was her mess to sort out.

He went out to buy fresh ingredients and was back an hour later. Snowy had been a good girl Sooty hadn't seemed to have eaten anything new. He picked her up and gave her a huge hug. Sooty was jumping up and down like a lunatic carrying Kevin's Y Fronts in his mouth.

'Birds and Bees my young pup' he said laughing. He lit a Benson and poured himself a glass of white. Mary turned up at twenty-past six, told Kevin she needed a shower and for him to have a cold white waiting for her. Mary came out looking beautiful, she walked out naked first and Kevin's mouth opencd, not because of her immense beauty but because it was like dejavue. Mary winked at him and Kevin needed a double take, she looked like bloody Suzanne! He had to get that image out of his mind!

He checked on Snowy and Sooty before serving food, they were both fast asleep. He served quail and roasted vegetables, drizzled Madeira sauce over the top and around the bird. Mary looked at him in awe and told him that this was restaurant stuff.

She led him to the bedroom stripped and flung the bed clothes back. Kevin excitedly started to strip. When he looked back up Mary was stood there, face like thunder holding a pair of black and red silky, lacy panties.

'What the hell are these Kevin?' She said almost spitting with anger. 'I don't know Mary, I really don't know.' Kevin replied honestly. 'Well I do Kevin, these are my mother's panties Kevin, I was with her when she bought them. What I want to know is why the fuck they're in your bed?' She screamed at him. 'Mary I don't know.' He pleaded. 'I never want to see you again Kevin!' Mary bellowed as she stormed out of the house.

....

31st March 1999

It was pouring outside but Kevin took Sooty out regardless. Snowy stayed at home. They got back soaking wet two hours later. Sooty was now actually living up to his name and as black as Snowy. Kevin toweled him down explaining he would be having a bath later. Sooty raised his eyes at Kevin suspiciously.

He fed Snowy and prepared the bath. Sooty was giving him the evil eye of all time. He spoke to him gently and led him into the bathroom. Over an hour later Kevin needed a Benson. Sooty was still black but dry. Kevin was clean and soaked. He stripped down to his pants. His new ploy was to get into the bath and see if Sooty copied him.

Success, as he got in Sooty jumped in with him. Kevin got out. Sooty jumped out before Kevin had even turned around. Three goes later at this new game and Kevin had a bath with Sooty and showered him down so he was white and golden again. The bathroom a different story, there was dripping dirty water everywhere.

As his PC warmed up he rang Mary. 'Mary, it's me.' 'Hi Kevin' 'Last night Mary, I can explain.' 'I know, I've been speaking to my mother today, she told me she stayed and she told me you were the perfect gentleman.' 'Sooty grabbed her underwear. He's taking to carrying panties around and leaves them in places he sleeps.' 'Oh' 'Please Mary, it's the truth.' 'Kevin I do believe you, I'm sorry for not talking to you last night but I saw red.'

'That's ok Mary, I understand' 'I don't think you do Kevin. This thing with my mother is still so raw, I'm not past it. I can't be rational at the moment.' 'What are you saying Mary?' 'We need to have a break Kevin, go back to being colleagues. In a few weeks, months, I don't know, maybe.' 'Mary, we were getting there, it was getting special.' 'I know Kevin but for now you're going to have to let me have my space, ok?'

'Mary, it's not ok but if it's what you need then I'll have to.' 'Thanks Kevin, oh by the way, I think Daniellie wants you to go to Canada on your return, I think he's going to ring you this week.'

He put the phone down and hit the vodka, why did everything always cock up for him? First Jo, then Alexis, now Mary, was he destined to be single forever?

....

01st April 1999

New month, new start, Jo had agreed to meet him for a drink tonight at eight-thirty, god Mary was still warm but hey ho. Today he was going running. He hadn't run in something like five years but he was starting back, it was his new thing, he needed to be fitter. He ran a good half a mile in about thirty minutes and went back to his apartment for a long soak in the bath.

He decided on a power nap, just to make sure he was on top form tonight for Jo. Kevin hit the bed with Sooty jumping up to be with him, Snowy quickly followed. He cuddled into his boy and girl and drifted off into a peaceful sleep.

He turned over and stretched and opened his eyes. He felt great. He checked the clock and screamed. It was quarter past eight. He jumped out of bed, threw some clothes on and was out of the door by twenty-past. There were no taxis so he hit the gears in his legs.

The pub was two miles away, if he pushed himself he'd make it in forty minutes. He arrived out of breath at just after nine totally knackered! He walked in, no Jo. Shit, shit, shit he thought. He turned around to walk out, another cock up with Jo ringing in his ears when he saw her walking out of the ladies toilet.

'Jo, I'm sorry, I, I fell asleep, ran all the way here, out of breath, sorry.' She looked at him, a smile returning to her face 'Kevin Julie, you are a dick, a real dick. Buy me a drink and I'll think about forgiving you.' Jo said looking smug.

He looked at her 'Shit Jo, no money, sorry, left my wallet in my rush to get here.' He replied still panting. Jo went to the bar and ordered two ciders, Kevin sank his in one and Jo gave him a fiver to go and get another. After he'd told her the whole story she was far more upbeat. 'It wouldn't be you if it wasn't nearly a disaster Kevin would it?'

They had a few more drinks and Jo told him to take her back to his. They got back about ten-thirty. Kevin protested he needed a shower. Jo agreeing on the proviso she joined him.

Three hours later they were lying back smoking on his bed. 'Kevin, they say some things are worth the wait and that was certainly one of them. How'd you get so smooth all over?' She asked taking a drag. 'Practice darling, I got waxed once, don't ask, and liked the feeling in the end so continued doing it.' 'Will you do me Kevin, next time? I mean if there is a next time?' Jo asked a little nervously. 'Kevin looked at her, kissed her and said tomorrow?'

02nd April 1999

Sooty was having his mad moment and running around the bedroom, Jo's underwear dangling from his mouth, Jo and Snowy watching from the bed. Kevin joined in watching Sooty do the most bizarre routine he'd seen yet. He took him out realizing he needed to release energy, Jo staying with Snowy saying she'd tidy up.

Jo had really cleaned his place up and was holding three pairs of panties in her hand, one white, one pink and one black pair. 'Where, I mean whose, I mean what?' Kevin spluttered. 'Under your bed, behind the toilet and behind the bin in the kitchen.' 'Jo, I'm going to have to teach him to grab something else, its bred into Labradors to retrieve and his purpose in life seems to be retrieve women's smalls at all cost.' 'Whose are they Kevin?' Jo teased him. 'Jo, a gentleman never tells.' He replied not wanting to say one pair were Jane's, one Mary's and one Mary's mothers. 'We'll wash them and you'll have to return them to their owners!'

They left his place at one and headed into town. They decided to split up when they got there. Jo was buying underwear and didn't want Kevin to see. He called her a spoilsport but she was adamant she'd get something he wouldn't be disappointed with. His jobs were to decide on a meal, buy the ingredients, the wax strips and razors. They parted at two o' clock and arranged to meet in the pub at four.

Kevin went to the pub first, had a beer and listed what he was going to cook and where he needed to go to get everything. He was struggling to think of his recipe. He had another beer, it normally gave him inspiration. He decided on Fillet Steak in a Red Wine Sauce with Potato and Parsnip Rosti's and Baby Caramelized Carrots. He was still struggling on his appetizer. Jo had said she didn't want a dessert.

On his fourth beer the idea for the appetizer hit him. A scallop and smoked bacon salad, no bones in there he thought smugly to himself. He had one more beer for the road and left the pub at twenty past three. He had all his ingredients his wax strips a pink girl's razor and was back in the pub by ten to four.

Jo arrived and asked Kevin what he was cooking. It was Kevin's turn to be secretive now, 'Ah, well that would be like me choosing your sexy undies with you, you know, spoil the surprise!' He said with a wicked grin.

They were back a couple of hours later and already feeling the effects. Once Kevin had fed both his babies he led her to the bedroom carrying a bowl of hot water, some strips, a pink razor and a small electric clipper device. 'You need to be still and trust me' he said seriously, his hands were still steady even if his head was a little alcoholised.

Jo was in fits of giggles as Kevin started with the clippers. He was a master at work however and had her ready for the wax inside of thirty minutes. The first pull nearly frightened Sooty and Snowy out of their minds, fireworks wouldn't have been that loud. 'You evil bastard' came spitting out from Jo's lips. He finished thirty minutes later, he had been called a sadist, a prick, a total cock, a 'c' word Jo said she had never used before and a fantastic man by the time he'd finished.

'Right my little beauty, the first course is minutes away, how are your bits?' He asked, already knowing the answer. 'Kevin, I must say, you are a genius with the whole thing, I'm as smooth as a babies bum!' Jo said in appreciation. 'Yup, I am the shave master, comes with practice dear, my mistakes on me weren't passed onto you.'

They finished the wine after Jo had confirmed Kevin no longer a cooking klutz and went to bed at ten past midnight. Jo kept the light on and showed Kevin the white see through panties she'd bought. They didn't get to sleep until three!

....

03rd April 1999

On the off chance he phoned Alexis, still the bloody answer phone. He didn't bother with a message this time. Kevin sat down with his third wine and his phone rang.

'Hello' 'Well hello stranger, I thought you'd disappeared off the face of the earth.' 'Mum!' 'Yes I still command that name, even if my only son doesn't ring me from one month to the next.' 'Oh mum, you know I don't mean anything by it, I'm just crap' 'Stop your excuses, I'm having my rant, how's my daughter in law and grandchild search going?' 'Well I'm working on that mother.' 'You're always working on it, when am I getting some results, even to meet a potential candidate would be some progress.' 'Look mum, its complicated.' 'It's always complicated with you my number one and only son.' 'You know me mum, searching for perfection.' 'Yes I know you a little.' 'Mum, seriously, I am seeing someone, it's in its early days yet, and I'm off to Canada with work for the next couple of weeks. When I get back I'll come down for a weekend, hopefully with Jo, if not on my own.' 'Kevin, that's wonderful.'

Before he knew it he was on his second bottle and had forgotten about his defrosted dinner in the microwave. He turned the computer on, he had lots to talk about and felt the urge to hit the vodka as the PC warmed up.

> Yo Peepsters
> Kevster here and on one again and this time a happy one. I have a new interest on the female front, don't worry all yous single gals, it's not serious, just some fun at the mo. On a serious note Peeps, I spoke to my Mum today, it's been a few months and I'm on a guilt trip. All yous special people out there pick up the phone tonight and be like ET. For now

though my lovelies I'm on a vodka fest and it's going to scare the pulp out of the orange juice Peeps. Love to yous and your families.

....

04th April 1999

He was ready for Jo, she was coming for a walk with him and his boy today she just didn't know it yet. Jo knocked the door at five-to nine and she was in a knock out dress. Kevin told her he needed her out of the dress and she beamed. He showed her the lead and collar. 'Kevin Julie, I didn't know you were into bondage, I'll do most things but I'm not playing a dog' Jo said looking really worried.

After they got back, Kevin took her into town. He asked her foot size, and walked into a sports shop. Ten minutes later he returned with two huge bags taped up so she couldn't see what was in them. He ordered the taxi and they got back to his apartment at three o' clock.

Kevin unpacked the shopping and shouted 'open your eyes' and Jo opened her eyes to see him standing there holding two pairs of roller skates. She squealed with laughter. 'Are you for real, we're going roller skating?' 'Correction darling, we're going street roller skating' he said as he opened the other bag which contained pads and two helmets.

'You're mad Kevin.' Jo said. 'One of my many middle names Sweetie.' Kevin replied as he put her pink trimmed pair on her feet. He then put his black pair with white wheels on and they both padded up.

They skated to the park and had an hour pretending to be teenagers again. They had a ball, Jo telling Kevin it was really romantic. 'My fourth or fifth middle name' he added to her squeals of laughter.

They got back at six o' clock, Jo telling him it was the best day she'd had in ages and they hadn't even had sex. 'I'm going to redress that now'. Kevin said stripping her out of her sweaty clothes. They showered at seven and Kevin went to work in the kitchen as Jo sorted Snowy and Sooty out.

He announced Chicken Livers to start, and Fillet a la Keviano for the main course. Jo clapped and said she'd repay him in kind later. He returned fifteen minutes later with chicken livers on a bed of lettuce. They looked stunning. They both started and kept with the white wine. Kevin had cooked the livers in chili and dressed the lettuce with garlic, olive oil, chili and sugar that he whisked together.

Twenty five minutes later he served two fillets in his home made pepper sauce with asparagus and cubed sautéed potatoes. This was first class food Jo had proclaimed, he had mastered this cooking thing somehow.

'Kevin, I know I said gently, gently and a bit of fun but if I said I'd pull a sickie for the rest of the week, well what I mean is, if you're ok with it, can I, I mean, can I stay here with you until you go to Canada?' Kevin beamed and led her to his bedroom.

....

06th April 1999

They both got up at ten o' clock and showered. He said he'd take Sooty out whilst Jo had some more sleep, she was ill after all! Kevin and Sooty went out at ten-thirty and got back just before one o' clock. Sooty had his mad moment and snuggled on his and Snowy's bed soon after.

Jo was still out for the count lying naked on his bed. She was drop dead gorgeous and he was falling for her. He thought she felt the same way but didn't want to broach the subject with her, not yet, it was far too soon. He heard his phone go at one-thirty, it was Daniellie. He'd agreed to go and see him on Friday to talk about the Canada trip. Daniellie had also told him America was such a success Kevin was going places.

He repeated the detail to Jo. 'Wow Kevin, that's amazing!' 'Yeah, I suppose it is. Jo, can I say something I promised I wouldn't?' 'That depends what it is Kevin.' 'Christ Jo, I can't put it any other way, I'm falling for you in a big way, really big. I know you said no big commitment but I want more with you Jo, much more.'

'Kevin, what I said to you last night, I thought it might frighten you away. The last days have been, well, amazing. I don't get it this good normally.' They held each other for ten minutes without speaking. Kevin broke the silence. 'Jo, when I get back, will you move in with me?' 'Christ Kevin, did you just say that?'

'Say what?' 'Move in with you when you get back from Canada?' 'Yup, I think that's what left my lips, is it too much, too soon?'

'Kevin, you are a klutz, I'm head over heels with you, I wish you weren't going away but yes, when you're back I'd love to move in with you.' 'Jo, wow, that's wonderful, brilliant!'

....

07ᵗʰ April 1999

After breakfast they decided on a dog walk. For the first time in ages Snowy decided to come. Kevin was sure Jo thought he had exaggerated when he said Snowy had previously been out for walks with him and Sooty. Jo was absolutely amazed.

When they got back the phone rang. 'Hi Kevin, I haven't got much time at the mo but I'm coming round tonight for tea and am staying, ok Babe?' 'Jane, hi, yeah, of course, what time?' 'Seven ok?' 'Fine, what's the rush at the moment?' 'Nothing much, I'll tell you later ok?' 'Ok' 'See you later Kevin, bye.' 'Bye Jane.'

Jane came bursting in shouting 'Mad bloody woman! Kevin, please get me a vodka, a bloody large one, and go easy on the orange.' Jane looked up, saw Jo, did a little double take and said 'Jo, hi' and ran over kissing her on the cheek. Jane looked at both of them and said 'Is someone going to explain or do I have to beat it out of you? If so I'll start with the weakest. Kevin?'

Laughing, Kevin said 'Jane, please can I introduce you to my girlfriend Jo Webster.' Jane screamed, hugged Jo, hugged Kevin and screamed again. 'Explain, explain, I want to know it all, but first Kevin a bloody large vodka, like I said, easy on the juice.'

'Easy really' he said handing her a very large vodka. 'When I get back from Canada Jo's moving in!' Jane did some kind of jig, similar to Sooty's morning routine.

She then spent the next ten minutes explaining about Suzanne, the woman was now stalking her. She needed a break from it tonight and that's why she'd asked to come over. Suzanne wouldn't dare come here.

By ten-thirty they were back on the vodka and Jane insisting they all played spin the bottle. At midnight the three naked friends went to bed, Kevin and Jo in one room, Jane in the other, Kevin had been insistent on that. Jane had suggested something different but Kevin shot her down. He did tell her she needed to be up early with them as she needed to see Sooty's morning madness before she looked after him and Snowy next week.

....

09ᵗʰ April 1999

He walked into Daniellie's office bang on ten o' clock. 'Kevin thanks and I really mean thanks for coming in on your holiday. The Company's taken your idea as the strategic worldwide plan. The CEO even called me personally to say how happy he is with you and with me for pushing this.' Daniellie said beaming. 'Thanks' Kevin said as he sat down.

'You will leave on a first class flight Monday morning from Heathrow to Quebec. You will be there almost three weeks and I'm afraid you will have a crazy schedule again Kevin. To compensate you, I'll give you three weeks leave when you get back to go with the bonus.' 'Daniellie, that's great, thanks' 'That's not all Kevin. On your return I have a new job offer for you. Head of HR UK! This comes with a basic of 75k plus a D band car, up to 45k.' 'You're shitting me boss?' 'No Kevin, salary starts from Monday.'

Kevin didn't really take it all in but asked if he had a pick on his team. Daniellie confirmed this and added he had to choose a deputy to act in his absence; this role warranted 40k and two assistants at 28k a head adding that he'd have a month to sort his team out when he came back in May. He then hit Kevin with the biggest shock yet. 'Kevin, the bonus payments have been announced this morning. You're getting ninety thousand, before tax of course.' Kevin nearly choked and he somehow spat out 'thanks boss.'

He took Sooty for a long two and a half hour walk. He wanted the time to digest today's events. He got back with an exhausted and filthy dog at four o' clock. 'Bath time' he shouted to Jo as he walked in. 'Let's get ready to rumble!'

Some hour or so later they discovered two washers were worse than one as all three of them had to sit in the bath to wash Sooty. He just wasn't having it any other way. After they were dressed Jo went to start the dinner. Kevin said he'd update his Blog as he wouldn't have time tomorrow. He lit a Benson as she brought him a large white.

My dearest, nearest and Peeps

The Kevster's back off across the big lake in less than forty eight hours. Whist I'm away this time Peeps I will be able to log on, the big boss has put Kevster into the twenty first century with a lap top. Can yous lot all believe it, me, walking around with a bloody portable computer, the world needs warning Dudes and Dudesses? Gals, I'm sorry for yous but happy for me that I'm in luv, my new girl is top totty, first class, sex siren, yous get the drift.

When I get back April will almost be over, that means we're heading into the summer Dudesters, the Millennium approaches Peeps, please be mindful how quick the year's gone already. I want the short list for locations done whilst I'm away yous lot so get cracking. I'll need a day or two to acclimatize but will be nagging yous all again by Wednesday next week, super party planning luck.

Jo announced she was the dessert after their food by grabbing him and taking him to the bedroom, he had no objections, none whatsoever! They fooled around until the early hours. In the end Jo screamed 'Enough Kevin, where the hell do you get your stamina from?' 'Long times of abstinence' he giggled back.

....

10ᵗʰ April 1999

Jo was taking Sooty out so Kevin could pack and figure out his new lap top. By the time he'd read all the instructions he was no better off. He binned them, turned it on and spent an hour playing. This was far more fruitful. He had it doing all he wanted well within the hour.

He told Jo he'd booked Salvatore's tonight as a surprise. He'd used some favors he had outstanding. Salvatore's was one of the top restaurants in the area, all the celebrities went there. Jo gasped 'Kevin, we can't go there, we're not stars.' 'We will be tonight, come on I'm buying you a dress.' He said feeling like a millionaire.

He took her to Jaeger and walked out eighteen hundred pounds worse off. He'd bought her a dress, coat, shoes and a bag. Jo said she'd make him feel special tonight. Kevin asked what that meant. 'You'll find out' she said looking smug.

The taxi picked them up at seven and they were in the restaurant by seven-fifteen. The menu wasn't huge but the food described sounded fantastic. They viewed the menu and were still unsure. Their waiter came over and introduced himself, his name was Michael. Kevin explained that they were unsure what to have and asked for his recommendation.

Their table was in the corner, a dimly lit area and out of sight of the main body of the restaurant. Michael arrived with the appetizers. He placed their plates down and walked away. Kevin looked at Jo and gestured for her to try hers first. Jo tasted her meatballs and looked at him and silently nodded. Kevin started on his.

Michael said he'd leave them for thirty minutes before bringing their main courses and to finish their champagne. He asked Kevin if he would like to see the cigars. Kevin nodded and five minutes later had chosen one of the smaller Cubans. As he lit it Jo moved her chair. Before he'd realized it she'd got under the table, undid his pants, and was, he couldn't quite believe it, giving him a blow job!

Three minutes later to his horror and champagne induced head saw Brooke Charlie, an actress from a popular soap approach him. 'Hi' she said as she got closer. 'Hi' Kevin somehow managed to respond in a high pitched voice he didn't recognize. 'I hope you don't mind me interrupting you, I was just wondering what cigar you have, it smells amazing and wanted to get the same for my boyfriend.' She said smiling brightly. He just about managed to tell her which cigar he'd chosen and she said if he and his partner wanted a drink after their meal they were welcome to join her. Kevin thanked her screwing his face a bit as Jo increased the intensity. Jo emerged from under the table giggling. 'I told you I'd make you feel special tonight Kevin!' She said as she lit a cigarette.

'Shit Jo, whilst you were going for gold, bloody Brooke Charlie came over and started a conversation with me!' Kevin said in an alarmed tone. 'I know darling, I heard her, that's why I increased the intensity, I thought you'd scream baby, but you held it together. Can you imagine her face if I'd got you done quicker?' Jo said now looking really naughty.

'After the main course I want the favor retuning.' Jo said grabbing his hand. 'Are you serious?' 'Deadly' she replied. Following their beautiful food Jo pinched his cigar and said seductively 'Your turn now baby.'

Fifteen minutes later he nearly fainted with embarrassment. Jo had screamed out loud. He had got her off but she was making a noise like a fire alarm. Kevin just got back up to the table as Michael arrived. 'Is everything ok?' Michael asked really panicked. 'Fine, sorry, I burnt my hand on the cigar.' Jo said coolly. Michael asked if she needed any first aid and Jo asked if she could have some ice.

Five minutes later Jo had the ice but it didn't go anywhere near her hands! 'I nearly died Jo, you were so loud.' Kevin said grabbing the cigar off her. 'I know babe, you just got me badly!' Jo replied and they both went into fits of giggles.

Brooke Charlie, true to her word joined them half an hour later with her partner. Kevin bought a bottle of pink champagne. They all chatted and smoked for over an hour, swapping turns to keep the champagne coming.

At midnight Jo said she was pooped and they went to say their goodbyes. Brooke turned to Kevin and whispered 'I'm having that table next time, God I can't believe what you two did, absolutely fucking brilliant.' Kevin looked at her and said 'You knew?' 'Of course I knew I could see her bum waggling under the table. I knew she'd made you do the same when I heard her scream. As I said, brilliant! I can't wait until next week to try it myself.'

....

10th April 1999

This was it, just one night to go and he was off again. The day went quickly and he needed to update his pages before he left.

> To all Peeps across the world
> It's the Jet setting Kevster here, on the eve of my departure across the pond again yous lot. I am as prepared as one can be. Packed what I can, got my winter warmers to keep me warm. Yous lot will know how hard that is for one as cool as I! There we go though, my cool self will be in the land of the Mounties in less than twenty four hours. Guys and Gals, I have listed all the suggestions for the big party to date. I have a short list I want all your opinions on. Here

goes then. Edinburgh, Glasgow, Manchester, Cardiff, London, Birmingham, Sheffield, Bristol, Norwich and gay Paris!

Jane was bang on time carrying more bags than Kevin had ever seen. He helped her in and had to go to the taxi with her for the rest. They got her huge haul in and shut the door. Jane spent an hour sorting her bags out and asked him for a glass of white.

He sorted her drink out, told her food was ready forty minutes from when they wanted it and held two pieces of paper in his hand. 'Jane, before food, before more drink, I need to go through the lists I've written for Snowy and Sooty.'

Jane looked at the instructions and told him sincerely she would be there for them and be alert and wouldn't let any of them down. 'Right then darling, we're having lasagna, salad, a chili lemon dressing and homemade garlic bread. How's that float your boat?' Jane looked at him, smiled and said 'Floats it right to the top my hunky baby.'

....

11th April 1999

Kevin boarded the plane at half past one after several champagnes in the First Class Bar. He was sat in front in seats bigger than his arm chairs at home. He also noticed he was sat next to a very pretty lady. The plane taxied and they were soon airborne. The pretty lady's name was Claire. She was off to meet her husband Paul who she hadn't seen in six months. Claire, as it turned out was really good company. They chatted about their lives and before Kevin knew it the pilot was talking about the descent plan.

The descent was not a pleasant one, unexpected turbulence caused them to rock all over the place. Claire was petrified but Kevin held her hand and told her not to worry, he had it all under control. 'Kevin, you're bullshitting me!' Claire said still absolutely petrified by the plane's dramatic falls and bumps. 'No Claire, I'm not, I'm the Kevster, the super hero name I use on the days I'm needed talk to higher authorities.'

'Who the hell are you talking to now then?' Claire asked in almost a delirious state. 'Well Claire, my first task as a Super Hero is to talk to you. Then I have a telepathic link to the pilot and a supernatural link to God.' Kevin said looking deeply into her eyes.

'Kevin, we're going to crash I know we are, you've got no fucking link to anywhere you crazy fool.' Claire said in a desperate tone. 'Claire, sometimes you have to have faith. Remember the Force from Star Wars? Remember Jesus Christ? Miracles happen, you just have to believe.' She tried to pull her hand away from him but he continued relentlessly. 'Claire the vibes are good, God has spoken to the Kevster, the pilot has spoken to the Kevster and the world has spoken to the Kevster.'

Claire looked at him and was about to call him all the false, bullshitting, nasty bastards she'd ever met when she realized they'd actually landed. She grabbed his hand tightly and kissed him on the cheek. 'You did all that to calm me down?' She asked still panting. 'No I did that to make the time go so you didn't fret Claire. I was shitting myself and it helped me to help you.' Kevin said with a huge sigh himself.

'Wow Kevin, you thought of all that under stress?' 'Yeah, somehow, I hope it helped you Claire.' 'Helped me Kevin, I was ready to kill you, I forgot all about crashing!' Claire said as they shared a long hug.

They grabbed their cases and Kevin asked where Claire was staying. He laughed as she brought out the same pack he had for the Hotel Quebec. 'Wow Kevin, we're in the same hotel, how uncanny is that?' Claire said and looked elated. 'Amazing Claire, I've got a car waiting for me. I can give you a lift.'

His Driver, Carl took them on the pretty route, there was snow everywhere. Kevin thanked Carl and handed him a fifty. Carl gave him the wink and said softly 'Thanks Mr. Julie, the guys in the States said you were top notch, they weren't wrong.' Carl carried their baggage in and left them in reception.

Claire asked Kevin if she could buy him dinner tonight. Without reason to object he agreed. They were checked in and heading to their rooms by six o' clock. Kevin got to his room and unpacked. He knew he had weeks of long hours, tonight's meal with Claire would at least be some respite. He knew he fancied her but he was in control. For once in his life, his cock was staying firmly put in his pants. The attention however was really flattering.

He showered and was in the bar at seven o'clock. He was chatting to a chap who was in for a sales conference. His Company sold clothes hangers. His name was Brian and he was a typical sales type, added to the fact he was born in New York and had lived in Canada for the last ten years OTT was an understatement.

Kevin was glad when Claire arrived, God all he had to do was not shag her, and it would be easier than talking to Brian all night. Claire went and sat at a table and gestured Kevin over. Brian looked at him and said 'Yo Kev, Fucking A man, top, titty totty.'

Claire started to tell Kevin about Paul. He'd been in Canada for six months with work. He was a Meteorologist for the National Oceanic Atmospheric Administration. Claire strongly suspected an affair as he had spurned opportunities to return home for short spells saying he was too busy.

She went to the bar and ordered them a bottle of wine, fifteen minutes later Claire had asked the barman to bring another bottle over. Kevin could see where this was going. She was already two to one on each of his drinks.

They went into the restaurant at eight. Kevin ordered squid to start, Claire melon. Claire had the sea bass and Kevin buffalo for the mains. They both abstained from dessert. Two more bottles of wine later he half escorted her, half carried her to her room.

He'd just got her through the door when he heard the retch. He felt the warm gush as he was splattered with sea bass and melon soup! It was all over his face, his hair, her dress, his shirt, everywhere!

Just as he thought she had finished she heaved again, something like out of the Exorcist and covered them both further. Kevin was nearly sick himself. Ten minutes later the sickness had eventually stopped. He took Claire to the bedroom and took off her dress. God the woman didn't mess around, she was starker's underneath it. Kevin turned her on her side, just in case, and left a note.

Dear Claire
You had one too many last night. Your honor is intact but I had to take your dress off to wash the sick out of it. I'm afraid you puked for London! I will be back later tonight and will check on you. I hope you're ok and your day is fruitful.

He took his shirt off, exited her room and closed the door. As he was walking down the corridor Brian collared him. 'Yo Kev, look at you, skunk up a trunk eh?'

....

12ᵗʰ April 1999

Despite hardly any sleep in the last twenty four hours he was up and waiting in the reception area by seven-thirty. At quarter to eight a large thickset man in a padded coat came into the lobby carrying a card with Mr. Julie on it. Kevin introduced himself. The Driver's name was Jack and he was a man mountain. Jack seemed pleasant enough though and said in his deep Canadian accent. 'We've got a one hour fifty minute journey Mr Julie, cold one today.' 'Kevin, please call me Kevin.' He said as he held out his hand again. 'Thanks Kevin that makes it easier. Sometimes I get the pompous bugger's who must be Mr or Sir. You and I will get along fine.' Jack said with a grin. Secretly Kevin feared for the sanity of anyone who didn't get along with Jack.

Kevin found out that Jack ferried all the bosses of the Company around and was a trusted confidant. He was married to Katie and they had three children; Josh, Alex and Alicia, five, three and eighteen months. They lived in a remote area by the sound of it.

Kevin explained about his circumstances and talked about his babies, Snowy and Sooty. 'You like animals then Kevin?' 'Yeah wouldn't be without them.' 'You should come see my gaff before you go then.' Jack said in an inviting tone. 'Why, what you got?' 'What haven't we got?' Jack replied. Kevin laughed but said he'd love to take Jack up on his invite explaining his last trip for the company to the States he didn't see any of the country. Jack said he'd sort it as long as Kevin didn't mind being away from his luxury hotel.

Kevin delivered his first presentation in just over two hours. He knew he'd nailed it though. Getting back to his room he opened a bottle of white from the mini bar. He turned his lap top on and went for a shower as it booted up. He got out of the shower, sipped his wine, lit up a Marlborough, he couldn't find any Bensons to buy, and opened his Blog Page.

Howdy Dudes and Dudesses

How are yous lots, any bears on the horizon? There's plenty where the Kevster is. Well as I told yous lot I'm in the land of the bear, the maple, the land of make believe Peeps, boy its cold out here. Minus thirteen this morning my warm sun loving friends, to say the old balls had shriveled a bit is no understatement, had to check there were still there! Joking Peeps, I'm suited and booted for expeditions into the wild. My driver's a cool dude, just like yous lot and has invited me to his primitive domain up in the hills and woods to spend a night with his family.

Tried the buffalo last night, well Dudes and Dudesses, that's gotta be on the old menu for the big bash at the end of the year, how many others will be having B B Q buffalo man, come on I ask you! Well that's it for now but fear not again my friends the Kevster's on the trail, on the nail and ready to sail man.

He got to the bar at just past five o' clock. Claire was there already. She grabbed him as soon as he got there and asked him to sit at her table whilst she got the drinks. 'Firstly Kevin I want to know what the hell happened last night, if you don't mind telling me. I know I was on one but . . .' Claire said going bright red in the face.

Kevin looked at her and said softly 'Do you want the actual or my gentlemanly take on it?' 'No, hit me with it full force please Kevin.' She said as she took a huge gulp of her champagne and lit one of his Marlborough's.

He sank his first glass, refilled it and started his story. By the time he got to the bedroom part Claire was in stitches, Kevin too couldn't keep hold of his laughter. 'So you've seen me at my worst then Kevin?' Claire said still smiling. 'Ah, don't worry about that, lots of people puke for their country from time to time.' He said smiling back. 'No, I didn't mean that Kevin, I meant you've seen me starker's!' 'Well that can't be your worst.' Shot out of his mouth before his brain had engaged. Claire blushed and looked a little down as he sank the champagne in his glass.

Kevin then told her about Brian and how he'd left her room topless. The smile returned back to her face as he repeated Brian's comment 'you got your skunk up a trunk then Kevin?' Claire burst into laughter, tears were streaming down the side of her face.

It took him a few moments to realize but the tears were actually tears of despair, she was quivering and shaking and really upset. 'What is it Claire?' He asked gently. 'Kevin, can we get another bottle of champagne and go to my room, I need someone to talk to and I don't want to be the public entertainment tonight?'

They got another bottle and an ice bucket and went back to her room. Claire started to tell Kevin that she'd met Paul and he had told her he was leaving her. He asked her if there was any chance of reconciliation. Claire shook her head and continued gulping the champagne.

'Come on Claire, there must be some hope. He wouldn't ask you all the way out here just to say it's all over, surely?' He said holding her hand. 'Well I thought that Kevin but the fact he introduced me to his boyfriend sort of sealed the deal!' She said in fits of new tears.

Later when Kevin got up to leave, Claire kissed him softy on the cheek and said 'Thank you Kevin' 'For what?' 'For being so nice' 'my sixth middle name I think' 'God you're funny Kevin' Claire said looking brighter again. 'That's my real middle name' he said as he left her room.

....

13th April 1999

He got to the foyer at five-fifty nine, Jack was sitting there reading a paper looking as if the day was already half old. 'Just in time Kevin, late night Buddy?' 'Something like that Jack.' Jack hit the heaters on full and they were on their way by six-ten. Jack was good company on the journey and talked about his life for the first hour. Kevin took the second. Whilst Jack was settled he wanted to know about Kevin's lot. Kevin tried to explain. They got to the site just after eight-fifteen. Jack told Kevin he'd be ready when Kevin was. His last session finished at seven-thirty and Jack was waiting for him as he came out just shy of eight o' clock.

They drove back and it was a slow affair, the road conditions were treacherous. Although Jack and he were now great talking partners Kevin sensed they both felt the strain of the length of the day and the conditions they were driving in. They got back to his hotel at just before midnight. Jack had already pre-booked a room. They had to leave again at five in the morning!

....

15th April 1999

The next two days were about the same but they did get back earlier. Jack said he was off home tonight to see his family and Kevin had four days off so he would see him on Tuesday. Jack added Tuesday was a breeze; a one hour drive, so he wouldn't pick Kevin up until seven. 'Hang on a second Jack, what about tomorrow, Saturday, Sunday and Monday? I thought I had one day off in three?' Kevin said looking confused. 'Easter mate, tomorrow's Good Friday, didn't you know?' Jack smiled then added that the day for Kevin's visit to his home, if he was still interested would be Wednesday next week.

He was a little worried about Claire so dialed her room. She sounded ok but asked him to pop around as soon as he could. Kevin got there five minutes later. Claire opened the door and hugged him. 'Thanks Kevin. Thanks for coming so quickly. I met Paul again and he's wants a divorce.'

'Oh Claire, I'm really sorry. This wasn't what you expected when you came out is it?' Kevin said holding her hand tightly. 'Not quite, I thought there was a chance, I didn't realize though that my husband and childhood sweetheart would turn out to be a poof Kevin, no; how the hell do you compete with that?' Kevin had tears in his eyes for her. Before Kevin knew it they were making love on her bed. They ordered room service and stayed close all night.

....

16th April 1999

He left Claire's room at nine fifteen and sat in his room with his head in his hands hitting on his personal blog, he needed a debate with himself.

>   Dear Kevin
>   What and I really mean what are you doing? Are you destined now to become some kind of sick stud that shags anything that moves? Keep your cock in your pants, how hard

can that be? Too hard, in your case Dude; what were you thinking? Do you love Jo or do you love Alexis? We need to bottom this out now Dude, once and for all. Claire is beautiful but only short term, even though she shouldn't be any bloody well term at all.

So what's next Stud Muffin? The first part of the year we were talking of nearly a year of abstinence and now we can't go hours Dude! Well for now it's easy, you've given this poor woman Claire expectations, the least you can do now is to help her, it's a one off, no strings, no ties, one sincere adult helping another in her time of need. It's the noble thing to do. You can't let her down now.

He phoned Jane after his rant at himself, she seemed a little off and he heard another voice in the apartment, her life he thought. Putting the phone down the pangs of guilt reappeared as did his debate between Alexis and Jo. He shut them down, everything was too complicated, he decided on simplicity for the next few days and that was in the form of Claire.

They met in the lobby at two and were both dressed for the cold. To his horror though, Brian was sat in the lobby drinking a beer. He called Kevin over. Despite just wanting to go he trundled over.

'Hi Brian' 'Hi Kevin, see your still pumping the puma you dog, bet you've got beaver watch all sorted hey?' Brian said with a wink. 'Na mate, no beaver, I shaved it off her last night, she's as smooth as a pool ball now, know what I mean?' 'Shit Kevin, you're really on one with this babe aren't you?' 'Don't you know it Brian, her sister's here tomorrow and I've been given the nod. Two sisters, one bed, one night, know what I mean?' 'Fucking A Kevin, you're a stud, what's your secret?'

'Shave too Brian, women go mad for the bald guy look.' 'What, you shave your nads?' 'Na, wax them mate' Kevin said as he left a speechless Brian gulping his beer.

Kevin left with Claire and she asked what all that was about. Claire laughed when he told her but then said, 'will you get me as smooth as you later big boy?' 'If you desire it, I'm here to meet your expectations hairy girl!' He replied and squeezing her bottom.

They stepped outside and the wind and coldness hit them like a lead balloon. Kevin couldn't remember it being this cold, even in the early morning's he'd been out with Jack. Claire said there was a bus stop down the street that went into town, she gestured him to follow her.

He kept a smile on his face as Claire dragged him around the shops. On the upside she bought him a hat, another extreme coat and also some new gloves. He tried to protest but Claire showed him Paul's gold card. 'The poof's paying.' She said determinately.

Kevin used the wax strips and razor on Claire and asked her to check his work. 'No Kevin, you check it!' Claire said as they then spent the next two hours exploring each other all over. Claire told Kevin Paul was treating them again tonight, a restaurant in town called Seaside, an apparent Mecca for all fish lovers.

They both showered together, Kevin used the robe to go back to his room to get his clothes. In the corridor he bumped into his favorite friend, Brian. 'Hi Brian, just been dogging the hyena, know what I mean?' 'God Kevin, do you ever stop?' 'Yeah, sleep, work, toilet and social duties, but otherwise no, ramming the ram all the time Brian.' 'God Kevin, you should be in films.' Brian said again looking gob smacked. 'Already there Dude' Kevin said as he carried on down the corridor smiling to himself.

Kevin and Claire had a quick drink and hit the taxi into town. They walked into the restaurant, Kevin thinking the food must outdo the decor and surroundings. It looked like a fisherman's cafe.

Their food arrived and Kevin looked at Claire, looked at the huge plate and looked at her again. It was loaded with Lobster, Cray Fish, Crab, Madagascan Prawns, Mussels, Clams, Oysters, Scallops, Razor Clams and what Kevin assumed was Squid, Octopus, and some meaty fish steaks he again assumed was a large sea fish such as a Wahoo or the like.

An hour into eating, their plate was a pile of shells, pincers and lemon pieces. Although it was a mammoth plate it was light food and washed superbly down with the champagne. At eleven o' clock they'd done the lot. Kevin lit a Marlborough and Claire asked him for a whole one too.

The bill was five hundred dollars and this included the taxi back to the hotel. Clair put another hundred on as a tip. 'Let that sit with his new limp dick partner!' She said still looking a bit upset.

....

20ᵗʰ April 1999

Claire and Kevin had spent the entire previous day in bed with room service. Jack picked Kevin up at five and dropped him back at the hotel after another successful day at seven. During their journey there and back Kevin told Jack all about his current predicament. Jack was cool about it but then Jack was cool about everything.

Jack said Kevin should bring Claire with them tomorrow; he'd entertain her whilst Kevin worked and she could stay at his with Kevin. Their plan for tomorrow wasn't a long one. An eight o' clock pick up and as the office was small, one meeting, there was a two and half hour journey there and back though.

Kevin told Jack he'd decide tonight and if Claire was with him in the morning she was and he would be extremely grateful, if not it would just be him. Jack winked and said 'Up to you Kevster!' 'Shit Jack, where'd you get that name from?' Kevin asked in complete shock. 'We Mounties do have computers Kevin, it's not all bears and beavers you know!'

'Look Kevin, Katie and I have been talking about a trip to the UK, her parents will look after the kids and I have a Ranger mate who'll take care of the animals, can we come to you for this Millennium party?' 'Jack, I'd be more than honored, in fact it would make my year.' Kevin replied. 'Deal then' Jack said, adding 'Deals are deals with me Kevin, once agreed binding.' 'My kind of deal mate.'

He got back to his room, fired his lap top up as he poured a white wine and lit a cigarette as he also turned the shower on. He smoked his Marlborough, hit the shower as the lap top warmed up and was back in front of it fifteen minutes later. He refreshed his glass and his cigarette and went to his Blog Page.

> My most Sincere Peeps
> Not only is the Kevster having a ball in the land of the beaver, the bear, the moose and the maple. My new friend Jack (man mountain who'd pass for a bear) and his beautiful wife Katie are crossing the pond to join our big party Dudes and Dudesses. That's some commitment Dudesters I think you'll all agree!

I'm off to the wild with Jack and his family tomorrow night Peeps, right deep into the hills. Bet there's bears up there, know what I mean. What I must also tell you is this place is still cold man, the UK weather's going to be a breeze for our party, and I can't wait for the planning to start. Well Edinburgh and Cardiff are tied on ten votes each. All the others are only into single figures. God Peeps where'd Cardiff come from, do yous lot know something I don't?

He was down in the bar by ten to eight. Claire was already there in a stunning short dress. She was on her own but he saw Brian ogling from the seat he was sat in. Kevin called Brian over and they sat down, Claire opposite Brian. She hitched her skirt up and crossed her legs slowly. Brian's drink went down the wrong way and he coughed lager all down his front. Kevin suspected Claire was pantless and had given Brian a good view.

'Hi Clairvin, I mean Keviare, I mean hi both of you. God it's hot in here, God, I wish I had less clothes on, I mean I've got pants on but shorts, yes shorts would help. Are you ok you three? God it's bloody hot, really hot in here.'

Claire spoke first, 'gosh Brian, your glass is empty. Would you like a long one?' 'Yes please, a cool smooth, I mean hairy, no I don't mean hairy I mean smooth long one please.' Brian said in desperation.

Claire made a point of uncrossing her legs slowly again as she got up, Brian went purple. Kevin jumped in as she was off to the bar. 'So Brian, what's up?' He said keeping a straight face. 'Nothing's up Kevin, I mean definitely nothing, I mean I've been busy but nothing up, nothing, really.' Brian spluttered back at him.

Claire sat down, gave Brian his drink and opened her legs wide as she gave him the glass. He tried to gulp it down but spilt it all down himself again. Claire grabbed a napkin and tried to wipe him down. Brian ran from their table saying he felt ill clutching hands in front of his crutch area!

They had a light dinner, salmon and salad and Kevin offered Claire the invite from Jack. She was made up and lit a Cuban for him. God this was something Kevin thought to himself and got engrossed in all Claire. They didn't turn the light out until two in the morning.

....

21st April 1999

Jack told Kevin he was pleased he'd brought Claire as Kevin introduced them. They were on the road by eight-fifteen. They all chatted all the way there and Jack endorsed Kevin's view of Claire winking at Kevin. They got to the site at ten-thirty. Kevin eventually finished his presentations and found Jack and Claire. Jack got them into the car and they were off. Some hours later they stopped, Jack just winking at them both.

Jack then dropped the car off in a lot and came back five minutes later with a monster truck. They transferred their luggage and were off again ten minutes later. Jack then put icing on the cake even before it had been baked by saying their trip tomorrow had been cancelled, there was a flu epidemic on the site, and their next session was now Friday.

Jack got them to his house forty bumpy minutes later. Katie came out to greet them and gestured them inside out of the cold. As they got into the huge pad, no wooden shack, Katie took Kevin and Claire to their room.

....

22nd April 1999

As they walked into the kitchen the following morning the whole Black family were there, the animals as well as the children, Josh, Alex and Alicia. Kevin was amazed at how the animals just enveloped the children and provided a shield, not one you'd see but one you knew was there. Katie served them bacon, eggs, pancakes and syrup and said they were all going out for a walk afterwards to see their other animals.

Claire dropped him a minor bomb shell during breakfast. 'Kevin, I've changed my flight, an open booking. I'm going back when you go back. I know there's nothing afterwards but I'm making this last as long as I can.' Kevin couldn't argue this was somehow right.

The Black estate as well as their huge house came with in excess of fifty acres. As they went out into the cold Jack showed them his chickens, cows, raccoons, skunks, the beavers in his brook and then introduced them to Lennox. The kids and the animals ran to him and he nuzzled into all of them. The problem

Kevin saw was that Lennox was one huge, bigger than big should be grizzly bear!

Jack then told everyone to sit. They all sat like dogs, even Sadie the cat and Jack said 'Lennox, wrestle.' The huge bear ran at Jack and for five minutes they had a play wrestle. No one won and no one lost and in the end they hugged, actually hugged. Kevin nearly fainted.

Jack grabbed him and said seriously 'Kevin, I want you to meet my first baby pet, Lennox Black, please meet my friend Kevin Julie.' Despite himself Kevin peed in his pants. Jack saw, smiled and whispered to Kevin 'Don't worry mate, I've seen shit before now!'

They went back inside and Katie gave Kevin a large short, Kevin didn't know or care what it was but sank it asked for another. He sank that one too and asked for another, this time though in a more dignified way. Claire was as white as Kevin and hadn't spoken. She just sat there.

Alex sorted the silence out by saying, 'Most people are 'fraid of Lennox, he's a puppy tho, and he won hurt no one.' This kicked Kevin and so it seemed Claire into life, a three year old telling them not to be frightened. Kevin asked Jack if he could go and see Lennox again, now he was prepared.

He asked Jack if they could take a camera so he could put the photos on his blog page and also print them to keep forever. Jack took him back outside. This time now he knew what to expect Kevin met Lennox feeling more secure. Lennox growled and Kevin nearly lost control of his bowels, never mind his bladder. Still, Jack encouraged him forwards. Lennox approached on all fours and Jack told him commandingly 'Stand' Lennox obeyed and stood on his back legs, Kevin reckoned he was at least ten feet tall. Jack then told Kevin to walk towards him and stand in front of Lennox with his arms out in front of him.

Despite nearly peeing himself again Kevin followed the instruction. Jack told Lennox 'Hug Lennox, hug and kiss.' Lennox moved closer to Kevin and put his paws on his shoulders, surprising lightly and licked Kevin right on his lips. Jack was snapping away but Lennox was unperturbed, all he seemed to want to do was kiss Kevin.

Jack then told Lennox to sit. He did as he was told like a dog. 'Climb on him Kevin' Jack shouted. Nervously Kevin climbed on top of the grizzly bear! 'Horse' Jack shouted and Lennox moved with Kevin on his back like a horse!

Kevin jumped off and Lennox nuzzled up against him. Kevin couldn't believe it. Lennox wanted attention, like his Snowy, like his Sooty. His fear disappeared immediately and he hugged Lennox of his own volition. Jack snapped as they hugged, kissed, shook hands and the best one yet, Lennox allowing Kevin to hold him in a mock bear hug.

They walked back together and Kevin hugged Jack and said 'Mate, that's the best night I've ever had in my life.' 'Kevin, for you I see it. For me, one of mine too, a new friend, my family, it just doesn't get better for me.' Jack said with his knock out smile.

....

23rd April 1999

Jack hit the gas at four-thirty after they'd swapped vehicles, telling them both it was a four hour drive at best but with the weather probably four and a half. Kevin was glad he could smoke. They got to the site at ten to nine, Jack telling Kevin that that was some going. Kevin was in his first meeting at ten, his second at one and his third at three. They left at five-forty.

Jack drove like a demon and got them back to their hotel at just before ten. He told Kevin they had the same journey type tomorrow. They got to Claire's room and Claire said in a slight huff 'I don't know how you do it Kevin.' He held her and said softly 'Stay in bed tomorrow Claire and I'll be back as quick as I can.'

....

24th April 1999

After another long day Jack told Kevin they had another day off tomorrow followed by two more days and then they were done. Kevin was going to fly back on Thursday. Jack asked if they'd both spend another night at his place on the Wednesday. Kevin thanked Jack for the offer and said he couldn't think of a nicer way to end his trip and would be honored to join his family again, but told Jack he was buying the drink, the food, and he was cooking.

Claire spent the next two hours showing him how much she'd missed him today and they both fell asleep just before one in the morning. Kevin just remembered to tell her he had the day off tomorrow.

....

25ᵗʰ April 1999

They got up and showered and went to the restaurant for brunch. Claire said she'd been awake since nine o' clock but had been wait-ing for him to wake naturally, she'd known how tired he'd been.

God this woman was making life difficult for him. The more time he spent with her the more time he didn't want to be away from her. His head was in a complete mess. Kevin got back to his room, lit a Marlborough and turned his computer on. Although it was early he also cracked open a bottle of red from his mini bar.

> Dudes and Dudesses of the World
> Kevster here, rocking and rolling, shaking and making waves across the big pond. I can't keep up with the days to date so don't even know about yous lots. When I get back though Peeps I'll be posting the pictures of me with the bear. No Peeps, not talking anything dirty here but talking about my bond with Lennox, the real life, bigger than big grizzly who's as soft as a puppy!
> Just a few days left here everyone, be glad to get back, Canada's cool man but home's home if you know what I mean. Got to go now Dudes and Dudesses but will be in touch, keep the party locations coming Peeps, not long before we decide where we party like Nineteen Ninety Nine Dudesters.

He had another shower and changed, checked his watch, it was four o' clock and decided on a few drinks in the bar before Claire arrived. He got to the bar and saw a sheepish looking Brian already there. 'Hi Brian, you're still here?' Kevin asked in a friendly tone. 'Here all week Kevster.' 'Brian, when did you log on?' 'A while now but only sussed it was you Bro when I was on this afternoon. Yo Kev, you're the man, man. And if I can I'm coming to the party.' Brian said now back to his over the top best.

'Brian, I'm gob smacked, you're really going to come, all the way over and we haven't finalized the location yet?' 'You bet ya Dude' Brian said in Kevster speak.

'Wow mate, I'm impressed and I'd love to see you there, with you and Jack and his wife that'll be three new friends from this trip alone, awesome.'

'Do you really mean that?' Brian asked going back into his shell. 'Yeah, really Brian, you're a good guy.' Kevin replied. 'The other night though, I thought you and Claire were taking the piss.' Brian said still looking a bit down. 'Of course we were taking the piss Brian, you're a piss-taker, you should understand.' Kevin said giving him the wink. 'Fucking A Kevin' Brian said and headed straight back to the bar.

Claire joined them at five. She looked knockout and had a dress on again. To Brian's apparent relief it was below the knee and he went and bought her a drink as soon as she sat down. Brian came back with the drinks and they all sat and chatted for a couple of hours. Brian joined them both for dinner. They all chose the steak, Brian recommending the T Bone. None of them were disappointed as they finished their meal, Brian and Kevin sucking on big cigars and all of them sipping top quality French red wine.

....

26th April 1999

Jack had told Kevin their last day would be a long one and picked him up at three in the morning. Kevin was grouchy. 'Jack, three o' clock, I doubt the Devil gets up this early!' Jack smiled and led him to the car.

They hit the road just gone three and arrived at the site at just after eight-thirty. They spoke the whole way, Kevin trying to get an objective view on where he was with life and what he should and shouldn't do.

Jack was a great listener but didn't have the answers. He started with 'Well mate, from a blokes point of view, I'd go back with Jo, see Claire as and when you can, grab Anne in-between, collar Jane again and wait till Alexis comes back and throw her into the mix. If Suzanne grabs you in between, then do as the Romans do!'

Kevin had told Jack that this advice wouldn't get him any further than he'd got on his own. Jack reflected, said he'd have a think about it and they'd talk again on the return journey.

Kevin nailed the presentations and they got in the car at two-thirty. Jack told Kevin he'd been considering his lot and had a few ideas. 'I'm all ears Jack.' Kevin said wondering what on earth Jack could have thought about.

'Well for me mate its Claire. Go home, explain to Jo, get hold of Alexis and tell her the situation and go full bore for Claire!' Jack said really confidently. They hugged before Kevin got out of the car and Kevin said sincerely 'Jack, you've been a rock for me out here and I really consider you a friend now, not just a colleague. You and your family will always now be part of my life that is if you feel the same?'

Jack looked at him before responding 'Kevin, I drive all the big wigs around, all the time, you came as the new superstar and I just think of you as Kevin, you're a top bloke and my family and I would be honored to consider you a new lifelong friend.'

Kevin headed straight to Claire and was wrapped up within her persona in ten minutes. Claire handed him a parcel. Inside was a beautiful and soft tan leather jacket. 'From me to you.' Claire said smiling. Kevin hugged and kissed her hard. They decided on room service as he didn't have to get up for work again this week and Claire opened a bottle of champagne as they perused the menu.

The door knocked and the waitress delivered the steaks and two bottles of red. Kevin gave her a fifty dollar tip and took the tray into the room. He felt like this was real, but then worried as Alexis had felt real and Jo still felt real. He fell into a disturbed sleep.

He woke up at about two in the morning and needed a walk. It was freezing so he dressed up really warm. He walked around the grounds smoking and thinking. Things weren't getting any clearer. He just couldn't get it in his head and was looking for some divine intervention. None came.

He got back to bed about four. He'd been out in the extremities for two hours and hadn't realized. He realized soon enough as he got back in and was shaking uncontrollably. He thought he might have over done it but the heat inside and the fact he'd had warm clothes on he managed to control his shakes inside five minutes.

....

27th April 1999

Whilst Claire was in the shower he went looking for a bag and found one in her cupboard. Ideal, he thought to himself and emptied the contents. There was a label and receipt in the bag. The label said Hugo Boss the receipt said six thousand dollars!

As she came out of the shower he looked at her showing her the receipt. 'Claire, this jacket was six thousand dollars!' 'Yup, I know honey, I bought it for you.' She replied nonchalantly 'Claire, six grand!' 'No not really honey, its Canadian dollars.' She replied looking bored. 'But Claire that's far too much, especially on me!' Kevin argued. 'Look Kevin, I know what I said but I haven't given up on you yet, we've still got a few days for me to persuade you too.' Claire said determinately. 'Shit Claire, we agreed, we agreed, shit Claire, shit.' He replied horror struck. 'I take it you don't want any part of me then, I'm just the holiday shag for you?' Claire said now getting emotional. 'Claire, for God's sake, I think you know that's bullshit.' Kevin said angrily.

She hugged him and held him tighter than she'd ever done before and said softly 'Kevin, I came out here to repair a broken marriage. Deep down I knew there was no chance. I've had my suspicions for a while. Don't interrupt me.' She said as he tried to say something. 'Meeting you wasn't planned, how on earth could it be? But I love you Kevin.'

Kevin put his head in his hands and said 'Claire, it can't be, it just can't be, I can't be in love with you after two weeks. I just can't be!' She grabbed him again and said softly, 'Yes you can, yes you can.' Kevin held her tightly and asked that they continue as they had and discuss serious stuff another time. Claire smiled 'Of course darling.'

Kevin lit a cigarette and said 'Planning my sweet, is the key to cooking well' Claire looked at him funnily. 'Honey, if we that is to say I am going to impress the Black's it's all about planning.' He said now reenergized. 'Oh I see' Claire said getting with him. 'Now my sweetheart we go shopping!'

They got dressed and Kevin ordered a taxi into town. It arrived on time thirty minutes later. As they got in to the taxi Claire asked 'Are you going to tell me what we're after?' 'Nope' was his short reply. They got dropped off and the first place Kevin looked for was an outdoor specialist. He purchased two of the biggest cool boxes Claire had ever seen. They then found the fishmongers and Kevin went into the back with the fishmonger himself. He came out empty handed and Claire looked at him and asked 'And?' 'Nothing honey, just preparation.'

They headed to the nearest bar and ordered two large wine spritzers. Kevin then hit Claire with his menu idea. 'Right for starters I'm doing seared lobster salad with a sweet chili dressing. Then, wait for it, grilled Argentinean T bone steak in a green peppercorn sauce with Kevin's steak house chips, peas and onion rings, and for my finale, homemade apple pie.' He said proudly.

'Right then Mr know it all cheffy bloke, why the boxes, is my first question and my second and more serious one, why the hell are they empty?' 'Ah, that would be because I had a chat with the fishmonger and he's going to get me live lobsters tomorrow before we leave and a few just caught salmons I'm going to put into ice and take for Lennox. Then as I've given him such a good order, and he liked my accent he said he'd sort the T bones out for me, twenty eight days hung he reckons.'

Back at the hotel bar, Brian as always was there. 'Drink Kevin, drink Claire?' He asked. 'Yes please' they both replied. Brian came back with two large vodkas and a cigar for Kevin. 'Right you guys, you're off soon aren't you? I want to stay in touch Kevin, you know in preparation for the party Dude.' Brian said excitedly. Kevin gave him his mobile number and they both stayed with him until nearly eleven-fifty. Brian was now a friend and not a pain in the ass.

....

28th April 1999

They were up and on their way. 'Tell me again Kevin.' Claire had asked. 'Easy Babe, in the first box are the live lobster's, you know, in the water, in the second box are this morning's caught salmon, dead but fresh with the ice on the bottom and on the top layer the well hung meat!' He said with a wicked grin. 'Oh Kevin, what are you like, I suppose you think that was funny?' 'Me, well now you mention it, yup bloody hilarious actually'

They arrived just before five and the whole family were there to greet them. Kevin and Claire handed out their presents first. Josh, Alex and Alicia were over the moon, Katie told them they shouldn't have, Jack called them too generous and they all had a great time with the kids as they ate their dinner.

Katie took the children up to bed at seven and Jack told Kevin he was going to get Lennox and bring him into the yard, under the light. Kevin stopped Jack in his tracks and said 'Bloody drink first Jack and a large one at that. I've bought Lennox a present too and I want to give it to him, but I need some Dutch courage first.'

'Right you two, this is vodka Jack style.' He said handing them the huge monstrosities imitating glasses. Kevin sipped his, gulped some and then said in a whisper 'How much orange's is in that Jack!' 'The juice of quarter my friend and topped with ice, half a bottle of vodka between the two glasses, good stuff hey?' Jack said sinking his own. 'You wanted to be on the on the way to see Lennox again, I just helped.' He added. 'Helped Jack, if I cook after this it'll be a miracle.' Kevin said through a hoarse throat.

Nevertheless he sank it and told Jack he was ready for Lennox as they walked into the yard. Claire, who had only sipped her drink, wincing said she'd do the video shoot.

Jack was back five minutes later with the huge as a tree Lennox. Lennox was following him like a dog then saw Kevin and roared. 'He likes you.' Jack shouted 'he remembers you.' 'Yeah, I remember him too Jack.' Kevin replied but his nerves fading with the alcohol intake.

Kevin walked straight to them and had a hug with Lennox, all captured by Claire on camera. Kevin then said 'Lennox, sit!' Kevin grabbed his salmon box and presented Lennox with the first of the two huge salmon he'd bought him.

Lennox took the fish out of Kevin's hand and ate it, not like the wild animal that he was but like a child eating an ice cream. Kevin asked Lennox for another hug and the bear hugged him immediately, again all caught on camera by Claire.

Kevin hugged Claire and said the dreaded words before he had chance to think 'I love you Claire.' 'Shit Kevin that was one off the left.' She replied. 'Sorry Claire, it slipped out, the experience, you here to share it, God I didn't want this to happen but it has and yes Claire I am in love with you.' He said this time more sincerely. She grabbed him and said, 'I love you too Kevin, more than I've loved anybody before.' 'Shit we're in trouble then!' Kevin said and let it hang. 'Probably' Claire replied. Jack came back bear less and said to them both 'Party time Dude and Dudesses.' Kevin smiled and said 'lead me to your kitchen big man.' Jack escorted them both back inside.

Kevin started by laying all the non live ingredients out. He asked Claire to rip and dress the salad. As she was ripping he was preparing the dressing. Jack had put the music on and Bruce Springsteen was coming into the kitchen from speakers they couldn't see.

'Salad done Chef' Claire said in double quick time. 'Shit Babe, I mean well done.' He said realizing this woman knew what to do in a kitchen. Bruce was now belting out Born in the USA. Kevin asked Claire to crush his peppercorns, chop a garlic clove and finely slice some parsley. She completed this in a few minutes.

Everything was ready now so he set about the lobsters. There were four of them still moving inside his watered box. 'Boil them don't we babe?' He asked Claire. 'Shit no Kevin, that's cruel. We kill them with a sharp knife, instant death, no screaming, like from the boiling method.' She said commandingly.

'Ok Honey, can you do this for me?' Kevin asked nervously. 'Yes darling, pass me the large strong big knife.' Kevin did as he was asked and Claire took the four lobsters out one by one and put the knife straight through their backs, killing them instantly.

His huge T bones had marinated perfectly, all he had to do to his pepper sauce was reheat and add cream. He was ready to serve his idea of a classic American type dinner for his Canadian audience.

The starters went down a storm, the main course something else. Jack kept telling Kevin it was the best steak he'd ever had. 'No mean feat that Kevin, I've had lots of good steaks and the fries, so big, so crunchy on the outside so fluffy in the middle' He kept adding after almost every mouthful.

Claire was sniggering but Katie interrupted his repeated drabble by saying 'Don't worry about Jack you two, when he's drunk he forgets what he says.' Jack looked horror struck and said 'I don't. Great steak Kevin, probably the best I've had and I have some good steaks and the fries, so big, so crunchy on the outside so fluffy in the middle.' They all roared with laughter, even Jack although he didn't know they were laughing at him and not with him.

Katie was giving Jack the evil eye as he opened a bottle of Jack Daniels. 'You'll be sick big fella' she warned him. 'I'm fine darling, I've been eating.' Jack said as he opened the bottle and filled four glasses. Kevin took a sip and felt the burn as it slipped effortlessly down his throat. Jack threw him a Cuban and they chatted, drank and smoked for ten minutes.

At two o' clock in the morning Katie pulled rank on Jack and said 'Bed big boy' 'Awe Honey, not just yet, I'm cool babe, sober man. Cool babe, sober, fine, come on darling just a bit longer please?' Jack replied or that's what Kevin thought he said through his slurs. 'Jack Black if I say bed, then I mean bed. You know not to argue.' Jack followed immediately.

....

29th April 1999

They joined the whole Black family for lunch at one-thirty. Jack said through dark glasses and a groan he would be taking them back to their hotel to collect their stuff and dropping them off at the airport. They drove back to the hotel after saying their good-byes, Kevin insisting on seeing Lennox one more time before going and promised they'd stay in touch. Jack got them to the hotel at four o' clock and was waiting for them as they arrived with their luggage at four-thirty.

They checked in and sat in the VIP lounge quietly. The moment of departure had finally arrived. They boarded the plane at six twenty and took off at quarter to seven. After they'd been airborne for half an hour Claire broke the silence. 'Kevin this is shit, I can't control what I feel for you and not knowing what's going to happen is killing me.' Trying to think of the right thing to say he paused, held her hand tightly and said softly. 'Claire, this is right, we both know it. Give me a few days and I'll sort something out, I promise.' Holding him tightly and kissing him softly Claire said 'Ok, if it's a few days I can cope.'

They landed at what was now ten-thirty in London. They hugged and kissed and went in their separate taxis. As he got into the car a sense of loss was already upon him.

He was back at his place just before one o' clock. Jane opened the door and then the madness started. Sooty went on the most ballistic crazy session Kevin had ever seen. He was running forwards, backwards, spinning around, jumping to get to Kevin's face to give him a kiss and then repeated the show. He seemed to be going for a third rendition when Snowy came out, looked at Sooty, somehow telepathically told him to stop and went to Kevin for a cuddle.

After he'd cuddled her and put her down Sooty came charging for his own hug. Snowy just looked at them and Jane as if to say 'Boys!' Kevin hugged and kissed Jane. They went to the kitchen and Jane made coffee.

Jane had already committed to staying tonight and said she was cooking for him. As he was so tired, he'd lost a day somewhere, he thanked her saying 'Jane, you've just made my day.' He went for a shower and spent half an hour letting the water soak him through. He shaved and waxed and came out of the bathroom an hour and a half later.

He knew he needed to ring Jo but was dreading it. What the hell did he say to her? He took a sip of his wine, then another, then downed it and went into the kitchen. 'Out, out you, it's a surprise.' Jane screamed at him. 'Sorry, I need vodka Jane and strong.' He replied a bit taken aback. She gave him his drink through the half closed door.

Kevin walked back in, looked at Sooty and said. 'Glad to have me home boy?' Sooty waged his tail furiously and nuzzled into his legs. Kevin turned to Snowy 'You?' He asked her. She purred and sat on his lap. 'Task master then yeah guys?' He said to both of them. Their eyes were enough to confirm their answers.

He took a large pull on his vodka, lit up a Benson and hit the dial buttons for Jo's number. 'Hi Jo, it's me.' 'Kevin, when did you get back?' 'Now and I'm completely knackered.' 'I bet. It's always worse coming back from that side.' 'Yeah, tell me and my body about it. Anyway how are you?' 'Ok' 'Just ok?' 'Well no really.' 'What does that mean?' 'Kevin, I don't know, I really don't know.' 'Woe a second, what don't you know Jo?' 'Kevin I don't know.'

'Hang on a second here, we can't keep going with this Jo.' 'No Kevin, I need to see you, not today, I know you're tired but tomorrow. Can you meet me for coffee in Alexandra's at two?' 'I can but why not here or at yours?' 'Kevin I don't know, please . . . ?' 'Ok then two o' clock at Alexandra's.' 'Thanks Kevin, bye.'

Jane came in minutes later carrying two plates. She set them down and to his delight it was a shish skewered kebab with salad and pita bread. 'Jane that looks perfect' he said and gave her a kiss on the cheek.

He devoured the food inside five minutes and asked for more vodka. Jane still eating her food said 'Legs Kevin, you do have them.' 'Shit, sorry Jane, you've rooted me here for so long I forgot about them!' 'Funny guy' 'My middle name' Kevin said as he got up a little wobbly and headed towards the kitchen.

She lit him a cigarette and said 'Come on, finish your drink, smoke this and then bed!' Jane said assertively. 'Do you think you're Katie?' He spluttered back.

....

30th April 1999

Sooty had been on one since their walk and was running around the apartment going wild. Kevin heard Jane shout 'No Sooty, no underware! I thought we agreed!' Sooty jumped onto Kevin's lap and presented his master with the pink silkies as Jane screamed louder again and Sooty ran for it. Kevin shouted back 'Jane for God's sake, I've got them, Jesus, I'll give them to you now.' He grabbed them still wanting to play Sooty's game and opened them in his hands. 'Wow nice Babe' he said as he held them in front of him. Jane tried to grab them and Kevin pulled them away quickly.

He looked at Jane with the most serious eyes he'd ever looked at her with and said slowly and calmly. 'Jane, why are Mary's undies in my apartment?' She went from a screaming mad woman to a woman in despair and sat down opposite him. 'Kevin, they aren't Mary's they're mine, you must be confused.' She said but her look said she was lying through her teeth. Jane then sighed deeply.

'Kevin, when you left, Mary came around for a meal. We got drunk and slept together. We both said it was a one off, you know

Suzanne and all that and we decided not to mention anything to you. Thing is she's stayed with me every night since. Kevin we're in love' Jane said quietly.

'Oh great Jane, I suppose the next thing is you'll get married and ask me to be the best man, and for fucks sake her mother to be maid of honor.' Jane burst into tears, 'Kevin, please don't be like this, it wasn't planned, I've lost Alexis, I've lost you, and Suzanne. Mary and me are for real, forever, you know, real commitment. We are going to get married, we've decided but first we're buying a place together.'

Kevin jumped into the shower, changed and left to walk to Alexandra's at just after twenty past one. He got there at ten to two, early for once in his life and ordered an espresso. He needed something to lift him, he was as flat as a pancake at the moment.

Jo arrived bang on two o' clock, she looked really white. She sat at his table and he asked what she wanted but she just shook her head. As he looked at her he knew what was coming. Jo though ploughed on to tell him what he thought he already knew. 'Kevin, Michael my ex finance has come back. We've agreed to give it another go. I didn't want to tell you whilst you were away but I sensed you knew something was up when we spoke.'

Sitting there wondering how this had turned around, he left the coffee shop and found the nearest pub. Inside of five minutes he had a pint of cider and a vodka chaser on the go.

He sat talking to an old fella called Mick, who he supplied with cider, vodka and cigarettes. Mick was a good listener, he heard Kevin's full story over two hours and told Kevin he was right, bang on and to keep to his principals. Kevin knew Mick hadn't understood a word of what he'd told him but the thirty quid he'd spent getting Mick to listen for two hours was the best investment he'd made for a while.

He grabbed a taxi home and as he sat down, opened a bottle of red and rang Claire. The number was dead. He tried again, the same tone. He sat in his chair and thought of what had happened in the last twenty four hours, how the hell could it have all have gone so shitty in such a short time. If your name's Kevin Julie he thought. Despite his turmoil he needed to speak to his Peeps and now.

My dearest and nearest British and Worldwide friends

The Kevster is back from the land of the Moose, Mounties, Beaver and Bear. What a trip peeps and I mean what a trip. Where to start, well I suppose from the beginning, it always seems to help me anyway. Firstly there was a complication on the love front, someone new in dire straits and yours truly a good shoulder, yous lot know what I mean. Then there's new friends Jack, Katie, their children and the Dudester Brian. And my newest biggest buddy Lennox, wait until you see me with this Canadian giant (pics to follow soon). Party ideas have been coming in bestest buddies and buddiesses. Cardiff's now top of the tree, on the left side if you ask me but that's the leader at the current mo.

....

03rd May 1999

Kevin had laid low for two days but Jane had called and said she'd come round tonight with Mary if Kevin was ok with it. He took Snowy and Sooty out and had their longest walk ever. He loved being with his animals, especially when they both went out for a walk with him.

He was cooking curry, a new dish for Kevin. He started on the red and was in control and was happy. Company tonight would be nice, something to stop him brooding about Claire. Tonight wouldn't be the night for him to confide in Jane, he just couldn't do it in front of Mary.

They both arrived at eight-thirty. Kevin poured red wine, he was confident it went with the richness of the chicken curry. As it was, soon after they arrived the potential awkwardness disappeared. They were all like long lost friends. This made Kevin really happy. He served up at nine-twenty and they all tucked into his curry, rice, bahjies and mango and garlic accompaniments. Nobody spoke as they ate a really good sign in Kevin's mind.

Even though the situation felt weird, they all chatted, drank and smoked until midnight. Kevin knew it was a start but had found it really difficult. They all kissed goodnight and Jane and Mary went to the spare room. Kevin went to his bedroom with his cat and dog.

04th May 1999

Kevin got up feeling absolutely knackered and totally horny. His unused rise was higher than normal. He walked to the bathroom rubbing his eyes and on the way literally bumped into an equally naked Mary.

They both supported each other and apologized for not looking. At that, that's exactly what they did, looked at each other's nakedness and Mary specifically noting Kevin's uncontrollable morning rise.

'Wow, Kevin, I'd forgotten how impressive that was!' 'Mary, you look good too, but I hardly think a quick grope and remembrance does us any favors at the moment.' Kevin said trying to hide his now very interested rise!

Mary went to make tea. Kevin opened his PC. He saw a large file, an e-mail from a source he didn't recognize. Opening it he saw there were ten photo attachments. There was no message. Kevin opened the first one. It was him and Lennox. He quickly opened the rest. There was him with Jack, Katie, Josh, Alex and Alicia and loads of photos of him and Lennox hugging. He knew where they'd come from. Claire had taken all the photos . . .

Sitting at the table, sipping a far too strong vodka he opened the rest of his e-mails. He got rid of the dross and then opened the ones that counted. There was one from his mum, he knew he was going the week after next to see her so left it. He concentrated on the e-mail with the photos of Canada.

He tried a response, it read 'Hi Claire, please give me some contact details, I miss you, Kevin.' He watched his in-box for well over an hour but nothing, bloody nothing. Why oh why had she disappeared on him? He knew if he brooded, he'd be in a bad place. Feeling lower than ever, Kevin hit his own page:

> Dear Kevin
>
> Lost count on the sexless days but for once not really interested. How on earth have we lost Claire? Jo's gone, Alexis gone, Mary seeing Jane and Claire in no-man's-land. Dude we've hit the wall! How we get over it is another matter and one we'll have to think of seriously Dude. Battle on is what we

need to do, concentrate on work, Snowy and Sooty and have
a break from bloody women.

He decided on hitting the Vodka again tonight. He contemplated ringing his mum but thought better of it. She'd be asking who he was bringing with him. Shit, it had just hit him! He didn't have anyone to take. He went through his phone menu and hit on an inspiration.

Within minutes he'd arranged to take Anne and she'd demanded a session before a dirty weekend away. So much for staying away from bloody women he thought silently as he staggered to bed.

....

05th May 1999

Kevin told Snowy he was taking Sooty to help him buy a car as it was important that the car suited the family. 'You'll fit in any car Sweetheart, but Sooty will need some consideration, yeah, we don't want him doing the Sooty Show in the car do we darling?'

They started at the BMW garage, a short walk from Kevin's apartment. He walked in with Sooty and the first thing he was asked, or rather shouted at was 'Sir, get that dog out of here' Kevin looked at the shouter and saw it was one of the Salesmen. 'Excuse me sir would have been more appropriate.' Kevin said really miffed. 'Well sir, there are no dogs allowed in here.'

Kevin looked at him. 'What if I want to buy a car?' 'Sorry sir no dogs are allowed in our showroom.' Feeling frustrated Kevin took Sooty and walked for forty five more minutes before getting to the Mercedes garage. As they walked into the showroom a young salesman greeted them immediately. 'Hello, my name's Jason, very pleased to meet you. Can I ask you your name sir and the name of your stunning looking dog?' 'Yes of course Jason, my name is Kevin and this is Sooty.' Kevin said feeling warmer already.

Jason took them both to a seating area, arranged coffee for Kevin and a bowl of water for Sooty. 'Right Kevin, what can I do for you today?' He asked patting Sooty continuously. 'Jason, I need a new car, well a car actually, I haven't got one at the moment and I need it to fit with mine and Sooty's needs.' Kevin replied feeling a whole lot more comfortable.

Jason smiled brightly and said 'Kevin, don't worry, you're with me now, and I'll sort it. How much wonga do you want to part with my man?' 'I've got a forty grand budget but I can go over if the car's perfect.'

'Kevin, Kevin, you're with me now, forty grand's what you got, I'll get you what you need for that my friend, don't you worry.' He took Kevin and Sooty to a black estate car, the windscreen price said forty five thousand and nine hundred pounds. 'Look at this Kevin, an E class 350 sport estate. Got all the modern cons, air con, cd, sports suspension and Sat Nav. Look at the boot area, it's got a special net for Sooty. And if you want him inside its top quality leather Dude.'

'Ok, I'm really interested.' Kevin said. 'Good my man, shall I get the paperwork?' Jason asked now so excited Kevin couldn't tell him from Sooty's OTT behavior. 'Not quite, I need the car by next week, you deliver that and I'm in.' Kevin said waiting for the 'I'm sorry sir' speech. 'Deal, next Wednesday for delivery confirmed' Kevin smiled and said 'Jason you've just sold yourself a car.'

He jumped in the shower, knowing he needed to phone his mum tonight so made sure he was clean. Why he did this he didn't know but wanted to say he'd washed if she asked. After two more wines and three Bensons he decided mum before food and picked up the phone and dialed her number.

'Hi mum it's me.' 'Kevin, my beautiful and less than contactable son.' 'Thanks mum but we did speak a month or so ago.' 'Thank the lord, my son rings twice in the same six month cycle!' 'Mum, come on please, we could keep this going all night.' 'I know Kevin but I do like to wind you up.' 'Mum, you're so funny.' 'My middle name Kevin' 'What Kevin's your middle name mum, when did that happen?' 'Kevin, you are funny.' 'I know mum but nice to bounce off yeah?' 'Yes, absolutely great, my lovely but distant son.' 'Still want to end on your note as always mum?' 'Always' 'Good to know some things never change' 'Yes but with you my dear is change an occupational hazard?' 'What do you mean mum?' 'Well, I've heard nothing of Jo since we last spoke.' 'No, that would be because there's no Jo mum, not any more anyway.' 'Well I'm shocked but not that shocked really. I take it you're coming alone with the dog next

week then?' 'Ah no, I'm bringing Anne, Snowy and Sooty too.'
Who's Anne and you're bringing the cat?' Anne is a friend mum
and yes I'm bringing the cat.'

....

08th May 1999

He packed his overnight bag and checked the clock, it was
already gone six o' clock. He changed and fed Sooty and Snowy
and cracked a glass of white open at six-thirty. He ordered his taxi
for seven-thirty and sat and relaxed for the first time of the day.

He was knocking on Anne's door at five to eight, carrying
a bottle of red and a bottle of white. Anne answered and Kevin
nearly dropped the bottles of wine he was holding. What she was
or wasn't wearing was totally gob smacking! Anne had some see
through negligee on and was completely naked underneath.

'Thanks for the wine Kevin, but that can wait.' She said
leading him by his cuff. 'Put those down in the kitchen and follow me.' Doing as he was told Kevin followed her to what was
evidently her bedroom. 'Strip Kevin!' Anne said sharply. Completely overawed Kevin just complied.

She slipped her negligee off and jumped onto the bed. 'Take
me Kevin, take me now, take all of me!' She screamed at him. He
got onto the bed but didn't have chance to do anything. Anne had
jumped on top of him. She spent the next five minutes telling him
it was the best sex ever and how he'd satisfied her beyond all her
expectations and better than any one had ever done before and
disappeared out of the bedroom.

Lying in the bed not knowing what had really just happened or
what he was supposed to do he dressed and went into the kitchen.
He opened the red, sank a glass in one and poured another to sip
on as he lit a cigarette.

An hour passed and there was no reappearance so Kevin
went back into the bedroom. Anne was fast asleep on the bed
completely naked. After finishing the red, he opened the white,
finished that and still wasn't drunk enough so went searching her
kitchen cupboards. He found his staple head clearer, vodka, and
started on one no orange juice would ever consider entertaining.
After finishing the bottle he went to Anne's bed and fell into a
deep drunken sleep.

09th May 1999

Anne was on top of what was now his morning rise. She shouted and screamed how wonderful it was, and in Kevin's calculation, about two minutes later jumped off screeching 'Just showering you sex beast you' as she exited the bedroom. Now left there with a still fully usable morning rise and a headache Kevin didn't quite know what to think. Perhaps Anne had missed out for longer than he'd thought.

As he walked back home he reflected on the night and morning. Bizarre still stood high on the list of words that he could describe the experience. Entering his apartment, Sooty greeted him but Snowy was still in bed. Kevin hugged his dog, changed the cat box, fed Snowy and grabbed Sooty's lead taking him on a doggy long walk.

10th May 1999

He was in the office just after quarter to seven. He was really surprised to see Mary there. She looked great from a distance but as he got closer he realized there was something wrong. 'Mary what's wrong, you look terrible, I mean, have you, God you are, Mary what's wrong you're crying terribly?' Kevin said all a little awkwardly.

'Oh Kevin I'm sorry, you know what I'm like I hate to bring anything personal into work but, well what I mean, I mean, well, Kevin I've broken it off with Jane!' 'She's been seeing Suzanne on the side Kevin, I caught them yesterday. I said I was going to be out for the afternoon but the weather was crap so I came back early. They were having some hows your father as I walked back into our bedroom!'

He arrived home just after four-thirty and grabbed Sooty for his walk, Snowy showing no interest this evening. They were out by five and didn't get back until seven, Sooty finding the illusive dirty pond, puddle and stream again. By the time they'd had bath time fun it was nearly eight o' clock.

Opening a bottle of Chablis and lighting a Benson Kevin made his first call, expecting this to be one of the long ones. 'Hi Jane darling, it's me.' 'Kevin, are you ok sweetie?' 'Fine darling, what about you, and please Jane no bullshit!' 'Ah, well I wondered how quick it'd be before we got to that.' 'You did? Jane I do work with her.' 'I know sweetie, but still wasn't sure it'd be today, that's all.' 'Ok then, well now we know it is today Jane, give it to me straight please.' 'Ooh, someone is pushing tonight aren't they?' 'Jane, don't insult me with counter psychology, I've only started sipping my first glass.' 'Ok, no shit Kevin. I thought I was in love, and my actions proved I wasn't, that's the short and tall of it.' 'Oh come on Jane, you and Mary were going to get married but you still find it reasonable to shag her mother?' 'You did!' 'Don't turn this around, I've paid my price.' 'Oh Kevin, I don't know, I thought I was in love with Mary but it was more the fact she was straight. Suzanne's sex on legs. I don't think I'll love again the way I love Alexis. And for another point Mary fancies you more than me, it was like Alexis all over again.'

'Are you ok with everything?' 'Not really, I know I cocked it up but still saw Suzanne last night so God knows is the honest answer.' 'Do you want to come around? Fish pie on offer?' 'Can I Kevin? That would be great.' 'Get your rear into gear then, food in an hour.' 'On my way.'

Lighting up another cigarette and filling his glass up Kevin made his next call.

Mary was ok, she told Kevin she wasn't really a woman's woman but was deeply upset it was her mother again. Before he realized it he'd invited her to his mothers, Mary agreeing through some sobs. He called Anne and said he was ill and the trip was off, feeling somewhat guilty as he put the phone down.

Jane arrived at just before ten o' clock demanding to be fed. 'Kevin, you promised food and I'm starving.' She said as she bowled into his apartment. 'Chill babe, I'm on it, ten minutes ok?' Calming down Jane nodded and asked for a glass of wine.

They small talked for ten minutes and he served his fish pie by half past ten. Jane filled both their glasses up as Kevin sat with the dog and cat on the sofa. He lit up a Benson, handed it to Jane and lit one for himself. 'Jane, where the hell's your head now darling?' 'Truth?' She replied. 'Yes Jane, the truth, all of it!'

Jane sipped her drink and pulled on her cigarette before saying 'Kevin, I've cocked this up a lot. Mary was never a full on lesbian and would never really commit to a life time relationship. I knew that but still took advantage.' 'But Jane, you proposed to her for God's sake!' 'I know, and at the time I meant it Kevin, I was all over the place emotionally.' Jane said defending her position. 'But her mother Jane, after everything that's happened!' Kevin retaliated. 'Kevin, I know, I know, God how bad could I have got it? Suzanne's like a drug, and I take and can't get enough of her. Christ, I can't believe I let myself get trapped. The truth is though Kevin, if I loved Mary, really loved Mary I wouldn't have done what I did, would I?' Jane said in a desperate tone.

Seeing the look on her face he knew she was in turmoil and knew he just needed to hug her. They held each other for ages and Jane said after a long time 'Kevin, I really needed this tonight, I really needed you.' 'Jane, I'm always there for you, you know that.' Kevin replied and hugged her tighter.

'Kevin, can we go to bed please?' Jane asked tearfully. 'Of course babe, come on' Kevin said as he led her to his bedroom. They both slept naked together cuddled tightly and both Snowy and Sooty, realizing there'd be no humping joined them soon after.

···

11th May 1999

Kevin woke with the normal Julie rise. 'Kevin darling, are you propositioning me?' Jane asked with a giggle. 'Bugger off, you know I'm not, and shit its bloody late.' Kevin said checking his alarm clock. He jumped out of bed and was leaving by nine-forty five. Jane shouted she wasn't going to work and would take Sooty out and later would cook supper.

As he got back from work Jane was waiting for him with a glass of red in her hand. 'Wow, that's what I call a welcome honey.' Fifty minutes later, after a few more top ups of red, Jane came in with two plates. She had cooked him a Beef Wellington with red wine sauce with what looked like asparagus spears.

After they'd both eaten Kevin said 'Jane, that was bloody fantastic but now I'm knackered, I need bed,' 'Great babe, because I'm shot too. They both had a cigarette and headed to the bedroom. As they both stripped and were about to get into bed the doorbell rang.

Kevin went to the door and looked through the peephole and saw Suzanne staring back at him. 'Who is it?' Jane shouted from the bedroom. 'Suzanne' Kevin shouted back opening the door but forgetting he was naked. 'Hello Kevin, what a welcome.' Suzanne said looking at his freshly shaven bits. 'Oh shit, I forgot' Kevin said retreating back to the bedroom to get his jogging pants.

Suzanne followed him and said 'Wow, a naked Jane, a naked Kevin, this could be really interesting.' 'Not going to happen tonight Suzanne.' Kevin said strongly but with a slight smile. Jane got out of bed and said 'Suzanne, why are you here? I told you I was staying at Kevin's tonight' 'I can see that, both naked and getting ready for good shag I take it?' 'Suzanne, we're friends, we've always slept together naked.' Jane replied coldly. 'Apart from the time you did shag that was.' Suzanne said scowling.

Kevin said 'Suzanne, look, I'm not prepared to argue all night, I'm going to bed you're welcome to stay, in the spare room.' He added quickly. 'Jane, you can stay here or go with Suzanne, I don't care, as long as I get sleep.'

'No Kevin, I don't want to stay, I wasn't checking up on you both but I want you both to help me. I want to bury the hatchet with Mary. Please can you arrange something for Friday night, a meal, here, on neutral grounds, please?' Suzanne said now sounding sincere.

....

12th May 1999

Kevin got out of bed reluctantly. He checked his watch as he had no idea where the alarm clock was and rang the office straight away. He told Mary he was collecting the car and offered to pick her up at four and take her for a meal.

He showered and was going to make breakfast. Jane came into the kitchen yawing at nine-fifteen. 'What's all the noise Kevin?' She asked sounding grouchy. 'It's me, I was thinking of making you breakfast.' 'You're too happy it's too early to be happy.' Jane said through a muffled yawn. 'Can you do it a bit quieter Kevin, I'm going back to bed' Smiling he fed Snowy and Sooty and changed Snowy's box. As he was going to deposit the bag to the outside bin he saw something that made him jump out of his skin. In front of his door was a rat, not only a rat but a great big, furry, big scary dead rat.

He ran backwards so quickly Carl Lewis would have nothing on him. 'Jane, Jane, Jane, quick!' He screamed still holding the dirty litter bag in his hand. Jane jumping out of bed naked ran to him shouting 'Kevin, what's wrong, what's wrong?' 'It's out there, out there! All big, furry and dead Jane!' Kevin screamed back. 'What's dead? Kevin you're not making sense.' Jane replied. 'It's out there, in the hall Jane, in the hall!' Kevin said still screaming.

Jane walked past him into the hall and returned holding the dead rat by its tail. 'Kevin, it's a dead rat, Snowy brought it for you as a present.' She said standing there naked holding the stiff as a board rat. 'Jane, I don't do dead things, get rid of it, please.' 'Give me the litter bag Kevin.' He put it on the floor and retreated. Jane walked past him two minutes later, still naked but at least rat less.

She was back another two minutes later laughing uncontrollably. 'Kevin Julie you total poof.' 'I don't do dead things, there's nothing wrong with that.' He tried to retaliate. 'So if I wasn't here would you be stuck indoors all day?' She teased further. 'No, of course not, I'd have called maintenance.' He replied deadly seriously. 'Oh Kevin you are so funny.' Jane said still giggling loudly and headed for the shower.

> Rock and roll Peeps
> Kevster's here and singing a song, 'Lord won't you buy me a Mercedes Benz.' Yes Peeps, today's the day I get my dream car. Blood, sweat and many tears over many years Dudes and Dudesses, but I get my rewards in the end. That's the persistence of the Kevster Peeps. I've had loads of updates everyone's on the party locations.
>
> Look my super party Peepsters, the year will run away so get voting. Yours truly will keep yous lot informed but need yous to vote my special Dudesters. Love and good luck to the special ones of the world.

He arrived at the garage at quarter to three. The paperwork took fifteen minutes to sort then he was shown all the basic functions.

Kevin drove out of the garage in his gleaming black brand new Mercedes feeling particularly pleased with himself.

The car was a joy, automatic but really powerful. He'd have to be careful with speeding with this beast. It wasn't the power that got him though but the refinement and the smoothness and the total luxury feel the whole thing had about it. Heading to pick Mary up he was really pleased with his choice. Mary jumped in and kissed Kevin on the cheek. 'Wow Kevin, this is special, really special.' 'I know Mary, really, really pleased with it. It's got everything I want.' Kevin said as they headed out of town.

After a long drive Kevin drove back to his apartment. Sooty was waiting at the door and Snowy even came out when she recognized Mary's voice. Kevin fed them both and poured two huge glasses of red plus a couple of strong vodka chasers.

He drank his two drinks before Mary had even got half way through her wine. Topping himself up on both glasses and lighting up a cigarette Kevin started his speech.

'Mary, Jane was here last night.' He said as openly as he could. 'How is the scarlet cow?' 'Not as you'd think I suspect.' Kevin said leaving it lie. Mary considered this for a few minutes before saying 'What does that mean?' 'Well it means she's a bit upset too but really thinks what you two were doing wasn't the real deal, she said she didn't think you'd ever really settle with a woman.'

Mary grabbed one of his Bensons and lit up. Kevin knew she was being serious now. 'She did, did she?' Was all Mary could manage 'Well, was she right?' Kevin asked softly. 'Of course she was bloody well right, but my mother Kevin, why does everyone have to fuck my mother?'

'Ah, that's the next part of what I want to discuss with you.' He said again quietly. 'No Kevin, you didn't did you not my mother, not again?' 'Woe Mary. No and never again. We can't keep bringing this up. Its history Mary, dead, do you understand me?' Kevin said so forcefully he actually frightened himself.

The effect hadn't been missed by Mary who sat back not speaking but looking intently into his eyes. 'Mary your mother came round late last night, she came in and stayed for an hour and left again, she realizes how she's been letting you down and wants to meet up for a meal here on Friday with Jane, you and me. I said I'd arrange it.'

Mary stayed silent for the longest time of the evening and eventually said. 'Kevin, you'd do that for me, despite everything that's gone on?' 'Yes Mary.' He replied softly hugging her.

....

14th May 1999

Kevin jumped out of bed, looked at the clock and held his head in his hands. 'Shit, shit, shit.' He shouted. Mary waking rubbing her head said 'Kevin what time is it?' 'It's nine Mary look we're working at home today, ok?' Kevin said convincingly. 'We are?' 'Yes Mary, today we work at home.' 'Kevin, I got drunk last night didn't I?' Mary said. 'Yes, a little, you were off your face but you didn't do anything silly or make a fool of yourself, you just slurred and repeated yourself a bit, that's all.' 'Shame' she said as she went to the shower.

He knew he had to call his mother. 'Hi mum, it's me.' 'Kevin darling, don't tell me you're pulling out at the last minute?' 'No mum, just a change of plan with the guest list.' 'Oh, well, it won't be a change of pet so it must be a change of woman.' 'Mum, you're so astute. Mary's coming and it's a long story so please no dramatics.' 'Kevin isn't Mary the colleague you've worked with for years' 'Yes mum and you'll meet her tomorrow but please don't probe, it's too complicated, even for me!' 'Ok darling, I'll be on my best behavior.'

Jane and Suzanne arrived at seven-thirty. As they entered the whole ambiance changed. The warm feeling that had been there mere minutes ago was replaced by the coldest of Jack Frost's Kevin had ever known. Trying to be some kind of mediator, but realizing he was one of the two least qualified in the room Kevin managed to get them all a drink and to sit down on the sofa.

Jane grabbed a cigarette and whispered 'Babe, this is hell, whose bloody idea was it?' 'Well it wasn't mine honey.' 'Kevin, it's just as bad for me you know.' She replied a little upset. Kevin decided action was required and stood in the middle of the room looking directly at Mary and Suzanne. 'Right, this stops now, I'm not prepared for us to sit in silence and maybe kill each other half way through the meal I have cooked. Suzanne, you called almost in the middle of the night to set this up. You have to take the lead here.' Suzanne looked at him nodding but still looked defeated.

'Mary, you agreed to come, maybe kicking and screaming but you came. Silence and bitchy looks won't get any of us anywhere' he continued. Mary nodded but still didn't take the disgusted look off her face.

'Right, let's put it more into the real world. Mary, I'm seeing you at the moment and want it to work. Jane, you're seeing Suzanne, you want that to work. The fact that a few weeks ago you and Mary were going to be married now needs to be irrelevant. The fact I've recently had an affair with both you and Suzanne needs to be irrelevant. We are all going to have to be involved in whatever the future holds so the past stops now!' Kevin boomed to all three of them.

Mary stood up, walked to her mother and hugged her. She then stood back and addressed all of them. 'This has to be the weirdest arrangement ever all of you. I have started to see Kevin again and I warn all of you, yes you too Kevin. If there is any further physical contact with whomever I see now or in the future then I'm off and will disown all of you. Is that crystal clear?'

By the time he served the cheesecake it was gone eleven. Jane and Suzanne left at midnight, Kevin secretly glad the offer to stay he'd half suggested was rejected. Perhaps this was the best end to the evening.

....

15th May 1999

Things were going surprisingly well on the journey until he heard a retch, followed by another and looking through his rear view mirror saw a panicked Sooty projectile vomit through the netting and hit the top of Snowy's cage. She meowed in disgust as the sick dripped all over her.

Kevin stopped at the next service station. It took half an hour to clean the mess up. The most part of that was cleaning Snowy. The seats were easy enough but the netting took some time. He took Snowy out of her cage and put her in the back with Sooty. Sooty calmed down immediately. They were back in the car fifteen minutes later ready to go on route again. 'Kevin, Snowy's so cool, going for a walk with Sooty, it's like a film.' Mary said really happily. 'I know it's just the way they've been since I brought Sooty into my apartment.'

His mum came out to greet them as they pulled into her drive. She hugged Kevin first. Then turning her attention to Mary she said 'Well then you must be Mary? My name's Felicity, you know, like the actress, only prettier and less country. I'm really pleased to meet you, especially as Kevin didn't say how beautiful you are.'

Blushing Mary said 'Hi Felicity.' and followed her into the house. 'What's for dinner mum?' Kevin asked about twenty minutes later. 'Oh whatever you choose darling, I'm not fussy and now you can apparently cook I thought I'd leave it to you. There's loads in the fridge, surprise us darling.'

He fed Sooty and Snowy and set her cat box up before washing and looking in the fridge. He saw a few joints and decided on the huge beef rib. He rubbed it with some anchovy, garlic and some herbs and put the rib into the aga for three and a half hours.

At ten past nine he served the roasted rib, vegetables and his wine gravy reduction. There was still enough meat to serve about ten people. The praise he wanted though came from the empty plate of his mother. 'When on earth did you learn to cook like that?' She said smiling brightly. 'See mum, I can be busy when I say I am!'

They finished the bottle of expensive red he'd bought and headed off to bed just after twelve. He kissed his mum goodnight and he went into his old bedroom, Mary, Snowy and Sooty following.

....

16th May 1999

Following breakfast they all piled into his mum's jeep and drove to the beach. Snowy jumped out quicker than Sooty when she saw the sand and sea and trotted off like a little dog. Sooty followed, playing minder.

Mary had offered to cook and drive back later so Kevin could have a catch up and drink with his mother. He sat back, lit a Benson and waited for his mother's onslaught. It didn't take long, just as he'd anticipated. 'Thank you darling for last night and today, it's been a brilliant few days. And Mary Kevin, why oh why didn't you tell me how cool and fit she is. She's daughter in law and mother material that one.'

'Mother' he always used this phrase when exasperated with her. 'Can't we just enjoy what we've got and see what happens?' 'Knowing you Kevin, seeing what happens normally involves you and your overactive loins with someone else.' She replied on the attack. 'Mother, how dare you, are you insulting my fidelity?' 'Yes Kevin, for once my darling son, keep it in your pants, other than for Mary whenever she wants it.' She added smiling.

They loaded the car and put Snowy and Sooty together in the boot area so she could keep an eye on him if he got over excited. They left waving to his mum just on six o' clock arriving home about three hours later. Mary came in for a glass of wine and ordered her taxi.

> Hi Peeps
> Number one son and chef Kevster here. My mother was bowled over by my culinary skills this weekend all yous Dudes and Dudesses. On the lady front well the partying playing rocking and a rolling Kevster's back in the game Peeps (Sorry all yous single Dudesses) The beautiful lady is keeping me on my toes and keen as yellow mustard all yous lot. That's it for now though and remember if you haven't made that call yet, there's still time. Your mother's deserve it Peeps.

He considered updating his own page but decided on making a call instead. He dialed long distance It was nine-forty so he figured about lunchtime, early afternoon in Jack land. 'Hello, Jack?' 'Kevin, is that you?' 'Yeah, how are you and the family big man?' 'Oh great Kevin, listen, I don't know if you've been told yet but I'm coming to the UK next month?' 'When Jack?' 'Look Kev, I'm tied up at the mo but will call you soon to let you know.'

21st May 1999

Following a week away Kevin had all his meetings wrapped up and was back home and in town by two o' clock. He went to Vivian Westwood's and bought Mary a black dress, shoes and hand bag, spending seventeen hundred pounds! Jane had arranged a table at the Ivy for him. It was Kevin's special surprise for Mary.

He laid out Mary's presents praying they fitted. He had champagne on ice all ready for her arrival. Mary arrived and went straight to the bedroom. She came back in screaming.

'Kevin, look what you've bought me!' 'Yeah, I know, I bought it darling.' He replied nonchalantly. 'I'm thrilled, more than thrilled, I'm, well I can't even say what I am.' Mary replied in splutters. 'You like it all then?' He said now with a huge smile on his face.

They left bang on time at seven forty-five and were there at half past eight for their nine o' clock reservation. As they entered the door the head of house asked their names. 'Kevin Julie' Kevin said a bit nervously. 'Oh the Kevster, Jane's told me all about you and I follow your blog page, Cardiff's my vote too. My names Richard, welcome to the Ivy. And this must be the beautiful Mary' he said to Mary's absolute astonishment.

Beaming Mary followed Kevin and Richard into the waiting area. There was pink champagne on the table waiting for them and Richard turned up with a Cuban for Kevin. As they were looking at the menu Mary tried to speak to Kevin but nothing came out.

Richard showed them to their table. Oliver James, the chef was sat on the table next to them. Mary went silent again. They had some superb food and sat back just looking at the surroundings.

Richard was back and whispered in Kevin's ear 'I don't normally serve Kevin but for you it's been a pleasure.' 'Thanks Richard, I'm really pleased you're a party goer and hopefully I can repay the favor,' Kevin replied.

'Now you mention it Jane says you're a demon in the kitchen yourself. A home cooked meal with me coming as Jane's guest would be more than repayment.' Richard said still whispering. He served their main courses ten minutes later. They swapped and changed the Venison and Lobster between them. Mary was back to being speechless. By the time their dessert came she was starting to get her voice, that was until Oliver James approached their table. Mary went white!

'Excuse me' Oliver said looking at Kevin. 'Hi there' Kevin said in return. 'Richard tells me you fancy yourself as a bit of a chef, I know Jane too and she's eaten my food so if she reckons it mate you must be not bad me old chucker.' 'Wow, Oliver James talking to me about my food, someone wake me up when I stop dreaming.' Kevin said now completely red in the face.

'Look Kevin, if Richard's coming to yours for a meal then I'd like me and Jude to come too, and I'll reciprocate for you and your lovely lady.' Oliver said smiling. 'Oliver James and his wife at mine for food, well I'll have to check my diary but I might be able to fit you in.' Kevin said smiling back.

'Jane told me you were funny Kevin.' 'My middle name Oliver' 'Yeah she told me you'd say that too me old matey boy.' Oliver said but was now laughing loudly. 'Ok Oliver, deal on one condition?' Kevin said regaining his composure.

'What me funny friend, tell me.' 'The thing is Oliver, if we're now on first name terms, I've got a great friend, Jack coming at the end of the month from Canada can I bring him with Mary of course? He owns a bear called Lennox.' Kevin said a little bit out of context. 'Kevin, you're on me old mucker, if Jack's here then let's do it.' 'Great, right then you and Jude a week Saturday?' 'Deal Kevin' Oliver said as he left.

Thanking Richard for everything Kevin and Mary left and saying they'd see him a week Saturday. He nudged Kevin and whispered 'Make sure it's good Kevin, I don't get many Saturday nights away from here.'

....

22nd May 1999

After his shower he felt alive. He knew what had happened last night but didn't quite yet want to contemplate it. He walked to the door to collect the post. There was the usual crap but also a thick letter addressed to him in hand writing. Knowing what lay in store for today and the rest of next week he put the letters in the kitchen draw. He could deal with them another day, there was too much to consider at the moment.

Kevin and Mary set about trying to create a menu for the dinner party. Following detailed debate and argument they both settled on chowder to start, Arbroath Smokie Chowder. Scottish Highland Beef Olives stuffed with a wild mushroom risotto hinted with chili and a white wine sauce with lemon and cream with char grilled asparagus. Finally Chocolate Scottish Single Malt Whisky Slice with cherry jus and whipped whisky cream.

23rd May 1999

They both had a quiet day and Mary left at tea time. Kevin had a few beers and went to his blog page.

> Yo my special Peeps of the world
> Firstly my deepest and most sincere apologies Dudes and Dudesses, it's been a week since I said hello to yous lot. All I can say Peeps is it's been a mad one, right up there with the Max series. I have another one coming and a major challenge at the end of it yous lot. Guess who's cooking for an International Chef and his trouble and strife? Yup me Dudes and Dudesses, the Kevster is doing the meal of his life and praying he doesn't cock it up in Kevster fashion.
> Love fronts still on the up Dudes (Sorry Dudesses) major wow at the mo. All is rocking and rolling in the right places and in the right time if you lots know what I mean! Well we're into the second half of May. Can yous lot believe no new votes other than Cardiff, who's now in the hugest lead Peeps. If that's what yous lot want then that's what the Kevster will plan. Two weeks left yous lot.

Grabbing a wine Kevin opened his own blog page and opened the mail he'd hidden in the kitchen draw. The large letter was intriguing him so he opened that one first. It was several pages long but what grabbed his attention was the name and address on the top of the letter.

It was from Claire and it had her address, e-mail and new mobile number as well as a land line. He didn't get past this to look at the words as it split his head in two. Why now, why after so long, what could she say that would make any amends, any difference? He decided to ignore it, the next week was mad enough without this new distraction. He took the bottle of vodka out of the kitchen filled his glass and started to write.

> Dear Kevin
> Things with Mary are top draw Dude, keep hold of this thought, you wanted it when it started so why not want it now when you've got it and its working so well? We know

we have the skeletons of Claire and of Alexis but Mary's real, she is here and now and wants you as much as anything. Stay with reality for once Dude! Shit, shit and more shit, we know you want to read the letter but leave it a week, store it, don't do it until after next weekend, there's too much going on. Hold it together Bro!

....

24th May 1999

Kevin, Mary, their new recruits from marketing, Deb and Jamie were off on a week's presentations in Scotland. Something Dani-ellie had handed Kevin at the eleventh hour last week. Despite the short notice all the sessions had gone bang to plan. Kevin finished early from the last one, leaving Mary Deb and Jamie to do the last presentation.

They met in the bar later. Mary went to bed first at ten o' clock. Kevin stayed with Deb and Jamie until ten-thirty telling them he needed to go to bed as had had a big night the night before. They both said they weren't tired and would stay a while longer.

Kevin said goodnight back and headed straight for Mary's room. He knocked the door gently. 'Hello, who's there?' He heard Mary's voice say from behind the door. 'Well that would be me!' He replied in a soft short tone. 'Well me, I'm not sure I should let you in. Me could be anyone, try persuading me differently' she said again from behind the door. 'Ok, a different tact then, well my sweet, if you don't let me in our new colleagues might walk past and ask why the boss is camped outside the deputy boss's door.' 'Oh that's easily explainable Kevin you were just checking if I was ok, I did leave early!' Mary said again from behind the solidly closed door. 'Yes, fair point, but why would the said boss be naked?' Kevin replied waiting for her response. 'You wouldn't, you just wouldn't' Mary said but checking her peep hole and seeing a fully naked Kevin standing in the corridor!

Mary opened the door as if her life depended on it and grabbed him and his clothes into her room. 'Kevin, you bloody idiot!' Standing still naked in front of her he replied. 'It's late darling and I've got a late rise, interested?'

He lay there, not sleeping for hours. He just couldn't dismiss the feelings in his brain. He was here with a stunningly beautiful lady who now seemed to love him but there were doubts, doubts because of other people, fuelled by the letter from Claire he hadn't even read yet.

....

27th May 1999

Kevin was still up by six and sent a quick message to his Peeps.

> Ock Aye all you Southern Beauties
> Yup it's the Kevster, all the way up in the beautiful and I mean beautiful Dundee Folks. The Dudes and Dudesses up here are top notch Peeps, really friendly. We've also been to the equally beautiful Edinburgh and Glasgow and I must say being a Southern Softie myself I am enthralled by the whole country. One bloke in Glasgow even offered to kiss me. Top Scottish Peeps the lot of them.
> Well as yous lot already know I'm cooking for a Superstar this Saturday and am as nervous as a scared rabbit Peeps. What better place though than to source some top quality Scotch ingredients. Off to Aberdeen tomorrow yous lot and yup I'm going for the authentic Angus Beef Dudes and Dudesses. I also need to find Arbroath Smokies and I'm going to turn them into a chowder Peeps.
> Listen yous lot, I know Cardiff's way out in front for the party of the millennium but perhaps lots of yous lot ain't seen the beautiful Scotland yet so take a look on line Dudes and Dudesses. I'm not trying to push anywhere but thought I'd share the beauty I've seen this week with all yous lot. Knowledge is power Peeps! See yous Jimmy's

....

28th May 1999

Their new driver, David, was there as they'd been told. He drove them to the office and dropped Mary, Deb and Jamie off at nine-thirty. They had another two meetings and he was collecting them at two to get to the airport by three for their four o' clock flight.

Kevin asked him for a favor, explaining about Oliver James, adding he needed to source some real Arbroath Smokies. David looked at Kevin and said 'I shouldn't really but we wouldn't want to let Mr James down would we?'

He drove them from Perth to Arbroath, approximately forty miles back towards Aberdeen but out onto the coast. Kevin bought the meat and whisky here and they went to the local small smoke house for the Abroath Smokies.

Despite David's worries they were back on schedule and he had them all at the airport well before three o' clock. They all said their goodbyes and Kevin thanked David for being such a star.

Kevin and Mary were back at seven o' clock. As he opened the door Sooty came running like a deranged rhino and knocked them both over. Snowy stood behind and smacked his back leg with her paw. Being told off he sat patiently waiting. Snowy walked forward to be picked up by Kevin and purred as he held her.

Sooty followed them all in and Kevin could tell he was desperate for a hug. He handed Snowy to Mary and called Sooty to come. He didn't disappoint and jumped onto Kevin's lap licking everywhere he could reach. An early night followed.

29th May 1999

Sooty was pulling the blankets off the bed and almost dragging Kevin out by his arm. Taking the hint he left Mary in bed sleeping with Snowy and got up and dressed. He put Sooty's lead on and they went for a long walk, they were gone for three hours and Sooty was flagging about ten minutes before they got back. Today was a day he wasn't protesting that he was going home!

Kevin thought he had it sussed, Oliver James was going to have his socks blown off. Kevin might be a novice but he felt he was going to be the rookie of the year. Nothing would stop him making this special.

Kevin showered first and looked at the clock. It was now nearly six o' clock. He shaved and dressed and then Mary got ready whilst he sorted the table out. He opened his first beer of the day, well a cider in fact and went through the ingredients again to make sure there were no cock ups.

Mary came out into the kitchen at seven o' clock and asked for a white wine whilst she finished dressing. Kevin did the honors and gave her a glass of the chilled Jerome Garnier Magnums 1997. As she sipped it she shouted 'Oh wow Kevin, that's absolutely divine.'

As she disappeared to finish getting ready Kevin poured himself a glass of the same and lit a cigarette. She wasn't wrong, this stuff was the dogs! The door went at seven-thirty and Jane was stood there with Richard. Kevin welcomed them in and asked what they wanted to drink. They were both giggly so obviously had one or two already and asked for vodka's.

Richard pulled out a box of Cubans with eight cigars inside. 'Cost me a fortune this box but worth it for a special occasion.' Richard said handing Kevin one of the fine cigars. It was now ten to eight and Kevin wondered if the famous Oliver James and his wife would actually turn up. Richard noticed Kevin's apprehension and said 'Kevin if Oliver says he's coming then he's coming. He doesn't make light of any personal arrangements, let me tell you.'

Kevin refilled all their glasses and sat down to relax. At one minute past eight the door bell went. Kevin answered with Sooty and Snowy by his side. True to his word Oliver James was stood there with his wife Jude.

Oliver said 'Richard, can I smell your Cubans in the air?' 'Oh Oliver your never one to miss a free cigar are you?' Richard said throwing him one. Jude tutted and started to speak to Jane and Mary.

Kevin walked into the room and asked the guests to sit at the table. They all moved immediately to his command. As they sat Kevin asked them to review the menu and choose their wine or champagne for the first course.

After a few minutes silence Oliver spoke first. 'Kevin me old mate, did you have all this wine and champagne in your place before you invited us?' 'No mate, I bought it for tonight, I wanted tonight to be special for all of us but especially Mary.' He replied honestly.

'Well matey boy this lot's cost you a small fortune and I have to say I'm honored to be here.' Blushing Kevin said 'Thanks Oliver, I do want this to be special for all of us though. Please can I have all of your preferences for the wine for the first course?' He said checking his watch nervously. Richard jumped in and said may I suggest the Louis Roeder Cristal for the chowder?'

Following general agreement Kevin returned with two bottles and two ice buckets. He opened the first bottle with no issue but the second cork escaped him and smashed Oliver right in the head. With all the guests screaming in laughter, including Oliver, Kevin tried to pour the champagne through shaking hands.

In his panicked state he overfilled Jude's glass and spilt it all over her lap. Trying to redeem himself he started wiping her. Oliver shouted 'Oy Julie get your hands off Jude's legs!' Looking horrified Kevin replied. 'Oh God I'm sorry.' Then looked at Oliver who was laughing uncontrollably and realized he was taking the piss.

Regaining his composure he looked Oliver right in the eye and said softly 'Chowder coming sir, in your case you can eat it from your lap!' He roared and said 'Kevin, you are funny, now go on and nail the food. It don't matter to me what's it like me matey but the effort you've put in I'll never forget.'

With his confidence returned Kevin poured them all a glass of the expensive champagne and returned to the kitchen to finalize the chowder. He started bringing in the bowls in less than five minutes, Mary had served the Soda Bread just before. They all ate and chatted about everything but the food. As nervous as Kevin was, he knew this was good.

All the bowls were cleaned and Mary and Kevin cleared the table. Mary washed the dishes while Kevin set about doing the final cooking for his mains. He got the risotto through its final stages and put the sauce on to heat and to reduce further.

He fried the slithers of Angus Fillet for less than a minute on each side and let them rest. The risotto was now ready and cooling and he finished the sauce. He griddled the asparagus for two minutes on each side and then asked Mary for help with the serving.

He rolled the beef with the risotto stuffing and trimmed each one. He put two on each warmed plate and then added four spears of asparagus. He then drizzled the sauce over and took them into the room. He hadn't asked what wine they wanted but was serving the Clos du Marques regardless.

They all sat and ate and sipped the stunning red wine. Kevin was desperate for feedback but the silent eating really said it all. Nobody left anything. Jude, Jane and Richard cleared the table.

Oliver looked at Kevin and said 'Matey boy, you've got some nuts doing that meal for me.' Kevin looked at him horror stuck. Oliver then smiled and said 'Kevin Julie, welcome to my world, you're good enough to go professional.' Kevin beamed and for once was lost for words.

Mary came back in, grabbed one of the stubbed cigars and lit it up taking a huge puff, sighing and then grabbing a full glass of white and nearly sinking it in one. 'Oliver if you didn't like that you should never write another book!' Mary said loudly. Oliver looked at Kevin and smiled brightly.

Oliver and Jude stayed until midnight and then arranged a taxi. They all swapped numbers and promised to keep in touch. Richard stayed with Jane and they all had a few more reds and some more of Richard's Cubans.

....

30ᵗʰ May 1999

Mary had gone home. Jane had walked Sooty and they were sat looking at Claire's letter with drinks in their hands. 'Do we have to read it Jane?' He said looking worried. 'No Babe, we can bin it, drink some more, smoke some more and forget you ever got it, your choice darling.' Jane said and pulling a huge gulp of the strong vodka.

Kevin lit a cigarette and passed her the letter. 'You ready babe?' He looked at her and responded 'Not really honey, but yes, please read it.' Jane composed herself and took the letter from him. 'Are you sure?' She said looking at him one more time. Kevin nodded and sat back in his chair. Jane opened it and started to read:

> Dearest Kevin
> Firstly I write to apologize for falling off the face of the earth. It was a completely cowardly action and one I'm not proud of at all. When I met you on the plane on the way to Canada, when we had the dodgy conditions I wanted to kill you for being so clam and in control. I quickly realized though

you did it all for me, to make me get through a frightening experience. I should have known what I was dealing with then but I didn't.

When we we're paired in the same hotel by chance I should have also realized destiny was taking over and again I didn't. When I found out about Paul you were a rock and despite your objection and defense I pushed you to get involved. This I am really sorry about, you had something and somebody, I didn't and I grabbed onto you like a baby to its mother.

You though took a while and begrudgingly got involved with me. I know this challenged everything you are about because you were at that moment in time falling into love with someone else. I know as the days progressed we found something not many people find in a lifetime and both made huge commitments to each other.

When I got back however I realized you already had someone and I was muscling in. I'd just lost my husband to a gay relationship and was grabbing the nicest alternative that could ever present itself. The problem was though that I fell hook line and sinker for you. Something I wasn't prepared for.

As we spent more time together I realized I wasn't just fling with you, but I had gone completely over, more so than when I met my husband. I can't tell you how much this feeling meant to me and I foresaw the rest of my life with you. As the time continued and we went to see Jack and his family nothing changed in my mind. I was in love with you more than I've ever been in love with anyone.

At the end of the trip, on the plane, I meant every part of moving to be near you. I got home and slept however. I was going to impose on a life you had and could make work. What was I thinking? You had a partner and I was pushing to take you away from her. How hypocritical is that. I'd just lost my husband to another relationship and was trying to force you to come away from yours.

When I woke up the following morning I knew I couldn't do that, not to anyone, even though I knew what I felt for you. I had to let go Kevin, I let go for you. Every day and night I miss you and cry myself to sleep more often than not due to what I perhaps could have had.

I follow your Blog page religiously and can gather where you are emotionally or partner wise but it seems you have moved on and that I'm really pleased about. I've left it this long because I wanted you to have time at home in your own surroundings and I understand if you want to sever ties but I had to let you know where I have been emotionally and sincerely apologize for changing my number and the like.

If you can forgive me and want to stay in touch my address, my e-mail address and my mobile number are at the top of the letter. Kevin I can't believe what I've done but can only apologize it's related to what I've been through. I do hope you forgive me?

Love Claire

'Jane, please can you read it again, I missed the essence of what was being said.' Kevin said looking confused. Jane nodded at him and reread the letter again. When she'd finished Kevin asked to look at it himself. He read it silently again and looked at Jane blankly. 'Jane, is it me or does it just not make sense?' He asked still confused. Jane looked at him and said 'Kevin, it's crystal clear.' 'What's crystal clear in that?' He exclaimed grabbing a cigarette and filling both their glasses up.

'Kevin, what's crystal clear is this woman is totally in love with you.' Jane said a little bit shortly. 'Where's it crystal clear Jane, she says all sort of things and eludes I was a mistake, a rebound from her husband.' He retaliated.

'Kevin you blokes are just nutters, Claire poured her heart out there, she sounds like one really special lady.' Jane said looking at him straight into his confused eyes. 'She is Jane. I fell for her in days and perhaps felt more in love than I've ever felt. I was prepared to drop everything for this woman and I mean everything, well apart from you, Snowy and Sooty.' He said still a little dumbfounded.

'Kevin you're going to have to face it, you love this woman. I know you think you love Mary but believe me as a woman I know the difference.' 'Ok, I accept what I feel but I still have a choice and I'm not leaving Mary, I'll make it work.' He replied defiantly. 'Kevin darling, it's the wrong choice honey.' Jane said as they went to bed.

31ˢᵗ May 1999

Kevin phoned Mary and told her he had some kind of flu and she instructed him to stay at home. Jane took Sooty and Snowy out and didn't return for a few hours. Kevin used the time to think but didn't get anywhere. Jane returned and disappeared just as quickly.

As he sat back with his wine as the phone went. 'Hi Kevin, how are you feeling?' 'Not too bad Mary, I was just about to ring you. I spoke to Daniellie today and he wants me to work from home so I don't spread any germs around.' 'Yeah I know, he told me this afternoon.' Anyway darling how are you?' 'Well that's why I'm ringing so early Kevin, not great actually.' 'Why what's wrong, there's nothing wrong is there?' 'Not with me darling, but it's my mum Kevin. She's on some kind of a downer, she's reflecting on her whole life and saying she doesn't deserve to live, never mind have a daughter who still speaks to her. She's that bad though I've asked her to move back in with me.' 'That's understandable Mary.' 'Is it Kevin?'

'Darling if it's upsetting you let it out, there's no point bottling it up.' 'Not even if it hurts me too much to say?' 'What does?' 'Kevin, I have to stop seeing you, she's in a real state, I fear for her sanity and if I still see you she won't recover.'

'Mary, there must be a way?' 'I wish there was Kevin but there isn't, not for now anyway.' 'Mary!' 'Kevin, please don't make it any more difficult than it is, please can you go back to being a brilliant boss to me, it's all I can offer at the moment, if you can't and I'd understand I'll hand my resignation in, I have no other choice Kevin.' 'Mary surely there must be a way?' 'No Kevin, I need your assurance or I walk.' 'Mary, you've got it but can't we speak face to face first?' 'No Kevin, I'll see you next Monday in work, sorry!'

01ˢᵗ June 1999

Hi first job today was an update to his page.

Dear Kevin
Where on earth have we got to Dude? We had Mary, lost her, had her again and lost her again. Claire, Claire, Claire,

what are we going to do? Whatever though, silence is no justifiable revenge Dude, she did pour out in the letter and was in a bad place. You need to ring her Dude, have a heart to heart and see where that goes. No commitments on the phone Dude, gently, gently approach, you know maybe five or six calls and perhaps arrange a coffee if those calls go well. Pecker up Kevin.

He checked his watch it was just before five. Jane was still out with Sooty so he hit the shower. Jane arrived back with Sooty and he watched laughing as she tried to get him to bath. 'Kevin, help please?' He eventually went to her rescue.

He then told Jane he'd decided to ring Claire, adding he could start by getting friendly with her again over several telephone calls before either of them committed to meet again.

He checked what he had in front of him, cigarettes, ashtray, wine and very strong vodka. Before he dialed the number he read her letter twice more. He lit a cigarette and took a large gulp of the strong vodka and dialed the number.

'Hello.' 'Kevin is that you?' 'Hi Claire, yes it's me in the flesh, well on the phone anyway.' 'Oh Kevin, you rang, you really rang, I didn't think you would, I thought you'd want to punish me, I thought you'd bin the letter and I'd never see you again, oh Kevin, I can't believe you've actually rung.' 'Claire, slow down, you're going ten to the dozen, I can't keep up with you.' 'Kevin I'm sorry, so sorry. I'm sorry for everything. I can't believe how I treated you and you've still called.' 'Claire you're not calming down, take a break, light a cigarette or grab a drink but slow down.' 'Kevin I'm sorry, can I have five minutes to compose myself?'

Checking his drinks he realized he'd sank both of them without realizing and felt more nervous than he'd ever felt before in his life. He walked into the kitchen refilled both glasses, looked at Jane, put his finger to his lips and said 'Shush.' Ten minutes passed and he was about to throw the towel in and go and tell Jane when the phone started to ring. For some reason he left in ring seven times and then picked it up.

'Claire?' 'Yes Kevin, sorry I was late calling you back I just couldn't compose myself.' 'It's ok, I felt something similar.' 'You did?' 'Yes, this is a little bit awkward for the both of us I think.' 'Yes I know Kevin and I'm sorry.' 'Claire, please can you stop apologizing?' 'Ok Kevin I will but I was such a complete wimp when I got back, I needed to see you but got embroiled in self pity, then doubt and then remorse that I'd bullied my way into your life.' 'Claire, I am a grown man and have got a voice and a mind, I chose to let what happened between us as much as you did.' 'Ok, but I didn't deliver Kevin, I got home and froze.' 'Yeah, I got that message.' 'Oh Kevin what must you have thought?' 'All sorts but why was the biggest one.' 'Fair enough, I tried to put my reasons in the letter but reading it back in my head I realized it was weak, unfair and pathetic. Somewhere my head was at the time.' 'Yeah about what I thought and agree with Claire!' 'Shit Kevin, you should want to kill me?' 'It did cross my mind at the time but I decided why waste someone who looks so good!' 'Are you being funny?' 'You know it's my second name.' 'Oh Kevin I miss you.' 'Ok Claire, Jack's coming over next week and we're going to the Ivy. Will you come?' 'What, just you and Jack?' 'No, Jack, me and Jane, my friend I talked to you about.' 'Yes Kevin, I'll come, I'll book a hotel.' 'Great Claire, I'll speak to you at the weekend to arrange the details and Claire I really can't wait to see you.'

Jane and Kevin sat and smoked and Jane then found her voice 'She's the one isn't she Kevin?' 'Jane, I think so, I've thought it from days after meeting her, but when she disappeared I sought of thought she couldn't be, not if she'd do that to me.' 'That's a bit selfish mate, you needed to consider what she'd been through, you needed to be the bigger person and tonight you have been.' Jane said but trying to keep her tone soft.

'Jane, what does that mean in man speak?' He replied now a little bit drunk. 'Well honey, we women have feelings too, her situation was something way off the scale to deal with and whilst she fell for you she got home and had to deal with the reality of the shit hand she'd been dealt.' She replied strongly. 'Ok in English?' He said still looking confused.

Jane sighed, sank her vodka and lit one of his Bensons up and said with a hint of a laugh 'Kevin Julie, for an intelligent man you are such an emotional klutz!' 'One of my middle names but I can't remember which one.'

02nd June 1999

Needing a long walk to clear his head Sooty and Kevin set off at eight-twenty and didn't return until eleven o' clock. Jane was up waiting for them and looking worried. Kevin explained he'd needed the time. Sooty was as black as Snowy.

Kevin got Sooty into the bathroom, filled the bath and turned the shower on. He looked at Sooty and said 'Remember what we said when we were walkies?' Sooty looked at him and jumped into the bath. Kevin showered him clean and then towel dried him.

Jane looked on gob smacked 'What did you tell him Kevin?' She said looking amazed. 'Only if he didn't do as he was told for bath time he'd have Snowy to answer to!' He said laughing. 'What and he bought that?' 'You haven't seen her with her right hook, have you Jane?' He replied and Sooty looked up checking he wasn't going to get one.

They both sat down after his take on Lasagna and lit a cigarette and sipped on the nice red wine. 'Shit Kevin, we need to sort out the restaurant and Oliver.' Jane said as if she'd been hit by a bolt of lightning. 'Ok Miss Panicky, I'll ring Oliver first, then you can ring Richard, it's not that late.'

He dialed Oliver's home number. 'Hello.' 'Hi, who's that?' 'Oliver its Kevin Julie, I thought you might be in work.' 'Wanted to speak to the trouble and strife then did you Kevin, follow up on mopping her fanny me old mucker did you?' 'Oh Oliver you're vying with me for funniness now then are you?' 'Kevin you are so funny and before you say it Dude, I know it's your second name.' 'Oliver have you been on my Blog Page?' 'Damn right Kevster, it's a blast.' 'Glad you enjoy it.' 'Nah mate its great and makes me laugh, God you make me laugh Kevin.' 'Compliments from a legend, I'm doing ok here.' 'Anyway me old mucker what you after?' 'Well you know you'd said you'd reciprocate the meal?' 'Yeah, and I meant it Dude.' 'Well next week Jacks going to be here, any chance I could bring him with Jane?' 'A week Sunday Kevin, looking forward to it.'

03rd June 1999

Kevin woke up to a call from Mary. She'd asked for a sabbatical to look after Suzanne. Kevin agreed it and with full pay. He rang

Daniellie and told him. Daniellie backed his decision one hundred percent telling Kevin Mary was worth her weight in gold. Next he checked his mobile looking to see if there was a message or a text. To his delight there was a text. It was from Claire and it said she was sorry she missed his call and would speak to him tomorrow.

'How the hell can I sleep with that smell going on?' Jane said grumpily but with an interested look on her face. 'Ah see, the smell of the ancient probes the mind of the sleepy.' He said back in some strange accent. 'Kevin have you been on something?' 'Oh the morning woman of angst is divided by the smell of the righteous path.' 'Oh Kevin, you are a prick sometimes, when's it ready?'

He stood back and gave her a horrified look. 'Well when the lady of the night desires it my sweet Scarlet!' 'Well make it now then if you want to avoid the Scarlet's wrath.' She replied but now smiling into almost laughter. 'My sweet lady Jane, please sit and your banquet will arrive my dear.' He finished before turning his back on her and actually finishing the cooking.

He got back into real mode and served Eggs Benedict with homemade hollandaise sauce, smoked crispy bacon and a chili dressing. Jane sat and ate still giving him the eye for waking her up so early but after tasting the food melted again. 'You bastard, how do you do this? I've tried to do this about ten times and failed every one.' She said in-between mouthfuls of his fantastic breakfast.

'Ah see Grasshopper, those things of the exquisite come to those who study the ancient methods.' He said in another trance like tone. 'Ok. That's it, what's floating your boat Kevin?' 'Ok, ok, when you went to bed I rang Claire, I know you said not to but I did. She didn't answer, don't worry.' He replied back in normal tone. 'So what's got your cock up then?' She said a bit confused. 'Well Grasshopper the worldly wise that wait get what they deserve.' 'Kevin, I'll slap you in a minute, so spit it out unless you want blood to go with the spit!'

Regaining his composure and normality Kevin said 'Jane, she left a text!' 'And that's makes you like this?' She replied a bit taken aback. 'Yes Babe, on top of the world!' He shouted back.

Kevin served roast belly pork, homemade stuffing, roast parsnips and fresh greens in a red wine sticky sauce. Jane was in pieces as she ate and kept saying 'Kevin, you need to change jobs, you need to change jobs.'

He lit up and looked at the phone, he so wanted to speak to Claire it hurt but the minutes ticked by as he smoked and drank. Eventually he picked it up at nine-thirty. He dialed the number slowly, it connected straight away. As it answered on the second ring he heard her voice. Somehow through the conversation he had agreed to see her before the weekend, right on plan with his slowly slowly approach!

....

05ᵗʰ June 1999

Kevin spent the previous day in work mode. He finished at seven, had two drinks, a sandwich and bed. This morning he had other things to do. Jane took Snowy and Sooty out and got back an hour and a half later.

'Kevin, that's the best walk and experience I've ever had. Sooty saw a squirrel and went tearing after it. Another dog, a Jack Russell came straight up to Snowy. She started to get into defense mode but Sooty abandoned the squirrel chase and came back quicker than I thought he could run to protect her.' Jane said beaming.

'Then what happened?' He asked a bit alarmed. 'Well firstly Sooty growled so the Jack Russell backed off. Then he looked at Snowy to check if he was quick enough to protect her and sort of hid his face in case she was going to hook him for being late. Then the owner of the Jack Russell Karen asked if they could all be introduced.' Jane said still looking like a smiling child.

'Well Kevin, Snowy, Sooty and Charlie all got along famously and I'm off out with Karen tonight, she's really hot.' 'Wow Jane, a really good walk then, we'll have to catch up tomorrow to compare?'

Jane left at one o' clock. Kevin did his things and sat and waited. He poured himself a white wine and lit a Benson. The door bell went just before two o' clock. He went to answer to answer it all excited and was about to say 'Hi Claire' but the name changed in mid sentence to 'Jo.' He must have looked as he felt because she said 'Bad time Kevin?' And burst into tears. 'No, well yes, but Jo come in please.'

He asked her if she wanted a drink. Jo replied she'd like something as strong as he could do and grabbed one of his cigarettes. She sat down and re-associated herself with Snowy and Sooty. Kevin sank his white and poured himself another. 'Jo, what's wrong?' 'Kevin, we've split up, we were talking about marriage and children and I realized I loved you not Michael. I finished it with him telling I wanted to marry and have children with you.'

He was trying to process this through his confused brain when the door went again. This time it was Claire. Looking horrified he said 'Claire!' He didn't get chance to reply, Jo came to the door and introduced herself.

Jo continued in tears saying she was Kevin's ex girlfriend and had just split up with her fiancée that she'd gone back to when he came back from Canada. Then in her upset state and to Kevin's horror she asked 'How do you know Kevin Claire?' He didn't have chance to influence anything before Claire replied 'We met in Canada, on the plane out there actually.'

'So you two had a thing when we were together then, whilst you were in Canada and I was left alone at home?' Kevin looked at Claire, then Jo and was left speechless and knew Claire wouldn't take this lying down. 'Was that about the time you were getting it back on with your ex, soon to be reinstated fiancée Jo?'

Kevin was still playing head tennis, looking at Jo, then Claire, then Jo, then Claire, then Jo and Claire again. Again before he had time to intervene Jo launched herself at Claire trying to punch, slap, scram or do whatever she could to her.

Kevin still looking on helplessly saw Claire overpower Jo, push her back on the sofa and before he knew it Sooty was growling at Claire. Kevin finally managed his voice and shouted 'Sooty, no! Room! Jo, grab your stuff and leave.' Jo grabbed her bag and left silently.

Claire made a grab for her bag but Kevin still now in assertive mode said 'Sit Claire.' She sat as quickly as Sooty would have and he went straight to the bedroom to get his dog. 'Sooty, this is Claire and she's special, she is and will be one of your best friends ever. Please go see her and be nice.' Sooty doing as he was told went over to see Claire and within five minutes was licking and jumping on her for attention.

Kevin looked at the scene, the dog by her feet, and the cat on her lap and knew it was right. After chatting and catching up for an hour they got onto the return home and Claire's disappearance. This was an uncomfortable moment for both of them but in the end they both said, almost simultaneously that going backwards wouldn't do anything for either of them.

Another hour later with the wine flowing they were both laughing about the mini fight. 'Claire, it's taken me thirty years to get two women to fight over me and wow it was worth it.' He said in fits of giggles. Claire looked at him realizing he was joking and said. 'That's what I missed a lot Kevin, how funny you are.' 'Is that all?' He said but grabbed her hand and led her to the bedroom.

....

06ᵗʰ June 1999

They went on the Snowy walk and were back just over an hour later. Sooty did his show and Snowy turned her nose up, she must have thought it was a bit boring today and wanted to sit on Claire's lap as soon as she sat down. After his show Sooty sat by her feet. 'Didn't take them long to love you did it Claire?'

After another hour Kevin reluctantly took Claire to the train station, insisting she wasn't using the tube and to make sure she rang him as soon as she got home. Keeping an eye on the time, it was now four-thirty Kevin opened his lap top to update his blog page.

> Well hello Peeps
> Kevster here, and all over the place on the romantic ride of the roller coaster big dipper, but yous all that's for another time. Less than twenty four hours to decision time folks, our party of the millennium will have a destination soon Peeps so this is the last call for the votes to come in. Big Jack, you know guys and gals, the one with the bear is here tomorrow for a month and I know yous lot will be pleased we get someone so cool to sample the city before we party on Dudes and Dudesses. Right, don't forget, votes close at midnight

Monday night. For now though yous lot please rock and roll and take a stroll on the wild side.

....

07th June 1999

He had to wait until two o' clock to see Daniellie but was invited in by his boss with the biggest smile Kevin had ever seen on his face. Kevin walked out two and a half hours later as HR Director in waiting, a salary of over a hundred grand, and a car budget of seventy to eighty. Mary had to replace his current role and take his current car.

As he was walking home with his head in the clouds his mobile went, it was Jack. 'Kevin, I'm still in Canada, stuck at the bloody airport, delays mate. I won't be touching down until the morning now.' 'No problem Jack you're still staying with me though?' 'Yeah mate, until Katie and the kids arrive.' Look Jack, I'll sort something out for me, when they arrive I want you lot to stay at mine, at least until you move on.' 'Kevin, you mean that?' 'You know it big fella.'

Snowy and Sooty sat on the sofa with him as he relaxed fully for the first time in a long time. The wine flowed as he smoked a cigar in stages and ten o' clock came without him realizing. He knew he had to log onto his blog page now and watch the results. Kevin was watching intently when his door bell went at five to twelve. Claire was stood there 'Kevin, four minutes to go, sort it out and send the list just after midnight as you promised everyone.' Getting back onto it he checked the scores at eleven-fifty nine got the draft ready to send.

> Yo Peeps
> Scores in and we have a decision, the winning city location is only Cardiff, the capital of Wales Dudes and Dudesses. Well done all of you for a definitive decision. I must say yous lot, Scotland came close and Edinburgh was only pipped by two votes. Well my loveliest Peeps we've got it, we're going for it and now we've got to plan it. Welcome to the party of 'Nineteen Ninety Nine in the capital of Wales Cardiff.
> We will now all need to add ideas Peeps and we also need to finalize the numbers. Votes suggest we have in excess of

one hundred and fifty Peeps, so with momentum we could be in to the two hundred mark! I want to thank each and every one of yous for making this so successful, yous lot are truly my friends and I want to meet each and every one of yous. Love, peace, rock and roll and to all party planners of the world!

Hitting the send button at one second past midnight, Kevin poured himself and Claire silly strong vodka and led her to bed some ten minutes later.

....
08ᵗʰ June 1999

Jack couldn't have come across any directional problems as was at Kevin's door at just on ten to eleven. Jack and Kevin hugged. 'Where's your babies Kevin?' Jack asked as he came into the hallway. 'Out with Claire mate' Kevin replied. Jack nodded but then said 'Claire? Kevin, I thought it was off?' 'So did I mate but a long story, come on. Let me show you to your room.'

Claire returned some ten minutes later and shouted 'Jack, you're here, wow. Let me get cleaned up and I'll be back in a jiffy, I can't wait to catch up.' Kevin asked Jack what his itinerary was and Jack asked him to pass him his brief case. Jack pulled out a diary planner and showed it to Kevin. Kevin reviewed the locations and said 'you'll need a hotel for the North West and for Cardiff.' 'Why Cardiff?' Jack asked a bit confused. 'Because that's the night my man we get to check out what Cardiff has to offer Jack, you know, in preparation for New Year's Eve.' Kevin said with a cheeky grin.

Kevin showed Claire Jack's itinerary and said 'Right, firstly we're in the Ivy Thursday night. Then on Sunday we're off to Oliver James's for dinner, cooked by the maestro himself.'

Kevin suggested they went to a traditional English pub for a few drinks. Jack was really up for it and Kevin decided on the Red Lion. They arrived back at his pad some hours later. Jack said he needed a lie down and Sooty followed him. Kevin checked them five minutes later and asked Claire for her camera. They were both collapsed on the bed and cuddled up like partners, the big man and the big dog. Kevin snapped this and put it straight onto his blog page.

About eight o' clock Kevin started the food, Jack was still sparko but Kevin guessed the smell of the food would wake Sooty and in turn Jack would follow. Sooty entered the kitchen within a minute of the food smell and Jack as Kevin predicted followed a few minutes later.

Kevin fed Sooty and showed Jack the blog page and picture. Jack roared, not in anger but in laughter. 'Katie's going to kill me!' He said still laughing at the picture. 'She told me I had to behave and not get too drunk and here I am on the first day appearing like I'm out for the count.'

....

09th June 1999

Kevin drove to Greenstones and asked for Jason. 'I'm sorry sir but he no longer works here can I help you?' 'Yes you can, you can tell me why Jason has gone as he was the only reason I bought a car here last time.' Kevin replied a little miffed.

'Well sir, he was a little off the cuff and the management thought not in line with Mercedes expectations.' Kevin saw red and asked for the manager of the showroom. Michael Thomas came out five minutes later and said 'Hello Mr. Julie, I'm the General Manager of Greenstones, can I help you?' 'Yes you can, you can tell me why your best asset has been sacked!' 'Oh Mr Julie, I see, Jason was uncouth and not befitting of Mercedes standards, I'm sure you understand.' He said in such a posh voice Kevin knew it wasn't his own. Kevin asked him to accompany him outside. 'Well Mr Thomas, see my car over there.' 'Yes sir one of our very good models and very new.' 'Mr Thomas, or can I call you Mike?' 'Oh Mike please sir.' 'Well please call me Kevin then, Mike, I spent this money merely weeks ago and now I have seventy plus grand to play with.'

'Oh Kevin, that's amazing and of course I want to sell you one of our finest models.' 'Well then Mike, you'd better get Jason back by tomorrow then hadn't you, cause me old Mr too important guy, no Jason, no sale.' Kevin said as he turned around and walked out.

Kevin's phone went off less than thirty minutes later. 'Kevin, Jason here.' 'Jason how are you my friend?' 'Better now Kevin, I've just got my job back, a five grand pay rise and if I seal the deal with you tomorrow a five percent bonus on that sale and the one I sold you the other week.' 'Jason that's great, I'll be back tomorrow, let me give you a heads up though, I will want the car quick yeah?' 'No probs Kevin, the Jaester will sort the Kevster out and I'm looking forward to Cardiff man, stick my name down on the top the list Dude, yeah?' 'Deal Jason, see you tomorrow.' 'Kevin . . .' 'Yes?' 'Thanks a lot man.'

Claire arrived and Kevin explained that Jane and Karen were coming for dinner and told her what he was cooking. He showed Claire the steaks and she nearly choked. 'Why not just bring the cow home darling?' 'Well it's for Jack isn't it, he loves big food.' Kevin replied defensively.

They both showered and were changed and decent by the time Jack walked in at ten past six. Jack had a quick beer and told them how well his day had gone and then said he needed to shower.

Jane arrived with Karen at quarter past seven. Kevin realized Jane wasn't lying when she'd said Karen was hot. She was about five foot five, blond, big busted and had legs and a bum that didn't know the meaning of the word fat.

Jack came out at about half-seven and Kevin introduced him to Jane and Karen. Karen was mesmerized. Kevin could see it even if Jane couldn't. They all sat and chatted with Oasis playing in the background and getting on very well. Jack had started on the red and was getting louder by the minute. Claire nudged Kevin to start the food.

They sat down at just gone eight-fifteen. Jack was in heaven telling Kevin he hadn't had such a good steak for a while and it wasn't a bad size either. The rest of them toiled through their own monstrosities but all made comment how good it all was. Claire served one of her special bottles of red and it went down a storm.

The conversation was getting ruder and cruder. Karen was holding Jack's hand without Jane seeing. Kevin and Claire though saw the danger and recommended an end to the evening. Karen suggested she and Jane stayed over. Jack being drunk agreed readily. Kevin managed to get Jack to sleep on the sofa so Karen and Jane could have his bed and he went to his own with Claire, Sooty and Snowy.

....

10th June 1999

Jack had gone, off on one of his site visits. Karen walked into the kitchen looking almost naked. She had a tee-shirt on and it was short. Both Claire and Kevin both noticed she wasn't wearing any pants. They couldn't help it, her tee-shirt didn't cover enough!

Kevin spoke first 'Karen, I don't mean to be rude but your flange is hanging out dear.' 'Oh shit, sorry, please give me a minute.' She replied running back to the bedroom with her smooth firm backside in full view.

'Well if you don't mind me saying Claire, she's got one hell of an ass.' Kevin said blowing his cheeks out. 'I know what you mean Kevin, enough to challenge anyone, man or woman.' They ate breakfast and Claire said she'd take Sooty out. Jane asked if she could go too. They were bonding and Kevin was really pleased. They left about ten minutes later, Snowy stayed behind with Kevin.

He sorted the kitchen out and was grabbing the rubbish when Karen exited the bathroom completely naked. She looked at Kevin, smiled and said softly 'Do I look nice Kevin?' 'Very.' He said. 'You look nice too Kevin, you could come and moisturize me, my skin needs it after a shower and your hands look very capable.' She said looking right into his eyes.

Kevin stared for what seemed like minutes before recovering and responding 'Karen, that would be lovely and if circumstances were different I would jump at that invitation. The fact that I have someone and you have someone however necessitates a no I'm afraid. God, I'll always think of this moment but no.'

Kevin went for a shower himself and made sure the water ran cold. He stood in it for a long time until he was composed again. He shaved and was relieved to hear Jane and Claire's voices. He got into his bedroom and changed and went to greet them. They were both wet through, it had been pouring. Karen was trying to dry Claire with a towel but Claire blushing grabbed the towel from her and dried herself. Jane showered first and left with Karen about eleven-thirty.

Claire showered and came into the lounge area in her towel. 'Kevin, she's something Karen, isn't she?' She said still looking flustered. 'Yes she is.' He replied still in a sort of a trance.

'Kevin, did she try it on with you whilst we were gone, Jane reckoned she would?' Claire asked but not looking jealous. 'Yeah, full on and naked!' 'And you didn't bite, not even a little?' He looked at her and said very carefully 'No, not even a nibble but don't ask me to promise I won't ever put the experience into the wank bank Claire.' Smiling she said softly 'that'll do for me darling.'

They decided to go and look at the car together. They drove to Greenstones and arrived just around lunchtime. Kevin walked in with Sooty with Claire following behind. As they walked in the first person they met, a receptionist said 'I'm sorry Sir, no dogs in here.' 'How dare you, she's my partner.' Claire laughed as Mike Thomas and Jason came into the showroom two minutes later and Kevin asked Mike to leave. 'Right me old mate, sixty grand, seventy at a push, if it fits what Sooty wants and delivery in a week, and by the way I want black metallic Dude.' Kevin said smiling brightly at Jason.

'Give me two hours Dude?' Jason said brightly. 'You got it. I'm off for some lunch but want it sorted by two o' clock, yeah?' Kevin said knowing Jason would have Mike running after him like a whippet.

Kevin, Claire and Sooty went for lunch around the corner, a pub called the Pig and Whistle and who had no problems with dogs. Kevin ordered three steaks, two medium rare with chips, peas, mushrooms and onion rings and one rare with nothing.

All three of them had a pint of Ale, Sooty's being put into a bowl by the barman. When the food came Kevin cut up the rare steak into dog sized chunks and gave Sooty the plate on the floor. If the dog could have spoken Kevin knew he would have said Christmas had come early.

When they got back to Greenstones, Jason was there waiting for them. 'See I knew you were good Jason.' Kevin said and shook his hand. 'Listen Kev, I've got you what you want but the timing may be a little off. Let me talk you through it and you decide.' Jason said looking really confident.

'Ok, hit me with Jason.' Kevin said now interested. 'Well mate, what I've got you is an E class 350 Sport AMG estate, top of the range Dude and retailing at sixty five grand. For delivery next week however in metallic black I get you the same car with all extras on the list for fifty nine, nine, nine five.' Jason said looking like a cat that got the cream.

'Jason me old mucker, you got a deal if I get the car Friday and I'll pay sixty one.' Kevin said as he really wanted to deliver his current car to Mary on the weekend.

Jason asked for an hour again and Kevin asked him to get hold of him on his mobile.

They drove back home and Snowy was waiting for them at the door. She checked Sooty and realized he'd had a drink and spent the next ten minutes checking he was ok and fussing all over him. Claire said the cat could rival a wife and they both laughed out loud.

The phone went an hour later. 'Hi Jason, how are you?' 'Better now Kevin, I've got the car for tomorrow and at fifty nine flat.' 'Jason you're doing yourself out of bonus here.' 'Yeah but for you it's worth it, deal Kevin?' 'Deal Jason, I'll see you on Friday, how's Mr too important Thomas with you now?' 'Oh Kevin, he thinks the sun shines out of my backside at the moment.' 'Good Jason, you deserve it.' 'Kevin thanks for everything.'

Jack got back twenty minutes later and they had a beer and catch up. They had an hour between them to get ready. The taxi taking them to the Ivy was coming bang on seven. A couple of glasses later they were all in the taxi and arrived at the Ivy at seven-thirty. Jane was already there and Richard greeted them as if they were stars.

Claire spotted an actress from one of the popular soap operas. Richard sighed but told them the Head Chef was cooking for them and had chosen what to serve them, all a surprise. Jane had told them there was only one dietary requirement, Jack's, and his was big!

Richard sat them at a table and Claire noticed Kelly John from the Gramophonic's with Stuart Wire. She was star struck. Jack not knowing what or who they were just sat and looked around saying 'not a bad place, I hope the nosh is good and lots of it.' Kevin laughed and Richard was impressed by Jack's total under estimation of the famous Ivy.

Richard started them off with a couple of bottles of the Ivy House Champagne and served them an entrée of smoked salmon parcels. Jack's face was a treat when he saw the delicate little things. Kevin told him not to worry as it wasn't even the starter. Jack's face brightened a bit after this.

Next up was soup, a consommé that Jack liked the taste of. Kevin noticed him polishing his champagne off as quickly as the broth. The main starter was lobster claw salad. Jack had no complaints with this saying it was one of his favorite starters of all times.

The main course came and Jack actually stood up in his full hugeness and applauded. It was a four bone rib of beef on a huge platter with roasted vegetables. The guest list in the restaurant looked at the man mountain and applauded with him. Stuart Wire from the Gramophonic's actually came over to introduce himself.

By the time they'd eaten the stars in the restaurant were all chatting to the group and absolutely endeared by the photos Jack had shown them with him and Lennox. Kelly John reckoned he could get Lewis Lennox to have a photo with Jack so he could put it on his mantle piece with the picture of him with his bear. To everyone's amazement Kelly gave Jack his number and said 'Ring me next week and I'll sort it, Lewis is in London at the moment and as you're Canadian as well would love to be part of this name sake memoir.'

They left the Ivy with Kevin telling Richard it had been one of his most memorable occasions ever. Richard said the whole night was worth it when Jack called Kelly John Keith and that Kevin owed him another home cooked meal.

....

11th June 1999

Claire took Sooty and Snowy out, Kevin needed to update his blogs.

> Hello world
> Kevster here and now on top of the world in the way I feels Peeps. God this week couldn't have gone any better. New job, new car, new friends and new love yous lots. I suspect the Kevster will be off the list as an available male forever, sorry good looking Dudesses, yet again, but I have the confidence this time that this will be the real deal, the sure thing, the one that's stops the squirrel hibernating, the bear's bollocks, yous all know what I mean!

Party plans are trickling through but we need a base Peeps, some where's we can congregate before we party like it's nineteen ninety nine. Don't yous lot worry though the Kevster will prevail.

Kevin got to Greenstones at ten past one. Mary was already waiting outside with Jason making a fuss over her. Jason told Mary that whatever she wanted from this garage in future to go straight to him. 'You're now on my list of VICD.' He said. Mary looked at him and asked politely 'What does that mean Jason?' 'Well Mary, kind of obvious I thought but it means Very Important Customer Dudess.'

Kevin drove out in his new car forty minutes later. He couldn't believe the difference. He'd have to be careful with this machine as he ran out of road before the car ran out of power. Claire said she was cooking tonight and popped out in his new car to get her shopping list.

She was gone for over two hours and Jack got back well before her at six. Kevin cracked open a few cider's, Jack commenting he liked this stuff and they were three in by the time Claire got back at quarter to seven.

Claire told the boys to carry on drinking and chilling. She was doing chicken stew, a family recipe that had been handed down over years. It was a spicy dish so she told them to be prepared as she went to the kitchen.

Jack and Kevin were on a cider fest and getting drunker by the minute. Claire finding this hilarious kept feeding them with fresh top ups. When she went in with her fourth top up the pair of them were giggling uncontrollably. 'What's so funny guys?' She asked. 'Raining frogs Claire.' Jack replied as Kevin giggled like a teenager.

Smiling she asked Kevin to pop into the kitchen. He followed her still laughing. 'Pants down please Kevin!' Doing as he was told he stood there with a mini rise. Claire caressed him quickly and then said 'Pants up Kevin.' Less than a minute later he was running around the apartment like a headlight dazzled rabbit. 'What have you done to me, I'm burning, burning, on fire!' He screamed. Claire held up the scotch bonnet chili she'd used and showed Jack. He roared with laughter, getting what she'd done.

'Put it in a glass of milk Kev.' Jack said laughing. Kevin was about to swear at his friend but Jack seemed serious. Kevin went into the kitchen, scowled at Claire, poured a pint and put his throbbing bits into the glass of milk. Jack was only bloody well right, the pain diminished almost instantly.

Standing in the kitchen with his pants down, his nowhere near of a rise dipped in the milk, Kevin told Claire she was having some of that medicine when she would least expect it. Eventually pulling his pants back up Kevin rejoined Jack who was still giggling. Claire served them food at eight-thirty and both boys were in bed by nine o'clock.

....

12th June 1999

Jack got up and joined Kevin. 'Kevin, what the hell did you give me last night as my head hurts like Lennox has caught me with one of his haymaker paw swings?' 'Cider Jack.' 'Man that stuffs good in the night Kev but kicks like a mule in the morning mate.'

Kevin and Claire went out to buy wine for dinner with Oliver tomorrow.

Jack said he'd stay back and call Katie and the kids adding 'I'll look after the animals whilst you're gone.' Claire spent the first half an hour as they wandered holding hands taking the mick out of him and Jack last night. 'What on earth was the raining frog's thing about?' She asked smiling. 'What raining frogs?' Kevin asked honestly and Claire smiled back saying 'God, I wish I'd videoed it.' 'Just don't forget I'm getting you back for the chili trick.'

Kevin wanted to get food and the wine for tomorrow. He asked Claire what she fancied and she surprised him by saying curry. 'That'll be different for Jack, good call darling. I can call you darling again can't I?' 'If you think I warrant it Kevin.' Hugging her tightly he said sweetly 'Claire, you rock my boat every which way there is.' 'Is that a suggestion for a Clint Eastwood sequel darling?' She replied and poked him in the ribs.

Claire was in charge of food and Kevin beer and wine. They decided to split up to ease the time and agreed to meet back at the pub in an hour. Kevin adding he could do with the hair of the dog.

Kevin got a case of Chateau Medoc, it cost him just short of five hundred but he reckoned it worthwhile. He'd take three bottles to Jamie's and open a few tonight. He was in the Slug after twenty minutes and ordered another cider, if he was grabbing the hair he might as well go the whole hog and start off where he'd finished.

They got back several drinks later. Jack, seeing their red faces jumped in at two to one, staying on the cider as well. Before long raining frogs were in the conversation and they were both singing to the tune of the Weather Girls. Dinner was eaten and bed beckoned early yet again.

....

13th June 1999

They arrived at Oliver's at half-one. 'Kevin me old blind date, how they hanging? This must be the lovely Claire?' Oliver said offering his hand to Jack with a wink. Jack laughing replied 'Yeah man, that'd be me.' Claire held her hand out and said 'Hi, I'm Jack.' Oliver now in fits said 'we're going to have a good time, you're my kind of people.'

'Kev, Jack and Claire, what would yous guys like to drink?' Oliver said with a little bow. Kevin looked at Jack, Jack nodded and Claire shook her head as they both said in unison 'Got any cider Oliver?' 'Got any, don't you believe it me old mate's, I've got some scrumpy in the cupboard, that do you guys?'

Oliver announced his menu an hour after they'd arrived. 'Right me old mates, to start we're having a sexy salad, it's lovely man, Parma ham, mozzarella, figs with basil and lemon and olive oil. It's gorgeous.' They all looked impressed but Jack said 'Ok, after the rabbit food?' Laughing Oliver said 'Ok big man, I'm doing me old man's chicken for the main course. It's chicken in puff pastry with a mushroom stuffing. I'm doing that with the best roast spuds with garlic and thyme and braised greens.'

They ate, drank and were finished by about five o' clock. Jack told him the food wasn't bad, nearly as good as Kevin's. This brought hysteria from everyone but Jack.

Oliver told Kevin and Claire they were welcome anytime in the future but Jack needed special invitation as he needed to make sure he wasn't working the next day. Jack, standing up asked why? 'Cause if you're here I need to drink big fella, you bring me right back to where I need to be in terms of just being normal.'

Pacified but not quite understanding Jack said 'Cheers Mate, when you come to me in Canada Katie will show you how to cook a pig roast my friend.' Laughing Oliver said 'great with that recipe I might just write a book.'

Oliver had a bottle of Jack Daniels in his hand. 'Jack for Jack me old matey.' He said with a smile. Kevin tried to say Jack wasn't good on whisky but the two new best friends wouldn't have any of it. Kevin whispered to Claire 'Watch this blow up babe?' Jack and Oliver were sinking the Jack Daniels in single gulps and cheering the world on each one.

Jack stood up, wobbled and said 'Where's the can Olly?' Laughing he replied 'In the cloakroom Jack, where's it's always been.' 'Why's it with the coats?' Jack asked but sounding off. 'Sorry Jack, out of the door turn left and last door down the hall on the right.' Jude interrupted.

Jack stumbled off and was really heavy footed. They heard him clatter into the walls in the hall. 'I hope he doesn't lock himself in Claire.' Kevin whispered to her. Several minutes passed and they heard nothing. Kevin was starting to get a bit concerned and looked at Claire. She was giving off the same vibes with her look when all of a sudden they heard a huge crash.

Kevin, Claire and Jude ran out and Oliver followed slowly behind them. Jack must have fallen out of the toilet, his pants were around his ankles, and he was flat on his back and was still peeing, all over his shirt! Laughing out loud he managed to say 'I fell over going for a pee, I fell over.' Oliver was in fits and Claire looked at Kevin and said 'You'll have to sort him Kevin; it's not fair on me or Jude, not with his cock hanging out and piss all over him.'

Kevin sorted his big friend out. If he did feel drunk this sobered him immediately. Jack went for a bough in the toilet and had a good go at clearing the whisky from his system. An hour later they left, Claire and Kevin laughing about the three J's, James, Jack and Jack.

....

14th June 1999

Claire left for home and Kevin for work. The morning went well enough. He spent the rest of the afternoon going through plans with Deb and Jamie. They didn't stop and before they realized it was six o' clock. Kevin told them they needed to wrap up. He asked them both to come to the Slug with him to meet Jack. Jack arrived about seven-thirty and joined them for his first and much needed drink of the day. Deb and Jamie stayed until nine but Kevin and Jack carried on until ten.

As they left Kevin promised Jack a real treat. Donner Kebab and headed for Kebab Land. Jack was amazed and ordered two large Donner's, no salad but with chili and garlic sauce and a large chicken shish kebab. He asked for onions separate and extra pita. Kevin stuck with the large lamb Donner with chili and Salad. They got back and Jack had eaten his first two before Kevin had got through half of his.

....

15ᵗʰ June 1999

He was in work by ten past seven and went straight at what they'd left last night. They slogged away for four and half hours when Kevin cracked and said at half past twelve. 'That's it, I need a smoke!'

Kevin called halt at four and they left it for the evening. He was home by five o' clock and jumped in the shower. He cracked open a bottle of red and set about preparing his ingredients. He was making his take on Lamb Balti, served with Egg Fried Rice and Home Made Nan Bread with accompaniment of dips.

Jane and Karen arrived about quarter to eight. Jane had two bottles of red in her hand. Karen had the shortest skirt Kevin had ever seen on and Jack's eyes nearly popped out of his head. Sooty and Snowy ran to Jane. Kevin wasn't sure who had the most puppy dog eyes, Jack, Karen or Sooty.

Expecting another interesting night Kevin got them drinks. Karen was sat next to Jane and opposite Kevin and Jack. Her short skirt and lack of pants left nothing to the imagination. Jack was mesmerized and Kevin, if truth be told was enjoying the show.

Kevin asked Jane for a hand in the kitchen 'Jane, she's flashing her bits, and she hasn't got any bloody undies on. I'm getting it full on and Jack's getting it full on in more ways than one.' Kevin said lighting a Benson and sighing. 'Oh the cow, I warned her.' Jane replied.

Kevin served a stunning balti curry with perfect fried rice and homemade nann bread with homemade dips. Jack was the most impressed, he had three helpings. Karen was now nearly sitting on jack and making no effort to hide her attraction. Jane had a huge row with Karen and Karen left in a huff. Jane went to Kevin's room looking evil. When he eventually got into bed with her Jane half suggested a friend shag. Kevin told her his interested rise was staying firmly in his pants. They laughed as they fell asleep.

....

16th June 1999

Kevin was in work just after six-thirty. He nailed their outstanding plan by eight and waited for Jamie and Deb to come in. They arrived together with smiles on their faces at seven-thirty. Kevin knew the look. The two of them had obviously got it on the night before. 'Right you two love birds.' He said half smiling. The expected protests and denials followed but Kevin continued 'Look, what happens outside work is not my concern, just what happens inside. As it happens I think you two make a great couple. Now we've got that over, Jamie, you can take that smug look off your face and Deb, please take that I've been shagged look off yours!'

Kevin got home and had a chat with Jack about Karen. 'I was worried last night big fella. I thought you might cross the line with Karen the way she flirted with you. Jack considered what Kevin had said and thought about it for what seemed like several minutes before saying 'Kevin, God she looked good and I was tempted but since I've been parted from Katie all I've done is self relief. Last night maybe three times but was only self relief!' 'In my sheets?' Kevin asked horrified. 'No mate into your, what do you call it, toilet roll?' Jack replied before they both knew the conversation needed to be changed.

Claire arrived as Jack was in the shower, Kevin couldn't believe he'd missed her so much in mere days. He decided on a Chinese takeaway tonight. The food arrived twenty five minutes later. Kevin and Claire ate a large plate of the mixed food and Jack ate the rest before retiring and to ring Katie. Kevin shouted 'Remember the Andrex Jack!' As Jack headed off giving Kevin a filthy look.

Claire didn't even bother to ask about this male humor. 'Before I forget Claire my mother's coming back when I go to Cardiff with Jack, I want her to meet you.' Kevin said all of a sudden. 'Kevin, that's brilliant, but can we go back to my house, I want you both to see it?'

....

17th June 1999

They both showered and Claire took Sooty out, Snowy stayed in today and sat with Kevin as he logged onto work. Deb and Jamie had it all sorted. Claire arrived home with Sooty. The little bugger had got her and him so messed up they looked like a pair of vagrants. 'What on earth Claire?' Kevin asked looking at his dripping girlfriend and dirty wet dog. 'Pond again, he knows Kevin, he knows how to get me.' She replied looking desperate and upset.

'Right, Claire don't get changed, you, sit!' He said to Sooty and put his shoes on. Sooty didn't move. Kevin grabbed Claire and said 'Come on, we're going back out.' He grabbed Sooty's lead but to Claire's and Sooty's surprise he handed the lead back to Claire. 'Come on, to the pond.' He said so commandingly they both followed without question.

Just as they got to the front door Kevin shouted again, this time to Snowy and said 'Snowy, you're coming too.' Snowy didn't argue and followed them all out of the apartment. They all walked for twenty minutes until they got to the infamous pond. Kevin told Claire to let Sooty off the lead, true to form he dived straight into the pond and sat there. Kevin told Claire and Snowy to join him on a park bench twenty foot away and they both followed. Sooty sat in the pond barking for the next ten minutes. Kevin told Claire and Snowy to ignore him.

Kevin said they were off and Snowy and Claire followed him away from the pond. Claire was panicking for Sooty who was barking in the distance, still in the pond. Kevin put his finger to his lips to indicate sshh and they walked away. Snowy seemed to be with Kevin, looking disgusted at what her dog was doing.

They walked five minutes away and sat on another bench. Kevin looked at Claire and said 'five minutes maximum and he'll be back, tail between his legs, watch and see!' Claire didn't look convinced and even had a worried look but Kevin ignored this. Snowy purred.

Three minutes later Sooty came bounding out of the wooded area looking as panicked as any of them had ever seen him. He saw them after looking around three hundred and sixty degrees and bolted towards them.

Snowy hissed at him and Kevin made him sit and told him what he'd been doing wrong. Sooty looked between Kevin, Snowy and Claire and Kevin knew he'd got the point and learnt the lesson.

When they got back Kevin told Claire to bath Sooty and tell him she wouldn't put up with any nonsense in the future and threaten him with Snowy if he tried to object. Fifty minutes later a clean Sooty and very clean fresh smelling Claire exited the bathroom. 'Sorted Kevin, I don't know how you managed it but he's a different dog with me now.'

They both laughed and Sooty nervously cuddled up to Kevin first and after his acceptance sought Snowy's. She cuddled into him and purred loudly. As Claire was commenting how sweet it was Jack came through the door.

'Hi both, second meeting got cancelled so I had to come back, good morning session though. You two been up to much?' He continued. 'Dog training lesson.' Kevin said with a grin. Jack showered before Kevin and Kevin put the oven on for his leg of lamb. When Jack did get out of the shower he smelt the meat and shouted in to them 'Whole lamb roast?' 'No Jack, a leg.' Kevin replied 'What are you two eating then?' Jack shouted back to Kevin and Claire's loud laughter.

....

18ᵗʰ June 1999

Kevin and Jack drove to Cardiff. The meetings were pretty intense and they left the office at five. Their hotel was right in the centre of Cardiff, an old building called the Angel and was opposite the famous Arms Park.

Jack joined Kevin in the bar at six. After an hour and three ciders later they hit the town. They headed first to Sam's Bar but soon realized that although it had a good buzz about the place it was too small to fit two hundred odd extra people and create a party scene that Kevin was looking for. The same could be said of Life, Walkabout, O Neil's, The Philharmonic, Kiwi's and eventually The Continental.

Kevin sat with Jack drinking vodka. It hadn't worked. He couldn't think what to do next. Just as he was about to give up and grab Jack to go back to the hotel, two pretty girls Emma, and Kate, who they'd been talking to earlier came to him with an idea.

'Are you prepared to part with some cash Kevin?' Emma asked 'Depends on how much and why but in essence, yes.' 'Right then, I've agreed with the bar manager to supply us two bottles of champagne and four glasses for one hundred and fifty quid. If you agree, I'll take you somewhere to show you my idea.'

They left the club at twelve-thirty and Emma led them on a ten minute walk. They arrived at what she called the Civic Centre. There were some fantastic buildings, apparently the City Hall, the Crown Court and the Museum. There was a huge lawned area in front of the buildings and long roads in-between each of them.

'Where we are now will be decorated and called Winter Wonderland, there will be an ice rink and shows and stalls selling food, drink and entertainment. The streets or roads you see in-between the buildings will be full of more stalls and more show rides. There's going to be a stage at the end of the road we're opposite' Emma said excitedly.

Kevin sank his drink and topped all their glasses up and considered for a moment before saying. 'Who's playing on the stage?' 'Not sure yet Kevin but what I'm suggesting is a barbecue, cool boxes full of beer, wine, champagne and all two hundred odd of you can be together with enough space, see in the New Year with thousands of others and can all celebrate your party together.' She replied looking really positive.

Kevin realized it was right all of a sudden. Two hundred people, a barbeque in the middle of winter, lots of local people around and a concert, what more could a party ask for?

....

19th June 1999

Kevin dragged Jack to breakfast and four plates later he resembled something like human. 'Jack mate, I forgot to tell you we're picking my mother up from the station, she's coming back with us.' Jack grunted something in response. They were in Cardiff Central Station by ten to nine.

Kevin told Jack to wait in the car and went to find his mum. She was outside as he got to the entrance of the station. 'Kevin darling, how are you?' She said giving him a huge hug. 'Hi Mum, it's great to see you and I'm fine, how are you, it does seem like ages since I've seen you and dare I say it missed you?' 'Oh Kevin so nice, OTT but nice' 'OTT is my tenth middle name mum.' 'Stop it. Come on take me to meet Jack.'

They walked back to the car and Jack was comatose in the passenger seat and the idiot had locked the doors. Kevin knocked on the window to no avail. He banged the door, rang his mobile but Jack didn't budge.

As mothers do, his sorted it in two seconds by whistling at the window. Jack jumped, saw them and unlocked the doors. He apologized profusely as he saw the look of anger on Kevin's face. Kevin's mum though laughing said 'Ah the famous Jack, without his bear but just as dull, I'm Felicity.' They got back to his pad at just after twelve.

Kevin introduced his mother to Claire and they hugged. Pulling no punches Felicity said 'Kevin was definitely right about one thing Claire.' Claire looking blankly replied politely 'He was?' 'Yes Claire, he said you were gorgeous and he wasn't lying.' Blushing Claire replied 'Thank you Felicity.'

They got to Claire's at five o' clock. They drove up the drive, Kevin saying 'this isn't a drive darling it's a bloody road.' Ignoring him she got out of the car and opened one of the huge oak doors and led them into a hall way bigger than Kevin's and Jane's apartments put together. 'Where's Jeeves?' 'Oh Kevin, get over it, there are no butler's, no maids, I do have a cleaner and a gardener but I don't use hardly any of the house.'

Claire took Kevin to the bedrooms and helped him carry the bags as they left Felicity chilling with her wine. They dropped Felicity's bag in her room which was on another wing. Claire saying she could scream as loud as she liked without Felicity hearing a thing. 'Oh I like your style Claire.' Kevin said with a wicked smile. 'Come on, we need to cook for your mum first, well I need to cook anyway.' Claire replied and led him back downstairs.

'No time for a quickie then?' Felicity said to the both of them. 'Not really mother but Claire's put you in a room where you won't hear her scream later.' Kevin replied with Claire going bright red. 'Oh Claire, you're not just beautiful, you're considerate, a real quality.' She said looking at Claire. 'My middle name' Claire replied a bit skeptically. 'Perfect' Kevin and Felicity said together.

Claire said she needed to prepare food, Felicity wanting to unpack. He decided he'd find his babies and feed them and make a few calls whilst chilling over lots of wine and Bensons.

He found Snowy first and asked where Sooty was. She meowed and Sooty came running. Kevin told them both it was dinner time and they followed willingly. He set their things up in the study, off the main hall entrance before going back to the Drawing Room as Claire had called it and dialed the home number first.

'Hello, Jack Black here, how can I help you?' 'Jack you dick, it's not an office, you're not my bloody secretary, you're my friend and my home is yours.' 'Kevin, you ok, yeah sorry, a bit of a work habit, everything ok your end?' 'Yeah we're all here and safe, but Jack this is a mansion, never mind a house.' 'Everything cool though?' 'Yeah fine, when are Katie and the kids arriving?' 'Tomorrow, I can't wait Kev, I really can't and thanks again for giving the place up to me, Katie and the kids.' 'Least I could do mate'

He set his lap top up and began to write his Blog.

> My dearest and most special Peeps
> What the Kevster's arranging is an outside extravaganza in the centre of Cardiff with shows, stalls and a concert Peeps. How cool's that? Yous will all need your winters finest but we're there Dudes and Dudesses we're there! So that's it all yous lot, party planned, all I need now is confirmed names. I've already paid for the drink and food up front. What we need now Dudes and Dudesses is commitment. I hope I've met your expectations and I know this will be a rocking, rolling, shaking experience we'll all never forget. Make peace with the world and love to all those who are close.

Felicity got a little drunk and was ready for bed by ten. Kevin went with her just to make sure she was ok. With Snowy cuddling into his mum, he cuddled her too and told her he loved her. He got back to Claire and she was sat snuggled up to Sooty on the sofa and to his total disbelief they were both asleep and snoring.

....
20th June 1999

Claire took them out for the day. She drove to a so called nature reserve which from what Kevin could see was a bloody big forest. As she parked and opened the back Sooty went bounding off into the unknown with Snowy having a sedate look around near the jeep.

They walked for two hours and had several looks from people seeing a cat walking with a dog. Sooty was in his element, fending off any canine attempts to get at his cat and loving every second of it. They were back early afternoon. After more drinks in the pub they decided on a siesta.

Kevin and Claire took the opportunity to use his afternoon rise and surprisingly fell asleep about six o' clock. Kevin woke at ten o' clock and went for a cigarette but nobody else stirred. He got back into bed and fell back into a deep sleep instantly.

....
21st June 1999

Felicity said she wanted a serious chat with her son. Claire, taking the hint went for a shower. Kevin lit a cigarette and said 'Hit me with it mum, whatever you think won't change my mind but I want to hear it anyway.'

'Well son, I'm off today, I've booked a train on the internet at five fifteen so I need a lift to the station. That's number one. Number two is I'm going to give you guys more time together, you never know what might happen! Number three my darling son is a warning, you mess this beautiful, stunning woman around and I'll disown you. Number four my baby boy, if you don't marry this woman and give me grandchildren I'll kill you.'

Claire volunteered to take Felicity to the station. Snowy and Sooty were going for the ride to say their goodbyes. 'Kevin, your mum's brilliant, well apart from talking grandchildren to me, she's great.' Claire said returning with a smile. 'She is darling and I agree about the grandchildren bit, I think she thinks I'm past it.

I'm not thirty until December the twenty fourth.' Kevin replied with a slight sigh.

Claire gave him a hug and said 'For a minute there I thought you were going to tell me you were a Christmas baby, I knew I was wrong though, you're too naughty to be a Jesus child.' 'Yeah I've had that connection all my life. I was close though babe, eleven-fifty!' 'God, ten minutes Kevin, you could have been a different person, a saint or something.' Claire carried on ribbing him. 'Ok sweetheart, I'm no saint and never will be but I'm no devil either.' He responded defensively. 'Oh yes you are Mr. Julie, you're a bedroom devil!' Claire said now changing her look of amusement to one of desire. 'For that darling I'll make sure I'm on form tonight, but only after you've fed me, I'm starving.' She gave him a hug, poured him a large red and even lit a Cuban for him. 'I've got a Stroganoff in the freezer, will that do?' 'Brilliant darling, thanks.'

Kevin sat smoking his Cuban and sipping his wine for five minutes contemplating life. Claire was the biggest thing that had ever happened to him and he was definitely not going to do anything to jeopardize this. His phone went and he answered it without a care in the world. 'Jane, hi honey, how are you darling?' 'A bit of a mess actually Kevin, can I see you urgently?' 'Jane that sounds serious?' 'It is or I wouldn't ask Kevin.' 'Can't you say on the phone?' 'I'd rather not babe, not on this, can you come back tomorrow?'

Claire came back from her bath and noticed the look on Kevin's face. 'What's wrong darling?' 'To be honest Claire, I don't know. Jane's just rung in bits and wants me to go to her tomorrow and come back here on Wednesday. I've never heard her sound so distressed.' He replied looking blank. 'Well you've got to go, I'll look after Snowy and Sooty and have you back Wednesday.' Claire said supportively.

....

22nd June 1999

They hugged as he arrived at Jane's door and Kevin followed her in to her apartment carrying his bag on his shoulder. He dumped it into the spare room and said to Jane. 'I promised Claire I'd ring when I got here.' 'Ok darling, you ring Claire, I'll grab us a wine, a box of cigarettes and an ashtray.' Jane replied still flatly. He rang Claire feeling lost for some reason.

'Come on then darling, I know this is something big so spit it out!' Jane mouthed silently. 'Jane, take a breath and tell me please.' Kevin said firmly. 'She's back Kevin, she's back!' Jane said and burst into tears. 'Whose back Jane, Suzanne, Karen?' He asked trying to grab her arm softly. 'No Kevin, Alexis is back, she's back Kevin!' 'When Jane, how, how do you know, did she contact you?' 'No Kevin, Anne rang me and told me, she got back two days ago and has rented an apartment, that's all I know.'

Kevin sat back, lit a cigarette and gave Jane a huge hug. 'Darling, what can we do, she's excluded us from her life. We need to move on' he said in control of his emotions.

Jane took a cigarette and sank her glass and then managed in full control 'Kevin, that's bullshit, I've loved her since I met her and you two have loved each other since you can remember feelings. You know neither of us can ignore her return and she knows it, that's why she hasn't tried to get hold of us.'

'Do we have her current number Jane?' 'No Kevin, Anne wouldn't give it to me.' 'Ok darling we can't sort that out now. Come on let's go to bed and we'll think in the morning when we've not got too many glasses of wine inside us.' Kevin said and grabbed her by the hand.

··

23rd June 1999

As soon as he got up he lit up a cigarette and put the kettle on and Jane walked in rubbing her eyes. 'Clothes darling' Kevin said looking at her naked body. 'Shit, I forgot, I normally walk around naked.' 'Well unless you want a quick rogering I suggest you put some on darling.' Kevin replied laughing back. 'Is that an offer?' She replied but was running from the cushion he'd just thrown at her.

Jane came back in a minute later, at least with a tee-shirt on that just covered her bum. 'Underware?' He asked suspiciously. 'Of course darling, I don't do rejection very well.'

They agreed to go separate routes in their search and meet at Henry's bar at four. Kevin let her go and dialed the number he knew would net the right result. 'Mum, hi, it's me.' 'Yes darling I know, after thirty years I do tend to recognize your voice.' 'Mum, no bullshit, I need to get hold of Alexis.' 'Ok darling, she knows it too, she's given me a number for you to call her on.' 'Mum, thanks.'

He lit a cigarette, he'd known how Alexis would play it, and she hadn't changed since they were children. This would allow him the opportunity to see her before Jane, something he was determined to achieve. Throwing his cigarette aside he dialed Alexis's number. It rang three times and she answered. 'Hi Kevin.' 'How'd you know it was me?' 'I only gave this number to Felicity.' 'Oh, planned then?' 'Yes.' 'Alexis, I need to see you, I don't want to talk on the phone.' 'Me neither Kevin, when?' 'Now' 'Ok, where?' 'Do you know Henry's Bar, just off Bush Street?' 'Yes.' 'How long before you could get there?' 'Thirty minutes.' 'Ok, see you there in thirty minutes?'

Alexis walked in about twenty minutes later and all who were in the bar stopped and looked at her. Hating himself he thought that she was the most stunning person in the world. She walked up to him and he stood to greet her. They hugged for well over five minutes before she sat down and Kevin went and got her a large glass of white wine.

After an hour of Kevin's attacks she tried to say she couldn't explain. 'Kevin it's too difficult, I can't, just can't!' 'Not good enough Alexis, tonight I'm cooking at Jane's and you're coming and you're going to tell us both why you shat all over us. I won't take no for an answer, is that clear?'

Jane arrived, bought them drinks, Kevin sipped his wine and lit his Benson 'Jane, I've found her, met her and she's coming to yours for supper at seven.' Jane looked at him in amazement but nodded silently.

Kevin used the opportunity to call Claire. He explained he needed a little longer and Claire agreed immediately. They walked back slowly and not talking. Jane went for a shower and Kevin to the fridge hitting on a glass of white.

Jane emerged from the shower naked and had made an effort and shaved everywhere. 'How'd I look darling?' She asked doing a pirouette. 'Naked for one, sexy for two and bloody well smooth for three' Kevin replied shaking his head with a smile. 'Shower's all yours babe.'

He showered and shaved and made sure he looked his best, again he hated himself for still trying to impress Alexis. His rationale was he'd always done it, ever since he was a child. Just as this was computing this in his head the door bell went. As he opened it Alexis walked in looking down trodden. 'Hi Kevin, God this is difficult. You both probably want to kill me. I wouldn't blame you either.' She said looking at both of them, tears trickling down her cheeks. 'I'm so sorry, so sorry. I can't change how I've been only how I can be.' Kevin walked towards her. She looked really worried but he held his hand out and hugged her with all his might and gestured for Jane to join them.

He served the king prawns on a bed on sliced spring onion, celery, cucumber and lettuce with a sweet chili sauce. This went down a storm. Alexis and Jane were now chatting like old friends and Kevin also managed to release the cramping feeling in his stomach.

Jane offered to clear the starter dishes up leaving Kevin and Alexis alone. She lit him one of her Marlborough's and one for herself and held his hand tightly. Gripping it back twice as hard he whispered 'You hurt me badly babe.' 'I know Kevin, I'm so sorry, I really am.'

They all chatted and smoked for a while before deciding to go to bed. Kevin checked the clock some time later and saw it was five in the morning. He got up to have a cigarette. Alexis joined him sometime later as he was drifting off to sleep on the sofa. 'I decided to join you.' She said and kissed him softly on the cheek.

Kevin held her and burst into tears. 'Alexis, I love you but I love someone else.' 'Kevin, I know, I have already let you go as husband material. I know you love Claire and I'll hold back, meet her and be both of your friends.'

....

24th June 1999

Kevin grabbed Jane and gave her the biggest hug ever just before he left. He didn't say anything but didn't need to, he'd put all his love into this hug to tell her she was still his best friend, it was just his other best friend had returned. 'Why don't you come around Friday night?' He said still hugging her. 'Ok, do you mind if I bring Karen?' 'Karen!' 'Yeah, she's been texting me and says she's changed and misses me.' 'Your shout darling' He said as Alexis came back in with her bag.

On the way to Alexis's apartment he asked her if she'd come and meet Claire at his on Saturday. She agreed and true to her promise hugged him and pecked his cheek as she got out of the car.

Kevin drove to Claire's far faster than he should have and checked his trip computer, he was averaging eighty miles an hour. As he pulled up to the huge entrance of Claire's house she was there with the dog and the cat looking out of the open door. Sooty won the race to greet him and knocked Kevin flat on his back with a humungous leap at him to welcome him home, then proceeded to kiss him all over to check he still smelt and tasted the same. The two ladies walked sedately to meet him. Claire hugged and kissed him hard on the mouth and Snowy meowed until he picked her up for a cuddle.

He put Snowy down and followed Claire to the kitchen. Kevin grabbed her from behind and hugged her as he kissed the back of her neck. Claire turned around and kissed him hard. 'Missed me then have you?' She said with a surly look. 'Nah, not really but thought I'd check out your pretty neck out anyway.' Claire blushed with a huge smile on her face.

Kevin then told her about the dinner party's with Jane and Karen and Alexis on the Friday and Saturday nights. Claire thought it was ideal, 'I want to meet them and be involved Kevin, I don't want separate friends.'

Claire got a bottle of Champagne out and asked Kevin to crack it open. 'Darling, this is Dom Perignon!' 'Yes it is darling and it's a special occasion, you're back so I want to celebrate.' Claire replied giggling. It was now eight o' clock and Claire said she was going to cook the food as Kevin updated his blog page. He turned his lap top on and sat back thinking as it started up.

Yo Dudesters
Kevster here with a huge apology, far too long has passed and I haven't said hello again. Let me promise yous all this will change and I will be better! Well Peeps, another five days of roller coaster ups and downs for the Kevster. Although not for general release the Kevster's had a few things to deal with

and knocked him about a bit. Still as ever, the rubber man bounces back and as you will no doubt tell is now back on the up.

Well Peeps we've got our plan and names are drifting in, and the names that have come so far have all coughed up. Thanks to yous guys and gals who've backed their boasts with cash. The rest of yous need to take note, the Kevster's set aside enough to cover it all but wants to use your cash to make it better for all of us Dudesters.

Claire made sure Kevin had an evening rise and told him to do things to her she'd never done before. It was midnight before they knew it and both had a Benson before they went to sleep completely exhausted.

....

25ᵗʰ June 1999

Kevin and Sooty went on a walk of Claire's grounds and out into the countryside. Snowy had turned her nose up at them and cuddled into Claire as they left the bedroom.

Claire met them as they returned and said she needed another hour in bed. He fed the animals and walked back upstairs. As he approached he bedroom he stripped naked, screamed a Tarzan call and jumped right on top of her. Claire was now giggling and asked him to do the rude things to her that he'd done last night again!

After half an hour's nap they both showered and started to get ready to leave. They were all packed and ready by twelve and left at ten past. They arrived back at Kevin's by three o' clock. He said he'd go and get the food and Claire sorted out his apartment for new guests.

Claire told him she felt horny 'Again, now?' He replied a little aghast. 'Yes again and yes now!' Claire replied without blinking. 'Only if it's a quickie' Kevin replied looking at his watch. 'For now darling that'll do as my middle name.' Claire said laughing and dragging him in to the bedroom.

Claire was still getting dressed when the door bell went. Sooty went running to the door and Kevin followed. He opened the door for Jane and Karen and Sooty did a show. Jane joined in and Sooty and Jane did their own show as Kevin took Karen into the kitchen to get them all drinks. 'Kevin, I'm sorry for the way I've behaved before, I've been a real tart.' Karen said holding out her hand. Kevin shook it and said 'Let bygones be bygones darling.' Smiling at her

Claire came out ten minutes later and topped them all up. They chatted for ages before Kevin announced the food ready. They all ate and Jane proclaimed this the best meal he'd cooked yet. Kevin did ask if they were staying but Jane said they weren't. Perhaps she didn't quite trust the new Karen, he thought to himself.

....

26th June 1999

Over breakfast Claire looked at him in a considered stare and said 'Kevin, tonight's going to be really difficult for me, you know that don't you?' 'I thought you wanted to meet Alexis darling?' 'I do darling but only because she's important to you.'

They spent the rest of the day preparing and Kevin was ready for seven when the door bell went. Feeling more nervous than he'd ever felt he opened the door. Alexis was taking the piss. She had the shortest skirt and tightest top he'd ever seen her in. She definitely didn't have any underware on. 'Hi Kevin' She said as she walked in as if she was on a catwalk. 'Alexis, what are you playing at?' He asked her in a whisper. 'Nothing darling, I just want your love of your life to know what's waiting for you if she lets you down.'

Claire came out a couple of minutes later and if it was possible had a shorter skirt on than Alexis and a tighter top. She too seemed not to have any underware on. Following introductions Kevin went to the kitchen. He listened closely at the door and heard soft voices, a good sign.

He then heard Alexis say something that made him cringe and wish he hadn't arranged their meeting so soon! 'So Claire, you're married right?' 'Well technically yes but going through a divorce.' Claire replied curtly. 'Oh I see, why a divorce Claire? You look like a woman no man would want get rid of.' 'It was complicated Alexis.' Claire said in a hiss.

Kevin jumped into the room and topped up their glasses to their false smiles. Getting back to his sanctuary of the kitchen he eaves dropped at the door again. They weren't letting it go. 'So it was complicated was it Claire?' 'Yes, it was as a matter of fact.' 'We'll what can be so complicated then Claire?' Alexis asked 'He was seeing another man if you must know!' Claire said a bit defensively. Alexis replied with what Kevin knew was a sneer. 'Ooh, that's different, I take it he didn't like your bedroom moves then?' Kevin was just about to run in and intervene before Claire got her confidence back and hit Alexis with 'Well coming from you dear, that's a little rich. My husband was a bit like you, gay but couldn't come to terms with it so tried shagging around with the opposite sex and fucked more than one person's life up!'

Kevin nearly fell over behind the kitchen door as he leaned closer to hear Alexis's reply. 'Claire for your information I'm not gay, I just happen to have found women attractive along the way and thought I'd give them a go.' 'Don't give me that crap Alexis, you're a muff muncher, you always have been but you've got this childhood thing with Kevin and now you worry life is passing you by and your biological clocks ticking so you're reverting to Kevin as some seventh or eighth choice!'

The next thing he heard was tears. They were Alexis's. Following the tears he heard her say through broken sobs 'It's not like that Claire, I do love him, and I've always loved him. I'd rather be involved with him as a friend and put all that to one side and let him go to you than think of losing him, does that make any sense?'

Kevin listened at the door and there was silence for what seemed like ages before he heard Claire respond. 'Yes it does Alexis, but you've got to decide if you're willing to spend the rest of your life with him as a lover or a friend. I want both from him and don't want any other man or woman.'

Kevin witnessed another silence and decided to enter the room. Claire and Alexis were hugging and from what he could see both crying. Claire waved him away so he went back and finished the food.

When he did go back in five minutes later Claire and Alexis were eventually chatting like friends. They ate and drank and all went to bed by midnight. Claire made sure Kevin had a rise and made use of it, kissing him nonstop telling him how much she loved him.

....

27th June 1999

After they got back from lunch Claire told him she needed to go home today. He asked her if everything was ok and she replied by leading him to the bedroom and having an attempt at his initially reluctant afternoon rise.

She left two hours later and Kevin sat down on the sofa in his room silently with a glass of red and two vodkas. He needed a sleep before he made calls or updated any of his blog pages. He woke up on the sofa at eleven-thirty and knew he needed to go to bed. He had work early in the morning.

....

28th June 1999

Kevin had his meeting with Daniellie at two o' clock and was out of his office just before four. He updated Deb and Jamie on the meeting he'd had and again thanked them for their efforts and the quality of their work.

He was home by seven and asked Sooty if he wanted another walk, the bark and wagging of his tail gave the answer. The three of them went on the shorter route. Kevin sat down with a glass of red at half past eight with two very strong, orange juice worried vodkas and set to write his current update.

> My dearest most special Peeps
> Just keeping in touch as the Kevster promised. I can't believe the names still coming through for the party Dudes and Dudesses. Before I continue I wish to share with yous lot the new grand total Peeps:
> Well what can I say Peeps, the new grand total is, wait for the drum roll . . . fifty seven all you party mad Dudes and Dudesses in just a few short days. We're going to party Peeps, we are really going to party.
> With a list building so quickly I reckon we can be seen as being the party extravaganza of the whole of the UK Peeps. We're all into the home stretch of June Dudesters and we'll be counting down into the second half of the year before any of us can say party! Well my favorite Peeps, fifty seven names in and we're on a roll.

It was still early enough to make a call, who though he mused in his confused head, Alexis or Claire? 'Hi Darling it's me.' Kevin, are you ok?' 'A little drunk but other than that sort of.' 'You sound hanging darling.' 'Well, a few things on my mind, that's all.' 'Ok sweetie as long as you're ok.' 'Yeah fine darling, look the reason I'm ringing is to ask if you're free tomorrow night.' 'Yes I am. What are you proposing?' 'Dinner here' 'Wow, that'd be fantastic, I want sea bass Kevin.' 'Consider it done Alexis.'

29th June 1999

He rang work and spoke to Deb, everything was under control. He told her he had to finish the next plan. He spent two hours solid sorting it. He didn't think, smoke or move until it was done. By the time he'd finished he thought about making a few calls.

Thinking about things he decided not to ring his mum, she'd ask too many relevant questions. He was sure she was an evil fortune teller, always able to predict what he was up to so settled on ringing Jack.

'Hi Fella' 'Kevin my buddy, how are you?' 'Brilliant Jack what about you and the family?' 'Would you believe it Kev, we've all met Lewis Lennox and he's coming to stay, as well as Oliver, to see our Lennox!' 'Yes for you I'd well believe it Jack. You know who Lewis Lennox is now?' 'Shit no Kev, he's a big bloke who originated from Canada and is ok. I know he's famous as a boxer but that means diddly squat to me.' 'Jack, your naivety makes you so special.' 'What's that mean Kevin?' 'Don't worry Dude, a good thing.'

At six o' clock he had everything prepared and went for a shower. He was out by ten past and drying when he heard the doorbell go. Going to the door in just his towel he opened the door to Alexis standing there in a dress so short it needn't have been there.

'What a welcome darling.' She said as she walked in and grabbed Sooty first and then Snowy. Alexis looked at Kevin and said assertively 'Food later darling and took his towel from him. Hating himself but feeling as excited as any man can he followed her without comment or question.

An hour later they both showered and Kevin said he was making the food. He served grilled bass with a garlic, wine and shrimp sauce with sautéed potatoes with some flash fried garlic asparagus.

He opened the champagne as they sat at the table and ate, drank and chatted like a conventional couple. The food was stunning. Although Alexis said it, Kevin knew; he knew when he'd nailed something and this was one of those occasions. They sat smoking and drinking the champagne, getting tipsier by the minute.

Three hours later he knew this woman was his forever. He loved every single part of her. He fell asleep knowing what was right and what was good. Two hours later Kevin woke up, lit a cigarette and felt Claire was the perfect woman, the woman he was going to marry. He then thought of the woman he also loved in his bed and wished for divine intervention, none came. He got back into bed and just smelt Alexis, she belonged there, but so did Claire. The only person he couldn't see who was worthy was himself.

....

30ᵗʰ June 1999

He turned his lap top onto work ten minutes after Alexis left. Jane opened the door coming in about twelve minutes after Alexis had left. She seemed a little off as she walked in but wouldn't elaborate. Kevin knew something was wrong and suspected he knew what it was.

Jane took Sooty out for a few hours and Kevin sorted everything he needed to for work, it was surprising how much he did without distraction. Jane got back at about twelve-thirty and sat down in the chair looking mean. 'Spit it out darling.' He said waiting for her to let go. 'Well Kevin, the cow's only gone and done it again.' Jane said angrily. 'Karen?' He replied knowingly. 'Bloody right Karen, yesterday I caught her in a pub with a man, her husband Kevin!'

'Did you approach her?' 'Well if you call punching her lights out, then yes I approached her.' Jane said now looking seething. 'You hit her?' 'Twice in fact, two left hooks, the second one knocked her out!' Jane said but now a little calmer.

Trying to take all this in seriously and daring not to laugh he asked 'Then what happened?' 'Well her dozy bloody thick husband got up and tried to grab me.' Jane replied still calmer than earlier. 'And . . . ?' Kevin said now really interested. 'Well I knocked him out too! I then asked the barman for a piece of paper and a pen and left a note on their table.'

'Didn't anyone try to stop you or call the police; what about the bar staff?' Kevin asked but couldn't now hide his smile. 'Well firstly darling, the staff didn't think a scorned lesbian lover was worthy of the police. Secondly I think they were scared of me and thirdly darling, it appears the super hubby didn't know about the flings his wife had and is a well respected local. They asked me to leave and suggested I shouldn't return.' Jane said and now was smiling herself.

Kevin walked over to her, hugged her and kissed her on the cheek. 'Let me look at your hand darling?' He said grabbing her left one. Sure enough her knuckles were really bruised. 'Jane, what are you like? I'll make sure I never get into a fight with you!'

Jane laughed with him and then said out of the blue, 'it's not me you want to worry about Babe, its Claire!' Kevin looked at her and said worriedly 'what do you mean darling?' 'Oh Kevin, I can smell her, I lived with her for years, I know she's been here and by the smell, in the last few hours.'

Kevin sat back, lit a cigarette and said softly 'I'm in a mess Babe.' 'I know. I could see it coming as soon as she got back Kevin. Both of you have feelings which are too deep routed. All I'm going to say is that Claire is the one darling, not Alexis.' Jane said and pinched his cigarette from him. Jane went out for food telling him they'd talk later.

He picked up the phone making sure he had cigarettes, wine and his animals; he knew his mother would give him a hard time. 'Hi mum.' 'Kevin my darling son, how the devil are you?' 'Absolutely top of the world mater' 'Bullshit Kevin, I can tell by your tone you're in distress.' 'How mum, how'd you know, how'd you always know?' 'Mother's instinct darling, it's inbred, can't change it dear.' 'Ok mum, I am in a mess.' 'Let me guess, Claire and Alexis?' 'Mum, how do you know that?'

'Kevin, I'm not stupid and know you, look we both agree you're in a mess. The next part is how to deal with it and I need some time to think on that.' 'Mum, Claire's here tomorrow, can you think quickly?' 'I'll ring you later darling, if that's ok?' 'Well it'll have to be but thanks mum.'

Jane got back at eight and Kevin was on his way to drunken oblivion. She made herself a drink, a large red and asked him 'Are you ok to make dinner darling?' 'Do bear's shit in the woods?' Kevin cooked food and they ate in near silence. He was nearly out on his feet, full of food and alcohol.

'Come on darling, shower, I'll join you.' Jane said leading him away. Jane stripped him and washed and shaved him all over, she then took him into the bedroom and took advantage of him.

An hour later, lying naked in the bed and smoking with Jane he asked 'How's that helped darling?' 'Well it's made me come and I feel better darling. Look Kevin, I love you as a friend, we aren't getting married and having babies but I needed sex. You haven't committed to Claire or Alexis so whilst you're putting it about I wanted some. My promise not to do it again is on condition you have a partner you are true to.'

The phone rang and Jane answered. 'Hi Felicity, yes, he's just cooked me chateaubriand with a spicy Madeira sauce and these really neat cabbage rolls, it was the best food I've ever eaten. Yes, I know about Alexis and Claire. No, I'm not really helping as I've just shagged his brains out. I know Felicity but until he commits I think he's fair game. Yes and always.'

Jane handed Kevin the phone and he took it with trepidation. 'Hi Mum.' 'Kevin, how could things have gotten so much worse since I last spoke to you a couple of hours ago?' 'You know me mum, life on the edge.' 'Kevin, Kevin, Kevin.' 'Thanks mum, I do know my name.' 'Oh funny man again now are we?' 'Yup, middle name mother.' 'Kevin are you drunk?' 'Very mum and still a long way to go to where I want to get to' 'Oh honey, you are in a mess aren't you?' 'Big style mum.' 'When can I come and see you?' 'Mum, if you could come next week after Tuesday that'd be fantastic.' 'I'll be there darling, in the meantime, be careful, I can't think of anything else to say.' 'I know mum, me neither.'

....

01ˢᵗ July 1999

Jane left at three-thirty and Kevin was about to go out to get food ingredients for tonight when he heard the phone. It was Jack

'Kevin I tried ringing last night to tell you we have a date tonight, you, me, Claire and Katie in the Ivy. Lewis is coming!' 'Jack you're shitting me?' 'No Mate, we get on like a house on fire and he's really keen to meet you, he's bringing some other bloke called Bruno, a friend of his.' 'Did he say his second name Jack?' 'Yeah, something like Franks, I can't really remember.'

Claire arrived at five. Kevin held her, smelt her and from that moment realized she was the one, it wasn't Alexis it was Claire! Somehow he now knew. This was his woman and he would be true to her forever from now on. Why he'd been the way he had he just couldn't contemplate.

They spent the next ten minutes hugging before Kevin remembered about tonight. 'Shit darling, we're out tonight and if I've got it right with Lewis Lennox and Bruno Franks.' 'Kevin you're playing with me?' 'No Darling, well not yet anyway' 'Do you ever stop?' 'For food and sleep, look joking aside Jack's invited us and it's a freebee at the Ivy.'

The taxi arrived on time and they were outside the Ivy earlier than any of the others. Richard was still manning the door and embraced Kevin. He didn't even ask why they were there but Kevin told him anyway.

The next guest to arrive was Lewis Lennox himself, Richard showed him to the table they were waiting at and he sat down, looked at them both and said 'You must be Kevin and Claire, I've heard so much about you.' 'I hope it's all good Lewis, of course I know a little about you.' Kevin said shaking his hand.

Claire seemed to be shaking but Lewis was really cool. 'Why are you nervous about me Claire, I hear you've met the real deal Lennox?' Lewis said kindly. 'Oh you mean the bear, yeah I've met the bear, and he's gorgeous.' Claire said finding her feet and her voice.

Jack and Katie arrived and Jack and Lewis exchanged high fives and Claire, Kevin and Katie hugged like the long lost friends they now were. Richard brought champagne and joined them for some photos. Bruno arrived last and about half an hour after Jack and Katie. Claire was in star struck land, Kevin impressed and Jack just as non plussed as ever. Bruno said 'Hello, nice night for it.' 'Jack shook his hand and replied as quietly as Jack could 'You're a bit late mate, we nearly had to order without you.'

Bruno looked at him, barked a laugh and said to Lewis, 'is he the dude with the bear?' 'Yup Bruno, I told you man, takes no shit this guy, and he's a rock man.' Bruno said hello to everyone as if they were his best friends and charmed the ladies. He sat next to Kevin and asked sincerely 'So you're the one with the blog, the party idea?' 'Yup that's me.' Kevin replied. 'Look Kevin, I hear your funny man, I like funny guys, but I wanted to meet the bear man, that's why I'm here.'

Kevin dragged Bruno's huge head to one side and whispered 'Bruno my friend and here was me thinking you made all this effort to meet me!' 'You are funny Kevin, Ha, ha, ha . . .' Bruno replied in a mock growl. 'Look you, if we weren't with company, and I didn't have my etiquette to think about I'd offer you outside for that!' Kevin said staring at Bruno with his hardest stare!

Bruno looked right back at him and barked 'You are really funny man, they got that right.' 'I'm glad you think so friend cause there'd have been a mess in the car park otherwise.' Kevin said still eyeing him full on. Lewis by now had heard the banter and shouted 'Can you two stop trying to be the funniest guy here, I'm starving!'

Kevin and Bruno chuckled and banged knuckles together, followed by a man hug. Lewis told them to get a room to huge laughs and barks by Bruno. Jack told all of them to shut up as he was hungry. It seemed nothing got in the way of Jack's food. Richard was soon over, sensing Jack's apparent hunger and said assertively 'Food will be served shortly' and showed them to their table.

Jack rubbed his hands and the waiters brought out some ribs. They weren't baby back ribs like Kevin was used to, these things were huge! Richard proclaimed 'The best, biggest and tastiest beef ribs you'll ever eat!'

Lewis and Bruno nodded, Claire, Katie and Kevin just looked but Jack shouted 'Starters at last!' After their monster beef ribs Richard brought the main course out. It was a sea food fest. Lobster, crab, muscles, oysters, razor clams and the biggest prawns Kevin had ever seen. 'Compliments of Michelle, our Chef tonight, who says he's heard Jack's got an appetite!' Richard said smiling brightly.

They all sat and chatted and laughed out loud. Bruno was still vying against Kevin on the jokes front, Kevin was keeping pace but Bruno then got Lewis biting and he got a little bit pissy. Jack looked at Lewis and said calmly 'I'd be a bit careful mate, have you seen the size of his muscles, that Dude'll be hard as nails, mark my word mate!' Bruno laughed louder than ever, Lewis joining him.

They left the restaurant at ten to one and had had a memorable night. Claire told Kevin it was probably the best night she'd ever had. 'Mine too babe.' He replied as they got in the taxi to go back to his apartment.

Although he'd had far too much to drink and had the most beautiful woman ever next to him, who he now knew he loved beyond reason, he couldn't sleep. All he could think of how he was going to tell Alexis. He'd always thought of her as his dream woman, and now she eventually wanted him and he was going to decline.

....

02nd July 1999

There was a note from Claire to say she'd taken Sooty out. Kevin grabbed his lap top and a glass of beer. He knew it was early but he needed some light intervention into his thoughts. He updated his Blog Page first, again knowing he'd left it too long:

> Howdy Peeps
> Kevster here and been rubbish again in my communication over the last few days again...I hope yous lot forgive me these indiscretions, they're not meant. More names are coming in for the party. Last bit of news on the Kevster front Peeps is last night I met Mr. Lewis Lennox and Mr. Bruno Franks. Two nicer gentlemen you couldn't never wish to meet. Hi yous two and thanks for a good night!' Well Peeps. Signing off for now and speak soon. Remember to keep the names coming in; we're on the party countdown of the millennium Dudesters!

....

03rd July 1999

Kevin got up and took Sooty out for a quick hour's walk. He couldn't believe he was off with Claire to meet her estranged husband. As they walked into Claire's house Kevin could sense her nerves. As it was Paul was in the drawing room having a drink and was mildly pleasant as Claire introduced Kevin to him. He did ask why Kevin was there and Claire diplomatically said 'He's my boyfriend Paul, life does move on you know.' Paul nodded and even looked a bit ashamed.

Claire asked Kevin if he minded her leaving him with Paul so she could prepare the food. 'No worries darling, Paul seems ok. We'll have a chat, man to man.' 'Are you sure Kevin?' Claire asked looking worried. 'Course babe, what can go wrong in a few minutes?'

Claire came back in ten minutes later and topped them both up with wine. Paul asked her very nicely if she could also bring in a bottle of whisky. Claire looked at him and asked just as nicely 'Are you sure Paul?' 'Yeah, I'm bonding with Kevin, every man who's a man won't say no to whisky.'

They sat drank and smoked for over an hour with Claire popping in every fifteen minutes or so. Claire looked worried but Kevin gave her the don't worry stare every time. After their second cigar Paul started to change in his approach to Kevin.

'So Kevin, you're going to marry my wife are you?' Paul said now with a definite snarl to his voice. 'Yes Paul, when your divorce comes through, I thought she'd told you all this.' Kevin said softly and calmly. 'She has Kevin, look, let's put it straight. You can have her, but I've still got right's to the cash!'

'Look Paul, I thought the reason you guys spilt up was your sexuality, if you do favor men, that's fine, but it should at least allow your partner, your wife, to move on. I don't need and have no interest in money and property, I just love Claire.' Kevin said but now his voice getting animated.

Claire came back in and Paul burst into tears. He shouted how sorry he was and how much he loved Claire and what a huge mistake he'd made. Claire broke down too and held him tightly.

Kevin stood up and shouted 'Claire, he's lying, it's all an act, he's spent the last half an hour telling me how you're a cow and he just wants your money' 'Kevin, please don't. Paul's sensitive, he always has been, this is hurting him.' Claire said defensively.

Kevin tried in vain to explain but Claire was blinded. She asked Paul if he wanted anything to help and he asked for a cognac, one of the special ones. Claire rushed off and Paul looked at Kevin and said really slyly 'See my man, these women are so easy to bullshit. She thinks I'm upset and I'm going to blame the breakup of our marriage on her to get top cash my man!'

Kevin looked at him and said 'You make me sick.' 'So pretty boy, what are you going to do about it? 'Kevin grabbed him by the throat and said 'watch and find out you horrible man.' Paul screamed and screamed and Claire came running in to see Kevin holding Paul by the throat. Claire added to the screaming by shouting at Kevin to let Paul go. Kevin did as he was asked and threw the piece of scum to the floor.

Claire was now really upset and asked in a tone of desperation 'What happened, you two were getting along so well?' 'Claire, he tried to rape me, he said he wanted a piece of me now he's had you. It was all I could do to fight him off, he's so strong!' Paul said in fits of tears.

This was too much for Kevin and he did now attack. He grabbed Paul and hit him hard in the face several times and drew blood on both his hands and Paul's face. Paul slumped into the sofa and Kevin looked at Claire, right into her eyes.

Claire looked at him and her defenses seemed to drop. 'Kevin, that's my husband you've just battered. Just because he's gay doesn't give you the right to hurt him!' She said and rushed to Paul, holding him in her arms. Kevin protested loudly, trying to explain she hadn't heard everything but Claire was livid. After a few silent moments Claire said convincingly 'Kevin, go, we're through, I thought you were different. Please go and don't contact me again.'

He wasn't sure how much he'd had to drink but didn't care and drove his car back to his apartment like an idiot. He got home and started a bottle of vodka opening his personal page.

Dear Kevin

As an intelligent man how on earth do you get into these situations? Firstly you can't keep your cock in your pants, which needs sorting Dude and secondly you keep leaking girlfriends when you get them! How can you move on in life if you don't change Dude? It starts tonight, focus everything on Claire, don't let Jane bully you into a shag and whatever you do don't go back to Alexis as a lover. Now we've got that sorted, get back to work, get back to routine and get Claire back!

....

05th July 1999

Following a day of brooding Kevin phoned work and spoke to his boss. Daniellie told Kevin that things were going bang on plan but he needed him to go to Spain on Wednesday until Friday and really wanted Mary to go with him if possible. Kevin said he'd talk to her and if she couldn't he'd take Jamie or Deb. Daniellie made it clear without saying that he'd promised Mary.

He phoned his mother and left a message to say he wouldn't be around until next week due to work so they'd have to catch up soon. He switched his mobile off and unplugged the phone. Snowy and Sooty joined him for his earliest night of the year.

....

06th July 1999

Kevin finalized the plans for the sessions and checked in with Deb to confirm the travel arrangements. Deb had sorted it all out. Kevin was picking Mary up at six to be in Stanstead for eight for a nine o clock flight. They were flying back on Friday and back in Stanstead for eight o' clock in the evening. He put his blog page up and prepared to update things that had been going on and how the name list was progressing.

> Yo Dudesters
>
> Kevster here and back on the rock and roll stroll Peeps. The week's been a disaster but then lots of what I do with the Dudesses ends in carnage. You lot don't really want to hear about the Kevster's Dudesses disasters though do you? Let's talk about the party then Peeps. More names have come in and at the mo, one dropped out.
>
> Well Peeps were up to wait for the drum roll . . . Seventy five Dudes and Dudesses confirmed and paid up folks. Keep them coming, yous can all see this will be the party to eclipse all parties my mad for it party Peeps. Well other news Peeps, the Kevster's off to Spain tomorrow for a few days. Yes the plane to Spain without the rain all yous lot, how lucky am I?

Before yous all get too jealous, it is work Peeps, you know a hard slog in high temperatures and only three hours every afternoon to take in the rays! I may not be able to update yous lot any further until the weekend Peeps and if I don't, stay cool, stay dry and stay happy.

Dialing Claire's number with huge trepidation Kevin expected it to go to answer phone. To his surprise she answered on the third ring. 'Claire, it's me.' 'I suspected you'd call today.' 'Claire how have we got to this, please tell me?' 'Kevin, you battered my husband.' 'Claire I know what you saw but you don't know what I heard, he's after your money. I snapped, I'm not proud of my actions and it's not how I normally behave.'

'Kevin you battered another human, just because Paul is a man it could be me the next time you lose your temper, I can't live with that.' 'Claire it's not like that, what happened was provoked and intended on his behalf, he looked for it for effect and it's working.' 'Kevin no matter what you think you heard I've known Paul for fifteen years and he wouldn't do that to anyone, never mind me.' 'Claire you're being naive.' 'Kevin, you have no right to say I don't know my own husband!' 'Claire, he held a gay secret from you for years.' 'That's different Kevin. He says it was an experiment that went wrong. He's told me he could never expect to be with me again but needs help to set up on his own, a very reasonable request in my opinion.' The phone line went dead.

Kevin knew he wasn't finished, when he got back from Spain he'd drive to Claire's and really convince her. He was contemplating calling her back when his door bell rang. Opening the door, Kevin saw a disheveled Alexis stood in front of him.

He invited her in but knew what was coming, she'd been speaking to Jane, he could tell. Alexis had the look of disappointment on her face. He grabbed them both a glass of white and sat next to her. He held her hand and said softly 'Are you ok Alexis?' 'Not really Kevin, not now I know you chose Claire.' She replied with tears starting to appear at the corner of her eyes.

Holding her hand tighter than ever he looked into her eyes and said as softly as he could 'Alexis, I've loved you since I was five years old, I always dreamt of marrying you, you know that. The fact you spurned me for so many years didn't deter me, I had a goal. That goal was nearly realized and even when you came back after spurning me again I had hope. What really sealed it though was Jane, you and her have a different sexuality and I can't satisfy you one hundred percent of the time.'

She looked at him, tried to speak, knew he was right and sat back. 'Kevin, can we have some strong vodka's?' She said through streaming tears. Kevin made them what he called super silly vodka's and they drank them down in one. He made another two and sat and talked to Alexis for another hour.

They both went to bed naked as normal but just cuddled. They knew their future together was as friends.

....

07th July 1999

Kevin drove to Stanstead and was pleased Mary seemed to be back to her normal self. They checked in on time, flew on time and were in their taxi an hour ahead of schedule. They arrived at the office in Barcelona by ten to two and had a session booked for three o' clock.

The session went very well and they were out of the office on their way to the hotel by twenty past five. Kevin led Mary to the restaurant and they were shown to a table. Kevin ordered a bottle of Rijoca as they perused the menu. The wine came and the waiter asked if they were ready to order. They both nodded. Kevin chose the squid in a spicy sauce and vegetables and Mary the catch of the day with the same sauce.

The food took about twenty minutes but when it came was fantastic. They ate, drank and chatted and Mary invited Kevin to her room for a night cap. Carrying a new bottle of red and two glasses Kevin followed Mary to her room.

Mary helped herself to one of his Bensons as Kevin poured the wine. As he sat Mary's whole demeanor changed. She burst into tears and said 'Kevin, I'm sorry we didn't work.' 'Hey, me too Mary, it was just timing, no one's fault, it just the way it goes sometimes.'

Mary looked at him, right into his eyes as she sipped her red wine and then stripped naked. Kevin looked, he couldn't help it and stood up to leave ready with his apology. Mary beat him to the door and locked it. 'You're not going anywhere tonight

Kevin!' He tried to protest but Mary was too intent on her prey. Kevin was naked with her five minutes later and involved in wild sex a few minutes after that. He lay back some hour or so later and he thought, shit, how the hell have I got to here!

....

09th July 1999

Yesterday was all work and no chance to play. Today they were going home. They got through luggage and customs and were in his car by eight-forty five. He dropped Mary off at nine-thirty and was home before ten. Jane was there waiting for him. As he walked in and to his huge surprise he saw Alexis.

'Hi Darling' she said as Sooty did a double take and charged at Kevin. Before almost falling he knelt down and hugged his dog. Snowy walked casually to him for her welcome. Several dog and cat kisses later he was able to respond to Alexis. 'Hi Hon, wow, I didn't expect to see you here.'

Jane sat next to Alexis and spoke first 'Kevin, we're back together. We've talked it over for the last forty eight hours and it's what we both want.' Kevin stood up and walked to Jane first, knelt and hugged her tightly, he repeated this with Alexis.

Nothing was said for who knew how long but there were tears and hugs all round, Sooty didn't understand and Snowy was just looking in shame at all of them.

They decided to order a takeaway and sat talking over several glasses of wine. The food came and they all ate well. Kevin insisted they stayed. They said they'd sleep in the spare room but he flatly refused. 'Tonight my Shelia's you can forego sex and sleep naked with me. I need to know I can still do that without any of us falling to temptation.

....

10th July 1999

He left all three girls in bed and took his boy out. They went on what Kevin told Sooty would be the biggest doggy long walk ever. They walked and walked and Kevin thought and thought. Three and a half hours into the walk Sooty protested he'd had enough. Kevin hugged him and headed home, his head was now clear, for the first time in months.

Dinner, drinks and cigarettes later they were all in bed by ten o' clock and Jane said she'd take Sooty out in the morning.

....

11ᵗʰ July 1999

He'd decided to treat Alexis and Jane to a rib of beef. Going to his favorite butchers, Prings, he bought a three bone piece. He was doing beef and Yorkshire puddings with red wine gravy.

Kevin got back at four and wasn't sure where the time had gone. He told them what he was cooking and they both whooped in delight. 'You've got to taste it first girls.' He said back to them in a sarcastic tone. 'Kevin everything you produce is tasty!' Alexis said with Jane nodding and returning to their girly giggles. 'Now now love sick fools, too much of that and I'll eat my own meat!' Kevin said feeling back on form.

He had the food ready by eight o' clock and they all ate like pigs and drank too much red wine. He was exhausted by ten and said he needed to go to bed. Jane promised they'd take Sooty out in the morning and Kevin hit the bed with too many thoughts on his mind.

....

12ᵗʰ July 1999

He arrived in the office at twenty past six and was at least an hour ahead of anyone else. He caught up on e-mails and prepared the week ahead for Mary, Deb and Jamie, he was working from home all this week once he'd set them off and spoken to Mary.

Leaving the office at four-thirty he was happy with his day. Getting home he fed Snowy and Sooty, prepared himself some fish and a salad and sat on his own with a glass of white wondering whether to ring or write to Claire. He decided on neither and ended up turning his lap top on to update his Blog:

> Hello to the Peeps of the World
> Kevster here and firing on all cylinders. Yous may have noticed I've been a little down of late and if yous did, yous lot were right. The Kevster bounces though Peeps, like a rubber ball and has bounced back into the land of the living Dudesters.

There is a lady out there that thinks I don't care but she's wrong Peeps, she's wrong. I'm marrying material me as all you single Dudesses keep telling me when yous write to me, I do have to say sorry Gals, the Kevster's chosen who he wants to marry. We do have one little issue in that she's dumped me but we live in hope Peeps, we live in hope.

To celebrate the Kevster's return to form the Kevster has come up with a cool idea. A pre-party party Dudesters, a picnic in Hyde Park Sunday 25th of July Peeps. This will be a chance for all us local Dudesters to try before we buy and tell all the others how cool our Millennium Party will be. For nows though yous lot I'm signing off, I've only got a party to plan! Happy summer lovin.

He knew he needed to update his own page but was struggling with words to type. He called on his friend Mr vodka for advice. Making one strong enough to make the orange scream in protest sat back at his lap top.

Dear Kevin
Perhaps this is the biggest mess you've ever been in, it can't get worse. That said we have to move on, change and fight. Claire is all that you want and need to stay focused on. Now is the time to listen to the head and the mother and keep the cock in the pants. We'll have to lie and put pride aside, her asshole of a husband is out to clean her out. That's not right or not fair, it's time Dude to take some responsibility and sort it out, just as much for Claire as for us Dude.

....

13th July 1999

He'd worked hard on the updated plan for work and spoke to Daniellie, getting his endorsement. Deciding the next approach to Claire was in writing he set about his best effort.

Dear Claire
I suppose I should try to start somewhere but there lies the greatest difficulty. How do I start to try to get back to you, to your heart and soul? As I write I'm still not sure.

Well, here goes for a beginning. The first thing I must do and say is sorry. Sorry for letting emotion overrule my head and actually engage in an act of physical violence. Despite my anger, I should have never resorted to act in this manner.

The second thing I have to say is also an apology, this time to Paul. Although I stand by what I said, reasoned argument and debate should have been my course of action. For my physical abuse of Paul I apologize profoundly and will accept any charges he may wish to levy against me.

I miss you Claire with all my heart and since our separation realize this more than ever before. You are the one woman in the whole world I see my future life with and I won't give you up without a fight. If I have to ring you daily, write to you daily to keep a flicker of hope alive I will do so.

I sit here and know you feel the same about me but have been clouded by my actions. I can only say this is out of character and not me. I can't believe we are where we are because of the actions I took. Please try to understand my side of the story, no matter how bad it looked and in fact was.

When I met you Claire, I told you I was a Superhero and I stopped the plane from crashing. You know this was me being me. Please can you be you and stop my plane from crashing, because the one I'm on now has no chance of landing safely.

All my love

Kevin

....

14th July 1999

He walked Sooty, Snowy stayed in bed. They had a great walk and Kevin met someone new whilst he was out, Emily. Emily had a Staffordshire terrier called Cassie. Sooty and Cassie played as if their lives depended on it and Kevin surmised Sooty had found himself a girlfriend. Emily however was a babe, only about nineteen with blond hair, huge, huge breasts and a figure most women would die for.

Kevin introduced himself as formally and responsibly as he could, trying with all his might not to stare at Emily's boobs. He knew he was failing miserably but carried on chatting anyway.

Emily broke the ice by saying, 'Don't worry about staring at my chest Kevin, everyone does, if I'm honest when I'm naked I take a good look too.' Kevin looked, initially a little red in the face and said 'Well it's ok for you, you've seen them in the flesh, and I've still got an overworked male point banging around inside my head.'

'Kevin, you're so funny.' Emily said laughing as the two dogs were still tearing after each other. 'My middle name Emily, my middle name'

They chatted for ages as the dogs played and Emily had agreed to meet Kevin on Sunday to take the dogs out and they exchanged numbers. Kevin looked at Sooty and said 'I think I might just have made a mistake there pup, she's a real demon. What do I keep letting myself in for?'

They both got back at nine-thirty and Sooty was ready for food and sleep. He worked the rest of the day at home. No response from his letter to Claire and went he to bed, again a forlorn figure.

....

15th July 1999

It was now just after one so he went out to buy the food for tonight for the meal with Alexis and Jane. He wanted to impress so went for something different. He bought everything he needed and had a quick drink in the Slug. He was on his first pint when he was taken from behind, his hand pushed up behind his back and walked outside. Kevin thought the police had arrested him until he felt punches to his head, neck, chest and stomach. He had been given a real beating.

He was left on the floor, not knowing what had happened but at least was conscious. The last of his attackers shoved a piece of paper in his mouth as he tried to get up and kicked him hard in the chest.

He was now angry. He managed to swivel on the floor and grabbed the guy who had kicked him last by the foot. He pulled at this guy's foot with all his might and kicked his ankles away from him. The guy crashed to the floor by the side of Kevin. Kevin managed to stand before his attacker and kicked him hard in the head. He heard a groan so kicked him again, this time even harder.

Kevin knew now he wasn't ready to fight on. He sank to his knees and grabbed the guy by his lapels. 'You'd better start talking you cock or I'll stand back up and stamp you into a position you never thought existed.' Kevin said in total surprise to himself.

The guy however bought it and said through a badly broken nose 'we were hired to do you over and leave a note. We got two grand. He told us to hurt you, leave the note but nothing else.' Kevin looked at the note and saw it was his letter to Claire all scribbled out.

....

16th July 1999

He woke up to the door bell ringing repeatedly. Kevin let his mum in and apologized. He'd been through the mill and not really realized it. He hurt from top to toe and it showed in his face.

His mum quickly rallied and said 'Kevin, Snowy and Sooty look starving.' 'Sorry mum, I know, I've just got up, and I'm not really sure where I am.' He replied still very groggily, 'Leave it to me a minute Kevin and sit down, grab a cigarette and I'll bring you coffee in a few ticks.' She said and leading the hungry animals to the kitchen. Kevin sat in his chair, lit a Benson and thought his head was on the verge of exploding.

His mother brought him coffee ten minutes later and this had an effect on perking him up a bit. Felicity left it ten more minutes before demanding 'Tell me everything Kevin!'

With his head clearing he said 'Mum, shower first, check in with work and then we'll take Sooty out together, I'm sure Snowy will come too, she seems worried about me.' No shit she's worried about you darling, what the hell happened?' Felicity said. Kevin looked at his mum and pleaded for a little time, he did need a shower and he had to check in with work.

During their walk Kevin told his mum everything .When they got back he said he felt tired and went back to bed.

....

18th July 1999

Kevin had been in and out of bed for the last forty eight hours. Today he felt better and broke down in despair, not from the beating but the loss of Claire. His mother was a rock. Hugging her son she held him as tight as she could and said 'Kevin, Is it really worth it darling, to end up like this? And it could get a lot worse.' This was the catalyst that got Kevin back to normality. 'Mum, this dirty horrible man put a contract out on me and he wants to do Claire for her money. I will not stand by and let it happen mum, I love her. I love her with everything I've got.'

He regained more strength and said 'Mum, I need to ring her, I need to warn her.' 'No Kevin, this isn't over the phone stuff, we'll go to see her tomorrow, you and me.' She said commandingly.

Looking at the clock he nearly jumped, the time was already one o' clock. He then remembered something with Alexis and Jane and also some dog walking date.

She just looked at him and said 'Darling, Jane and Alexis pass on their regards and disappointment we're not hooking up. Emily rang too, I explained you were ill and would see her the next time you were walking your dog. Kevin she sounded about sixteen!' For the first time in a while Kevin was back on track. 'No mum, she's nineteen and has the best pair of bunnies I've ever seen!'

His mother gave him a hug and said 'Darling you need to think really carefully about what to do next.' 'I have mum, come on we're off!' Kevin said grabbing his car keys. Through repeated objections Felicity ended up following him to his car.

They drove to Claire's with Kevin not talking. Despite his mum's efforts to try to say it was the wrong thing to do at the wrong time, Kevin drove on like a man possessed.

They were at Claire's by three o' clock and Kevin raced out of the car. He pressed the doorbell and stood back and waited. The door did answer but it wasn't Claire, it was Paul, looking really smug. 'Still alive then prick are you? Well I've sent your darling away for a week, just in case she got any wind, know what I mean!' And spat in Kevin's face.

Felicity tried to scream to stop Kevin doing what she knew he would but it was too late. Kevin gave Paul the hugest punch to the stomach and Paul collapsed, doubled over. 'Right you shit, I gave them back your sick note, and I don't want Claire ever knowing how much of a monster you are. I do warn you however, I won't go away and if you try anything like you just did again, I'll kill you with my bare hands and go to prison satisfied!' Kevin said a little out of breath.

Paul was lying on the floor trying to speak and threaten Kevin again. Kevin kicked him harder than he punched him, again the stomach and Paul winced in real pain.

With his mother screaming Kevin played his trump card. 'Right you shit, you disappear tonight, if you don't I'll go to the police.'

'You don't have a clue do you, you prick of a man, there's no link to me, the money's Claire's, and it all goes back to her!' Paul said from the floor in a wheezy voice. 'All wrong again you excuse for a man, the hit was covered on the Pub's CCTV and for your information their system has a microphone. The whole things on tape and implicates you right up to your neck!' Kevin said now smiling.

Paul looked up at him from the floor and knew he wasn't joking. 'What do you want, how much? I can get it, I can get as much as you want. Name your price!' Paul screamed at him in panic. 'Right Paul, firstly I want you to stand up, you know, like a real man.' Kevin said calmly. Paul stood and looked at Kevin and his mother not saying anything. 'Secondly Paul, I want you gone from here tonight. No notes, no goodbyes, no nothing!' Kevin said again really calmly. 'Thirdly Paul, if you ever return to Claire's life I'll seek and punish you for attempted murder.'

Paul looked at him and said 'You bastard, I had her money, she was all hooked, another week, and she'd have signed over the two million I wanted.' 'It's a good job you fucked up then isn't it Paul?' Kevin said now with more emotion in his voice.

'Paul looked at him and said, 'she'll never believe you though mate, you've lost her!' Maybe she won't mate, but I hope I don't have to revert to the device that's switched on and in my pocket, picking up every word that has come out of your excuse of a mouth. I'm rather hoping she'll believe in my love, my word and my witness, my mother, if absolutely necessary.'

'Right Paul, grab your stuff because you're going now, in fact I'm taking you.' Kevin told him now with such a look on his face that his mum was even scared. Paul looked right into Kevin's eyes and said brashly 'Make me!' Kevin hit him with the best right hook he'd ever thrown and knocked him straight out.

Kevin gave a re-written copy of his letter to Claire to his mother and said 'Mum, please go in, drop this in the kitchen. I'll stay here and have a cigarette and make sure the scum doesn't choke. He's going from here tonight, whether he likes it or not.'

They dropped him in London, at Kings Cross. Kevin hugged his mum and said 'Mum, can you drive home, I'm not sure I can stand up.' She took the keys off him and led her son back to the car and got him home and into bed by nine o' clock.

....

20th July 1999

With yesterday a blur in his memory he got up and felt the best he had in days. He grabbed Sooty and went out early. They were out for several hours, Kevin using the time to think. On the way back they bumped into Emily and Cassie. Emily took one look at Kevin and screamed as Sooty and Cassie went all out for it, playing like long lost friends.

She ran to him like Sooty and Cassie had run to each other and jumped on him pretty much the same. 'You poor, poor baby, who did this to you? They need arresting, no in fact they need shooting!' She said in quick fire speed. Before Kevin had chance to catch his breath Emily was kissing him, full on the mouth. 'My handsome man, my poor handsome man' she kept repeating.

Kevin managed to shake her off, albeit a very delayed and lethargic attempt and said 'Emily, woe a second, just woe.' Emily gathered herself and went a bit red in the face. 'Sorry Kevin, I've been so worried since I rang and spoke to your mum, I lost myself a little.'

He was finding the urge not to look at her chest almost impossible. 'Checking them out again, aren't you Kevin?' She said adding to his total embarrassment. 'No Emily, I mean, bloody hell yes and I'm really sorry.' Kevin managed in response. 'I told you last time Kevin, don't worry, they're that good I like people to look at them.'

He nodded at her but thought to himself that he didn't just want to look at them but do all sorts of other things. 'Oh I see, you want to touch them now then?' Emily said fluttering her eyes at him. 'Stop, stop now Emily, God I fancy the pants off you but you're nineteen and I'm thirty, this can't go anywhere.' Kevin said sounding all adult and mature.

Emily looked at him, flashing her eyelashes again and said softly 'Kevin, I don't want a relationship, I just want sex and be friends afterwards.' Kevin looked at her feeling like a child. So much for his adult tone of a few seconds ago, he thought to himself. 'Emily, you just want sex?' He managed to spit out of his very dry mouth. Somehow, despite his desire to take her into the nearest bush Kevin asked her to come to his place tomorrow night, and said he'd cook for her.

....

21st July 1999

Felicity left and Kevin promised to phone. He then popped into work. Deb and Jamie were horrified by his bruises, but Mary burst into tears. He told them all not to worry and that he had sorted it all out and there would be no repercussions. Once they'd got this out of their systems they all enjoyed a two hour session catching up. He took Sooty out for a short hour and a half walk and promised him it would be longer tomorrow.

> Ola Peeps
> The Kevster's been rubbish again and neglected his duties to us all. Once again I find myself apologizing so just have to say I didn't mean it Dudesters. I won't bore yous lot with the details but I did have a bit of an experience whereby there were more of them, they had weapons, and they were professionals. Still the Kevster lived to tell the tale . . . Just!
> Onwards and upwards I say though Peeps and we plan on. Party planning expert, my new job for the big two thousand, at least I hope so. That I suppose depends on yous lot and experience in the biggest two gigs of nineteen ninety nine. Although I've been battered, bruised and knocked about the party's still on for Sunday all yous lot. Although I haven't had the time I need it will go ahead, two o' clock on Sunday Dudesters. See whoever's there.

Emily arrived at seven. He had no time to make dinner. Emily made use of his first second, third and even fourth rises. For the first time he could remember he failed on the fifth time of asking.

22nd July 1999

Emily left early a little put out saying she thought Kevin didn't think she was attractive. He tried to explain he was still a bit beat up but she was gone mid way through his attempted response.

Kevin needed a miracle for the party to still work so dialed his only hope. 'Hi Richard, its Kevin Julie' 'Kevin, are you ok, I heard!' 'Yeah, thanks Richard, I appreciate your concern. Look Richard, I need to arrange something for Sunday in Hyde Park, a summer barbecue.' 'Ok Kevin why ask me?' 'Well the thing is mate I don't know if anyone will turn up or maybe a hundred. I'm paying for the lot so want some help with suppliers.' 'Kevin, why didn't you say? Look, I know what you're trying to do. I know some Caterer's who are looking for publicity. What say I get them to do it for cost? They can take freezers for the food and if it doesn't all go they can take the unused food and use for profit on another gig, if it all goes they'll win on the day by the publicity it generates for them.' 'Richard, you can arrange that?' 'Not for anyone Kevin, but for you . . . with pleasure.' 'Richard, you're a star.' 'Yes and don't I know it, you owe me one of your nice meals.'

He couldn't believe his luck. He'd fallen in shit and come out smelling of roses again. His next job was checking in with work and then he spent the next four hours liaising, updating and getting back into the swing.

He called his mother as he promised he would. The phone call wasn't a long one, especially when he told her about Emily. His mother even took the mick out of him for failing a rise. He knew this was the conversation end, but decided he was going to have a real go with Emily and her Bunnies.

Before he knew it, it was eight o' clock. The day had escaped him. He'd made some good choices and some poor ones. Cracking open a cider decided he wasn't hungry and would have an early night.

23rd July 1999

He walked back from work and made use of the fresh air and had three Bensons on route. When he got into his apartment Sooty and Snowy came running as normal but there was an envelope on the floor. Picking the envelope up Kevin walked into the kitchen, opened a bottle of red and lit a cigarette. The writing on the envelope was distinctive and beautiful. He didn't want to open it. Two more glasses of wine and several cigarettes later he told his girl and boy he was going to go for it. Kevin opened the letter with hope, trepidation and fear on his face.

Dear Kevin

Thank you for your letter. I guessed you'd try to write as I haven't been contactable. This has been the worst few weeks in my life and I do miss you terribly. I suppose I should start somewhere myself. I do accept your apology Kevin, but physical violence is something I've never got along with. Something to do with my childhood but that's not for here and now. I accept this may have been out of character and have never seen this in you before.

As for Paul, he's disappeared and so I can't pass on your apologies. I am not sure what has happened these last days but don't think they are unconnected to the night we parted. Before he left there was no mention of pressing charges so I don't think you need to worry about that eventuality from your actions. I know something upset you and I know Paul could have been very vindictive in speech but he never hurt any part of me before our breakup and his confirmation of his sexuality. He's never asked for any money from our divorce. This of course I convinced him otherwise before he disappeared.

I have tried really hard to understand your side of the story and prior to Paul's disappearance was ready to accept certain parts of it. Since Paul has gone though I have received legal notice he holds no claim to anything from the marriage.

This must have been enforced Kevin, Paul and I had agreed to a settlement which amounted to a large sum of money. For him to run from this I think he was frightened away. Paul is a gentle man, he always has been and coming to terms with his sexuality caused him great distress, especially as he knew what it would do to me. Paul would never threaten me, my friends or try to get one over on me, I know this for sure.

You saved me once as a Superhero Kevin but have become the big villain and I'm afraid your plane might be struggling to land but mine has now crashed. I know and you know there was something special between us Kevin but I can't ignore what you've done to my husband and yes Kevin, at the moment he's still that. I can't see you again Kevin and ask that if you feel anything for me you respect this and don't try to contact me again.

Claire

He knew he'd got it wrong and his actions had caused it all. The alcohol kicked in and so did Kevin's resolve. He couldn't chase a dead cause so had to move forward. It was the only option. He put the lap top on and set about updating his Blog Page:

To my all partying Peeps

Less than forty eight hours to go to the Hyde Park affair. I've no idea how many of yous will turn up so I've gone for the conservative Dudesters. As I'm paying I've set it up for ten Peeps, Peeps!

Now I knows yous lot are thinking cheapskate and yous would be right if I'd done such a thing. Sorry all of yous, I'm drunk and emotional at the moment and was sharing a joke Peeps, yous lot know those things that make Peeps laugh, ha, ha de ha! What I've done is set for one hundred and coughed up the dough. I wish to see as many of yous as possible and look forward to the day.

Sorry again yous lot for the way I'm being, just major league dumped by the love of my life. Keep it fresh and open yous single Dudesses but I've already been snagged by a young busty beauty for the next few days.

···

24th July 1999

'Richard.' 'Kevin you ok?' 'Depends on what you tell me Richard.' 'Well if you want good news I'd try another call.' 'Richard!' 'If you want great news then you should be speaking to me!' 'Richard . . .' 'Ok, keep your pants on, it's sorted, my illustrious friends have set up 'Meals To You' they see themselves as high quality chefs who work freelance as opposed to the normal restaurant protocol. They've prepared for one hundred and fifty Kevin and done it for twenty quid a head.'

'Richard I love you.' 'Now now Kevin, your love life's complicated enough without same sex relationships.' 'You know what I mean Richard.' 'Yes, I do, I was trying to be funny.' 'Make it one of your very end middle names.' 'Ok, I know.'

Checking his watch, it was three o' clock he opened a bottle of chilled white and went to work in the kitchen. Emily arrived first at four o' clock. She was in the shortest tightest dress he'd ever seen and he was tempted to take her straight to bed. 'Hi Kevin' She said as she bounded in. Kevin greeted her and they shared a long kiss. 'Ooh Kevin, I can feel you're all ready, already. Have we got time?' Emily said beaming.

Kevin felt yes try to escape from his mouth but just managed to stop it. 'God Emily, I wish we did have time but not quite, can you store the desire for later?' He said blowing from the cheeks. 'Oh yeah, I can baby, it'll just make me hornier later, you ok with that?'

He told her about the party tomorrow and asked her if she would go with him. 'What like a girlfriend?' Emily said looking really excited. Not able to come up with any different response Kevin replied 'Yes Emily, like a girlfriend.'

He smiled to himself and wondered how Jane and Alexis would take to her. Sooty was already approving by licking her all over and Kevin was sure he saw him have a rub on her leg. This was a first for Sooty.

Alexis and Jane arrived at five and Sooty and Snowy went mad as Jane walked in. Emily got up to greet them with Kevin and Kevin saw both Jane and Alexis make a double take. He quickly sorted wine out and Jane said she'd help him in the kitchen.

Kevin had everything prepared and lit a Benson. Jane rounded on him and said 'Kevin, she is hot. Not just fit but really fit! God she's made me get all excited.' 'Hey, you have Alexis, any more of that and I'll tell her.' Kevin replied but with a laugh. 'You tell her darling, I wouldn't be surprised if she wasn't trying it on already, in fact we'd better get back in there, I don't trust her with Emily, not when she looks like that.' Jane said heading back with Kevin following.

Sure enough Alexis was flirting outrageously with Emily. Kevin called them both into the kitchen. 'Alexis, Jane, please read this whilst I go and have five with Emily.' He said handing them Claire's letter.

As he walked back to the kitchen they both hugged him and didn't let go for a long time. 'Is that it?' Alexis eventually asked. 'Looks like it doesn't it?' Kevin replied then added 'For now I'm going to have some fun with Emily and see where it goes.' By eleven o' clock they were in their separate bedrooms. Kevin was undressed by Emily as soon as their door was closed. By one o' clock he'd worn her out. She was sleeping like a baby. Feeling happy with his regained status as a bedroom demon Kevin closed his eyes with a smile on his face.

....

25th July 1999

Kevin was up in more senses than one, very early. He woke Emily and wore her out again. She was snoring as he got up and made tea, whilst bouncing around the kitchen like a mad dog. He was singing to himself that he was the man. Jane came out of her and Alexis's bedroom and told him to shut up. 'Who me?' He asked with a smug look on his face. Jane just stared at him with a scornful look on her face. Alexis joined them a few minutes later and told Kevin to put his smile away, somewhere other than on his stupid boyish looking face.

The four of them went for a walk, Snowy staying with Emily. They were gone for nearly two hours and Kevin was bragging all the way. The two girls got narked off with him in the end and threatened to both go to bed with Emily on their return to show her a real session. This shut Kevin up instantly.

Logistics for the shower was a chore and Kevin swore he needed to buy a house. The old apartment was getting too small for his needs. They all got ready by eleven and were in the taxi to Hyde Park by ten to twelve. As they walked through the gate into the park, Kevin was feeling more and more nervous. Richard had said there would be signs.

They walked fifty yards and his spirits rose to massive heights. There was a bill board on a weighted sand stand and it proclaimed

Kevster's Pre Party, Party. If you Know, You'll Go! Follow the Arrows.

There were arrows placed on trees every fifty foot or so. They all followed and then saw a mini marquee. There was another sign that just said 'Kevster's' Sponsored by Michael and James, Home Restaurateurs. Kevin looked at Jane and she beamed back at him. Emily hugged him and said 'Did you do this Kevin?' 'Yes Emily, I did.' He replied and wanted to thank Richard hugely. Kevin went and introduced himself to Michael and James. They had it all sorted and even had music playing to the levels the park would allow.

All Kevin needed now was people. They all had a glass of white wine and waited. One o' clock passed and there were no attendees. There were a few interested passersby but no party Peeps. At one-thirty Kevin was ready to throw the towel in. James told him to be patient. The next thing Kevin saw was a group of about ten people coming towards them. At the front was Richard and what looked like nine of his friends Kevin hadn't met before.

Next he saw Mary, Deb, Jamie, Steve and a few others, behind them were a group of five he didn't recognize. Kevin was busy speaking to people and Emily hanging on his arm, telling anyone who'd listen she was his girlfriend.

Kevin was chuffed, there were already nearly thirty people there. It got from good to great, another three separate groups of people arrived, each in groups between four and seven. Just as he got used to this there were more people coming from all sides. He couldn't count how many people there were but just tried to talk to as many as he could.

Before Kevin knew it five o' clock had arrived. He'd spoken to so many people and Emily was loving being by the side of him. By the time six o'clock came they all had to disperse. The day had been a resounding success and everyone who came said they'd be there in Cardiff. Kevin asked them all to log who they were on line so he could keep control for New Years Eve.

As the crowd slowly disappeared Kevin was left with Richard, Emily, Michael and James, even Alexis and Jane had gone. James came up to Kevin and patted him on the back. 'You want payment now then mate, bloody well deserved too, you guys were immense.' Kevin said smiling gratefully.

Richard winked at Michael and James said 'Kevin, there were about two hundred people here over the duration, we took four grand over the bar alone, here's your share.' Kevin looked at the three of them and said in shock 'I don't owe you anything?' Richard jumped in and replied 'Kevin, you owe me two meals mate, that's it.' Kevin looked at them again and said 'yeah, what about the food guys?'

Michael looked at Richard, then James and said 'Kevin, you don't get it do you?' 'No, I don't get it. I really appreciate favors but don't want to free load off anyone!' Richard intervened, 'Kevin, I know business and I knew this would work, the four grand the boys took in drinks was profit Kevin, not sales.'

Kevin still not sure took the money and hugged all three of them, more than once. He left with Emily about an hour later and he asked her where she wanted to go. 'Back to yours of course Kevin, I owe you for this morning.' She said with a huge wink. They both went to bed early, trying to outdo each other. After no one won they were both fast asleep by ten o' clock.

....

26th July 1999

He won the morning battle. He prepared to leave for work at six-thirty and left a note for Emily, she was fast asleep still and snoring. This made him laugh out loud.

Walking to work he arrived just before seven. By the time they'd agreed everything it was six o' clock. They all left the office completely spent and said they'd reconvene at eight in the morning. Kevin got home at quarter to seven and Sooty and Snowy greeted him excitedly. He looked around for a note from Emily and found it in the kitchen. It was short, sweet and nice. It just said she had had a great time, taken Sooty out fed them both and changed Snowy's box. She'd left lots of kisses and that he'd better ring her later.

As he sipped his wine he knew he had a couple of calls to make and an update on his blog. He rang Richard first. 'Richard, Kevin.' 'Kevin, I can't speak for long, I'm working.' 'Yeah I know, I just wanted to invite you for one of the meals I owe you this week, let me know a day?' 'Ok mate, Thursday night?' 'Deal

Richard, look I'll have Emily, Jane and Alexis here, do you want to bring anyone?' 'Yeah, I'll bring Jose, if that's ok?'

With one more call to make and update his Blog Kevin set his lap top up. He opened another bottle of white and felt okay with life. He had to let Claire go. He dialed Emily's number and she answered after less than two rings.

'Hi Emily' 'Kevin, I wondered when you'd ring, I've been waiting.' 'Look Emily, thanks for this morning, it was a huge help.' 'I was glad to do it, I love Sooty and Snowy.' 'Yeah still it was a real help.' 'No probs honey when can I see you this week?' 'Tomorrow; and Emily, are you ok for Thursday; I've got Jane, Alexis and Richard from the Ivy coming for one of my steak meals?' 'Kevin, ooh yes, yes, yes! Can you take me to the Ivy one day?' 'How about Saturday?' 'Yes, yes, yes . . . Kevin you're so cool.' That's definitely my sixth middle name.' 'Ok my honey bunny until tomorrow, kiss, kiss.'

Trying to remember if he'd ever been called honey bunny, he smiled to himself and sat back with a Benson and took a few sips on his Chablis. The Blog page was ready but he wanted to think what to write first. He was enjoying himself and the thoughts in his mind for the first time in weeks.

> My Perfect Party Peeps
>
> Wow, wow and an even bigger wow! Was it not a blast? I must admit partying Dudesters, I was a worried man, really worried. It was planned at the eleventh hour and I wasn't sure it would work. But did it work my beautiful Dudes and Dudesses, didn't it half!
>
> I know I tried to speak to yous all and may not have got around to it but I had a ball Peeps, if that's the kind of Peeps and party atmosphere we get for the party of nineteen ninety nine then I'm a happy Kevster. As I may have discussed with yous lot, I need names and comments to add to the plan for our Cardiff gig. I'm on line for the next two hours and really, really want to hear from yous lot. Party, party, party

He couldn't believe how excited he was. It only took ten minutes for the replies to start to flood in. From all the feedback they'd only well bloody actually enjoyed it. Everyone said they were looking forward to the New Years Eve party even more now. Kevin was elated. The last message though made him feel the best yet.

> Son didn't come to this but looking at the comments I don't know why though. I'll be in Cardiff. Love Mum. PS, Well done darling.

....

27ᵗʰ July 1999

Another slog later at five, not even stopping for a cigarette break Kevin had got home. Emily arrived and seemed intent on making him suffer for his earlier victories and won tonight's battle. This time she laughed as he snored alongside her.

....

28ᵗʰ July 1999

He arrived in work early again. To his huge surprise Daniellie was already in and beckoned Kevin. 'Kevin I've got good news, in fact great news.' 'Daniellie, what does that mean?' 'Well my son, I've lobbied for you to be MD of the UK my man. The European Board has accepted my proposal. I need to let go by October the first as there's too much going on over the pond my son.'

'Daniellie, what does this mean for me?' 'Well Kevin, firstly your salary, it shoots to two hundred and fifty grand with a twenty five percent bonus package, so around the three hundred grand mark. You get an upgrade on the car to eighty five to ninety five and all the trimmings.' 'Daniellie, that's fantastic, when does it start?'

'Well your salary next month, your car whenever you want but officially the first of January next year.' Kevin cracked open a bottle of champagne when he got home and rang Jack. It was still early afternoon in Jack land. 'Hi Jack' 'Kevin, I heard!' 'What did you hear?' 'You got the UK MD post, well done my friend.' 'Thanks Jack, God news travels quickly in this place.' 'Don't you know it my friend?' 'Jack, you and your family are fast becoming some of my best friends. Thanks for everything.' 'Kevin, you deserve every success you get and you are now one of my dearest friends too.' 'Ok Jack, stop before I get emotional.' 'Ditto friend, speak soon.'

....

29th July 1999

He was in work by six-fifteen and in dream land, he was going to be MD of the whole UK! He knew this was largely down to his team and wanted to tell them as soon as they got in. He told Mary first. Mary hugged him and kissed him hard on the lips. They both looked at each other and then broke apart as if it hadn't happened.

Jamie and Deb came in just before seven-thirty and Kevin told them the news. They were ecstatic, Kevin saying he had to leave at twelve as had a dinner party to arrange. He left the team at ten past twelve and said he'd work from home tomorrow as well.

He hit town by twelve-thirty and bought the steak he ordered from the owner of Prings a day ago. Not only was it the best steak available, the owner of the butchers had trimmed every last piece of sinew from it. He took his six pieces of finest quality steaks away and paid Mal, the owner sixty notes.

Next he needed wine. He visited Glasshouse, a place he'd been before for fine wine and ordered a case of Chablis and a case of Vosne-Romanee. He parted with seven hundred but they promised delivery in an hour. He was happy with what he'd done and then went to Birds for some fresh mussels. This he was serving in a cream, wine and chili broth. He got home by three and spent an hour solid preparing. Once he was done he took Sooty out for an hour's walk, he loved walking his dog and missed it when he couldn't.

Kevin had them sat at the table by seven-thirty and had the mussels in the dishes by seven-forty. Richard told Kevin he was a star and could come and work in the Ivy anytime. Feeling on top of the world he took orders for the steak at eight o' clock.

It was a little complicated as there were two rare, two medium rare and two medium. This for a restaurant chef would be easy, for Kevin though, it required thought and timing. Everything was perfect and he served at eight-thirty. The wine had been breathing in the kitchen and Kevin took three bottles in with him. They ate for well over half an hour, no one spoke but there were lots of ums and yums in the conversation. There was only one comment he really seeked and that was Richard's.

Richard was however engaged in conversation with Jose and Alexis. They'd finished eating and were now more than sipping their wines. Richard threw Kevin one of his Dunhill's and said loudly 'Mr Julie, not only was that the best steak I've eaten, the sauce recipe needs to go to chef at the Ivy, it's better than his! Don't you ever say I said that, because I'll deny it you lovely man.'

Kevin served the fruit mousse up at ten thirty and then Alexis and Jane left, Jane promising Sooty's walk in the morning. Richard said out loud. 'Kevin if you weren't straight I'd jump you for that food you just served, it was stunning!'

'Richard, thank you for your appreciation but I don't want a jump, what I do want is a table Saturday night, just for me and Emily.' Kevin said picking what he thought was the perfect moment. 'Kevin, you, and only you don't need to ask, I'll fit you in anytime. For Saturday however the food's on me, just pay for your drinks. You can come anytime and I'll keep you a VIP table.'

....

31ˢᵗ July 1999

Following a lazy day the day before Kevin and Sooty had a doggy long walk to match any one before. Emily hugged him when they got back and then hugged Sooty. 'Kevin, he's stinking, he needs a bath.' She said pulling her now muddy arms from the wagging tail of the excited dog. 'Right you bundle of beauty, here's your first challenge of our relationship, you can bath Sooty. If you get through that and still want to stay around then I'll be impressed.'

Emily looked at him and said with a wink, 'you think he's going to play me up don't you?' 'The thought had occurred, yes.' Kevin replied still smiling and heard the bath running and then nearly jumped out of his skin. 'Sooty here now!' Emily shouted but in a soft loud tone.

Sooty ran like the wind to her. The next thing Kevin heard was 'Sooty, in.' He then heard a splash followed by complete silence. Fifteen minutes later he heard the shower going. The next noise he heard was 'Sooty, out, and sit!'

Ten minutes after that a dry Emily and dry Sooty emerged from the bathroom. 'Want me to do Snowy as well?' Emily mocked him. Kevin was speechless but Snowy heard and ran into the spare bedroom.

They jumped in a taxi at seven-thirty and were outside the Ivy at ten to eight. Richard was on the door and gave Kevin a wink as he welcomed them in with open arms. Kevin followed Richard back to their lounge table. He was carrying a bottle of very special red and told Kevin this was on him, just because Kevin was such a special bloke.

Emily had no eyes other than for Kevin and she told him this was the best night she'd ever had and he'd better have some energy for later. They left at eleven. Kevin and Emily were back by twelve and he was surprised how much energy he had. Look out Emily he thought with a smile. Kevin did what he'd intended to do and made Emily sleep before him and hit the pillow with a smile on his face.

....

01st August 1999

Following his shower he turned his lap top on, he wanted to say another thanks to all that attended and especially all those that had commented:

> Well hello Party Peeps
> Sorry Dudesters but I've been poor on communication yet again. Firstly all yous party loving Peeps I want to thank those who posted comments. Secondly I want to thank all yous who came to the Perfect Pre Party Party Peeps. The third thing I want to say to yous all is the big one is on Dudes and Dudesses, just about five months to go. Those who came to this one please tell all yous knows.
> Following the do the Kevster's planning, scheming, wheeling and a dealing and has it all sussed Peeps. The party in Cardiff my super Dudes and Dudesses will be the party of Nineteen Ninety Nine! I will be working hard over the next few months and will need some help and support yous lot. Love and party pledges to the world.

....

02nd August 1999

Kevin was home from work by five and took Sooty out for his second walk of the day. It was a sedate walk and they were back just before seven. He knew he was outstanding a call to his mum, and one to Emily. He hadn't eaten properly for a day or so either so put some meatballs on to defrost.

'Hi Mum' 'Kevin, you ok how's the jail bait?' 'Mother, she's nineteen to start and yes she's cool, firm boobs and tight bum as you'd expect.' 'Kevin, are you really saying you are into this girl?' 'Mum, I tried not to be actually, but yes she's nice and she likes me so why not?' 'I can't argue with that but what about Claire?' 'Mum, Claire is all I love in life but she doesn't want me, what can I do? Emily does and she's fun and I'm not getting carried away.' 'Kevin I do understand but if Claire knew the truth?' 'Mum, she had an opportunity to ask me but she chose not to, she chose to disbelieve me.' 'Kevin, isn't that being stubborn, and is it the right way to go?' 'Probably not mum. I can't change her mind though and she's chosen not to listen to my side of the story.'

He cooked his meatballs and tomato pasta and rang Emily. She was as tired as Kevin was and asked if she could bring Cassie around tomorrow night to stay with Sooty and Snowy. Kevin smiled as he said yes, ate his food and was in bed asleep by nine-thirty.

03rd August 1999

Kevin had been instructed he needed to revisit Canada for the best part of a month. Daniellie had told him this morning. Daniellie also told Kevin he was making him rich and barked a laugh down the phone. Kevin spent the day sorting personal details with Jack, including extending the trip to spend time with Jack and Katie as Mary sorted his travel arrangements.

Emily arrived at five-thirty with Cassie. The first fifteen minutes was mayhem. It was like Tom and Jerry. Eventually the animals settled down and Snowy made a point of telling them both who was in charge. He cooked Emily and himself a chili with a jacket potato. They shared two bottles of red and were in bed by nine. Emily said she was staying until he left, she wasn't missing a minute. She started off the way she meant to go on and they were both exhausted by the time they finished.

....

04th August 1999

Kevin took the two dogs out, Snowy turned her nose up at them and went back to bed with Emily. He decided to take them on a fairly long walk. The two of them and if truth be told Kevin all had a ball. He was going to struggle with a month away from his dog and cat and now he actually thought of it, Emily.

They all got back by ten-thirty. Emily was up and had breakfast waiting, warmed scrambled eggs and some fresh toast. Once he'd finished eating Emily decided she wanted breakfast again, this time no food passed her lips. They both showered by half past twelve.

Kevin said they were off to look at a car next. He was going to see his mate Jason at Greenstones. As they got there Kevin was ecstatic to find out Jason was the new GM of the place. 'Kevster' Jason shouted as they arrived. 'And who may I ask is this beauty?' 'Jason, put your eyes away, this is Emily, Emily, Jason.'

They all shook hands and Kevin said 'Here's the deal Dude, I've now got eighty five to ninety five. I want something good for me but also for Sooty. As it is at the moment I'll probably need four by four. I'm looking to move' Kevin said as he saw Jason's look of confusion. 'You know, more into the country mate!' 'Ah' Jason replied. 'Give me twenty four hours Kevin.'

Emily said she'd pop out and get something for dinner, her treat and a surprise. Kevin caught up on work, quicker than he'd anticipated and was done and dusted an hour after Emily had left.

Emily came back and settled, putting the stereo on and turned the sound up loud. Snowy turned her nose up and went to bed. Emily had fifteen minutes of fun singing into her wine glass and being the lounge karaoke queen. She sang so badly Sooty joined in and it was like a cat's chorus without any cats. Snowy didn't even show herself.

Emily disappeared soon after Sooty had finished singing and came back from the kitchen ten minutes later. 'Ten minutes my honey bunny' she said bouncing around.

Emily served ten minutes later. Kevin looked at the food, it was finger picking paradise. She'd done chicken wings, ribs, battered prawns, onion rings, garlic mushrooms, chili tomatoes and cucumber and sour cream and chive dip.

She looked at him and asked 'Have I done ok?' Kevin kissed her hard and said 'No babe, not ok, bloody brilliant.' Emily actually burst into tears as they started to eat. He couldn't remember eating so much in a single sitting, and as soon as they had finished went to bed and fell to sleep instantly.

....

05th August 1999

They both showered at ten o' clock and Emily took the dogs out, Kevin catching up on work again and checking his mails. Jason was the one name he was looking for and Jason hadn't let him down. He rang him as soon as he'd read the mail. Jason had sourced a brand new S Class 6OOCLS estate. It had four-wheel drive, a six litre engine and every extra Mercedes could offer. The price was ninety grand but Jason could have it ready by tomorrow.

Kevin gave Jason a verbal contract over the phone and said he'd be there by three tomorrow to pick it up. Jason agreed adding he'd book his summer holiday as soon as the deal was signed. Kevin liked his style and asked if he was still coming to the Millennium party. Jason said he'd be there as long as rabbits still shagged rabbits. Kevin took this as a yes.

Emily was back with the dogs after what seemed like ages. Kevin checked his watch, she'd been gone nearly three hours. As all three of them came back in Kevin couldn't tell who was more tired. After ten minutes of their return, the sleeping Emily and Cassie answered his question. Kevin cracked open a bottle of white and turned his lap top on:

> Hello Peeps
> It's been a few days and they've been roller coaster rocking for the Kevster Dudesters. The first bit of news is that I'm off to the land of the Mountie, Bear and Beaver again next week folks, and this time for a month. Yes you wildlife followers I'll be catching up with Lennox again. Next is the job, yet another promotion Peeps, any more of these and I'll have to start ignoring celebrities in the street. Look all you party going superstars, we nailed the last one so the real one's going to be absolutely awesome, I may not have the time to go into details in the next month yous lot but I know yous

will still keep banging the drum. Peace, International coop-
eration and love to the world

Kevin thought about Claire again, as he did every day since
she'd been gone. Emily was giving him everything he wanted so
he couldn't grasp why it wasn't the same. They got ready to go out
and again when Emily emerged dressed. He thought she would
knock any movie star out for attention, she was that drop dead gorgeous. What she wanted with him he still couldn't fathom.

They were in Henry's by five o' clock and on the cocktails.
Three jugs later and they were both on the way and laughing
and shouting like teenagers. The barman even told them off.
Laughing now silently they ordered champagne and Emily's
idea, Red Bull.

By the time they left Henry's at nine, they were both drunk as
skunks. They were at Toni's by nine-fifteen and had his meat chili
deluxe and extra garlic cheesy bread. The walk home was only
five minutes but it took them twenty.

Kevin and Emily had devoured the pizza on route and had
three pieces of the bread left as they got back by ten o' clock.
Sooty and Cassie had a piece each, Snowy turning her nose up
at them. They were in bed asleep by ten-twenty. There were no
rises on offer!

....

06th August 1999

Kevin logged onto work and by two he was up to date realizing
he'd forgotten to tell Emily they were collecting the car at three.
Jason greeted them and told Kevin as soon as they arrived that
there was a problem. Kevin looked at him and Jason hung his
head in apparent shame. 'Kevster, Dude, I failed you, the Black
S Class I promised you for three didn't happen.'

Kevin took it in his stride whilst Emily looked horrified and
ready to say something. 'Ok Jason, I'm early, it's twenty past two,
you got it ready for two then. Not surprising, I know your style
by now.' Kevin said and mocked a yawn.

Jason looked at Kevin and said 'Dude that was my big finale!'
'Needs some work then Dude?' Kevin replied shaking Jason's
hand. Emily stood there looking confused.

Jason went through the detail of the car with Kevin for forty minutes and they swapped keys at three-thirty. He took Emily home and collected Snowy, Sooty and Cassie and all five of them went out for a two hour test drive. Snowy kept control of the dogs in the back.

As they were out Kevin's mum rang and said she'd be there in the morning. Kevin had forgotten it was so close to him leaving, he hadn't really done any personal preparation. Emily said she go in the morning before his mum arrived. He told her that wasn't an option.

....

06th August 1999

Felicity arrived at half past two. Emily was still holed up in Kevin's bedroom. He shouted to her when his mother came in and she shouted back she'd be a minute. Emily presented herself at twenty to three. She'd made a huge effort and done herself up very smartly with a pair of jeans, a nice top and just the right amount of makeup. She was stunning!

Felicity looked at her, then Kevin, tried to hide her shock, quite unsuccessfully and then managed 'Hi, I'm Felicity, Kevin's mother.' 'Hi Felicity, I'm Emily, Kevin's girlfriend!' Kevin sensed the standoff and jumped in. 'Look you two, for introduction purpose, one of you is Felicity and one is Emily. Can that do to start?'

They both put their bitch pouts on and said simultaneously 'Yes Kevin, of course.' He knew he had his work cut out this afternoon. He decided they'd all go out to Gio's he'd sorted the table as he'd waited for Emily to get ready.

They all had a drink by three and Kevin booked he taxi for four o' clock. After a few wines the two girls seemed to be speaking without hissing at each other. Progress he thought to himself.

A few more wines before the taxi came and it seemed Felicity was getting past Emily's age and actually engaging in real conversation. Kevin knew Emily was trying too hard but she still had her naturalness coming through.

As the taxi arrived Kevin could have been forgiven for thinking they were actually getting on. The wink his mum gave him as they left the apartment confirmed his thoughts. His mum had melted to Emily's charm. He knew this was easy but expected her to have put up more of a fight.

Felicity ordered a bottle of champagne. 'To welcome you Emily, from me' she said and smiled brightly. Emily burst into tears and the two women hugged. Kevin was losing the emotional control now, this was real woman territory. Once Emily's tears had subsided, Kevin asked an honest question. 'I take it you two are now ok and we can have a real evening together?'

As they went to bed Emily seemed to fall asleep immediately. Kevin was woken however some time into the early hours. 'I was waiting for your mum to go to sleep.' She said as she did things to him that she said she thought he would miss when he was gone. She wasn't wrong and Kevin eventually put his head back down to sleep at four in the morning.

....

07ᵗʰ August 1999

His flight had been delayed for fifteen hours. Despite the delay it allowed him time to think and it passed quickly enough. He boarded at midnight. He was in Vancouver for his connecting flight to Whitehorse by eleven o' clock and surprisingly still relaxed. There was no need for him to be a Super Hero on the plane, something that both amused and saddened him.

He decided to go to the bar when he got to the airport. It was one of the only places you could smoke. He hit on triple vodkas. He wasn't sure why but they were going down easily. He was on his second when he heard a voice he didn't expect to hear. 'Yo Kevin, Super Stud Muffin and Party Planner Extraordinaire' Kevin looked up, a little startled and saw Brian, bloody hell Brian, stood in front of him!

The hours he had waiting vanished in minutes, Brian was an ok guy and Kevin liked him. Kevin told Brian his movements and Brian said he might be able to catch up with him and Jack, he was all around Canada this month but wasn't sure if he could tie the times in. They checked mobile numbers and promised to keep in touch with each other throughout the month.

He landed in Whitehorse and was through customs by seven o' clock local time and Jack was there to meet him. They hugged and Jack drove them straight to the hotel. On the way Jack explained they had a four hour drive in the morning to Dawson City so had to be leaving at four in the morning. 'Nothing changes there then big Fella?'

09ᵗʰ August 1999

They left the hotel at four o' clock as planned and Jack started to explain to Kevin that they were now in summer and it would be far more pleasurable in terms of climate than the last time he came. By the time six o' clock came it was light and Kevin was starting to appreciate what Jack was saying. It was a pleasant four hour drive, partly because Kevin didn't know where they were going and had never seen any of it before but mainly because he and Jack were like a comedy double act.

By the time they arrived in Dawson City Jack was appraised with everything Kevin and Kevin everything Jack. Kevin was so looking forward to ten days with the Blacks and more so when Jack told him that he, Josh, Lennox and Kevin were going on a two night camping trip into the woods.

They got to the office at eight and Jack and Kevin separated by eight-thirty after they had been served coffee and bacon and eggs. Kevin was introduced to Julia, the General Manager of the site. She explained they had sixty on site staff permanently and one hundred drivers.

Julia gave Kevin a site tour and then he started on his sessions from ten o clock. By the time he'd finished questions and answers they were walking out to the car at five thirty. Julia joined Kevin and Jack and offered to join them for dinner at their hotel later. Jack was really keen, as was Julia. Kevin thought he'd have to referee later, especially when Jack had had a few. There was definite flirting going on.

Jack and Kevin were staying in Dawson's lodge, apparently a very good place for buffalo meat. They checked in at six thirty and Kevin was in the bar by seven o' clock. Jack was already there and on whisky's with Julia. Kevin sighed and knew he had a night and a half ahead of him.

Jack was on one of his drunken spats by twenty to eight. Julia was pushing and Kevin could see Jack was waning. Bloody whisky, what did it do to Jack! Kevin suddenly remembered he'd either puke or fall to sleep if he had too much so encouraged the rounds.

They ordered food at eight. They all had the specialty, buffalo in a cream pepper sauce. Jack had the thirty two ounce version and Kevin and Julia the sixteen. They ate the food. Kevin couldn't finish his so Jack did for him. Julia was getting more and more outrageous in her flirtation with Jack and Kevin could see the whisky working on Jack.

He changed tact and ordered a few triple vodkas. Julia didn't like vodka so Jack had hers. That was enough, he was now comatose on the table. Nothing would budge him. Kevin apologized to Julia and arranged help to get Jack to his room.

When Kevin got back down to the bar area he saw Julia with some local chap, both checking each other's tonsils out. Kevin smiled, retreated and went back to his room.

10th August 1999

They ate breakfast and chatted about last night. Jack asked Kevin what happened towards the end as he couldn't remember. 'I fed you vodka to stop you doing something with Julia you would have regretted.' Kevin said punching Jack on the shoulder.

'Thanks mate, God she was really into me man.' Jack said blowing his cheeks out. Kevin smiled, he didn't need to tell Jack that Julia seemed to be really into anything had had meat and two veg last night and giggled to himself silently.

They were in Whitehouse by eight o' clock and checked in to the Whitehouse Oakhouse at eight-fifteen. Tonight was a simple meal and into the office by eight the next morning.

11th August 1999

They arrived at the Whitehouse Office by ten to eight and met the Site Manager, Ian Elliot. Ian was a live wire and told them the next couple of nights he was taking the boys out on the town. Jack and Kevin left the site at just before seven o' clock. Ian said he'd pick them up in a taxi at nine and had a meal booked at a nice Italian restaurant at nine-fifteen.

Kevin showered and was in the bar by eight. Jack wasn't there yet so he ordered a local beer and sat smoking rethinking how the day and the sessions had gone. All in all he was pleased. Jack came down at half eight and they had a few beers but trying to keep it quiet.

Ian picked them up at nine as promised and they were in the restaurant by ten-past. They all had a three course special. Beef olives to start in a spicy sauce, King Prawn Risotto and ice cream. They shared a few bottles of wine and were ready to leave by eleven o' clock. Ian told them tonight was a quiet one but tomorrow they were drinking and going to a bar that had table service, followed by a wink. Kevin picked up on it straight away. Jack being Jack said that would be different and nice to be served at their table.

....

12ᵗʰ August 1999

Another long slog later Kevin and Jack were back at the hotel. Kevin was first to the bar at six. He started on the wine. He knew what kind of night tonight was going to be and decided to go with it. He was on his second by the time Jack came down. Jack had a beer and got Kevin his third wine. Ian was there on time and they left the hotel at just after half-six. They were at their destination before seven o' clock. Ian paid the taxi driver and led them to the entrance of Bouncers. 'Nice name.' Jack said and still no idea what place they were going into.

They walked in and their host Pammy showed them to their table. Jack nudged Kevin. Kevin checked Ian's face and he was just shaking his head. He whispered to Kevin 'I'll pay for his first one and we'll sit back and watch it should be fun.' Pammy brought them their drinks and asked if they had any preferences. Ian replied and said 'blond, very slim and buxom.' 'Is that a cocktail?' Jack asked to sniggers he couldn't see.

Pammy said she'd send Dolly over to check what they needed.

Dolly came over, stood in front of Jack and asked him if there was anything he wanted specifically. 'Yeah, can I have a beer and a vodka chaser?' Jack asked innocently. Dolly looked at Ian and Ian whispered 'Give him the works darling.'

Dolly took out her thirty eight double D assets and presented them to Jack's gob smacked face. Jack tried to look at Kevin but Dolly had taken her pants off and sat on Jack's lap. Kevin called Pammy back over and ordered a bottle of champagne, a bottle of vodka and a jug of iced orange juice.

Ian slipped Dolly four notes and she asked Jack to go for a walk with her. Kevin jumped in and said he wasn't walk material so Ian disappeared with Dolly himself. Jack looked at Kevin and slurred 'Kev, man, she was into me, she really wanted me man, I could have had a look, and you know window shopped?'

Kevin managed to escape with Jack with both their fidelities intact but they had to leave Ian there. He was sure he knew what he was doing so wasn't too worried. Kevin grabbed them a taxi and they were back in their hotel by eleven o' clock.

13th August 1999

They were back in the office for eight. Ian had called in sick and apparently had a doctor's appointment at a clinic out of town that he had to go to urgently. That's what his PA told Kevin.

He completed the final sessions by two o' clock and he and Jack left the site at half-past. They got to Whitehouse airport at three, their flight to Yellowknife due to take off at four. There were no delays and they touched down in Yellowknife at five. Jack sorted the car out as Kevin was left with baggage duties.

They arrived at the hotel, The Great Lake at just before half-six. Kevin and Jack unpacked and met in the bar at half-seven. They booked into the restaurant at eight and both commented they needed early nights.

Jack asked Kevin if he thought Ian would have been ok. 'You know mate, having to go that urgently, he must have had a real illness.' 'I suspect he did mate, something I'm sure could have been sorted with some pills or cream though.'

They were sat in the restaurant at eight and Jack's eyes lit up as he saw the menu. They only had a thirty two ounce T-bone steak on the menu. The comment read 'The Monster-Only for the Brave!'

Before Kevin could say anything Jack shouted 'I'm having that!' The waitress came over, her name was Lola, she was really pleasant and when Jack ordered the Monster she giggled and said 'Only real men have managed to finish that sir.' Jack replied 'Sounds good to me babe, can I have extra fries?'

Kevin waded into his own sixteen ounce slab of beef. Thirty minutes later he was spent, he had a quarter of his steak left. Jack was at the end of his and to Kevin's utter disbelief, burped, drank some red wine and said nonchalantly 'Finished yours mate?' 'What my steak?' 'Yeah, if you don't want it I'll finish it.' Jack said with expectant looking eyes.

Kevin pushed his plate to Jack just as Lola came over. She looked at Kevin, then at Jack and just said 'Wow, what a man, a real man! What's his name again?' Kevin was about to tell her when Jack stood up, empty plates all around him and said 'Jack darling, Jack Black.' 'Pleasure to meet you Jack, are you around long?' Lola asked him. 'Couple of days but will be here tomorrow night, you on?' Jack said sitting back down. 'Yeah honey, see you tomorrow big boy.'

They both went to their rooms at ten o' clock. Kevin had a quick chat with Emily. Apparently Alexis was being a bit off with her. Kevin told her not to worry. He closed the line wondering why Alexis was being funny. He thought about his blog but decided he wouldn't update it until Sunday though, they still had tomorrow night to go and he wanted to send a weekly report rather than a daily garble.

....

15th August 1999

Saturday had been a daze, three sessions, dinner and bed. They only had two morning sessions today before they were off on their next flight. These went well and Jack and Kevin left the depot by one-thirty.

They arrived in Prince George by five and in their hotel, the George by seven. They both decided on room service tonight and to be in bed early. Kevin rang Jane, he couldn't resist, and he wanted to know why Alexis was being funny to Emily. Now he was sober he was happy to have the debate.

'Jane, it's me.' 'Kevin, how's it going out there?' 'Yeah good darling, really good, the travel's hard but you know the rewards are there.' 'Kept your cock in your pants?' 'Jane. Are you insulting my fidelity?' 'Bloody right I am Kevin, yes or no?' 'Yes darling, apart from my right hand, it's been in its pants and being a good boy. Anyway sweetie, why's Alexis giving Emily such a hard time?' 'She's jealous babe, isn't it obvious?' 'Obvious to who Jane' 'Well me and your mother for a start, Kevin, I love her but she's still battling about you, she always will.' 'Shit Jane, I want her back as a best friend.' 'She will be darling, it'll just take time or she'll dump me and declare everlasting love for you.' 'Jane, I chose Claire, not Alexis, do you think that's hurting her?' 'What? God Kevin you can be daft, that's hurt her more than anything else ever in her life. The fact you then get a nineteen year old super looking girl who loves you as well! Come on Kevin!' 'Ok, I'm an emotional idiot. She will come round though won't she?' 'Yes she will. I've been having a word with her about Emily and Felicity's been helping too, she'll come round.'

As he digested the conversation Kevin loaded his Blog.

> Howdy Peeps
>
> Kevster here and back in the land of the Mountie, Beaver and Bear, yes folks back in the very, very beautiful Canada. Some of yous may know I'm here for a month spreading the Julie magic to the Canadian masses. Their good luck I tell yous lot. I must admit though Dudesters, these guys and gals are top notch.
>
> Been going for a week with the Big Man and he's been a star, super driver, super navigator, superman but lousy drinker. Mind you Peeps Jack holds the world record for what he can eat. So far been to Dawson City, Whitehouse, Yellowknife and now in Prince George. I've got a couple of days here and then we're off to Edmonton. I'll keep you Peeps informed but I'm passing the Julie word along as we travel. For nows though, keep safe, keep loose and keep happy yous lot.

....

17th August 1999

Yesterday had been a blur, a fifteen hour day, quick bite to eat and bed. They started their long journey and were like double act. Kevin eventually told Jack about Bouncers and the girls in there and why he suspected that Ian had to go to an emergency clinic.

Jack was gob smacked 'I thought they were just game birds.' He said as he drove on.

'Yeah mate, so game they strip naked in front of you and try to get your todger out?' Kevin asked still laughing. 'You don't know Canadian girls Kevin, not like I do anyway.' Jack replied and sort of stopped Kevin's laugh mid way through.

Jack was singing as he drove and Kevin joined in, the six hour drive went in no time and by the end of it they both reckoned they should form a group, they even came up with a name 'Kevajacksters', which they both thought was highly original and catchy.

They got into Edmonton at six o clock and were in their hotel at six-thirty. Again they plumped for an early night both going for room service. Kevin told Jack that in the next week or so they had to find a Karaoke bar, so they could practice their act.

....

22nd August 1999

After five days of total work they left Edmonton at ten o' clock for the six hour drive ahead of them. Jack hit the gas and they departed in relative silence. Kevin's mobile went whilst they were a mere ten minutes into their journey. It was Brian.

'Kevin, you stud muffin female stuffing man.' 'Hi Brian, nice to hear from you, where are you?' 'Vancouver Dude.' 'Brian, you're shitting me, that's where Jack and I are heading.' 'I Know, Jack told me Dude. What time you and the big fella arriving?' 'Bout four o' clock I think.' 'Kevster, that's cool Dude, I'll plan us a night out extraordinaire! I've booked us into Sounds, a karaoke bar and we've got VIP treatment man.'

'Jack you bugger, when'd do sort all that out?' 'When I knew what we'd be doing, we talked about a karaoke night and I thought it'd be a laugh.' They decided to use the remaining five hours of the drive to practice their songs for tonight.

Feeling better in himself generally and actually looking forward to seeing Brian, Kevin decided he was going to have a good night. The last few days had certainly knocked him around enough to warrant a night out with the lads!

He arrived at the bar ten minutes early feeling happy and normal. Brian was already there. 'Kevin, my man, the stud, the party planner, the dude, fucking A man,' Brian said as a sort of a greeting. 'Hi Brian it's great to see you.' Kevin said as he gave Brian a hug. Brian ordered triple vodka for each of them and one small bottle of orange. Kevin knew this was going to be a messy night.

They were in Sounds by just before eight. It was dead at the moment but Brian said he wanted to be there early so they all got their track lists when they wanted them. Judge was the DJ and Karaoke Compare and seemed like best friends with Brian.

Judge told them that as VIP guests they got to do what they wanted, when they wanted but the party didn't really start until nine-thirty. Brian took the boys back to the bar and ordered a bottle of champagne and a few real Cuban cigars.

At nine-thirty Brian got up and Judge introduced him as a closet Sinatra. Brian started on key and nailed New York New York. The place went wild, Brian was actually better than good, he was great. Kevin was really impressed and really worried how he and Jack would do.

He didn't have chance to dwell on his worries and Judge announced 'Next up is Kevin Julie and Jack Black with November Rain by Guns n Roses, please put your hands together ladies and gentlemen.' The place erupted in applause and Kevin walked up gingerly but Jack was playing the crowd with big waves.

The song started and Kevin had the first lines. He watched the screen and hit the first word, bang on time as it appeared on the screen, Jack was straight in and on time with his part and Kevin jumped back in seamlessly with his. Jack joined Kevin for the rest of the song as a duet as they bellowed out the words. The place went wild as they finished, Brian had held them with New York New York, Kevin and Jack had blasted them with Guns n Roses.

Brian conceded and bought more champagne. The three of them drank and smoked until midnight and then grabbed a taxi back to the hotel.

....

25th August 1999

Two fifteen hour days had passed and Kevin woke feeling surprisingly ok. He went for breakfast. Jack was already there and by the looks of it on his second or third plate. After yet another long day in the office Kevin and Jack returned to the hotel and Kevin went straight to his room. He set the lap top up and rang home first as it was booting up. It was only six o' clock their time so he wasn't sure who'd answer. To his great happiness Emily answered.

'Kevin, I wondered when you'd ring. I've missed and worried about you.' 'I'm fine. I wish you were here though to cuddle into me, still another week in work and at least I can have a chill with Jack and his family before I get back to you. How's my mum?' 'Your mum's brilliant and Jane too Kevin.' 'What about Alexis?' 'Nah she blanks me, her loss.' 'Ok darling, I'm sure it's nothing personal.' 'Kevin it is personal, she thinks I'm too young for you.' 'Ok, let me deal with that when I get back ok?' 'Sure babe.' 'Ok darling I'll speak to you in the next few days.' 'Bye baby.'

Kevin filled his second glass of red, lit a Benson and started on his Blog Page:

> My dearest and most sincerest Peeps of the world.
>
> Kevster here, still rocking and a rollin. On the Canadian front, still cool, very nice Peeps out here and a few adders on for the party Dudesters, the list is growing and a growing. Who'd have thought we'd be four months away in just a few weeks Peeps. I've checked the party list all of yous and can tell yous lot the new confirmed number of party mad attendees is . . . One twenty Peeps, that's one hundred and twenty! We're going to rock, roll, stroll and bowl the opposition party's into millennium oblivion Peeps.
>
> Keep it coming yous lot, I need to finalize arrangements by the end of October I'd say but we're looking cool Peeps, looking cool. I've got another few days work before I catch up with the Bear in Jack land. Me and the boys are off camping into the wilderness of Thunder Bay folks. That's me, Big Jack, even Bigger Lennox and the little fella Josh, he's only five all you Dudesses and a real cutie. Still with the big fella and the bear, he and I will be well looked after. That's it for now my party planning Peeps so be good, be clean and be seen.

31st August 1999

Day and days of work and nothing else they were at the airport by two and on an earlier flight at three. They arrived in Thunder

Bay airport at five. Jack had phoned Katie in advance and she was there waiting for them. Jack hugged her like he'd never seen her before. Katie didn't want to let go but did so to hug and say hello to Kevin. They got back to their pad by seven and Jack was over the moon to see his kids.

Kevin got big hugs from all the kids too. Katie put them to bed after half an hour and Jack let the animals in. Shadow came pounding towards him and went on a rampage Sooty would have been proud of. The cats then came and Jack seemed back in his place, his element.

Kevin didn't want to intrude tonight and wanted to get to his room. Jack spotted this and thanked Kevin but then said 'Come on, five minutes with Lennox' and led Kevin outside to the pen.

Lennox went madder than all of the rest of them when he saw Jack and ran to him at pace that frightened Kevin a little. He stopped short though and hugged Jack as if he was a dog. Jack told Lennox that he'd brought Kevin to see him. 'Do you remember boy?' He asked the bear. Lennox looked at Kevin and some recognition took place as he walked up to Kevin and gave him a pat on the shoulder!

'He remembers you Dude.' Jack shouted, 'Come over here and he'll give you a hug now he remembers, I've just got to tell him your name again.' Kevin stood tall and Lennox came over for a hug. Jack told Lennox it was Kevin and Kevin was staying for a few days.

Kevin made his excuses when they got back to the house. Shadow followed him but Katie shouted 'No Shadow.' 'It's ok with me if it's ok with you' Kevin said thinking of Sooty and Snowy. Jack looked at Shadow and said 'Ok boy, you can go with Kevin if you want to.' Kevin said goodnight and went to bed, Shadow followed and cuddled into him as he fell into the most comfortable of sleeps of the whole trip.

....

01st September 1999

Feeling like he was at home Kevin got up and made his way to the kitchen. Katie was making breakfast for Josh, Alex and Alicia. 'Hi Kevin, did Shadow wake you up?' She asked him as she kissed him on the cheek. 'Well yes, I suppose he did, but it felt like home.'

Jack came into the kitchen with a smile as big as Lennox's. 'Hi everyone' He beamed. Kevin could see how much it meant for Jack to be back with his family and felt a little bit like he was intruding on their privacy.

Jack seemed to notice again and said 'Right Kevin, after breakfast you're on a tour with me and the bear. We're going for a twenty mile hike today and on the way back we'll pick our camp site. It'll have to be within five miles though, too far for Josh otherwise.'

Kevin smiled; he was going on a boy's day out, him, Jack and the bear! What a start to a holiday or as Jack kept calling it, vacation. Katie made them eggs, bacon and pancakes and said 'when you two get back I'm roasting a hog. Dave and Jo, Mike, Lesley and Beth and Holly are coming as well.' Kevin was feeling comfortable until he heard the last two names, he was hoping Katie wasn't match making, she didn't really know much about Emily.

Jack went and changed and threw Kevin a pair of boots from the kitchen cupboard. 'They're brand new but I've got the same pair and they don't need breaking in my friend.' Kevin looked at these boots and realized they wouldn't have been cheap. 'Jack let me pay you for these?' 'No chance Dude, you're cooking tomorrow night and I want a special Julie treat.' 'Deal big fella.'

They collected Lennox from his pen and Shadow and Lennox had their five minute play. Lennox chased him like a dog and they had a ball. Kevin videoed this as people just wouldn't believe him. He had a morning hug from Lennox after the two boys had finished playing and then they all departed.

They walked, walked and walked further. Kevin tried to ask Jack how far they were going but Jack just said 'far.' Over two hours later they stopped. Jack said 'Lunch here and on the way back we'll pick our camping spot for the next couple of days. I need it near a river, Lennox likes salmon but he's a klutz and can't catch one for toffee, I'll bring a rod.'

An hour later they headed off and walked to a spot Jack said was perfect. Jack got his bearings and marked the location on an old map. They carried on walking for another thirty minutes and Kevin saw terrain he recognized and then Jack's house.

Kevin went to his room, changed and then went to the bath-room. As he got into the hot bath he didn't want to leave it. He hadn't realized how much he had ached. The only part of him that didn't hurt now he thought about it was his feet. 'Good boots Jack' he said out loud to no one.

He got out of the bath and the aches started to ping all over his body. If he had muscles where he was aching he hadn't real-ized before today. Throwing a clean pair of jeans on, some white trainers and a white tee-shirt Kevin hobbled into the kitchen. Jack was there having a beer and a Marlborough and Katie was giving the children tea in the next room.

'Kev, come have a beer Dude.' Jack said and getting up to go to the fridge. 'Jack mate, any chance of something stronger, you know drugs, anesthetic or raw alcohol?' 'Who's aching then Dude?' Jack said and went for the vodka instead of the beer. 'Jack, I can't believe how stiff I am, and for a change it's not Kevin junior. I thought I walked a lot back home but today . . .'

Jack was laughing, 'Dude that was the beginners walk, we can go for fifteen hours in a day my friend.' 'Don't invite me on that one please Jack?' Kevin said and sipped or rather gulped half of his strong vodka and orange. Jack laughed again and offered Kevin a Marlborough. 'Do you mind if I have a Benson mate?' Kevin said in a groan rather than his voice.

Katie joined them and asked Kevin how he was doing. When he said aching she played around poking him all over making him scream in pain and her scream with laughter. 'I love to do that to anyone who's done the short walk for the first time.' Katie said in fits of tears. Kevin looked at her and said 'I'll get you back Katie.' 'They all say that Kevin and they never do.' 'She does that, wait until the end of the night, you'll be calling her all sorts of names.' Jack said laughing.

Dave and Jo arrived at about eight and joined them by the fire. The night was pleasant and warm. Mike and Lesley turned up fifteen minutes later quickly followed by Beth and Holly. Kevin knew one thing, Katie was playing, Beth and Holly were both single, between twenty five and twenty seven and both attractive.

They all had their introductions and Katie started to carve meat off the spit roast at nine o' clock. They ate and drank well into the early hours. Kevin, despite himself was bonding with Holly who had taken Katie's lead and been poking him for the last hour.

Everyone left at two in the morning but Katie told Kevin she'd invited Holly over for supper tomorrow, she had apparently jumped at the chance knowing Kevin was going to be cooking.

....

02nd September 1999

He tried to get out of bed but his muscles weren't listening to his brain's commands. He literally couldn't move without wincing. Every muscle from his stomach down ached like there was no tomorrow.

Shadow wasn't having any of it and was barking at Kevin to get up. Somehow he did, threw a pair of joggers and a tee-shirt on and went into the kitchen. Jack was skinning something, something that bled a lot. Katie was also there humming a tune brightly.

Jack looked up and said 'Kevin, my man, managed to get your lazy behind out of bed then?' Kevin coughed a false laugh and before he could stop her Katie attacked, giving him multiple pokes. He winced, moaned and screamed he was going to get her but was too stiff to get anywhere near her. Jack was in fits of laughter. Jack jumped back into the conversation. 'Kevin, firstly, after yesterday's walk you are now the best getter upper. Our last guest, after that walk didn't move until six, the one before, three.'

'Great Jack, I am one of the better weaklings. That makes me feel so much better.' Katie ran around and poked his legs again, screaming in laughter. 'You cow, if I could move I'd get you!' He screamed at her with a huge smile on his face. Jack intervened, 'Come on you two, enough games. Katie's taking you into town in the truck. You've got to buy and cook dinner for the four of us, price of the boots, remember? And, yeah, whilst I remember you need to rustle something up for the kids.'

Kevin nodded and then replied 'Jack, tell me again why I like you so much? And Katie, you poke me once whist we're out and I'll find the strength to put you over my shoulder and smack your ass!'

Katie told Kevin she was now finished with her poking game but had been tempted by the smack on the ass, especially upside down. Kevin called her a cruel cow but they high fived. She got them into town and Kevin said he wanted to do fish, 'Jack's too much of a meat man, I want to surprise him, well all of you actually.' They went to the fishmonger and bought some allegedly freshly caught salmon, some prawns, some scallops and some monkfish.

They then hit the liquor store and Kevin bought a case of white and a case of champagne, this cost seven hundred dollars and a row with Katie. 'Look, it's what I like to drink and we won't do it all tonight so I can have it whilst I stay.' He argued back and eventually won.

Katie told Kevin that Holly was really sweet and fancied the backside off him 'Thanks Katie, here's me trying to be good and you're trying to set me up. God Katie, we live a million miles from each other.' 'Sorry Kevin, what I didn't tell you is Holly's not looking for any relationship, she just needs a shag Kevin!' Kevin looked at her and said 'Katie, that's a little bit direct isn't it. What about relationship and respect?' 'Bollocks to all that Kevin, she just wants no strings sex for a few days, what's wrong with that!'

They were back at the house by five-thirty, Josh, Alex and Alicia were waiting for their new uncle but more so for their mum. They ran to greet her and Shadow ran to Kevin, realizing he couldn't compete with the three children.

Jack helped them in with the supplies and asked if they'd had a good time. 'Great, thanks mate.' Kevin said, then adding 'She's stopped poking me now so she's my friend again.' 'Yeah until the next walk' Jack told him.

Kevin set to work on the food preparation, aided by a glass of white wine. He did Josh, Alex and Alicia's first and made them salmon fishcakes, twice cooked chips and some peas. The three of them loved it and all told uncle Kevin they loved him as Katie took them to bed at seven.

His menu was fairly simple. Thinly sliced and fried salmon with prawns and a sweet chili mayo dressing with lettuce followed by roasted garlic and dill monkfish and seared scallops in a white wine sauce with green beans and sautéed potatoes.

He had it all ready in thirty minutes and joined Jack for a wine in the yard. It was still pleasant and Kevin told Jack if he could choose anywhere to live and have a family it would be here. They shared a man hug and Jack said it would be good to go and say goodnight to Lennox.

They went to his pen and Kevin didn't need introducing tonight Lennox came out for a hug without request. 'Makes me miss home mate' Kevin said to Jack as he hugged the bear. Jack said in a low voice 'I know Kevin, I know.'

They walked back to the house arm in arm and as they got there Kevin noticed Holly with Katie. With what Katie had told him and his vow to stay celibate he was somewhat worried. Holly had the shortest skirt on he's seen for ages and was beaming at him. This won't be good he told himself inside his head.

First he served the starters. By his own high standards he was pleased; this was fresh, light and extremely tasty. Holly was already making a play and being encouraged embarrassedly by Katie. Jack wasn't defending him either.

He roasted the Monkfish in garlic and dill and seasoning, prepared the sauce and the vegetables and put the scallops on at the last minute in butter, just to brown them. He served up his fish treat, making sure Jack had the biggest portion.

Jack brought out the whisky and they all talked and smoked until midnight. Katie said she was tired and wanted to go to bed and Jack, yawning agreed and they both said their goodnights. Despite the alcohol Kevin did notice the subtlety that they didn't confirm any sleeping arrangements and Holly didn't appear to be going anywhere!

Kevin lit one of his Bensons and Holly asked for one. As he handed her one she lit it and said in a soft sexy voice 'Kevin, you know I like you, Katie should have told you. Please don't think I'm being a slut but we don't get to meet many men out here, I'm sure you've already figured that out. I know you're going back in a few days but I'd love a fling!'

Pulling on his cigarette Kevin couldn't even muster a response. Holly answered for him. 'Look Kevin, I want you tonight and for the next few days, no strings, I think you find me attractive.' He opened his mouth, trying to respond that he had a girlfriend back home but all he did was pretend to be a goldfish, no sound came out of his open and shut lips.

He still couldn't speak but let her lead him to his bedroom and into his bed. He went for a cigarette in the kitchen sometime later and checked the clock, it was five in the morning!

....

03rd September 1999

He walked into the kitchen and it was empty. There was a note from Jack. *'Gone out with the family, be back late, make yourself at home.'* He made himself some food, smoked a cigarette and decided to take Shadow out for a walk. They called by Lennox's pen and Kevin called him. To his huge surprise Lennox came out and made a roar of approval.

Kevin let him out and waited for the two boys to have their chase around. Then he took the bear and the dog out for a walk. It reminded him of Snowy and Sooty but looked at the difference and laughed out loud to himself, he'd just taken a bloody bear out for a walk!

....

04th September 1999

They had breakfast together and the three children fought over Kevin's attention, he felt broody for the first time in his life, but wouldn't dare admit it to anyone other than his subconscious self. Jack came in and said to Kevin they'd take a short walk today and set the camp site up for tomorrow. They were sleeping under the stars but Jack wanted to make the place safe enough for Josh before they got there.

Kevin checked his muscles and Katie poked him. As she did he picked her up and tickled her into submission. 'I told you I'd get you back.' He said as Katie howled. Jack was in stitches and added, 'reap what you sow honey!'

Katie got her voice back and asked if Kevin was up for a night in tonight, looking after the kids. She wanted a night out with Jack. Kevin agreed instantly. 'By the way, I asked Holly over to keep you company, if that's ok?' 'Cow' he said throwing a tea towel at her.

Kevin grabbed Shadow as Jack got himself ready to depart. They left at ten and Kevin asked if they were taking Lennox? 'Only if bears shit in the woods!' Jack said and roared at his hysterical joke. Kevin did find it funny and replied. 'Are you after my Crown Mr Black?' 'Only if it slips off mate.'

They grabbed Lennox and the routine of a play with Shadow was followed by hugs for Jack and Kevin. They walked to the site Jack had chosen the day they went on their hike only taking an hour. This was what Kevin called pleasurable, in fact a really nice time. The scenery and everything was so much prettier now he wasn't aching and thinking he'd have to walk all day.

Jack spent two hours though clearing the place they were going to sleep and lit seven small controlled fires. 'This, my friend will scare away the snakes and spiders, warn off the wolves and foxes and not harm the terrain' Kevin just nodded. Jack sat down and threw Kevin a Marlborough and looked at him seriously before considering and then saying 'Kevin, I know about Emily, Katie doesn't know that much at all, she still thinks you're single and grieving over Claire. You Dude have to start considering what you want though.'

'Jack, I love Claire, it hurts so much how much I want her, and I'm playing at everything else. The funny thing is though is that for years I thought it was Alexis. When Claire came though I was forced into a choice and I chose her over Alexis. The fact she's disowned me though hurts like nothing I can describe.'

'And Emily, surely she means something to you? You talk about her a lot.' 'I do care for her and I wanted it to work, it might still but it's not the same as Claire.' 'Kevin, answer me honestly, if you were with Claire now would you be playing with Holly?' Kevin lit another one of Jack's Marlborough's and replied carefully 'Jack, I can't deny I'd still find Holly attractive, she told me it was sex with no strings but no, I'd be bunking with the dog for the duration of my stay.'

They headed home at about two o' clock and put Lennox in his pen around ten-past three. Shadow disappeared for what Jack called a Doggy Nap. Jack disappeared to shower and change. Jack came back in, now smelling of aftershave. 'Smooth mate'

Kevin said as he lit his first cigarette for a couple of hours. 'I try sometimes, well every time I get to go out with Katie I do anyway.' 'Well I must say you look and smell great my friend, quite sexy actually.' 'Hey, don't push it!' 'Ooh, is Mr. Black getting embarrassed?' 'Ok Kevin, you win.' Jack said as Katie came in looking stunning in a pristine ironed top and skirt.

Kevin looked at Katie and said 'Wow, you look good, so clean and pressed, you'd impress anyone.' She beamed with a smile wider than he'd seen before and then he attacked her. Tickling her into submission, Kevin put her over his shoulder and smacked her ass. 'I think that's now a draw.' Kevin said to her mock scowl.

Holly turned up at seven-thirty and told him she was desperate for a drink. 'What do you want?' 'Kevin, strong vodka would be nice' 'Well I know how to do those!'

They sat down and Holly gave Kevin one of her Camel cigarettes and sipped on his frightened orange juice vodka as he called it. He went to the kitchen to check on the food. Kevin served ribs in his sticky sauce. Holly ate quickly as Kevin ate slowly. She was mesmerized by what he had done and stuffed her face. Kevin found this funny, she was a quarter of the size of him but ate about three times what he did.

The inevitable happened and she fell asleep ten minutes after eating. Kevin sat there sipping his drink and checking on the kids every half an hour.

....

05th September 1999

Holly left at six after saying a very physical goodbye and Kevin settled back down to his bed for another couple of hours much needed sleep. Nothing doing! Firstly Josh and Shadow joined him quickly followed by Alex and Alicia. They all wanted Kevin to make them breakfast.

Reluctantly he got up and went with the kids and the dog to the kitchen. He asked them what they wanted to eat. Josh chose bacon and eggs, Alex toast and Alicia wanted chocolate crispy cereal and then some jam on bread. Shadow seemed to agree with all choices and wagged his tail nonstop.

By the time the four of them were fed he found time to make himself a cup of tea and nip out for a cigarette. Katie came in yawning and looked at the table. 'Kevin you didn't make them three different breakfasts did you?' 'Well don't you normally make them what they want?' 'No darling, they have what they're given, they've been playing you!'

Kevin looked at the three Black children and growled at them. They all screamed and ran away laughing. 'They'll miss you when you've gone Kevin.' 'Me too Katie, me too' Jack came in about eight o' clock and said. 'Did I hear Kevin was bullied by the kids?' 'Yes darling!' 'Oh well, they used their initiative so I won't be complaining too much. Kevin, you are soft!' 'Jack my sixteenth middle name!' The three of them roared with laughter as Shadow barked along.

Jack had brought a rucksack which was as big as Kevin stuffed full, then handed Kevin one half the size. They were walking to their site an hour later. They arrived at the camp and Jack went to collect some more wood for the embers of the main fire they'd lit yesterday.

Once Jack was happy with the fire he told Kevin and Josh they were off fishing. Lennox and Shadow were told to guard camp. They both seemed to understand as neither moved to follow them and both stood looking alert.

Jack, Josh and Kevin took their rods to the river, a ten minute walk from their site. Josh was really excited and telling Kevin he was going to catch a fish. 'Have you caught one before?' Kevin asked him. 'Yeah, it was as big as my arm uncle Kevin.'

Jack smiled as he set them down at the place he'd picked to fish. They cast their lines and sat back and waited. Josh fell asleep and Jack grabbed a few beers out of his bag and a packet of Marlborough's.

Jack shouted and Josh woke up, 'Bite, bite, bite' He screamed. It wasn't just one though but four out of the six rods he'd set were moving. 'Josh, you know what to do, Kevin, follow what I do.' Jack hauled in the first one and put it into the net, Jack got the second and then helped Josh bag the third. Kevin with Jack's help eventually got the fourth and then the two other rods creaked and Kevin landed one on his own, as did Josh.

Jack was screaming 'Six my boy, six, a record, well done my darling son!' Josh was made up and hugging his dad and Kevin. Kevin was so thrilled, especially as he saw what it did for Josh.

Kevin was so excited he started to do some strut around where they were fishing. Josh looked at Jack and Jack sighed saying. 'Son, he's English, he doesn't get it.' Josh nodded as Kevin carried on with his ridiculous routine.

They walked back to site with six huge salmon. Lennox roared as he smelt the fish but Jack told him to wait. To Kevin's huge surprise Lennox obeyed. 'Right then all, two salmon for Lennox tonight, one for us, one for Lennox for breakfast, and two to take home to the family.' Josh was running around whooping and Lennox imitating him.

Jack gave Josh one of the salmon; it was still alive and said 'give it to Lennox son.' Without any fear or trepidation Josh walked up to Lennox, told him to wait and handed him the live salmon. Lennox took it off Josh so gently Kevin couldn't believe it. Josh even hugged the bear as he held the salmon in his paws before he started to eat it. 'Jack, that's just amazing mate.' 'It's all Lennox is used to Kev, Josh is like a brother to him but higher in the pecking order!'

Kevin sat back and just admired the scene it was totally surreal to everything he had learnt over the years. It was mesmerizing to watch. Jack moved first and said 'Our food now' and grilled a whole salmon for him, Jack, Josh and Shadow. As it was cooking he gave Lennox his second one.

Lennox slept after his fish and Jack served Josh first. He gave Shadow a huge piece of fillet and threw some potatoes in foil into the fire for Kevin and him. Josh fell asleep with Shadow cuddling him. Jack and Kevin sat up drinking and talking. They ate salmon, roasted jacket potatoes and some salad but didn't sleep at all through the night.

06th September 1999

Jack put the kettle on the still burning embers and made tea. The salmon they hadn't eaten last night he made into sandwiches for breakfast for him, Josh and Kevin, fed Shadow with the rest of the meat and gave Lennox his breakfast of a single whole salmon. Lennox sat and ate like a human, carefully and deliberately.

As they headed home Jack said 'Oh well, two to take home my friend, Katie will be well happy, one is a treat, two a real success.' All through the trip Josh had been taking photos and Jack said he'd upload them before Kevin left.

Katie said she'd freeze the salmon and asked Kevin if he minded babysitting again tonight, they'd been invited to a meal only last night and Katie would like to go. 'Katie, it will be more than my pleasure, I'll sort the kids out and catch up on calls and my blog.' Kevin replied relieved at the chance to have some alone time.

A full glass of wine later Kevin turned to his blog page and began to write:

> Hello Peeps
> Rocking, rolling and jiving Kevster here! Yous may be wondering where I've been Dudesters and you'd be right to wonder. The Kevster's been in the wilderness of Canada Peeps, fraternizing with the bears, the wolves, the foxes and the snakes. Don't worry though the Kevster's far too cool to get snagged by one of those beasts. Don't think the beasts didn't try though Peeps! But me the Jackster and the Bear saw off all comers and lived to tell the tale. Wow yous lot this is a cool country. Big ups to the Canadians Dudesters, top of the shop Peeps these.
>
> I'll be heading back in day's yous lot and then the party planning takes on a new dimension, less than three months to go when I get back. I'll give an update soon but for nows Peeps I have a dancing date with the bear!

He lit and finished a Benson, poured another wine and went and checked on the kids again. Jack and Katie came home at eleven-thirty and Kevin made his excuses and went to bed, followed by Shadow.

....

08th September 1999

Kevin had spent the previous day in bed with a migraine. He knew he had to get up today though. As he entered the kitchen Jack was there waiting. Kevin had somehow gone on a downer about Claire that he didn't see coming. He managed to spit his feelings out to Jack.

'Kevin, if you want Claire, you've got to fight for her. You're right about not messing around with others, it's not what you want and it's destined for failure. You have to get across to Claire what you feel for her and stop messing around with other girls, no matter what the temptation.'

'How can you fight for something that won't be fought for Jack, how?' Jack hugged Kevin closely 'Look mate, you're now the best friend I have in the world, you fight by being you and not having twenty girls as an alternative, you fight by letting Claire know she is everything, no matter what else happens. You fight dirty, if she won't speak to you, send someone she will speak to and don't give up Kevin, never give up on her.'

They shared a hug and Kevin thanked Jack. 'Look mate, without you and the way you are with your family I'd have given up a long time ago. I know what I have to do and I will do it!' Katie walked in and said 'Breaking something up boys? If so I want Kevin's ass after you Jack!' 'Oh now Mrs bloody Black's the comedian!' Kevin shouted in reply. 'My middle name Kevin' she said as she walked over and hugged him tightly.

Jack dropped him off at half-twelve and they shook hands. Neither said a word. Kevin went into departures and waited to be called for his flight home.

....

10th September 1999

Putting the key in the door he opened it with all sorts of emotions running through his mind. As he walked in there was a stampede, Emily, his mother, Sooty, Cassie and then at the rear looking extremely pissed Snowy! He quickly kissed his mum on the cheek, hugged Emily, gave Sooty a hug and then picked Snowy up. She was protesting louder than any one.

'Do you all know what I'd love to do now?' Kevin said. His mother replied 'It better not be rude Kevin!' 'Nah mum, I want to take my babies and the most important women in my life out for a long walk.'

Felicity answered first 'I'd love to darling but my trains booked for twelve, Jane's agreed to take mc.' Emily then shouted 'Can it just be me you and Snowy, Sooty and Cassie Kevin, please, I'd really like that.'

They went on a fairly medium walk and got back an hour and a half later. As they returned Emily took Kevin to the shower and then spent the next three hours showing him how much she'd missed him for the last month. His head hit the pillow about four o' clock. He was out like a light.

....

11ᵗʰ **September 1999**

Emily had gone home with Cassie. Kevin phoned the office with a Benson lit in his hand and blew out a breath of satisfaction. He had been on Marlborough's for a while and had missed his Benson fix. Mary answered, everything was ok.

He took both Snowy and Sooty out. They got home at just after lunch; he settled them down, showered, changed and left the apartment. He need to ring his mother and needed her to do him a favor.

'Hi mum,' Kevin darling so soon.' 'Yes so soon mother, I wanted to speak to you.' 'You mean you want something' 'Same horse, mum I really need you to do something for me.' 'You do?' 'Yup and only you can do it my beautiful, stunning, funny, slim, fantastic mother.' 'Compliments, it must be a biggy?' 'Well a little biggy mum.' 'Spit it out.' 'Ok, the party I'm planning in Cardiff mum, Claire promised me the use of a mansion, one of her friends. I can't think of an alternative and well, I was sort of hoping you'd go and see her and see if it's still ok?' 'Not much then darling?' 'You know me mum.'

....

15ᵗʰ **September 1999**

He'd spent the previous two days sleeping intermittently but phoned Alexis and Jane and arranged dinner. The phone rang immediately as he put the receiver down. 'Kevin.' 'Daniellie, hi, long time.' 'I know son, look the reports from Canada have been brilliant. I've been patted on the back by the big man himself.' 'That's great boss, where are you?' 'Italy at the mo but that's part of the reason for the call. The big man wants to meet you next week in Italy, I'm not likely to be back in the UK now so he wants you to take the MD role now. He's talking of another bonus for both of us, a big one too.' 'Daniellie, I'll sort out the trip tomorrow, how long do you want me there?' 'Say Tuesday to Thursday?' 'Deal, I'll see you Tuesday.'

He couldn't believe his luck with work. Still strike whilst the iron's hot he told himself and hit on his page:

> Beloved pretty and handsome Peeps
>
> Kevster here and on top of the world. The boss just told me I have another bonus coming, how cool's that you fun loving Dudesters? Well with the work shit sorted, my Peeps, excitement reigns. I'm hoping for details to come out next week but need to rally yous lot to nag all yous friends for commitment. The number's got to be decided by the end of the month Peeps. There's a couple more for the list. Dudesters that's one seventy strong and growing by the day. I'm so overwhelmed Peeps, it's going to be the party of parties and we're going to be there. Late summer lovin Peeps.

16th September 1999

He needed to settle down to some serious work. Not moving for seven hours solid he completed everything he wanted to and e-mailed Mary for her to check. She replied it would take her until noon tomorrow. Emily arrived about six and jumped straight into the shower. She seemed to be in a strange mood but Kevin dismissed it. He showered afterwards and they arrived at Jane and Alexis's a little after seven. Emily was still acting oddly. Kevin put it down to the Alexis situation and thought this would take time to heal.

As it was though Emily was absolutely fine with Alexis and as chatty with Jane as ever. Alexis had concocted a Sweet Chili Lamb and it was awesome. Kevin said it was better than any chili type dish he'd tasted. Alexis was made up by this. Emily though wouldn't drink and was distant all night.

They left at ten and got back to his about ten-thirty. Emily said she wanted to go to bed and said she was a little bit nervous about tonight and apologized for being a bit down. Kevin kissed her goodnight and went to have another drink figuring he'd call Jack. The time was fairly ok for a Canadian chat.

'Jack, my man.' 'Kevin, how are you?' 'Great thanks mate, you and the family?' 'Yeah we're all cool, want to say hello to Katie?' 'Yeah mate.' 'Kevin.' 'Katie. God it's good to hear your voices, I forget how much I miss you guys.' 'Me too Kevin, perhaps you can move out here?' 'Nice thought Katie but I'm an English man, the song an Englishman in Canada doesn't quite work the same as New York does it?' 'What you're moving to New York?' 'No Katie that was me being funny?' 'You were?' 'Are you taking tips from your husband?' 'You got it!' 'Well, I'm impressed.' 'Good, by the time we get to come and see you again I'll be competing harder than ever.' 'Bring it on Canadian girl.' 'Ok honey, look Josh is calling I'll put you back to Jack.' 'Kev.' 'Jack, you're back, God I've missed you.' 'Me too fella, been ages.' 'Yup, I'd almost forgotten how your voice sounded.' 'Ok, this could go on all night, what's new?' 'Nothing really, still happy and with Emily. Look, I'm off to Italy next week to meet Daniellie and the big cheese, apparently I'm going to be UK MD ahead of schedule.' 'Yeah, I heard.' 'You did?' 'Nothing gets past me my friend. I'm really pleased for you.' 'Cheers mate.' 'Kev you're currently number one mate, Daniellie's riding on your wave.'

....

17ᵗʰ September 1999

Emily was much more like Emily this morning and she again apologized for being a little off yesterday. Kevin brushed her comments aside telling her anyone could have an off day. She asked him if he minded taking the dogs out. Snowy heard and seemed to decide she was going as well.

Kevin took them out for a very long walk, three hours in fact and was back ready for Mary's e-mail on his proposal by one o' clock. He'd known she'd told him lunch time but Mary was bang on the nail at one o' clock with her feedback. They were off to Emily's parents later, something she'd sprung on him earlier and he felt the pressure mounting.

They arrived at Emily's parents at just before half-seven. Her mother, Nicola came out to greet them looking really excited and her dad, Bobby hung around by the door. They lived in a modern large detached house that had considerable grounds. Kevin also noticed a Jag, a Merc and a Ferrari in the drive way. Emily whispered as she saw him look 'Dad likes his cars.'

The first thing he noticed was the interior was almost palatial, these people had lots and lots of money. Cassie ran around like she owned the place and Sooty didn't need much encouragement to follow. Snowy turned towards Kevin and looked at him as if to say 'Dogs!'

He sat in the sitting room as they called it and Nicola offered him a choice of drinks. He was settled when she mentioned Chablis. Bobby sat next to Emily and asked Kevin what he did. When he said he as now MD of the UK operations of a multinational courier company, Bobby mellowed a bit. 'Earn cash then do you son?' 'A bit Bobby.'

As the evening wore on Kevin realized these were nice people, no pretence but just had money. He saw where Emily got her personality from and by checking Nicola's features in the light her looks. She was almost as stunning as her daughter, even with the generation gap.

Nicola served food at nine-thirty. Dessert was served but Kevin abstained, he'd also noticed Emily hadn't drunk all night, quite unlike her. Booby took him to the games room for vodka and cigars. They joined the others thirty odd minutes later. It was now two in the morning and Kevin was feeling the pace, as it seemed were all the others. Emily grabbed him, kissed him and said 'Bed darling, now.' He wasn't arguing and followed her to the bedroom.

As they got undressed Kevin asked her if there was anything wrong. 'I'm not sure Kevin, really not sure.' 'What does that mean Emily?' 'I can't answer that at the moment, what I can tell you is I'm pregnant!'

Kevin looked at her and asked as softly as he could 'Sure?' 'One hundred percent, I was telling mum when you were having the inquisition off dad.' 'I don't know what to say.' 'Are you happy, sad or horrified?' 'Well on the three options I'd choose happy but it's a lot to take in so suddenly darling.'

Emily grabbed him and asked him to produce one of his rises, she wanted to make love. Kevin managed the rise but Emily was fast asleep before he had chance to present it. He decided to go back downstairs and get drunker than he felt so far, this was huge, massive, off the scale, and he needed more vodka.

He got back to the games room and Snowy followed him. He found the vodka, didn't even look for the orange and also found the box of Cubans. Feeling sure Bobby wouldn't mind he helped himself.

He wasn't sure what time it was when he left the games room but he knew it was late, or early or somewhere in-between. He struggled back up the stairs whatever time later. He stripped and climbed into bed with Emily, a very early morning rise took over him. He tried to get Emily interested but got a slap across the face. With the lights turned on and he realized he had only been in bed with Nicola, not Emily! They both jumped out of the bed completely naked, Kevin with his rise in full view. Nicola covered her impressive naked body and Kevin tried to cover his hard on!

She eventually threw him a gown as she put one on herself, he put it on immediately. 'Nicola, I didn't realize, I thought I was back in my room, where's Bobby for God's sake?' 'Kevin, calm down, you came into the wrong bedroom, Emily's across the other wing, me and Bobby don't sleep in the same room, it was a mistake, calm it down, I just got a huge shock.' 'You did? Shit that's two for me in almost as many hours.'

Nicola looked at him and said 'Second shock?' 'Emily told me she's pregnant.' 'Come on lets go for a drink and a smoke.'

They went back to the games room, Kevin poured the vodka and lit up two of his Bensons handing one to Nicola. They sat down and Nicola said cheekily 'I can see why Emily likes you so much with tackle like that!'

'Nicola you're making me all hot and flushed.' 'Only joking Kevin, thought it would break the ice. What are your intentions with Emily now she's pregnant?' 'The whole nine yards Nicola.' 'Do you love her?' 'Yes.' 'That wasn't very convincing Kevin.' 'I think the world of her and the thought of a baby really excites me, you know the thing that will make me settle down.'

'Kevin that's very honest but are you sure it's what you really want?' 'Sometimes Nicola you have to go with what you're pre-sented and I want to go with this.' 'Good answer, you've satisfied my first inquisition anyway.' 'Thanks, what about you and Bobby?'

She considered his question and replied shortly 'It's been a while since we've been physical.' 'Isn't that hard in a relationship?' 'Yes I suppose it is or in this case it isn't, that's the problem!' 'Shit

Nicola I didn't mean to pry that deeply.' 'No worries a bit like my sex life no depth, rigidity or penetration.' 'Are you making a joke?' 'He eventually gets it, yes it was a joke but problem's real enough, how'd you think I felt with a fully erect boner sticking into me when I haven't sniffed one for years? Now bugger off before I do something I'll regret!'

....

19th September 1999

Emily had told him yesterday she didn't think she could have the baby and Kevin did what he did best and lost the rest of the day in drink. It was only half-nine today and he tried Emily's number, no bloody answer, this was driving him wild inside. How could he influence her? She was young but he had feelings too. He tried Jane and Alexis and again the same no answer. Before he could get too wound up, his mum was on the phone asking for a lift from the station.

He picked her up at just gone ten-thirty. They went to the local coffee shop Bellingos and sat at a table. Kevin lit a Benson. 'Ok, how'd you get on with Claire mum?' 'Ok, she's sorted the mansion out for you but dropped her name off the attendee list.' 'I figured that would happen. How is she mum?' 'She's ok Kevin, that's all I'm allowed to say, part of the deal of getting you the place in Cardiff, I'm not allowed to talk to you about her.' 'Mum, that's mad.' 'It's the deal I struck and I'm sticking to it.'

....

21st September 1999

He'd driven to Emily's parents yesterday to no avail, no one was home. His flight today was at seven, straight into Lineate. Daniellie was picking him up at ten-thirty Italian time providing there was no delay with the flight. He took off at seven and only took hand luggage to miss baggage collection either ends.

Daniellie greeted Kevin with a hug and gestured him straight out of the airport to the car park. He did promise breakfast before the office as Kevin was starving. They parked the car in the office complex in central Milan and walked back out into the busy morning city centre. Daniellie took him to a small Cafe he often went to and they had coffee, meats, croissants and cheeses. Kevin was fit for the day afterwards and Daniellie told him it would be all meetings.

They hit the meeting room on their own initially, at eleven thirty and didn't move until four when Kevin went for a cigarette. Daniellie said they had a few more things to agree today before they met the big boss, Jim Beamer tomorrow. They stayed locked in the room until eight o' clock.

They met in the hotel restaurant at nine-fifteen, they had a glass of wine, steak and another red before they finished their dinner by ten-thirty.

....

22nd September 1999

Daniellie was in reception and looking like a child waiting for a present. 'This is it Kevin, we're going places you and me, big places too.' 'You reckon boss?' 'Wait and see son, wait and see?' They were in the office well before six and after two coffees and two Bensons Kevin was ready for his first meeting with Jim. For some reason he wasn't nervous at all, Daniellie seemed the more on edge.

Daniellie went through everything they'd already gone through four more times. The more Kevin heard it though the more he started to disagree. He wasn't about to dump Daniellie in it though, the stakes were too high. He went for another Benson at eight-forty as Daniellie waited in the Board Room. Kevin met Jim before their meeting, he joined him for a cigarette at ten to nine.

Jim looked at him and said in his deep American accent that Kevin needed no introduction. He knew who he was and knew what he was all about. 'Look Jim, I don't mean to be rude, I know you would have heard but how'd you know what I looked like?' 'Ah Kevin, Jack is my greatest friend in the whole world.' Kevin smiled at Jim and said 'We've got a meeting at nine, shouldn't we be on our way?' 'Like your style Kevin, I knew I would, come on, let's not keep Daniellie waiting any longer.'

They walked up to the Boardroom together and Kevin knew this guy was for real and he actually for some reason liked what Kevin was about. They entered together and Daniellie nearly choked. 'Jim, you're here, I see you've met Kevin?' 'Yes Dan, I did, his reputation preceded him so I sort of knew what to look for.' The meeting lasted less than two hours, by the end of it they had agreed Kevin would take over the UK from the first of October, and that Daniellie and Kevin would both receive a monkey bonus. Jim laughed as he said it. Kevin took the bait and said 'Thanks Jim, five hundred pounds will come in really handy!'

Daniellie nearly choked for the second time of the morning before Jim replied 'Jack said you were funny Kevin.' 'My middle name Jim' Kevin said as Jim departed. Daniellie looked at Kevin and said 'Son, how the hell do you get away with it?' 'You know me boss, a break from the norm.' 'Yeah, don't I know it, we just secured a million pounds worth of bonuses between us son!' They got back to the hotel and Kevin spurned Daniellie's invite for celebration and rang home.

'Mum?' 'Kevin, it's so late.' 'I know mum, I'm sorry but has there been any news from Emily?' 'No darling.' 'I figured as much but wanted to know.'

....

23rd September 1999

As he got home he sat and talked to his mother over a bottle of wine. 'Mum, I'm in a mess. I love Claire, care for Emily but can't get my head around any of it. Emily is pregnant and if I'm not mistaken has had an abortion. Claire won't speak to me, Emily won't speak to me and Jane and Alexis are AWOL.'

She didn't reply immediately but had tears in her eyes. 'Darling it will work out for you, it always does somehow, God you fall in shit and always come out smelling of roses.' 'Not this time mum, I've got to accept it, I've lost with a capital L.' 'Not necessarily darling.' 'What does that mean?' 'Nothing other than things can change darling, I really believe they can!'

He was about to ask his mother which school of crystal ball studying she went to but the door bell went. Sooty went pounding to the door wagging his tail as if he knew who was there. Kevin dragged himself up and went to the door. Jane and Alexis were both standing there holding their left hands out!

He stood there and looked at them but not smiling. They both looked as if they'd explain but saw his face and asked softly 'What's wrong Kevin?' He shook his head and couldn't hold back the tears so gestured them in.

They walked in less excitedly than they'd been at the doorstep and saw Felicity. She went and got glasses and opened a bottle of red. Kevin then lighting a Benson apologized to his best friends and told them the Emily story.

Felicity stood up and said 'Look you three, she's so young, come on, it's not fair to make judgments against her. Kevin I love you with all my heart but she's only nineteen, give her some slack, even if she has made the wrong choice.'

Kevin was shell shocked, his mum, his number one supporter and his one hundred percent backer hadn't backed him. He was about to protest loudly to her and tell her she needed to be on his side when the penny dropped. She was right, his mother was always right.

He sat back and looked at all three of them before replying 'Sorry, all of you, I've been so selfish. Mum, you're right, bang on as usual but I've been a little dented by it all.' Before any of them could respond he added 'Jane, Alexis, I missed why you were so excited when you arrived but I've just noticed your rings, God I've been a cock. What happened, when, how, why and why wasn't I there?'

Jane answered 'We had a row again and decided it was make or break time. We booked a last minute trip to Barcelona and decided all phones stayed behind. When we got there we both realized this is for real and needs to be forever so bought engagement rings and we'll get married next year.'

Alexis then spoke and said 'Kevin, are you ok with this, we want you to be best man at the wedding and yes you have to organize the hen party!' He looked at her, had flashbacks in his mind of his experiences with the both of them and then replied 'I don't love anyone as much as I love the people in this apartment at the moment, sorry Claire aside. Well to be honest I'm happier now than I could have thought possible today. You two are the best friends I've got, want or could ever wish for, I'm over the moon!'

....

24th September 1999

Richard was coming for one of Kevin's meals tonight so he visited the best fish mongers his locality had to offer and the best butcher. It was a classic meal he was cooking, not over the top but quality and hopefully executed to perfection. His last but one stop was a local delicatessen and he picked up the last of the food ingredients. His menu was quite simple.

King Prawn, Scallops and Squid in a Chili Sesame Salad
Fillet Steak in a Red Wine Jus with roasted Vegetables
Sticky Toffee Apple Sponge and Custard

He'd neglected the Peeps again without meaning to and needed to explain. The lap top warmed up and Kevin set himself for one of the hardest updates this year:

Yo Peeps, hello from the Kevster

I know I told all yous lot I would be more consistent in my communication but as ever my Dudesters the Kevster's got it wrong. Personal stuff has yet again got in the way and I'm truly sorry' Well as always Peeps I pick myself up, dust myself down and fight on, I don't know another ways yous lot so some forgiveness for my silence the last few days would be a little welcome.

Well my Dudes and Dudesses the fact I carry on means we still have a party my friends and it's coming closer and closer by the day. I've had more Peeps confirm their attendance but will update yous lot on that in the coming days. Guys and Gals were on the road to the best party ever and its all cause of yous.

He wasn't entirely happy with what he'd posted but he had things on his mind he couldn't shake, he was hopeful they didn't notice however. He grabbed Felicity and told her who Richard was. She nearly froze with fear. Kevin told her not to worry and Richard was a friend and he'd cooked for him before.

The door bell went at ten to seven and it was Jane and Alexis. Felicity greeted them and hugged them, especially Alexis. Before they had chance to settle Richard arrived bemoaning the fact Kevin had forced him to take a Friday off. Kevin smiled and felt happy again, 'Richard, this is a special occasion that the Ivy will have to do without you for. So tonight my friend you enjoy the Julie experience with friends.'

Kevin served the starters and Richard sat silently eating. Kevin was desperate for his opinion but the bugger wouldn't talk. Kevin did the waiter honors and then said 'Before I speak and salute my best friends I want some feedback on my food from the silent professional.' Richard stood up and looked at them all and then said with a huge smile 'No fault so far!' He then left them and went and finished the main course.

They all sat down and ate and Richard again remained silent, Kevin knew though by this stance that Richard had enjoyed it. Felicity did the dessert and served it just warm with room temperature cream slightly laced with vanilla extract. It went down a storm.

....

25th September 1999

He woke up to a loud scream. It appeared Snowy and Sooty had attacked his mother. Felicity shouted at both of them and stormed into Kevin's bedroom. 'Can't you keep control of these bloody animals?' She screamed at him. He sat up and pulled the covers over himself. 'Mum, please can you take them this morning?'

She strutted and shouted 'I'll take them out but can you get out of bed and sort them out first?' 'Not really mum.' 'Why the hell not?' 'Well unless you want to see the underpants bulge from your nearly thirty year old son mum, I'd better stay where I am.'

Felicity huffed and shouted 'I'll bloody well take them then, men and hard-ons, always an excuse!' Kevin smiled as she got ready and took both of them out. After the door was closed he thought it a shame to waste the first morning rise for a while so stayed in bed a little longer.

Following a shower he felt alive again, he needed to know about Emily and he was going to find out, warts and all. He left his mum a note and jumped in the car heading straight to her parent's house. He got there in quick time, the Saturday traffic was nothing like mid week.

Knocking the door his heart was beating ten to the dozen. For a minute there was no response. Another minute passed and he was about to walk away before he saw some movement through the mottled glass of the door.

He waited and saw Nicola appear with a very sad look on her face. 'Hi Kevin, I thought you'd come. Come in please.' He followed her but was none too happy. They got to the kitchen and she asked him if he wanted coffee. 'Nicola, with all due respect no I don't want coffee, I think you've taken Emily away for an abortion and I want to know the truth . . . Please?'

She looked at his desperate face and said softly 'Wine Kevin?' 'Please.' She opened a bottle of red and sat next to him at the kitchen table. 'Kevin, what I have to tell you isn't easy.' He looked at her a bit crestfallen and nodded. Nicola poured them each another wine and sat down again. She asked him for one of his Bensons and he lit one up for each of them. Nicola looked at him with tears in her eyes. 'I'm sorry Kevin.'

He didn't ask for an explanation but asked 'When Nicola?' 'Last Wednesday.' 'Why?' 'She loved you but then realized she's still a girl.' 'I figured that would happen but I didn't figure she'd be pregnant when it happened.' They sat in silence for a few minutes and Nicola poured him another wine. 'I can't Nicola I'm driving.' 'Kevin you can stay, there are plenty of rooms, and I'll do my best to answer your questions.'

He lit another Benson, passed it to Nicola and lit one for himself. Nicola topped up their wines. 'You know what and honestly Nicola? Emily was and will always be special but I couldn't shake off my ex who I'm still in love with. How bad is that?'

Nicola laughed at him. 'What's funny?' 'You think she didn't know about Claire?' 'Yes of course she did, I told her.' 'Yeah but what you say with your mouth never hides your eyes. Kevin, she knew you cared for her but as young as she is she isn't dull. She knew you didn't love her, not like you love Claire.'

Feeling sorry for himself he went into the bedroom he stayed in whilst he was last there with Emily and lay there silently. The door pushed open some minutes later and Nicola was stood there almost naked. 'Mind if I join you Kevin?' His head screamed no! His mouth said 'Jump in pretty woman.'

....

26th September 1999

Kevin entered the kitchen and walked in with his head in shame. Nicola looked at him and said 'Look, last night and this morning weren't anything to do with Emily. I knew there was an attraction and I knew you were vulnerable, I used the circumstances to my advantage.'

Sitting down and taking a coffee Kevin asked 'If we'd been together, Emily and me I mean, would you still have, for a better phrase, had a go?' 'No Kevin, but I would have had some fun thinking about it.'

He got in his car and left for home at eight o' clock. He cursed himself all the way home. Why couldn't he use the word no? A mystery he couldn't answer now but needed to solve if he was ever to achieve happiness.

Felicity told him she was going home today, Kevin said he'd drop her to the station and asked if he could go and visit her next weekend with Snowy and Sooty. She beamed at him, 'Wow son, you getting soft on me with all this contact.' 'Make the most of it mum, I'll slip back into my old bad ways soon enough.' Over a wine and a Benson Kevin spoke to his world.

> Yo, Yo Party Peeps
>
> Kevster here and back in the groove yous lot. Single gals out there beware, the Kevster's on the prowl again and as free as a bird. Look bird watchin aside folks the party's coming and now I'm in the final stage of confirming guests. Names close at the end of September Peeps, that's it. That's to make this the bash of bashes and one we'll all remember.
>
> Peeps, I'm banging on the drum now, more committed than ever, it's going to be better than AFKAP ever said yous Dudes and Dudesses. We're going to be Kings of the party Peeps, never mind Princes. I've got a few more confirmed guests yous all but remember we're on the last run in, if yous knows followers of this and they are Gen Peeps then nows the time to let them know. Countdown is beginning Peeps. Remember Dudesters we've got days left to finalize the deal plan the Peeps and plan the party.

....

27th September 1999

After a busy day he got back and prepared for Jane and Alexis. Apparently they had another announcement. They arrived at eight and chatted happily for an hour over several drinks. He served the food at nine. Alexis proclaimed it was the best thing he'd ever done. Kevin knew it wasn't and waited for why.

After they'd eaten Jane asked for vodka, one of Kevin's specials, the ones the orange juice was scared of. He poured three and sat down with them handing round his Bensons. Two vodka's later their intentions started to materialize. Jane went and made another three drinks then asked Kevin to sit down, listen and not comment until she had finished. She made him promise. Kevin agreed but still wasn't sure where this was all going.

'Kevin, we, I mean Alexis and I are really sad about Emily, we think, that is both of us think you were probably ready for a baby in your life.' Jane said and let it sit. He was ready to respond but Alexis jumped in. 'Sweetie, I know how hard it's been on you and you would make a perfect dad.'

Jane went and filled up their vodka glasses again and kept with the Julie tradition of frightening the orange juice away. She sat back down, threw each of them one of her Marlborough's and spoke in a drunken but sincere tone. 'Kevin, there could be.' 'Could be what Jane?' 'A baby Kevin, well two actually.' 'Jane you're talking riddles here, I don't understand.'

Alexis jumped in quickly and said softly 'Darling, we both know what we want from you as a wedding present.' 'You do? Let me know and I'll buy the best version there is.' 'Darling your present won't cost you any money, well maybe a bit in years to come in presents but only if you wish to.' 'Alexis, you two are making no sense.'

Jane entered the arena and said directly this time. 'Kevin, we are getting married, we want children, one each in fact, no more no less. We want you to be the biological father to our children.' Kevin laughed, 'What you want me to shoot into a test tube for you?' 'Darling, that's not what we're saying.' Alexis replied. 'Then what are you saying?'

Alexis grabbed his hand and said softly 'Kevin, your present to us is to father both our babies and not through artificial insemination but through physical love making.' He looked at them both in disbelief and said 'I need to go to bed.' Jane nodded and said 'Look we're both staying for a few days to talk this through with you.'

28ᵗʰ September 1999

Alexis emerged from the bedroom first at seven-thirty. She asked him if he was ok. 'Yeah fine darling just need to get cracking on with work.' 'Jane and I thought we'd take Sooty out and then get stuff to cook for you tonight.' 'Ok, sounds fine Babe, I'll just be busy for a few hours ok?'

Alexis nodded at him as she went back to the bedroom. She and Jane emerged together half an hour later. Jane said 'Hi Hon, you ok?' 'Yeah fine darling just busy.' 'Ok darling we'll take Sooty out for a long walk and give you time to concentrate.' 'Thanks darling, that'll help.'

Jane and Alexis left with Sooty at just after eight. Snowy was staying behind with Kevin and sat on his lap to make this known. They got back with Sooty at eleven and they both went for a shower. Kevin acknowledged them but apologized he needed to concentrate one hundred percent and had a few hours left to complete it.

They both went back out at twelve and said they'd be cooking him a surprise later. He stopped for five minutes and thanked them and hugged them both, one at a time before saying. 'Look we need to talk later ok and not through copious amounts of vodka. A glass or two of red will be ok though as I don't think I'll be able to talk about it completely sober.'

Alexis and Jane got back at five. Kevin smiled but was still lost for words. Jane went into the kitchen and Alexis sat down in near silence. He didn't have to wait long before Alexis went back onto her sales pitch. He appeared to listen but didn't take in a word. This was so mad and he wasn't going to agree with it. Alexis finished whatever she'd said by hugging him. She smelt so nice and so natural and so like she should be there all of the time but he still said nothing.

Jane joined them after ten minutes, a pre arranged time gap he was sure and sat down. She started her speech five minutes later. Kevin paid the same interested look to her but again heard nothing, this was nonsense and he was going to tell them.

A couple of wines later Jane served the food, this helped him a bit, as his head had started to go fuzzy with the red wine. The food was good, very good in fact and they all exchanged small talk eating. Alexis took the plates away and Jane started on another attack.

'Kevin, there's no one better, this is biological, not like a normal situation, you won't be burdened financially.' 'Jane, for fuck's sake, how long have you known me, when has money been my driving goal, I could have had a baby and that was taken away from me and now you two want me to produce two I'll have nothing to do with?'

She looked at him and then the tears started 'Kevin, how can you say that, you are my best friend in the world, Alexis is yours, we love you and will always be part of your life.' 'So explain Jane, make me understand because I'm struggling with it all.'

Jane went to reply but Alexis jumped in. 'Let me answer that please.' She said to the two of them but not looking at either. 'Kevin, there are two people I've loved in my whole life, both are sitting here now. Although I know and always have done that I'm a lesbian I chose you, eventually I chose you. This broke Jane's heart. You chose another, Claire. Jane and I somehow regrouped and realized we were meant to be together.'

She let this lie and stayed silent for a minute or two. 'You are the most influential and important person outside the two of us and would be next of kin or our family, whichever way you want it explained. We want children of our own, our own family and can't do that without help.'

He wanted to run, he wanted to scream and say no but her argument was winning and Kevin couldn't think of anything to fight back with. He managed 'Guys, how I can just be biological when we're so close? Answer me that?' Jane jumped back in and added 'Kevin, we'll be the parents, Alexis and I but you'll be involved as much as you want to be, at worst you'll be Uncle Kevin, at best their dad who doesn't live with their mums.'

He wanted to say no, he wanted to tell them it wouldn't work, it couldn't work, there was no way but he sat back, filled his glass up, took a Benson from his packet and said softly 'Ok.'

....

29th September 1999

He arrived home from work and the two of them were fussing over him as he walked in. 'Right you two, stop the shit, come on let's talk about practicalities before I change my mind! Look the both of you, we're adults, God I've seen and done everything with you both sexually and the thought of doing some of it again is a nice one, so let's get on with the detail ladies.'

He sat back, checked his watch, it was still only three-thirty but he needed a drink. He opened a bottle of Chablis. After his first glass he poured himself another, they were still sipping away on their first glass. 'Ok, how's this going to work?' And directed his line of sight to Jane.

She gathered herself before replying and said calmly 'My menstrual cycle suggests next week is the best time of the month, Alexis's the week after.' 'Ok Jane so what, you take it in turns to stay here, one of you one week and one the next and all I have to do is shag you both morning, noon and night for a week each, for the first month anyway?'

Jane looked at him before responding 'we'd sort of hoped we could both stay, but apart from that, yes you're right.' It was settled, they were moving in on Monday when Kevin got back from the weekend with his mother.

....

30ᵗʰ September 1999

Kevin worked all day. By the time he'd showered it was half four, beer o' clock he told himself and cracked open a can of cider from the four-pack that had been in the fridge for weeks. Before he knew it, it was seven o' clock and the four-pack had gone. He didn't want wine at the moment so walked to Toni's the local shop around the corner and bought another four-pack from Toni's fridge.

He checked his chicken and it was doing nicely, no need to move or turn it. He prepared the salad and set his blog page up:

> My most wonderful and patient party Peeps
> Yet again I've let yous all down by not being on line every day the last days. I won't apologize yous lot as can't. Too much going on but the Kevster's getting there my guys and gals, he really is. Yous may think I've been against my word but trust me Peeps, what's happened in the last two weeks wouldn't even make a book, it's been that bizarre. Right nows though

I'm dealing with that and concentrating on the party Peeps, days to go before the final line up.

On another front you single gals out there the Kevster is open to invitation for flirtation. That doesn't mean the Kevster is easy though, available but needs chasing you beauty pups out there. We are having the party of Nineteen Ninety Nine folks, make no bones about it and when it's over yous lot will all say 'I was there!!!'

Now was the time if ever there was one to update his personal page. He sat at it for over an hour before starting to write what was in his head. As he started to write the first word Sooty barked. Not a hello bark but a mad panicked and repeated bark.

Kevin couldn't understand it until he saw the smoke from the kitchen, the chicken, the bloody chicken. He ran to the kitchen and opened the oven door. The smoke alarms were going ten to the dozen. He grabbed the tray and ran outside with the burning mess. By the time he got to the bins the heat had resided from the burning pan, he threw the lot into the communal bin. He trudged back to his apartment and made his mind up on his future.

Before he got back to his personal page he had a chat with Snowy and Sooty and told them about the plans. They seemed to agree!

Dear Kevin

We got where we got by being stupid and not able to say no. The rest of your life however can be changed, it starts with the plan and ends with the ability to love and be faithful. Do what you need to do for Alexis and Jane and walk away, be Uncle Kevin not father Kevin, it's for them and you love them both. Tell Felicity about the plan this weekend and Jane and Alexis, tell them too. Oh and talk to Jack about it all! Good luck Kevin.

....

01st October 1999

He took a steady drive and arrived at his mums at five-thirty, he'd been lucky with the traffic. She hugged him on his arrival and told him she'd cooked a curry for tonight. 'Perfect mum, thanks.'

He said as he hugged her in a way he hadn't since he was a child. Felicity wasn't stupid and noticed but let it ride for now.

She fussed over Snowy and Sooty for well over an hour, then Kevin suggested they all go for a walk. They all went to the beach and took two nice slow non complicated hours over it. His mum then sat him down with one of her legendry vodka's, threw him a Benson and said 'Hit me with it son and all of it!' He smiled at her. He knew it had been coming and why he had gone there in the first place.

'I suppose mum, I should start at the beginning, I love Claire and every day without her hurts. That said I hurt for the fact I could have been a dad, Emily took that away from me mum!' He let it sit and they looked at each other in silence for a few minutes.

Felicity did what she'd learnt to do for years and listened without comment. Kevin acknowledged this and carried on. 'Mum, I was dealing with it, somehow and I don't know how, dealing with it.' He paused, looked at her passive face and continued. 'Alexis and Jane are getting married and I've agreed to be a surrogate or biological, or whatever you call it, father to their babies and be their best man.'

His mother looked at him and said softly 'Darling, that's all ok, and not what's troubling you so please spit it out?' Kevin smiled, his mother was amazing, and she knew how he thought. 'Ok mum, here goes. I love Claire and I want to dedicate my life to trying to get back to her but I can't do that if I chase her.'

She looked at him, her son and said 'And?' 'Well mum, I'm going to father Jane and Alexis's babies, have the party of Nineteen Ninety Nine and then I'm going to quit my job, move down here and open a Bistro. It will be called 'Julie's.'

She looked at him and said 'That's what you want?' 'Mum, I want Claire but if she ever comes back to me it will have to be here and nowhere else.' They hugged and Kevin went to bed for a very early night.

02nd October 1999

Getting up early Kevin took Snowy and Sooty for a long walk. He knew he had a session of questions and answers with his mother later so wanted a few hours to clear his head.

He breathed in the air and knew instantly he'd made the right choice, had the right idea, the right direction. He was handing his notice in on Monday and putting his apartment up for immediate sale. Somehow it all made sense, the picture of clarity had hit home.

As expected his mother was waiting as they got back. She told him she wanted a serious talk with him. He showered and they left to go to the pub, neutral ground, about half an hour's walk away. Sooty went with them but Snowy stayed for a nap.

'Ok Kevin, can we start with Jane and Alexis? I understand why they've asked you to do what they have, it's logical and on the balance a very good idea. All I want to say is that good ideas in principal don't always become good ideas practically. There's going to be so much emotion involved, how prepared for that are you, think about it?'

He looked at his mother and saw all the concern etched over her face before responding 'Mum, I know, look this is what I've decided. I will be Uncle Kevin to the both of them, when they're old enough they'll know I'm their biological father but their mothers are their parents. I will be involved in their lives and they'll be being brought up by two people I love as much as family.' 'And you can cope with that?' 'Yes mum I can. I thought about it all before I agreed.'

Felicity saw his glass was empty and went and got them another drink each. Sooty was sleeping in the sun. When she got back she continued. 'Ok darling, I've got that bit, what happens if you meet someone before a double conception?' 'God mum, talk English here please, I know we're in Wales and all that . . . but!'

She smiled at him and asked openly 'Kevin, how long do you think it takes to get a woman pregnant?' 'Well if the timings right through the cycle month I think, why?' 'Kevin it can take months and months, what if it does and you meet someone and then you move here?'

He looked at her and his smile dropped a little. 'Christ mum, I hadn't thought about that.' 'No shit darling.' 'Ok, ok, I've made the commitment so I'm going through with it, my life will have to go on hold and I can travel back and for and stay with them if push comes to shove.'

Felicity nodded at him and then redirected her focus. 'Ok darling, have you thought out the resigning thing properly?' 'Yes mum, look I could work where I am for the next ten years and probably have a couple of million in the bank, as it is I've already got over half a million and my apartment is paid for. That nets me around the eight hundred thousand mark, enough to buy a business and home in my opinion and then I can do what I want.'

She nodded at him and then said something he was completely surprised at 'Ok Kevin, I agree but I have in excess of five hundred thousand I don't know what to do with and I want to go into partnership with you on the restaurant. They had another drink each and headed back, Kevin told his mum he wanted to make a call. He grabbed his phone.

'Jack?' 'Kevin, Dude, how's it going?' 'Jack, better than you might imagine, look buddy, I really need to ask you a serious question.' 'Fire away Kevin.' 'How long were you the CEO of the Company?' 'Shit Kevin, how'd you figure it out?' 'I did some digging.' 'Ok, I was the youngest worldwide CEO the company ever had. I did it for five years but realized it affected my family too much so stood down.'

'Jack, what would you say if I told you I'm quitting?' 'I'd say I was disappointed because you were being groomed as the next me.' 'Jack I am quitting though.' 'Well now you've told me then my second comment comes into play, Kevin whatever you do is fine by me, you are my friend.' 'Jack, that's all I wanted to know, thanks and I'll speak to you in a few days. I just wanted you to be first to know is all. Bye my big friend.'

Yo Peeps

Kevster here and life changing news to come in the coming days and I will tells yous lot soon what it is. For nows though we are fast running out of days for the final list of Peeps for the Party you Dudesters, yes I've extended the deadline. Therefore the first thing I shall do is update the list my party planning guys and gals. Right Peeps it brakes the two hundred mark with days to go. Well done yous lot for rallying around. This is going to be the party of all parties' yous Dudes and Dudesses, make no mistake about that.

04th October 1999

He'd spent the previous day thinking how he would do what he needed to. Today he was in work early at eight, Mary and Deb not long after. When Jamie arrived Kevin briefed them on his decision. They were really shocked and there was a little panic in the air. 'Look you three, it's your time now, work like you do and, well the worlds your oyster. You're all talented people so go and do it!'

Hugs, tears and more hugs followed and Kevin held up his hand. 'Look Guys, Daniellie doesn't know yet, I need to phone him. They all nodded as Kevin went into his office. He dialed his boss's number it went to answer phone. He left a message and then rang Jack, it was the middle of the night in Canada but he needed to speak to his big friend.

Jack answered straight away. He told Kevin he'd been waiting for his call all night. Kevin had asked why and Jack explained Daniellie had been dismissed. Jack had told Jim of Kevin's intentions. Jim had promised Kevin a quarter of a million as a severance package plus he kept the car if he went now. Kevin asked why the pay off. Jack told him it was what should have been the share of the million split between Daniellie and Kevin.

Kevin acknowledged what his friend had said and called Mary, Deb and Jamie back into his office. He explained the Company decision, in a bit more detail and the fact Mary would be put in charge. They'd all expected this but not the fact that Kevin had been advised by the powers that be, that he had to finish today!

Kevin walked home via the estate agents. He gave his details and asked for a quick sale. To his huge surprise he had an offer without viewing an hour later. Somehow he sold his pad for twenty grand over the valuation but had to be out within twenty four hours.

He told Jane and Alexis that he Sooty and Snowy had to move in with them, whilst he serviced their baby making requests this month at least. Jane started on Kevin as soon as they'd eaten and had several attempts.

07th October 1999

After two more days of baby making duties. Kevin did his morning routine again, twice. Jane and Alexis said they'd take Sooty and Snowy out, Alexis adding they were swapping beds tonight, Jane's time was over and hers was in. 'Great darling, great.' They got back at eleven and Alexis pulled him straight into the bedroom. 'Come on guys give the fellas chance to regroup.' Alexis smiled and replied 'No time like now Kevin.'

He produced his third performance of the day and showered again. By the time it was six o' clock he craved a glass of white. Jane frowned at him and said 'Not too much darling.' 'That's it, I'll bloody well quit if you start managing what I eat, drink and smoke, darlings, my cock's on fire and not in a good way, I feel like a machine!'

They both looked at him and gave him a 'Well this is what it takes Dude look' 'Look guys I know, but I'm me and me has faults and cravings, you play it my way or my cock stays in my pants!' This seemed to do the trick. Jane got him a wine and Alexis a Benson. They then took a foot each and massaged them to relax him.

Following two more glasses of white and a full body massage, he felt more alive again. Jane was cooking him steak and Alexis spent the time pampering him. By the time he'd eaten they had him in bed by nine o' clock and Alexis said he could sleep. Kevin dropped off without a second's thought.

08ᵗʰ October 1999

Alexis had him up and at it at two, five and seven. He got up and went to the bathroom, running himself a bath. He laid and soaked for over an hour. He was beat and ruing the day he could let a rise go unused. Jane and Alexis did take Snowy and Sooty out and he went back to bed, alone for the two hours they were out.

When they got back he demanded a night on his own tonight, he needed to recuperate. He also said that tomorrow morning was Alexis' only option. They saw the look on his face so didn't argue. He left their place at one for a slow bow legged walk to meet Steve. He arrived at the Slug at half one and went straight for the cider.

Steve arrived at two, looked at Kevin and asked him what was wrong. 'Nothing Steve, why ask?' 'Kevin you look like you're sitting on hot coals.' 'Steve, I thought I had it under control.' 'What under control?' 'Oh nothing much buddy just my swollen piece.' Steve looked at him for an explanation but Kevin shrugged and said 'Another day Steve, another day.'

When he got back the place was empty. He saw a note on the kitchen top. He read it and smiled. Jane and Alexis had taken Sooty and Snowy out to one of their friends. Kevin had the night to himself.

> Dearest Dudes and Dudesses
> Yet again I've been neglecting yous all and am not happy with myself. God there are reasons but no doubt no different to what yous lot go through on a day by day basis. Well Peeps the final list is drawn, there are a few more confirmed Peeps to add so here goes:
> That's it folks, the final Party Peeps and by my reckoning two twenty Dudesters, how cool's that? My next week is tied up but after that Peeps, I'm off to Wales to plan. This is going to be so rock and roll and drum and base Peepsters, we're going to party like its nineteen ninety nine!
> For now though yous lot that's as much as we've all got. Be good guys and gals, the time is almost here, we are having it, bigger and better than I could have hoped and it's all down to yous lot.

He closed the lap top down and went for a good night's sleep at half-eight. He knew he had chores in the morning but now felt ready, the day off had really helped. As his head hit the pillow he fell into a heavy and satisfied sleep.

12ᵗʰ October 1999

Following three more days of solid baby making duties Alexis had announced her time had passed. A relieved Kevin told them both he was driving to Swansea to stay at Felicity's. Jane jumped in and said 'Don't worry darling, we've discussed this and we'll come and see you next month, only if we have to though.' 'Great, thanks Jane, I'm over the moon!' He grabbed Snowy and Sooty and left feeling somewhat relieved. They arrived at his Mum's by six. She'd cooked stew, he ate hungrily and they had a few wines before he retreated to his bedroom at eight. Tonight he needed sleep and a long one.

....

13th October 1999

Sooty was on top of him and licking him as if his life depended on it. Taking the hint he woke up, got out of bed and jumped straight into the shower. Forty minutes later he emerged fresh, clean and shaven and feeling better than he had done in weeks.

He walked into the kitchen and his mum had a cup of tea ready. 'Darling, I took Snowy and Sooty out earlier for an hour and a half, we need to talk and start to make some plans. Your mother has been a busy girl.'

They arrived in St Anne's, a costal part of the area. There was a plot of land for sale. It overlooked the sea and was idyllic. Felicity looked at her son and said 'One fifty darling and in my opinion a bargain.' 'Wow mum, how big is the plot?' 'Just under three acres, for cash I reckon you'd get it for a ton.' 'Mum, this is perfect.' 'I know darling, told you I'd been busy.'

He looked around and smiled 'Mum, this is it, I want it.' 'Good job darling because I've bought it for one hundred thousand cash.' 'Mum, I'm a bit confused here.' 'No need darling my investment in the restaurant has dropped by the same amount but we're still fifty, fifty ok?' 'Deal mum, shit!' 'Thanks might have been a better word.' 'Shit mum, thanks!' 'Glad to see you're back on form.' 'You know me mum, like a bouncy castle, keep springing back up with enough air in me.'

'Come on. There's somewhere else I want you to see.' They walked for twenty minutes and came up to a rundown looking building, still by the sea. 'Don't look at the building yet darling but look at the location and its proximity to locals, visitors, passersby, the roads to it. This is location heaven.'

Kevin took in the scene and agreed with his mother before adding, 'Mum, two things, first this needs a lot of work and second I want it to be the start of many, isn't this a bit remote?' 'Kevin, think, this is so you, make this work and then decide on world domination, it's perfect.' He looked again and it hit him, this was what he wanted, where he wanted to be, the question was, he thought silently, did he have enough to make it work?

'Mum, it is ideal, but it's going to be too much to buy and restore into a restaurant!' 'No son it won't, I bought it for fifty grand, sold as seen. He looked around in awe of the view and for one of the odd moments in his life was speechless. His mother grabbed his hand and kissed him on the cheek. 'Well darling, spit it out!' 'Mum, shit!' They walked back to the car without talking. Kevin was on fire with excitement and just took in the scene. He was in a place he wanted to be and wanted to make his.

....

14th October 1999

It was raining hard but Sooty was undeterred as Kevin got him ready for his walk. They got to the beach and he went at it like a dog with two. The next thing Kevin saw was a black Labrador running towards Sooty. The two of them seemed like long lost brothers and ran and chased each other as if both their lives depended on it. Kevin was smiling and saw them heading towards him. Neither of the dogs slowed and both smashed into and pole-axed him.

His owner came running over to apologize. Kevin told him not to worry he'd stick it on his blog later for everyone to laugh at. 'Sounds like something the guy I follow would do.' The Stanger said before introducing himself 'Hitesh, Tesh for short.' 'Kevin, Kevster for long.' Tesh giggled.

By the time they departed they had agreed to go out tonight, Tesh had said he was going to show Kevin wild, wild Swansea. 'No better night out on the planet.' Tesh said as he left with his dog Rufus.

The taxi arrived at six-thirty and he was in Wine Street by ten to seven. He ordered a glass of Chardonnay to begin with and sat looking around. He lit a Benson and a young lady introduced herself as Louisa. She was blond and very pretty and asked if she could pinch a cigarette, Kevin winked, passed her a cigarette and they started to chat. Her friend turned up and they left before Tesh arrived.

Tesh ordered a bottle of champagne for the both of them and said 'Right my friend tonight is challenge night.' 'Sorry?' 'We have two challenges to complete, one each. I've put them on paper and we pick one. Whatever's on the paper is the challenge we have to complete.' He said and getting ten pieces of folded card from his inside pocket.

Kevin looked at him very skeptically but the champagne and wine were kicking in so he thought sod it. He picked a card. 'Don't open it yet!' Tesh instructed and then picked one himself. 'Right on the count of three Kevin we open each other's cards and then you read mine first, then I read yours.' They swapped cards, Tesh counted down from three and they both opened the cards.

Kevin opened his card and said strongly 'Monica Lewinsky' Tesh opened his and said 'Talking the Pants Off.' Kevin looked at him and said 'Ok mate, what next, what the hell do these mean?' Tesh smiled and said 'Kevin, drink some champagne, I'm off to get another bottle and a few cigars.' Lighting up a Benson he wondered what the hell Tesh was on about but liked the wicked smile he left to go to the bar with.

Tesh returned with another bottle of champagne and three Kind Edward cigars. Kevin looked at him but Tesh told him to drink whilst he explained. The Monica Lewinsky thing was all to do with the cigar and the accusation against Clinton. Tesh giggled and said 'Guess I drew the short straw buddy.' Kevin nearly swallowed the cigarette he was smoking. Tesh looked at Kevin with another wicked grin and said 'Your job is far easier all you just have to talk the pants off a lady.' Kevin gasped further.

Kevin looked at him blankly but poured them a glass each and lit up his cigar. Within five minutes two girls approached them. 'Hi my name's Wanda.' The one said 'Yeah and I'm Terri, can we sit with you two?' Tesh nodded and disappeared for a few minutes. He was back with yet another bottle of champagne and two more glasses.

Tesh was immediately after Terri and smoked his cigar giggling with her for well over forty minutes. She left to go to the loo and took the spare King Edward with her. She came back five minutes later, put the cigar in Tesh's mouth, lit it and said 'There you go darling, a Monica Lewinsky!'

This time Kevin did choke and coughed up half a glass of champagne. Tesh sat back pulling on his cigar and said 'See Kevin, that was play time, your turn now.' Kevin was ready to leave but saw Louisa and her friend Sally. Louisa made a beeline for him. Tesh was very drunk and kept nudging Kevin and asking him for a new cigar.

Louisa asked Kevin what on earth Tesh was banging on about. He went to go for a line, cocked it up from the outset and blurted the truth out. She looked at him, smiled and whispered 'My pants for your number and a meal tomorrow, deal?' 'You mean it?' 'Kevin I don't often offer my pants!' 'Ok, deal!'

Louisa disappeared and returned five minutes later and handed Kevin a bright white pair of silky panties. Tesh barked a laugh but added 'How do I know they're yours?' Louisa laughed and lifted her short skirt up. Tesh screamed in laughter, Kevin felt uncomfortable in his own pants!

15ᵗʰ October 1999

He wanted to make one call before Louisa arrived. 'Oliver?' 'Kevin, is that you?' 'Yup' 'Kev me old mucker, what's happening Dude?' 'Well, I've bought what will be my restaurant and would really appreciate some ideas, how'd you fancy a meal on me in Swansea?' 'Kevin, I don't get much time off but what about Wednesday next week?'

Louisa arrived at twenty to eight. Kevin was nearly finished on his first bottle of Chablis. She came in and Snowy and Sooty came out to check her out. She seemed to pass the first test, Snowy liked her.

Louisa looked stunning, dressed in a short black skirt and a bright red top, against her blond hair she rivaled models Kevin had seen on TV and in the highest quality Women's magazines. 'Shit Louisa, you look stunning!' Escaped his mouth before he got his brain into gear.

She just beamed at him 'Gosh Kevin you know how to give a compliment!' 'Well, the thing is my mouth engages before I think sometimes, I should had said hello and hugged you first, forgot my manners!' She screamed with laughter and said 'Kevin, you're so funny.' 'My middle name Babe' He replied without thought.

She hugged him and kissed him hard 'Didn't wear pants tonight either Kevin, thought at least that way I wouldn't lose another pair, that is unless you're going to give me back my pair from last night?' He looked at her, remembered and went red. 'Sorry Louisa, I think Tesh has them but I'm not sure.'

Kevin had invited her for the meal with Oliver. Just before she left she kissed him hard and pushed his hand onto her naked backside underneath her skirt. 'All to come, my dear Kevin, all to come.'

....

17th October 1999

Getting up he joined his mother in the kitchen. 'By the way mum, we have guests on Wednesday.' 'We do?' 'Yes, Oliver's going to come and look at the restaurant project. He's bringing Jude and they're staying the night, I'm going to cook.' 'They are, and you are?' 'Yes and Louisa's coming too.' 'She is?' 'Yes mum, why don't you invite your secret man?' 'That would be because I don't have one, Kevin who is Louisa darling?' 'I met her on the weekend mum, she's great.'

Felicity went for what Kevin called a Nanny Nap. He half drifted off himself when his mobile went off. It took him a while to resister what the noise was but answered a little groggily after several rings.

'Kevin, Kevin, Kevin.' 'Jane?' 'Kevin, Kevin.' 'Jane what, calm down, breathe, tell me because I can't decipher what you're currently gabbing on about.' 'Ok Kevin, Kevin, Kevin.' 'Jane?' 'Kevin God Kevin, God.' 'Jane, sense please?' 'Oh shit, here goes then, Kevin, I missed my period, I took the test Kevin, I'm only bloody well pregnant!' 'Shit Jane, shit.' 'I know, I know.' 'Shit Jane, shit!' 'Kevin, Kevin, Kevin.' 'Jane, we've been there.' 'No Kevin, no Kevin.' 'Jane, you're back to making no sense!' 'Kevin, Alexis went and took the test at the same time, she's pregnant too!' 'Jane, Jane, Jane!' 'I know, I know, I know!' 'Jane, are you winding me up?' 'No darling, no, it's all for real, all for real, can you believe it?' 'No, no, no!' 'Kevin, it's real, real real. We've done it, you've done it we've all bloody well done it!'

He hit the vodka with some vengeance, the orange as normal was a frightened partner. His mother joined him at six o' clock and saw him sitting there with the bottle of vodka on the table and an ash tray with several smoked Bensons in it.

'Join you darling?' 'Sure mum.' 'Come on what's happened?' 'Jane rang, she says she's pregnant and Alexis took the test on the off chance and she reckons she is too!' His mother looked at him before saying 'And?' 'Well mum, I'm a bit shocked it's so soon.' 'Me too Kevin but doesn't that make it a bit easier?' 'I suppose. Mum?' 'Yes Kevin?' 'You know I'm going to have to go to see them both tomorrow don't you?' 'I wouldn't expect anything else.'

18ᵗʰ October 1999

He used the car's power today, not holding back. The thing flew and hugged the road without effort. He was back at their flat by nine-ten. He opened the door and burst in. They were both sitting there, at the breakfast table with grins he'd never seen on them before. Jane spoke first 'Coffee daring?'

He spent the day with them and they all agreed some ground rules. He was Uncle Kevin and Felicity was Gran. 'The other condition is no more friendly shags and as you're getting married no more sleeping together naked, pants on at least!' Kevin said in his most serious tone. They burst into laughter and Jane and Alexis said together 'You're a funny guy Kevin.' They all then roared together 'My middle name!'

He was back at his mums at four o' clock. He hit bed some vodka wine induced hours later sort of elated, confused but elated he eventually thought before sleep came.

19ᵗʰ October 1999

He took Sooty out alone this morning and bumped into Tesh and Rufus. The two of them went at like the crazy dogs they were. He and Tesh watched them for the best part of an hour until both the dogs came back, completely beat. 'Tesh, look mate, I've got a bit of a dinner party tomorrow night, a trial for some of my food for the restaurant, do you fancy coming?' 'Wow Kevin, that'd be great, alone or with company?' 'Nah mate company please.' 'Great, I'll bring Clarissa, she works in London but she'll drive down for this no problem. I've got to warn you though she's a bit racist.' 'Tesh, I take it she's a girlfriend?' 'Yeah mate, been together over three years but she's definitely a racist.' 'I don't get it mate.' 'Me neither.'

20ᵗʰ October 1999

Oliver and Jude arrived early afternoon and Kevin took them to the restaurant or the shell that would become the restaurant. Oliver looked and looked but didn't say much. They stayed for an hour and he still hadn't commented. When they were back at Felicity's Oliver asked if he had a pad, he wanted to make some notes. Felicity sorted him out and Kevin opened a bottle of red and a bottle of white.

Oliver wrote notes on his pad and asked Kevin for a private half an hour. They both went to the dining room. 'Kevin, me old mucker, how the hell did you find that place?' 'Sorry mate, I don't understand.' 'The location Dude, it's perfect for what you're doing, twelve months ago it would have been worthless but the change in eating habits and fashion make it perfect Kevin, just perfect.'

Kevin sat back, looked at Oliver and said 'It was all my own work. Years of research and knowing what I wanted.' 'Shit Kevin, I didn't think you had that deep routed desire.' 'Well mate, have a mother like mine, set her on her way and she delivers, it was her idea, I can't take any credit for the location or the building.' 'Ok Kevin, at least you keep up with no bullshit, I like that about you.'

Kevin spent the next half an hour going through his ideas. Oliver was really impressed and asked if he could invest now. Oliver offered to finance the chain to ten restaurants if Julie's took off.

Louisa arrived at seven and was closely followed by Tesh and his girlfriend Clarissa. Louisa was in awe with the fact she was in the same room as Oliver James. Tesh didn't care, his girlfriend was really moaning at him. Kevin couldn't hear what, but the look on her face said it wasn't nice for Tesh.

Kevin introduced everyone and gave them champagne. Louisa was getting on like a house on fire with Felicity and Jude, Clarissa was telling Oliver all about her job, she entertained all top stars on several hospitality functions. Kevin looked at Oliver who whispered behind Clarissa's back 'Cow!' He nearly choked on his champagne.

Oliver turned to Tesh and asked him if he'd been to any of Clarissa's work functions. Tesh said he'd been once but Clarissa hadn't taken him again. 'Why mate?' Oliver asked intrigued. 'She doesn't like them knowing she's going out with an Indian, funny thing is mate I was born in Kenya!!'

Kevin retreated into the kitchen and didn't even get to the starters before he heard a large commotion. He ran into the room to see Clarissa grabbing her bag and coat and storming off. 'What the hell happened?' He asked the silent room.

Tesh answered 'Kevin, I think we just broke up!' Oliver roared and roared. 'Kevin, she punched him, she actually punched him, Tesh, I'm sorry mate but that's the funniest thing I've ever seen.' Tesh was laughing too but Louisa, Jude and Felicity looked horrified.

Kevin served his starter and had chilled Chablis on the table ready. As they ate Tesh started on his story. 'I asked her to calm down on the bragging as it was getting boring for everyone else. She told me to fuck off adding what did I know, I was just a stupid Pakki bastard.' They all looked at him horrified. 'Don't worry guys she's always been like that. I told her firstly I was born in Kenya and am now British and she needed to calm down.' 'Yes then Tesh?' 'She got all shitty and said she was going so I told her not to waste any time and take her fat ass out of here.' 'You said that to her mate?' 'Yup and it felt good.' 'Then mate?' 'She punched me Kevin, a huge swinging right.'

Kevin looked at all of them horrified and said 'then?' Oliver jumped in and with tears of laugher said 'He slapped her back Kevin, sorry Tesh but it was so funny and your slap wouldn't have hurt a fly.' 'Well I didn't want to retaliate in any way but it was a reaction shot and I tried to stop it mid action.' Oliver was now crying with laughter.

Kevin went back to the kitchen and served the main course, Oliver still refusing to comment and by nine he had dessert on the table. Felicity grabbed Louisa and Jude and they took the dishes to the kitchen.

Oliver asked if he had any decent cigars and a good brandy. Kevin grabbed a few Cubans and his mother's decanter. Oliver sat sipping his cognac and still smiling at Tesh. 'Right first boys, let's talk entertainment, my best night for ages me old mates, I haven't laughed so much in years. Tesh, sorry that's at your expense but it was so funny.'

'Kevin, the starters were good, a little obvious and safe but well executed. The cheesecake and vanilla cream divine, I was impressed with that. The pasta and sauce Kevin was the best I think I've eaten, it was perfection mate, top bol!'

Tesh left at midnight and Oliver and Jude went to bed not long afterwards. Felicity eying the scene went to bed at quarter past. Louisa looked at Kevin and said 'Wow, that was fantastic Kevin, all of it, I was so impressed.' Kevin smiled and led her to his bed.

....

21st October 1999

Felicity got back from walking Sooty at one o' clock. They sat down over coffee and Kevin told her of the way he was considering splitting his cash. 'No son, the house is a million, I've already advised Jeremy.' 'Mum, first of all who the hell is Jeremy and second I don't have a million.'

She looked at him and smiled. 'Firstly darling Jeremy is the architect and a friend and secondly I've already given him an advance of two hundred and fifty thousand, with your seven fifty that adds to a million in my head.'

Kevin was about to argue when Felicity dropped yet another bombshell 'Kevin, I've put another two fifty into the restaurant project, call it an early inheritance, I want you to have money left over.' 'Mum, it's all too much, what about you and the money you need?' 'Kevin, I still have more left than I can spend.'

They hugged but Felicity added 'Kevin, I want your heart and soul in this.' 'You've got it mum I'll change my middle name if you want?' 'Funny guy, look last night showed me what I'd already done was worth it, Kevin, you're going to kick ass on this one and we'll have more money than we can both spend in the next ten years, I'm sure of it.'

....

22nd October 1999

Hi Peeps, Kevster here

Yous lot will be pleased to know the Kevster's been a busy boy in the bed department. Hey, no puns, Peeps. As there are so many of us I've had to think how and where we all sleep yous lot. I sat here pondering and thought how can the Kevster get this sorted? I mean yous lot, how do you get two hundred tired Dudesters into one place without huge cost?

It hit me Guys and Gals as I took a walk in the park and saw a tent. I knows what yous are thinking, a minimum of probably one hundred tents for two hundred Peeps. So I thought again my party planning friends and came up with Marquees. The Kevster Peeps has secured enough Marquees for food and sleeps yous lot, all yous lot have to bring is a sleeping bag. If any of yous want to share a bag then feel free, it is the season of goodwill after all.

Right yous lot I have arranged us lot a Bar-B-Q before we go to Cardiff, rides into the Centre and rides back and full English in the morning Peeps. How cool am I? All I have next is the band Dudesters, yes, there's going to be a band Peeps, all courtesy of the Kevster.

Kevin was on his third cider by the time Tesh arrived at the Wine Press at twenty to eight. 'Sorry Kevin, one thing and another, you know?' 'Yeah mate, come on your round?' Tesh nodded and came back with a bottle of champagne. Tesh's mate Pete arrived at eight and said he was sorry for being late. Tesh told him that was rubbish as he was always late. Pete smiled a cheeky smile and Kevin realized straight away he'd get on with this bloke.

Pete bought another bottle of champagne and Kevin reciprocated before they moved on to the next bar. Before Kevin knew it they'd been to seven bars and he was as struggling to stand without swaying, Tesh was about twice as bad but Pete was on one.

Pete came back with a bottle of tequila, a bowl of sliced lemons and a bowl of salt. Tesh winced and Kevin just looked. He thought he felt drunk now but realized there was so much more to come with huge dread.

Twelve midnight came and Tesh and Pete were fit for nothing else other than a Kebab. Kevin was starving too. They queued up with the rest of the night owls. Kevin ordered a large donner with chili sauce and salad, Tesh a shish kebab with coleslaw and Pete a large donner, large shish, chips, a pie, fishcake and curry sauce. Kevin looked at Pete and said 'You'll eat all that?' 'You bet Kevin, I'm starving!'

23rd October 1999

Kevin woke with a head like thunder but Sooty and Snowy were making demands to go out. He dragged his hung-over body around for an hour and a half before slouching back feeling a little better.

Kevin set about creating one of his starter ideas for the restaurant, Fish and Chip. A small piece of cod in a vodka and tonic batter fried in beef dripping, served on one large potato fritter cooked three times with homemade tartar sauce.

The prep didn't take long and he served it at six. It was perfection, just enough for a starter. He did the math's on bulk buying and reckoned on just under a fiver he'd make around forty percent. By seven he was going to call Jane, Alexis and Jack but fell asleep on the sofa. Waking at nine he went to bed with Snowy and Sooty in tow.

24th October 1999

Felicity walked in as he got back from his walk with his two babies. 'Hi mum.' 'Hi Kevin everything ok?' 'Yeah, had a good night out Friday and spent yesterday recovering but did come up with a few more dishes for the menu. How was your trip?' 'Ok, I'm getting there I think.' 'Getting where mum?' 'Kevin not now ok' 'Ok mum, look I've invited Tesh and Pete around tomorrow night to try two of the new dishes, is that ok?' 'Yeah fine, it's good you're thinking that way. Look let me have a shower and I'm taking you to the pub.'

Three drinks in and Jeremy, the architect arrived. He joined them at their table and got another round in. He then put plans for Kevin's house on the table and spent two hours going through them. Kevin was in awe.

They got back and Felicity went for a nap, throwing a cushion at him when he'd shouted 'Lover boy wore you out did he mother?' He phoned Jack but got the answer phone before retreating himself.

....

25ᵗʰ October 1999

Kevin had sessions with two builders today and felt confident between them they could deliver the project, Gary from Cosgrove's and Roy from Silvers. They were going to get back to him with quotes and completion dates later in the week.

He was all set by seven and jumped in the shower and changed. By the time he got back down at half-past Tesh and Pete were already there and chatting to Felicity. The first course was on the table by eight-fifteen 'Evil Eggs Julie' he announced.

Each plate had half a fresh peeled avocado pear, wrapped in smoked salmon with a peeled soft boiled egg positioned in the pear half. He also served a homemade lemon mayonnaise with it. They had champagne with this and Pete was in heaven. 'Look Kevin, next time can I have two of these?' 'There's a couple left in the kitchen if you want more mate' 'Kevin, you joking I'll have whatever's left if it's on offer.'

Tesh looked at Felicity and sniggered as Kevin went and did Pete two more. The rest of them thought it was plenty for a starter. Pete finished and proclaimed the best grub he'd ever eaten. 'A compliment I think.' Tesh added.

Kevin smiled and went into the kitchen, returning with two bottles of Chilean red wine. 'Let them rest for five and I'll be in for a cigarette, just need to get the next stage going.' He said and went back into the kitchen. At nine he served what he thought would be one of his signature dishes. It was fillet steak, served on a potato cake with a red wine, port, chili and redcurrant sauce with steamed leeks.

They ate and drank for the next half an hour. Pete looked up and with a bit of an apologetic look on his face, 'Any more Kevin?' They all roared but Kevin had already prepared enough to give Pete a second helping. Pete's eyes lit up as Kevin returned with a second plate.

They all laughed but Pete stood up and held his glass up. 'Kevin, that's the best nosh I've ever eaten. Tesh said we'd be guinea pigs tonight. All I want to add is that I'll be your pig any time!' Kevin was made up his ideas seemed to have worked. As long as Swansea and the world weren't full of Pete and Jacks he might do ok.

....

26th October 1999

He rang Richard, knowing it was early and he'd probably be moaned at but didn't care. Richard's view was vital. 'Richard.' 'Kevin, is that you and if it is why the hell are you calling so early?' 'Nice to hear your voice too buddy' 'Kevin, for God's sake it's before twelve, I don't surface on my day off before three! Look Kevin, can you give me five to wake up and I'll ring you back?'

He smiled to himself and made a strong coffee. Richard would moan like a bugger when he rang back, he needed to be alert. His phone went off half an hour later. 'Kevin.' 'Richard, you're awake now?' 'Look you, anyone else who disturbed my sleep on my day off I'd tell to bugger off and stick my finger up to the phone.' 'Yeah, but me, you'll bitch and moan for a while and then be ok?' 'Kevin, sorry, I'm a complete grouch, you must have called for a reason.' 'Yeah mate, I need your help.' 'You do?' 'Yeah, I want you to review my menu.' 'Ok, look I can get Sunday off, will that do?' 'Richard, that'd be wicked.' 'Look Mr Julie, I'm not driving all that way, I'll come by train and you can pick me up from the station.'

....

27th October 1999

Dog and cat kisses stirred him from sleep. Getting the hint he got up and took them both for a walk. He was back by eleven-thirty and fed them both. He spent an hour on another menu idea and then turned his lap top to his blog page:

> Dearest beloved and betrothed Peeps
> Kevster here and only, might I repeat only seventy three days to go yous lot. Wow, wow and a big wow! Guys and Gals were nearly into two, that's two months before we party Dudesters. Everything yous lot is on song, food for cooking and drinks for drinking Peeps, but all in safe storage yous lot all under the Kevster control.

Moving onto serious notes, the Kevster will be opening the restaurant in Swansea next year Peeps, as the dates come in I will of course let yous lot know and yes Peeps, you will get discount, that is if you're a party Peep. Big loves to my Canadian friend and his family and his bear Dudesters. Jack's the man that can and he's coming to see the Kevster soon. Don't yous worry though the bear stays behind although this makes yours truly really sad, keep happy, keep party planning and keep loving the world and all its inhabitants?

Roy from Silver's rang and offered a job price of seven hundred and fifty for the house. Kevin relayed the information to his mother. She looked pleased but said she was going to ring Jeremy. He sat back and drank his red wine and lit a Benson. Felicity came back and said 'Jeremy reckons seven fifty is fifty less than the best he would have predicted but wants to check this Silver character out.' Kevin nodded and they sat and chatted over a couple more bottles of red. Kevin saw midnight before his head hit the pillow.

....

28th October 1999

Kevin met his mother at the breakfast table and asked if she'd take Sooty for his walk. She agreed and asked what he was going to do. 'Crack on with the menu mum, Richard's coming on Sunday and I need to be ready.'

Felicity left with Sooty at eight o' clock, Snowy was staying with Kevin. He went straight to work, firstly on a catch phrase for the restaurant. He nailed it by eleven.

'Julies'
Devilishly Good Food

His starters were almost finished so he concentrated on that part of the menu. He was sure Richard would like the taste but wanted gimmick in the menu to appeal to all comers. He thought about how he wanted it presented and put it to paper for the first time.

Julies Evil Starters

Fiery Fish and Chip
*Prime Line caught Cod in a Vodka and Tonic Batter deep
fried in Beef Dripping with a homemade Tartar Sauce
served on a thrice cooked single Chip Fritter.*

Evil Eggs Julie
*Absolutely ripe half an Avocado Pear, wrapped in finest
Scottish Smoked Salmon with a peeled Soft Boiled Egg
sitting in the well of the Pear with Homemade Lemon
Mayonnaise.*

Scary Salty Spears
*Freshly sourced Asparagus Spears, wrapped in the
Best Italian Pancetta and griddled. Served with a Blue
Cheese White Wine sauce.*

Killer Kebabs
*Top quality Lamb Shoulder, smashed wafer thin and
marinated in Chili and Garlic and Fried Golden. Served
in Bite Sized griddled Tortillas with Crispy Salad and a
Sweet and Sour Hot Sauce.*

Quiche Lucifer
*The best Chili, Courgette and Broccoli Egg Tart you'll
ever eat. Served with Marinated Beetroot, Onion,
Tomato Salad and a Chili Jam.*

Monster Mushroom Medley
*Fried Mushroom Extravaganza with Garlic, Cheese,
Wine and Fresh herbs. Served with homemade Garlic
Bread and Light Wine Sauce.*

His mother came back down after cleaning herself and Sooty
up and asked to see his menu to date. He showed her the starters
list and the theme of the restaurant. She took well over twenty
minutes reviewing the menu and concept and then stood up and
walked to the kitchen without saying a word.

She walked back in five minutes later smiling brightly with two glasses, and a bottle of champagne. 'Kevin my darling, you're nailing this!' They were on their second bottle when the phone went. Felicity answered. 'Kevin, it's for you, Gary Cosgrove.' Gary had offered eight hundred and twenty for the house but one hundred and fifty and a twelve week completion on the restaurant project. Kevin put the phone down and told his mother everything Gary had said. 'Look darling, I say we get drunk tonight and review it in the morning over coffee with Jeremy.' 'Deal mum.'

....

29ᵗʰ October 1999

He started to crack on with the menu and his mother asked if he wanted her to do the shopping. 'Mum, that'd be such a huge help.' He gave her a long list and several twenty pound notes out of his wallet.

Julies Hot Mains

Devil's Fillet Steak
The best Aberdeen Angus Fillet Steak, served on a Potato Cake in a Red Wine, Port, Redcurrant and Hot Chili sauce with Freshest Steamed Welsh Leek

Old Nick's Sweet Baby Lamb
Finest Welsh Rack of Lamb Roasted with Mint and Rosemary. Served with Garlic Thyme Potatoes and a Minted Red Wine Sauce with Seasonal Greens.

Julie's Hell of a Big Meat Pasta
Home reared Belly Pork and Skirt Beef Meat Sauce with Tomato, Oregano and Secret Spices served with Home Made Spaghetti and Freshly Baked Garlic and Parsley Bread.

Fiendish Felicity's Mushroom Bake
The best Flat Mushrooms the season has to offer with Asparagus, Leek, Garlic, Chili and Cream Saffron Sauce. Served with Home Made Crunchy Tortilla Chips.

Frighteningly Fishy Super Supper
Catch of the Day, coated in Secret Breadcrumb Mix with warm Green Vegetable Medley in a Wine and Dill Sauce with Parmesan Potatoes.

More Evil Eggs Julie
Two Sweet Creamy Fresh Avocado Pears, wrapped in Scottish Smoked Salmon served in individual Savoy Cabbage Baskets with Peeled Soft Boiled Eggs served with a Home Made Lemon Mayonnaise.

Julies Wickedly Naughty Desserts

Sacrificial Sweet Spicy Pudding
Syrup and Ginger Based Pudding sat on top of Crunchy Biscuit with Vanilla and Brandy Infused Cream

Killer Chocolate Surprise
Melted Belgium Chocolate over a cooked Pastry Case, cracked in the middle, stuffed with Strawberries and served with Whisky Butter and Clotted Cream

Fiery Pear Pie
Internationally Sourced Fresh Pears, peeled, halved and baked in a Puff Pastry Case and served with Homemade Rum Custard

Flaming Perfect Peach
Peaches and Peach Snaps in a Peach Vodka and Cranberry Cocktail. Light, Bright and packs a real Punch.

Prince of Darkness Pig-Out
Chocolate Cake, Vanilla Ice Cream, Ginger and Rum Sponge served in a Cream Strawberry Sauce with Chocolate and Biscuit Bombs.

Nastily Nice Naughty Nosh
Apples, Blackberries, Cherries and Brandy Liqueur on a crushed Shortbread base with Cherry Custard

Felicity got back and told Kevin she'd met Jeremy and he advised to go with Silver's for the house and Cosgrove's for the restaurant. Kevin dialed Roy first. He agreed seven hundred and forty and a three month completion deadline. Gary was next, answer phone, so left a message for Gary to ring back indicating it was good news on the restaurant project. 'Come on then mum, that's done we need to prepare for Pete.' 'Oh God darling I forgot he was coming, did we buy enough food?' 'Hey mum, back to being funny, I like it.'

Pete arrived at quarter to eight. Kevin laughed and gave him a large glass of red and told him he had twenty minutes to wait. He served the Mushroom mains dish first and had another plate ready in reserve. Pete ate the first without blinking, Kevin wondering if he actually breathed. Kevin gave him the second plate and then served the dessert. Pete ate it all and on cue asked for more. By the time he'd finished Kevin asked him what he thought. 'Kev, considering there was no meat man, top scran.'

....

31ˢᵗ October 1999

He'd had another lazy day yesterday and slept through it in the main. Richard was arriving at the station at three-thirty. He went shopping, he had a lot to do in a short space of time, food for thought for the future he thought and liked to pun too. He was funny after all!

As he was finalizing his shopping his mobile went. Jack had called to say he'd been asked to come to the UK early in November and was coming to see Kevin in Swansea. Kevin was made up. If only he could finalize the deal with Cosgrove's, he could show Jack his dream then. He suspected Gary didn't do business over the weekend. This gave him a little doubt about his commitment.

He got back at eleven. He saw a van and had a huge smile on his face. The name on the side of the van said Cosgrove's. He got into the kitchen with all his bags in one trip, some feat considering the amount he'd bought.

Gary was drinking tea with his mother and chatting away. 'Kevin, sorry for dropping in but one of the kids messed with my phone and I only realized you'd left a message this morning. I thought I'd better come over as I didn't want you to think I wasn't committed as it's the weekend.'

Felicity went to collect Richard. Kevin was ready in time for their return. 'Bloody trains, bloody weather, does it ever stop raining here?' Richard said quickly adding 'White wine please and large.' They spent the next hour going through Kevin's concept for the restaurant and the menu. 'I like it, I do, I really do, mm, yes more bistro than Michelin but I like it.'

Richard asked what he was sampling tonight and Kevin just said 'surprise but three friends are coming, Pete, Tesh and Louisa.' 'I take it the latter is a new Julie conquest?' 'Something like that Richard, maybe, I'm not that sure actually.' He put the menu cards on the table at seven and Richard ran to have a look.

Louisa arrived at seven-thirty and Kevin introduced her to Richard. Pete and Tesh arrived not long after so he asked Louisa to help him in the kitchen. 'You look lovely.' 'Thanks Kevin, you're looking pretty hot too.' 'Compliments, I am honored, no calls for a week or so but compliments.' 'Look Kevin, not now please, I'm here for the night, can we talk about that later?'

He carried on cooking and told Louisa he was loading the table a course at a time. There would be six starters, and then the same with the mains and desserts. 'That's a lot Kevin. I won't get through it all.' 'No need darling, taste is what I want discussed tonight and besides Pete will finish what's left.'

Pete and Tesh left at ten, Tesh complaining he was so full he wanted to burst. Even Pete said he needed a lie down as felt a bit full. Felicity and Richard stayed up talking as Kevin led Louisa up to bed.

01st November 1999

He got up and saw a piece of paper on the chest of draws. Louisa had left a note saying thanks and she'd see him soon. Sighing he walked downstairs and Richard was having coffee with Felicity. 'Kevin, God last night my friend the food, you're going to be a star.'

With his spirits lifted he asked if Richard would still come to look at the sites. 'Too bloody right Kevin, I've been waiting for some lazy sod to wake up though. I take it you scored and had a late finish?' 'Thanks Richard, right to the point and correct as always.' 'Kevin, she's hot, you know if I was that way inclined I'd give it a go.' 'Thanks for the vote of confidence mate.' Felicity just giggled in the background.

Kevin drove to the house site first and let Sooty go exploring. Snowy followed him but more nervously. Kevin went through the plans with Richard and he was in awe. 'This is going to be stunning Kevin and I'll be visiting more than I thought now I've seen where it is.' 'Richard you'll be welcome whenever mate.'

He then drove them to the restaurant. Richard ran out of the car and was doing some sort of Sooty jig. Sooty thought it was a game and joined in running after him. Snowy stood with Felicity and Kevin and looked skeptically at the both of them.

Richard came back panting some half an hour later shouting 'Kevin, Kevin, Felicity, Felicity, Kevin, Kevin, Kevin.' 'Slow down Richard, you're going to have a clutcher mate.' 'But Kevin, Kevin, Felicity, do you realize how prefect this will be with your menu and food?' 'We were sort of hoping mate, hence asking you to take a look.'

'Take me back to the house, let me catch my breath and give me lots and lots of wine please.' Richard said as he staggered to the car. Kevin looked at his mother, shrugged and they followed him to the car calling Snowy and Sooty.

It took Richard a full ten minutes to recover his composure and then he spoke. 'Kevin, Felicity, this is going to fly. The location first is breathtaking, the theme idea brilliant and the menu really good. Plus Kevin can cook some!'

Kevin replied first. 'So it gets your endorsement Richard?' 'Gets it Kevin, gets it, I want to bloody well invest in it.' 'You'll have to speak to Oliver on that mate, he's already said if this one works he'll finance another ten and let me take ten percent.' 'Ooh he's a shrewd bugger that one!'

Felicity took Richard back to the station at seven and Kevin set his lap top up.

My Dearest Party Peeps
What a week for the Kevster and I mean what a week. New house, new restaurant, party planning and trying to Rock and Roll yous lot. Yous will be pleased to know though that the

Kevster comes through all Peeps and can say today sixty one, I say sixty one days to go! Can yous believe it guys and Gals?

Big Jack arrives on Wednesday and the Kevster and the Jackster will check out some ideas Dudes and Dudesses. No bear this time but with the big man no bear is needed. For nows Peeps that's it and I'll update yous lot of any developments and info Dudesters.

....

05ᵗʰ November 1999

Kevin hadn't stopped for three days. Jack would be here soon but he'd invited Pete and Tesh tonight for another trial. He'd walked Sooty for a good few hours this morning. Getting home at two he showered and drove into town.

He was ready by seven and Pete and Tesh arrived at quarter to eight. Kevin knew Pete by now and knew when food was involved he'd be early. Felicity gave the boys drinks and Kevin set to work in the kitchen, tonight he was doing a meat feast, purely for Pete. He was cooking his Killer Kebabs and followed by his Big Meat pasta. Pete shouted he needed lots through the kitchen door and Kevin smiled.

Pete and Tesh left at nine fit to burst, his mother had already gone up, so decided on a glass of red and a Benson. As he sat relaxing his mobile went. 'Kevin.' 'Claire, shit, God I mean hello, how are you?' 'Sorry for ringing so late but I've been thinking and I wanted to apologize.' 'Apologize for what Claire?' 'For doubting you Kevin.' 'Claire. There's no need but I really want to see you.' 'Kevin, I can't, sorry but I just wanted to hear your voice. Bye.' 'Claire, Claire, don't go please!'

The dead phone tone rang in his ears. By the time he finished the wine and some scared silly orange vodka he headed to bed at four in the morning.

....

08ᵗʰ November 1999

He'd had two days of brooding over Claire and last night went to bed at god knows what time. Surprisingly he was up and out by ten-thirty today and had Sooty and Snowy with him. He walked and thought and thought and came up with the same answer.

Claire had phoned him, actually phoned him, not him ringing her but her ringing him. Was there hope?

He had meetings with Gary and with Roy and had to get food for Jack. He wasn't messing around with his restaurant food tonight, Jack could eat a horse and loved T Bone steak. Kevin was going to make sure he got what he wanted, especially as he'd invited Pete for a sort of eat off . . .

Jack arrived a little past half-eight. He looked well and was extremely pleased to see Kevin and Felicity. Sooty made a show of trying to impress Jack and Snowy gave him a slap as if to say 'Calm down boy.' Jack laughed 'Those two would love it up with me and that bloody cat would try to get Lennox in line. I'm sure of it.'

They had a half an hour catch up before the door went at a minute past nine. 'Felicity answered and Pete gave her a hug and presented her with a bunch of flowers as well as carrying a case of wine. The case was high quality red wine, Kevin could tell by the box. 'Pete, there was no need, that case must've cost a fortune.' 'Well don't drink it all tonight then Dude.'

Kevin introduced Pete and Jack and they hit it off immediately. About an hour later Kevin served. They all had T Bone Steak, Pete and Jack's some forty ounces each, homemade thrice cook chips, onion rings, whole brown cap mushrooms and Kevin's special hot pepper sauce.

Jack and Pete looked at their dinners with eyes wide open and licked their lips. An hour after he'd served Pete finished first, downed a glass of red and asked Kevin for a top up. After Kevin poured Pete held his glass up to Jack in celebration. Jack carried on eating silently, finished, took a sip of his wine and asked politely 'Kevin, any chance of any more mate?'

Kevin had been expecting this so went and got one of the sixteen ounce T Bone's he'd been resting in readiness. He asked Pete if he wanted one but defeated Pete just shook his head. Jack ate the second Steak with the remaining pepper sauce and left a clean plate. Pete stood and held his glass up 'A toast to Jack, I take defeat poorly as a rule but when the defeat is so colossal then I hold my glass up.'

They all toasted and sat for an hour more talking and smoking some Cubans Kevin had dug out. Pete left at midnight. Jack said one more thing before falling into one sort of a comatose sleep where he sat on the sofa. 'Nice bloke that Pete.'

....

09th November 1999

'Mum, Jack got up yet?' 'No sweetie he's still out on the sofa.' 'Still?' 'Yup, I did prod him but nothing. I sent Sooty in, he tried, nothing! That man can sleep.' Kevin attempted a go at Jack at nine-thirty but couldn't budge him. He took Snowy and Sooty out telling his mum to let Jack lie. They were gone for two hours and the peace of the walk reenergized Kevin on a few things. He had his party to plan, his home and restaurant projects and a small sniff Claire might be interested again, and he also decided he needed to meet Louisa, if he was serious about any sniff with Claire he couldn't mess anyone around.

The three of them got back at around noon. Jack was still sparked out and sleeping like a baby! 'Right mum, drastic action required now.' 'What's that?' 'Put some steak, eggs, bacon and sausage on the pan.' Jack woke up like it was smelling salts. 'Thanks Kev, breakfast!' 'You bet big man, feeling ok?' 'Yeah top of the world my friend, what time is it?' 'Well now Jack it's around half past twelve mate.'

They went to house and restaurant sites next and Jack was really impressed. They got back at five with Jack saying he had one night left and fancied a few beers, this time without food, he said he'd eaten enough today and had to watch his weight.

Pete wanted to win a battle so started the Tequila rounds early. Kevin knew the result on this one, Pete would win hands down. Jack was as drunk as a skunk by nine and Kevin managed to get him into a taxi at half-past. Felicity went to bed and he rang Louisa as the lap top warmed up. She'd agreed to come around tomorrow night.

He sat and thought and wondered if he should ring Claire or not before he started to write. He decided against it and ploughed on with his Blog Page.

> Well hi all you Party Planning Peeps
> So late I know and so ratted am I! Ha ha! Sorry all yous
> Dudesters but I've had a few, I'm a little drunk Dudes and

Dudesses but not too dizzy to chat to yous lot. Not that drunk as a raccoon's ass at all, not at all Peepsters. Well my ever following Peeps I'm on the road to restaurant and home in the green, green grass of Wales, no Peeps, not Cardiff, where we're all going but Swansea you special Dudes and Dudesses. The Kevster is going to build a house by the seas for his children to play on the beach yous lot, how cool is that? If I've rambled, then I'm sorry yous special Peeps yous. Lots of Julie, hugging, loving hugs.

10th November 1999

To his huge surprise Jack was already in the kitchen, drinking black coffee. 'Kevin, you're up, wow, you guys do get up early here!' 'And you Jack, yesterday we couldn't get you off the sofa until the afternoon.' 'Ah well that was because I was well fed, when I get drunk I don't sleep very well.' 'Oh right, so we have to stuff you to sleep and pump you with alcohol to make sure you get up?' 'Yeah, about right.'

Jack was going about two o' clock and wanted to go out with Kevin and Felicity for a walk with Sooty and Snowy. They all got ready just as it started to rain. Snowy turned her nose up but then realized everyone else was going. She shrugged and followed them into the rain. They only walked for an hour. Snowy looked like a drowned rat, she was so wet and her fur stuck to her making her look about half her normal size.

Kevin went into town after Jack left, every time Jack left him now he felt a void. By six he was done and had a Benson and a glass of Chablis with his mum. She asked him sincerely 'Kevin, I thought you were looking to try to get back with Claire.' 'Yes mum, call this a goodbye meal. I'm sure it's the same for her.' 'Oh!'

Louisa arrived a little early at twenty to eight. Kevin spent no time in getting on with the food, he wanted to eat and then Felicity could disappear so he could talk to Louisa. They all ate and chatted until ten. Felicity looked at Kevin, picked up on his silent facial hints and went to bed just after five-past.

He sat back, opened a new bottle of champagne, lit a Benson and said as softly as he could. 'Louisa, this isn't going anywhere is it.' 'Kevin, this is hard for me, I shouldn't be here with you now, and God I should have never been with you at all.'

He looked at her and gestured for more information. 'Kevin, I'm married!' 'Shit darling, that wasn't what I expected!' 'I know, I didn't expect to be here either, I've always had a laugh but never crossed the line before Kevin, and you make it too easy.' 'I do?' 'Yes!' 'How?' 'By being you Kevin.'

They sat in silence for a moment before she said softly back 'Kevin, I can't go on with this.' 'I sort of guessed that.' 'I want to spend the night with you tonight and then I ask that we just stop contacting each other, I'm not strong enough to stop otherwise.'

....

11ᵗʰ November 1999

Louisa showered and left with no goodbye, just a kiss and a wink. He showered and took Sooty out. Snowy still wasn't completely dry and turned her nose up at the great outdoors. He smiled and took Sooty to the beach. They were gone several hours.

An early night beckoned. As he thought of the little things he had to do he drifted into a sleep that involved a dream. He woke suddenly at two in the morning sweating profusely. He had dreamt that Claire was pregnant, Jane and Alexis were fighting with her over who he was the most committed to as a father, and Claire had shouted 'He's only an uncle to your sprogs lesbian vampires!'

The dream unsettled him so much he got up and went downstairs for a settling Benson and a strong vodka with just a hint of orange juice. It had been so real he could almost touch all three of them and their pregnant stomachs. It really freaked him.

Two vodkas with limited orange and five Benson's later Kevin dragged himself back to bed at three-thirty, this time falling into dreamless sleep.

....

12ᵗʰ November 1999

He arrived at the White Hart at seven-thirty Tesh and Pete were already there and giving him some sort of an eye. 'Kevin, so nice of you to make an appearance' 'Pete, wow, when did you get the funny tag added?' 'Children, please, come on Pete it's your round, go and get the beers in.'

Pete came back with twelve tequila's, on a large tray. Tesh groaned, Kevin laughed and fifteen minutes later the next round of twelve was placed on the table by Kevin. Pete led them to the Ritzy. Kevin was up for anything, Tesh wobbling a little too much to argue any differently.

They paid the five pounds entrance fee and wandered in. It was still early for a Night Club so Pete hit the Tequila rounds again. Kevin, now into the swing of being tipsy upped the ante for the next round. He ordered not only tequila's, but also a bottle of champagne. 'Tequila and Champagne Slammers' he announced in some sort of celebratory tone.

One o'clock arrived and none of them could really speak. Two came and Pete somehow managed to spit out 'Food!' They left at two and headed for the kebab house.

Kevin remembered ordering a kebab, with extra chili sauce but didn't remember eating it or getting home.

....

14th November 1999

Following yesterday's sleep in he was up and alive, more so than he could remember. Grabbing both Sooty and Snowy they were off early. As they walked optimism filled Kevin's head, he wasn't sure why but he felt better than he'd done for months. Things were going to change, he was sure of it.

They had a fairly long walk, just over two hours with no incidents. As they got back he fed both his babies and remembered his dream. God it wouldn't be long until he had real babies, not his, well not to call his but real human babies. His sudden thought of how good his life was took a little dent before he decided things were good and what was happening was planned and a reason for celebration, nothing else. Grabbing a bottle of red he set his lap top up.

> Well my super Peepsters, a strange couple of days.
> Peeps there's only bloody well forty eight days to go! Can yous lot believe that? The Kevster cant, he's just realized how much is left to arrange for yous Peeps to have the party of

parties. Don't worry any of your sweet selves on that front though, the Kevster has resources and contacts all in place but just needs to finalize some details Peeps. All in his capable hands though! No other news for nows yous lot, other than to tell yous all to get excited, get ready as we are going to party with a capital P!

His personal blog page was in his sights but he chose to ignore to update it again. He knew he had a call to make and wanted to be fresh and ready. 'Claire!' 'Kevin, sorry I didn't mean to answer.' 'Why? Please talk to me.' 'Kevin, I can't, not now, it's too hard.' 'No Claire please.' 'Kevin not now, sorry!' The dead phone tone rang in his ears again but tonight he wasn't upset. She'd answered and that was definite progress.

....

15th November 1999

Dog walk, dog bath, Kevin shower and he was out to see Roy. By the time he left Roy at three he fancied a pint so went to the local around the corner, The Bluebell. He hadn't been there before but soon mixed with the regulars.

On the way back he picked up a belly pork joint for dinner, he had an idea he wanted to try on his mum, not for the first menu but for one in the future. He grabbed his other things he needed for this meal and was home by five. 'Right mother, tonight I experiment.' 'You do Kevin, what now?' 'Well my nearest and dearest mother I'm doing sticky crispy pork with herby greens and potato and parsnip cake.'

What he was aiming for was a succulent pork rosette, perfectly round with the best crackling around the meat, on top of a potato and parsnip mash cake, topped with rosemary hinted peas, beans and baby courgettes with a bitter port and lemon sauce.

When he presented the dish to his mother at eight o' clock she looked at him in awe. 'Kevin, where on earth did this idea come from?' 'Not sure mum just woke up with it. They sat and ate and shared a bottle of French Medoc, 'God Kevin this is that good I could come.' 'Mother, please, it's me your son here, hello!' 'Still Kevin, sorry it tastes that good.' 'That's better thanks mum, I can put my heart attack on hold!'

He opened another bottle of red and sat reflecting. Did he try Claire again tonight or leave it a few days? The first glass told him to ring tonight, the second to leave it a few days and the last just to go to bed and rethink tomorrow. Kevin chose the last glass's advice and went to bed at ten.

....

19th November 1999

His mum arrived back from a few days away. He joined her for an afternoon coffee and asked how her business had gone. 'Progressing darling.' She replied a little secretively. Felicity went to shower and Kevin set his lap top up, he wanted to say hello to the Peeps and then make a few calls.

> Well Peeps, Rocking, Rolling and Jumping Kevster here
> Well the Kevster has to be a busy boy in the next couple of weeks but don't yous Dudes and Dudesses worry, the Kevster still has it all under control. By the first of December folks the Kevster will have all the detail, and all the arrangements sorted. What I can tell you Dudesters though is its getting bigger all the time, yous lot will know yous been to the party of Nineteen Ninety Nine. Let me here you all say Party, party, party . . . Peeps this gig is going to rock the joint, kick all assess ever kicked and yous lot will speak about it forever man, let me here you say Party, party, party! Dudesters I've added fireworks, it's going to be a Kevster special show and all on me yous lot. Keep counting down the days. Bang, bang folks.

He needed to update his page, he'd been in denial for too long.

> Dear Kevin
> Well long time no speak we have needed to talk but I know it's been tough. Life is now going ok apart from Claire, I know you need her, she is the one and no one else can come close. Keep close to the project Dude but you know life won't be the same unless you win her back. Keep fighting Dude. Good luck Kevin, you might need it this time.

He next made the call he had waited days for, he dialed Claire's number 'Claire.' 'Kevin, you've rung again?' 'Yeah, sorry but I really wanted to speak to you.' 'Kevin, I can't do this, I've told you.' 'I know but I can't do without you Claire, it's the part of my life I waited for and cocked it up royally, I wouldn't cock up again,' 'Kevin it's just too hard, too much has gone on, we can't, I can't, it just won't work.' 'Claire, please meet me, let's talk, it's hard on the end of a phone.' 'Kevin, I don't know, no I can't, not now, sorry.' Back on the end of a yet another dead ring tone he smiled, she wasn't only answering but engaging in conversation, he was getting there.

···

20th November 1999

Getting up and showering he met his mum in the kitchen at half-nine. 'Mum, can you take them out today, I want to go into town and buy some new stuff.' 'Of course Kevin, date tonight?' 'Na mum, just a tear up with Pete and Tesh.'

Kevin drove into the city centre. He hadn't really seen it by day so enjoyed the hours he walked around whilst he revamped his wardrobe. He felt good, he'd knocked two grand off his balance but was pleased with what he'd bought, and it had been a while since he'd spent out. As a final moment of madness he walked into the Swiss Watch shop and parted with another three and a half grand on a watch, a Brietling.

When he got home he showered again and changed into his new glad rags and paraded in front of his mum. She said he looked like chocolate and then noticed his watch. 'Kevin, that's a Breitling!' 'Yeah mum I know.' 'And you're wearing it out tonight, with the boys?' 'Yes, and?' 'Well you know how much they're worth?' 'Yes mum, I bought it today and I insured it too, I'm not so stupid.'

She gave him a raised eyebrow look but seemed more pacified. 'Sorry Kevin, I know you're a grown man and I shouldn't mother you so much.' 'Look mum I'm off now but why don't you come out with us, join us later? Get showered and changed and meet us in the Wine Press in an hour.' 'Deal darling, see you then.'

By one in the morning the giggles had set in and every time one of them went to the toilets to say they wobbled was an understatement. It got to quarter to two Felicity was drunker than the three of them and fell backwards off her chair. At first Kevin thought the worst and she'd knocked herself out. He ran straight to her and she just giggled. The rest of the bar was now laughing like hyenas. Felicity's skirt had wedged up and she was showing off a silky white see though G String showing all to the cheering onlookers.

He managed to get her into a taxi at two-fifteen. Tesh and Pete were going for a kebab with a strict warning from Kevin to never, ever mention this to him again.

....

21st November 1999

By the time he arrived in the kitchen his mother was up and moaning about a bad head and drinking black coffee. 'Hi mum, how are you feeling?' 'Kevin, do you have to shout?' 'Sorry mum, what did you say?' He shouted. 'Ok, yes I've got a hangover, no more funny stuff, please Kevin?'

Two coffees later Kevin said off the cuff 'So mum, still wear silky see through G strings then?' 'Who Kevin?' 'That'd be you mum.' 'Kevin, what have you been doing, going through my draws?' 'Nothing like that mum, how much do you remember about last night?' 'Everything Kevin, we had a good time and we sang into empty champagne bottles didn't we?'

He looked at his mum, knowing he'd been in the same place before and should apply sympathy but couldn't do it. 'How much does your head hurt mum?' 'Worse than any hangover I've had before.' 'Figures.' 'What does that mean?' 'Falling off your chair, ringing any bells mum?' 'No, what are you talking about?' Felicity looked at him seriously and said in a sort of a whisper 'Ok, I don't remember that much Kevin, don't play with me, tell me, warts and all?' He told her the whole story, leaving nothing out! She buried her head in her hands. 'Oh shit!' was all she could muster as a response.

He joined her in a glass of red and added 'There was me, out with my friends and my mother decides to show the whole bar she still wears G strings and see through ones at that and grooms downstairs!' 'We'll I'm not exactly geriatric Kevin.' 'Fair point mother, remember that guy?' 'What guy Kevin?' 'The twenty-something you tried to take his number from.' 'I did?' 'Yes mum.' 'Shit Kevin.'

They ate at seven-thirty and were both tucked in by eight-forty. Kevin thought about calls he needed to make and updates to his blog but the thought of sleep took over and won the fight easily.

22nd November 1999

Felicity was taking them somewhere new. Sooty was like a dog with two in the car until Snowy slapped him to calm down. Getting home at four he opened his lap top up just as the phone went.

'Kevin.' 'Jack, how the hell are you?' 'I'm great you won't be well I don't think so when I ask what I've got to ask.' 'Well no point Jacking around mate, hit me with it.' 'Ok, funny guy, Wednesday to Friday, would you come to Canada to do a couple of presentations? I wouldn't ask but Jim Beamer has begged me to ask you, on a consultancy basis. Kev, you could do the couple of days and then spend the weekend with us and fly back on the Monday.' 'Jack, now it sounds interesting.'

Grabbing a large glass of red and his packet of Bensons he updated his blog page.

> Hi Peeps
> The Kevster's just been told he needs to jet off across the pond for just under week yous lot. No issues with party planning my soon to be party Peeps, so don't worry yous lot that's all under full control Dudesters. One thing I do need yous lot to think of when I'm gone is how many cars yous are coming in, a slight oversight by yours truly but nothing the magic Kevster can't sort, just need the numbers Peeps. Can all yous coming together let me know and I'll sort out the rest Peepsters. I'll be seeing the bear next week and will post lots of pics for yous all to see, he's the best bear there ever was Peeps and of course he just luv's the Kevster. For nows Dudes and Dudesses, keep calm and keep cool and bear lovin.

....

23rd November 1999

Following a long shower and packing in anticipation he rang Mary. She had it all arranged. He was flying from Heathrow at two o' clock tomorrow morning. By five he had a light tea with his mum and left for a leisurely drive at eight. He got to the airport at around ten to midnight, checked in and went to the first class lounge. Its grandeur fascinated him and he had a thought that all people on eleven or so hour flights should be entitled to better comfort. The money machine of the world of course would not allow it. Still if he owned the world!

....

24th November 1999

After a hug Jack told him they should be off, they had a huge schedule ahead, Jim was getting as much out of Kevin as the twenty grand payment and first class arrangements would allow him.

They got to the hotel at three. After unpacking they had a grueling four hour meeting, Kevin was nearly out on his feet. They had two beers at seven-thirty and a steak dinner at eight-thirty. Jack told Kevin he needed to be ready at four in the morning. They had a three and a half hour drive and one long day thereafter. He was in bed at ten to ten and asleep immediately.

....

26th November 1999

An eighteen hour day followed by a three o'clock start this morning and they were departing the last office at half-eight. 'Right Kevin, that's it, we'll be at mine in three and a half hours. God you do those presentations so effortlessly.' 'Doesn't feel like it now mate!' He replied and lit only his second Benson of the day.

Kevin fell asleep, at some point in the journey but he didn't remember when, he did remember arriving at Jack's and checked his watch. It was just around midnight. The Black house was dark and he needed some real sleep. He hit the bed fully clothed.

27th November 1999

Katie greeted him with a huge hug, followed by Josh, then Alicia and finally Alex. Kevin grabbed the three kids and told them he was having a house built and they had to come and stay. 'If mum and dad won't bring you then I'll come and steal you all for two weeks' he told them quietly. They all screamed yeah and gave him high fives and Katie smiled.

Katie grabbed him to one side and said 'They love you Kevin.' 'Well the feelings mutual darling, God I love being here. By the way I'm cooking tonight you've just got to get me to a store.'

Katie, Kevin, Josh, Alex and Alicia all headed for town at eleven. Kevin bought what he wanted and also bought, despite Katie's objections an outfit and present for each of the kids. They were all back at half twelve.

He couldn't wait for Jack to get back, he wanted to see Lennox. Jack didn't get back until four. The kids all had their new outfits on to greet their dad. 'Wow, you three whose been buying you presents then?' He said as he walked in 'Uncle Kevin Dad.' They all screamed in unison. 'I told him not to honey.' Katie piped up. 'Look you guys I wanted to, I won't see them at Christmas so call it their Christmas and Birthday presents in one fell swoop.'

Jack smiled and nodded thanks to Kevin, he shrugged it off. 'Taken him to see Lennox yet babe? I know he's desperate.' 'No Jack, I waited for you.' 'Ok, Kevin, come on lets go see the bear. Bring your camera and I'll take some shots with you Lennox and the family. Come on kids, and you too honey.'

They all went to see Lennox, there was still enough light but Jack hit the old generator to light up his den even more. Lennox came out and was really excited the whole family had come to see him. He then spotted Kevin. He looked at him, looked at Jack and then bounded towards Kevin and stood on his back legs, at his full height right in front of Kevin! 'Hey buddy, he remembers you, God he's only done that to me before, he must really like you Kev.' Jack said and took a shot as Kevin hugged the stood tall Lennox.

They stayed with him for an hour, photos of Kevin with Lennox, Alex, Josh and Alicia in their new outfits, photos of Kevin and Katie with Lennox stood up between them, then one of Jack and Kevin hugging him from either side, a family Black photo, including Shadow the dog and finally a timer shot that had them all with Lennox lying in front of them. It was one of the happiest hours Kevin had ever spent.

Following dinner they spent the rest of the evening on the red and when Katie went to bed at ten, Jack got out the Cubans. 'Kev, have you enjoyed coming back?' 'Look mate, work wise it was nice but easy to forget. This, what you've got is what I'll miss. God I could come out here and live.' 'That's what did it for me Kev, when I came here for a release I realized I didn't want what I had but what I could have.'

'Jack, can I ask you a real personal question?' 'Shoot Kev.' 'Why me, what did I do to make you think I could be the next you?' 'Kevin, you being you is all. Sometimes you meet someone you think yeah, that's the one. That's what I thought when I met you.' They sat and smoked another Cuban before heading to bed at midnight. Jack telling Kevin they were going to go hunting early tomorrow and going to bag themselves a deer.

28th November 1999

Kevin walked down at four wiping sleep from his eyes. Jack was there fully dressed. 'Come on Kevin, the early hunter gets the deer.' They walked for two hours before Jack settled in a low secluded area. Jack taught him the basics of how to shoot, telling Kevin if he didn't hit the target he'd set from about fifty yards after two goes then he couldn't carry the gun.

Before Kevin took a shot Jack went through the detail of shooting such a powerful weapon for another hour before he let Kevin even hold the gun. Jack then showed Kevin five real examples of how to shoot and explained each shot. Kevin was eventually given the gun. He set himself for the first shot but nerves got the better of him and he missed by a few inches. Jack spent another thirty minutes going through the drill and how the rifle worked. Kevin had now relaxed and when he shot he hit the target four times in a row, on the last even with Jack kicking his foot.

'Ok Kev, were ready to go on, we walk downwind so they can't smell us and when we get over the next ridge I expect to see a couple of animals. We don't want calf's or parenting females but a male or older unattached female, my preference is the female, the meat's sweater.' As they got over the ridge they saw what Jack had predicted. 'This is it Kevin, go for it.' Kevin got the target in sight and pulled the trigger slowly and purposefully. He hit it right where Jack said he should have and it was down and still immediately. The others all ran off into the distance.

When they got back Jack told Kevin he needed to skin, gut and hang the deer. Kevin asked if he could help. Jack looked at him and Kevin said 'Mate, if you're going to eat it you should be prepared to kill and prepare it.' Jack hung the deer after they'd prepared it, adding they'd eat one he'd bagged a week ago tonight. Later, following a shower Kevin went back into the yard Jack was there with Katie and the kids and she was getting one big fire going.

Katie then got the freshest looking loins of meat Kevin had ever seen. 'Now we marinate Kev, then we put the potatoes and onions and mushrooms in foil with spice and seasoning.'

Forty minutes later he sat round the fire with the Black family and Shadow and ate the most delicious piece of meat he'd ever tasted. They sang around the fire until ten when Katie took the kids to bed.

Kevin and Jack sat, smoking his Bensons and drinking red wine. As the heat of the fire resided it was one o' clock. 'Kev, what's happening on the woman front, I forgot to ask?' 'I'll tell you in the morning, let me sleep now ok?' 'Sure mate.'

They were about to walk into the house when Kevin said 'Jack, can I see Lennox before I go?' 'Only if you take him some barbequed deer and an onion, he'll get up for that.'

They took some hunks of meat and four roasted onions to Lennox's den. He growled to start with before his nose smelt the food. Jack turned the lights on and Lennox hugged Kevin before looking at him for the food in his arms. Kevin gave the bear the food and he ate it quickly. He had one last hug with Lennox and promised to come and see him next year.

29th November 1999

Jack told him they were late and needed to kick ass. Kevin didn't have chance to say goodbye to anyone else. They were on route to the airport when Jack said 'Come on then Kev, what's happening with Claire?' 'Jack it could be Emily or Louisa!' 'No shit Kev, Claire?' 'Ok mate, I'm trying and getting tiny steps, she answers my calls now.' 'Kev, keep at it, she's the one for you, I knew when I met her but you needed to know it more!'

Kevin looked at him 'What, I didn't at the time?' 'Not lock, stock and barrel Kev, no.' 'Jack I wish someone would tell me when I'm being such a cock.' 'Kev, it's something you need to work out yourself, like the rest of us.'

He nodded at Jack and then realized they were at the airport. 'Jack I'll miss you guys.' 'Us too Kevin, we'll have to get an arrangement next year for alternate visits.' 'You bet my friend, Jack thanks for the last few days, it's been great.' 'Feeling's mutual pal, now bugger off catch your plane and get Claire back.'

He got home at six and Sooty did some kind of show Kevin hadn't seen before and Snowy wouldn't leave his feet. His mum hugged him and asked him if it was a good trip and worthwhile. 'Yes mum, on both counts but I'm totally knackered so I'm off to bed.' 'Sure darling.'

....

30th November 1999

He managed to wake up fairly early, aided by Sooty half dragging him from his bed. Snowy was already waiting and seemed to have sent Sooty to get him. She purred as they left. As they walked he told them both about his trip. They only walked for two hours and Kevin felt like he was home again. What he wanted now was breakfast with his mum and then check on both his projects. He also wanted to make calls and update his blog page, especially with the new photos of Lennox.

Felicity must have read his mind, as mothers do, as by the time he walked into the kitchen she had bacon, egg and tomatoes ready for him. 'God mum, you must be telepathic?' 'Or know my son quite a bit.' 'Thanks mum, just what the doctor ordered.'

They ate and went to the house and restaurant sites. Things were really progressing. They got back into the house at four. Felicity said she was doing him a steak with pepper sauce and peas. 'Chips and onion rings mum?' 'Of course sweetie' Kevin cracked a cold cider and set his lap top up.

As he was on his third cider he thought of Claire, He rang her number and got really excited as she answered yet again. 'Hi Claire, I've just got back from Jack and Katie's.' 'Oh Kevin, how are they and the kids, and how's Lennox?' 'All on top of the world and all passed messages asking after you.' 'Well, I wish I could have been there.' 'What, with me?' 'Kevin, please don't?' 'Claire, don't what?' 'Get heavy.' 'Claire I need to see you.' 'Kevin, I still can't.' 'Will you ever?' 'I don't know Kevin, I just don't know.' 'But it's not no Claire?' 'No Kevin, it's not no. I miss you too but too much has passed and I don't know if I can deal with it.' 'Ok, but we have a chance?' 'Oh Kevin, that's too much pressure.' 'Claire, please, is there a chance?' 'Yes Kevin but I don't know when or if ok?'

> Yo Party Planning Peepsters
> Kevster here and back on top form, the trip across the pond was super duper and I'm totally regenerated yous lot. Look Peeps into the thirties, days that is yous lot, coming up to less than a month rocking and rolling Dudesters. I met the bear again Peeps and he hugged me hard, he remembers me you Guys and Gals as I hope yous lot will when we all meet soon.
>
> My house and business is coming on galloping guns and I must tell you single Dudesses out there the Kevster is again off limits. No current Gal but the love of my life Peeps hasn't said no about reconciliation. The Kevster's pursuing this with all his efforts Peeps. We're going to Party though Peepsters, let me here you say Party! Dudesters this is going to be it, Nineteen Ninety Nine done better than anywhere else, trust the Kevster! For nows again I go but will be in touch with yous lot soon. Hugs and loving Kevster style.

Felicity served him his favorite Steak meal and they shared two bottles of red. As he was smoking a Benson before bed he told his mother he'd spoken to Claire and what she'd said. 'Yeah, she told me she was getting there.' Felicity said.

Kevin looked at his mother and said 'Mum, please explain?' 'Oh Kevin, I've been visiting her ok, I've tried to fight your corner and she asked me not to tell you we'd been in touch.'

01st December 1999

It was a lovely sunny cold day and perfect for Snowy. Kevin took them the long walk and skirted the beach. On the way back at ten o'clock Kevin had his first scare whilst out with the two of them. A sheepdog really went for Snowy and when Sooty intervened had a real go at Sooty. Kevin jumped in, the sheepdog was out of control. The owner an elderly lady just screamed and did nothing.

Eventually the sheepdog caught Sooty on his neck and drew blood. Sooty pinned it down and looked almost ready to kill but just held it there snarling. The elderly woman eventually came over as Kevin told Sooty to go to Snowy as he held the sheepdog down.

Sooty obeyed immediately and the woman managed to get her dog on a lead. It was still deranged and snarling and foaming at the mouth. Kevin had a large bite in his forearm. 'You need to get that thing muzzled, it's out of control!' Kevin shouted as the woman ran away with her dog.

Sooty was sat protecting Snowy who was trying to lick him where he bled. Kevin hugged his dog and his cat and told Sooty he was a good boy, calling him Doggy Balboa, his fighting name and Snowy approved by licking her dog again.

They got to the vets at eleven. Sooty's cut was superficial and a cleanup and a course of antibiotics as a precaution was all that was required. It still cost eighty pounds. Kevin moaned to his mother he should go looking for the old lady for a rebate. He then went straight to the doctor's for a tetanus injection.

He got back home at two o' clock and went straight to Sooty. The vet had been right, it was a scratch, nothing else, Kevin's bite was actually bigger and he compared it with Sooty. He told his dog he was a good boy and Snowy was sat next to her dog grooming him. Felicity took a picture. Kevin looked at her and said softly 'Mother, pub, now!'

As they arrived Kevin bought them a bottle of red wine and two large triple vodkas each laced with a hint of orange juice. He told her to sink the first vodka and then the second and copied her. Next he poured two glasses of wine for them, lit a Benson and said 'Right mum, now you speak.'

His mother looked at him and said 'Honey what do you want me to say?' 'Well mum, please tell me about you and Claire?'

'Not much to tell really darling, I know you two are meant to be together so as your mother and someone who cares for Claire I decided I'd poke my nose in.'

'Ok mum but what does poke your nose in actually mean?' 'I've been to see Claire, a few times, the times I've been away for a few days at a time.' 'Ok mum and . . . ?' 'And Kevin she's emotional and not sure where her head is. I've been trying to help her see you are the real deal.' 'Mum, you did all this and didn't tell me?' 'Claire made me promise Kevin. If I told you, she said she'd stop seeing me.'

Kevin sank half his glass of red wine and said 'Mum, I love you, thanks, she's speaking to me now. It isn't close for us yet but she wouldn't even speak to me before.' They both embraced and Kevin told her she was a mum in a million. This made Felicity's night and the pair of them stayed in the pub until ten before swaying all the way home by eleven.

....

02ⁿᵈ December 1999

Kevin was cooking by the time Felicity came down. 'Mum, do you realize we didn't eat yesterday?' 'That's why I'm feeling hungry then.' He served a huge mixed grill at half past nine. They had sausage, bacon, gammon, steak, black pudding, chips, beans, tomatoes, fried bread and bloody Mary's, strong ones.

They ate and drank and it was instant hangover cure. Kevin showered after breakfast and said he was taking Sooty and Snowy out. 'Well I'm coming with you. You might not be able to punch the bitch's lights out but me Kevin, a whole different story.' 'Mother, calm down, if we see her I'll approach her. I'm not having my mum with a criminal record for assault!' As it was they didn't see the old lady and had a pleasurable stroll with no incident.

Following a visit to the house and the restaurant they ate dinner before felicity went to bed at nine. Kevin sat for another hour with some really strong orange juice frightened vodkas.

....

03ʳᵈ December 1999

It was raining cats and dogs today. Kevin donned his boots, coat and hat and gave Snowy the come on look. She ignored him as if to say. 'If you must boys but don't expect me to follow.' Kevin left with Sooty at quarter to eleven. The rain was really giving it some. By the time they'd walked for an hour Sooty looked at him with puppy dog eyes. Kevin knew from this look his boy had had enough. They battled back through the wind and rain and were home by just gone twelve-thirty. They were both soaked to the skin.

Snowy was hanging around and looking at them with a sort of I told you so look on her face. Kevin took Sooty for a shower and then dried him. He had a shower himself and by the time he got back downstairs it was already three o' clock.

Before he blinked it was six o' clock so he ordered the taxi. He tried to persuade his mum to go but she refused point blank. 'Kevin, I need a break before I show my silky's to that lot again.' 'Fair point my sexy mother, and perhaps chance to re-grow down below?' She hit him hard in the arm and called him a name he'd never heard her use before.

When he got to the Wine Press at ten to seven he wasn't surprised to see he was the first to arrive. Pete being on time the last time must have killed him. To his further surprise Pete was there five minutes later. 'Kevin, I was hoping to beat you here tonight.' 'Hi Pete, where's Tesh?' 'He had to cry off, I called him all the wimps under the sun but he wouldn't bite and said he just couldn't make tonight something to do with a reunion with Clarissa.'

Pete was in one of his funny moods, he was looking at every piece of skirt that walked past. It wasn't long before they were joined. Kim and Lisa sat on their table.

Kevin got another round in at quarter to eleven and when he got to the table Pete and Kim were close, very close. Pete's hands were everywhere and looked at Kevin doing some sort of a gesture with his right hand before disappearing with Kim. Lisa laughing said she was hungry so asked Kevin if he fancied going for a kebab. They got to the shop, both ordered large donner's with chili and garlic sauce and to be wrapped to take home.

Lisa held Kevin's hand and whispered 'You can eat that at mine if you'd like and what's left over we'll share for breakfast.' He looked at her. She was young, blond and extremely pretty. 'Lisa, I'd love to but I'm involved with someone.' She looked deep into his eyes, kissed him, moved his hand up her skirt to her pantless bottom and said seductively 'Are you sure Kevin?' 'God Lisa no but yes. He jumped into a taxi at one-thirty and was home by two. He shared a bit of his kebab with Sooty, knowing he'd fart like a bugger later.

04th December 1999

Jane and Alexis arrived at five. They both looked stunning and happier than Kevin had seen them together ever. 'Kevin!' They both shouted as he approached them. Then sooty came running and was quickly followed by Snowy. Felicity stood in the background.

She however guided them in and Alexis gave her a hug and a kiss like a long lost daughter with her mother. Kevin noted how much they meant to each other and felt warm inside.

By the time they were roomed and both Sooty and Snowy had given it their seal of approval it was six-thirty. The girls ate like Jack and Pete, he couldn't believe it, after they'd both eaten though they both got tired quickly and needed to go to bed. Kevin took them and tucked them in along with a purring Snowy. He loved these girls like his own family and then realized they almost would be. He kissed them both on the cheek and his cat on her head before going downstairs to his mum. They drank for an hour and talked about possible reconciliation with Claire. He hit the bed with his dog and felt on top of the world, this had been a good day. Sleep came before he knew it.

05th December 1999

Kevin was woken with a start, Jane and Alexis had crashed his bedroom, they had jumped in either side of him and were both naked pushing their bellies into his naked body. 'Can you feel our lumps Kevin' they both said giggling. 'No, but I can feel your boobs and bits I shouldn't be feeling again and it's giving me a morning rise!' 'Let me feel it?' Jane screamed, 'me too Kevin.' Alexis added. 'Out, out, the both of you. The only one who's feeling my rise this morning is me. Now you've made me get it I'm bloody well going to use it so out!'

They both ran out of the bedroom giggling, shutting the door behind them. He joined them shortly afterwards. 'Feeling better now?' Jane asked him. 'We'll a bit. After your two's rubbing I'd have been walking around with a gun in my pocket all morning if I hadn't used what you made come up.' 'What's that?' He heard from his mother's mouth. 'It's ok Felicity Jane and I jumped into bed with him this morning and our naked bodies got a reaction he had to sort before he could come for breakfast.'

'Oh, does that mean I have to wash the sheets Kevin, like I did every morning from when you were fourteen?' 'Enough, all of you, this discussion is over, let's talk about what we're doing today.' Jane jumped into the conversation and said 'Ok, ok, I need to go to the bank though.' 'That's fine.' Kevin said 'we can go somewhere from there, which bank do you need to go to?' 'The Sperm Bank Kevin!' The three women were giggling like teenagers.

Felicity knew a picnic site that had a great wood with streams, a river and a lake. It took them an hour to get there but it was ideal. Sooty thought it was Christmas. He was on one as soon as they unloaded the car. They all had sandwiches and flasked coffee and then Kevin took the dog and cat deep into the woods. They were gone an hour and a half and Snowy came back looking like a drowned rat. 'She knows how to swim.' Kevin said as they approached the girls.

He told them how Snowy had fallen in a deep part of the stream and Sooty had dived in after her. Rather than be impressed by his bravery she swam away from him to the other side. When they both got out she smacked him as if it was his fault she fell in. Sooty still looked dejected. Jane gave him a big hug and he soon brightened up. They left at four and Kevin asked what they wanted for food. Both Jane and Alexis said they had a craving for meat. 'Enough' he barked at them chasing them to the car.

He served the meal at half-eight and just like the night before Jane and Alexis were in bed soon after. He stayed up with his mum until half-ten, they were all going to see the house and res-taurant sites in the morning so he wanted to be up early to take Snowy and Sooty out.

....

06th December 1999

Kevin got up early it was another cats and dogs day with the rain so only he and Sooty went out. They managed two hours and were wet through and stinking. He put Sooty in the bathroom ready and sneaked into Jane and Alexis's room.

He jumped them in his soaked clothes. There were lots of screams then naked woman running away from the dirt monster as they were calling him. The bed clothes were covered in dirt and water. 'That'll teach you for jumping me, I always get revenge.'

They all had breakfast at nine-thirty and Felicity moaned about what he'd done to her bed sheets. 'Well mother dirty or soiled sheets is the same thing isn't it, they still need washing.' He said running away fast. He rang Oliver after the girls and animals all went for their afternoon snoozes.

'Oliver.' 'Kevin me old mucker how's it going' 'Good I think Oliver, I'm going to be two dads but as an uncle.' 'Kevin even by your standards that's weird.' 'Well you know me mate, nothing by half, how about I tell you about it over a free meal?' 'You want me to come back out?' 'Could you mate, it's important.' 'It'll have to be tomorrow Kevin, is that too soon?' 'Nah mate, fine, what time?' 'Again I'll get there for about three, it'll just be me though, Jude's busy.'

07ᵗʰ December 1999

He slaved all day until Oliver arrived at three. They went straight to the restaurant. He'd gone through Kevin's paper menu and catchphrase and loved the concept. 'And you change the menu every six weeks?' He asked Kevin. 'Yup, all in the sixes mate.'

Pete and Tesh arrived early at quarter past seven. Kevin smiled. He knew it wasn't Oliver that got them there early but Pete's desire to smell cooking food. He left them two bottles of red and two white and went to the kitchen. Felicity had gone away for a couple of days but hadn't risen to his bait that she was going to see Claire.

He worked hard to get the six starters onto the table by seven forty-five. The six mains were all presented by eight-fifteen and the six desserts by nine. Kevin joined them for a well earned glass of red and a Benson. He hadn't stopped.

Oliver was laughing. 'What's funny?' Kevin asked 'Pete mate, Tesh and I sampled each course for taste and Pete ate the rest.

He's sparko over there, look!' Kevin looked over to the lump that was Pete fast asleep in the corner of the large settee.

The three of them finished a couple of bottles of red before Tesh ordered a taxi at eleven o' clock. As it arrived he poked Pete who woke and said 'What's the next course?' Tesh grabbed him and said 'the next course is bed mate.'

....

08ᵗʰ December 1999

Kevin was up, out, back and back out again by ten, on his way to see Gary. 'Gary, did you see who I had with me yesterday?' 'Kevin I did, how on earth?' 'He's backing me Gary, financially.' 'Kevin, you're really going to put Swansea on the map then?' 'You bet mate, just keep to the schedule and we'll be fine.' 'Kevin don't you worry about that, I've got it covered.'

Kevin then went to see Roy and spent half an hour with him. Any more time than that and he thought he was just in the way. He knew he had calls to make later so dropped into the Bluebell for a quick pint. He ended up staying for four quick ones so left the car and walked home by six o' clock. He knew he had burgers and buns in the freezer and that would do for tonight.

Putting the burgers on to defrost and setting his lap top up, took another shower. He was thinking about calling Claire, he knew his mum would still be there and couldn't decide whether it was the right or wrong thing to do.

Felicity got back at seven-thirty and refused to talk to him about where she'd been and any details of her and Claire's discussions. 'Mum, you say you won't say where you've been but then say you won't tell me what you and Claire talked about.' 'Well just don't ask and then I can't get my answers wrong then can I darling?' He had his blog page open as Felicity shouted down she'd be ready for a drink in twenty minutes.

Hello my Party Planning Peeps
Kevster here and guess what Dudesters? Well there's only twenty three days to go. Count them Peeps, less than four weeks, only five hundred and fifty two odd hours and we'll be partying. Well all yous lot I'm rocking on the restaurant front and rolling on the house front but still shaking, rattling and

rolling on the Gal front. All will be ready for yous though for our progress into the Millennium Peeps.

Yous lots comments on the bear pictures have also been well received. The Blacks are like the Kevster's second family and I love them to bits. It's hard not seeing them Dudesters so often but all the more pleasurable when the Kevster actually does. Keep happy, keep counting and keep getting ready and mad for it.

He thought about his personal page but knew there was nothing to add, tonight had to be business with his mother. Felicity came down and asked him where her vodka was. 'On the table with your nibbles mum' 'Is it strong Kevin?' 'Well put it this way mum, I had to chase the orange down the street to catch it!'

Felicity took her first pull on the vodka and grabbed one of his Bensons. 'Oh Kevin, that is perfect and the mini spread?' 'All for my mother, mother.' 'Thank you darling it's great, now let's talk.' 'Ok mum, let's do the easy thing first, Pete wants us to go to El Ninio's on Friday, and he'd said he'd pay.' 'Well, that one is easy, he's almost eaten us out of house and home so the answer is a definite yes.'

'Ok mum, as you know Oliver came last night and I cooked the whole first menu.' 'Yes and . . . ?' 'Well mum he liked it.' 'And . . . ?' 'He offered to put two hundred grand in as working capital for a fifteen percent profit return but we keep the rights on the name.'

'Ok Kevin, I reckon we say yes but we need it in writing now, we need to protect ourselves.' 'You reckon mum, this is Oliver we're talking about.' After a heavy sigh she said 'Darling he'll understand he's a businessman. Do you want me to speak to him?' 'No mum, I'll do it now.'

'Oliver' 'Kevin me old mucker, how the hell are you?' 'Ok thanks mate. Look, I've been going over the offer you made with my mum and we are dead interested.' 'Good Kev, that's great news, look Kev, not to be a killjoy you need protection like I do so I want to get my Solicitor to draw a contact up and I want you to get it checked by your own legal people.' 'Cheers Oliver, you'll get it raised then?' 'Yup mate, leave that bit with me, it'll take a couple of weeks or so though.'

09th December 1999

Kevin and Sooty walked for nearly four hours in the rain, he was so excited. If he took the beginning of the year he was treading water in work, struggling to see where the next girl would come from and living in London.

When he thought where he was now, where he'd come from in less than twelve months it just beggared belief. He was more than pleased with himself but then remembered a lot of it was luck, the right place, right time, right ides and the right people. He owed people like Mary, Jane, Alexis, Oliver, Richard, and especially his mother and Jack a lot.

When they got back Felicity made breakfast whilst he bathed Sooty and showered. 'What are you up to today Kevin?' She said as he came back down forty minutes later. 'Well mum, my first job is to ring Claire.' She looked at him with raised eyebrows.

'Mum its professional, I need to go to Cardiff and have a look at the grounds Claire's friend is letting us use for the party.' Kevin ate his bacon and chili omelet and rang Claire at one o' clock.

'Claire.' 'Kevin.' 'Yup in the flesh, well on the phone in the flesh, but you know what I mean?' 'Are you trying to make me laugh?' 'What you haven't already?' 'Oh Mr Kevin Funny Julie, and I do remember it's your middle name.' 'Glad to hear you remember little things about me then.' 'Lots Kevin, lots.' 'Look Claire I'm after a favor.' 'Ok what?' 'Well you know the house near Cardiff where we can use the grounds for the party.' 'Don't ever let Vanessa hear you call it a house, it has twenty bedrooms she'll be horrified.' 'What should I call it?' 'The estate is a favorable term Kevin.' 'Ok the estate, I need to go and see it to plan the catering and the marquees.' 'Let me ring Vanessa and I'll call you back later.'

Felicity and Kevin were discussing what to have for dinner when Kevin's phone went. 'Claire.' 'Hi Kevin, how's your afternoon been?' 'So much the better now' 'Stop it you you'll get me all flushed.' 'Ok, I'll try not to make you flush again or anything else.' 'Kevin, that's airing on rude, look I've spoken to Vanessa she says you can go on Saturday. You'll have to stay there, she wants you to cook for her as payment.' 'A small price I think.' 'You think. She's a vixen that one.' 'She won't be with me Claire,

I'm a good boy, a one woman man,' 'Since when?' 'Since I met you Claire.'

....

10th December 1999

Settling down Kevin lit a Benson and dialed the number for Vanessa. Claire hadn't been wrong. She'd half seduced him on the phone. He felt all hot under the collar, he imagined a sixty year old sex starved widow and he as her prey. Still he was far beyond that now, everything was about winning Claire back.

He decided to go out and buy a case of decent champagne though. This lady was helping him out immensely. He also decided he'd be better off taking someone with him and rang Pete. Pete said he'd love to go, any opportunity to eat Kevin's food and liked the sound of this Vanessa.

His mother was back at six to see Kevin sat down, chilling with a glass of red, and a big cigar. He told her all about Vanessa. 'And you're still going?' 'Yes mum.' 'Kevin what about what you told me about not letting any woman getting between you and Claire?' 'Mum, I'm taking Pete with me.' 'Clever boy, you are learning.' 'My eighteenth middle name mother.'

Their taxi arrived at seven-thirty and they were at El Ninios by ten to eight. The first thing Kevin noted was the location wasn't as pretty as where he would be and it was in the opposite direction, quite a clear choice for possible diners.

Pete was already there. 'You're early Pete.' Kevin said as they walked in. 'Well I'll be eating won't I Kev?' 'Oh shit yeah, I forgot, what time did you get here, five?' Pete groaned some kind of a response.

The menu was a standard meat, fish and poultry British style affair with nothing really different on it. Kevin chose the steak, Pete the rib and steak combo and Felicity the fish. They all had different starters. The starters came separately and Kevin's was luke warm prawns that weren't very fresh.

His medium rare steak was medium well and just warm. But the pepper sauce was good. The vegetables were crisp and fresh but it wasn't singing and dancing. Pete and his mother's dishes were better from what they said and all in all it wasn't bad but as they said and Kevin concurred it wouldn't set the world alight.

They were home just after eleven. Kevin had agreed to pick Pete up at quarter to twelve tomorrow. 'Mum, what did you really think?' 'I think we have a chance of becoming the best restaurant in Swansea Kevin.'

....

11th December 1999

He took it easy driving into Cardiff and was at the junction Vanessa had said by just after one. Kevin rang Vanessa. She said she was on target to be there by five to two and she had a range rover with the registration plate VAN E5A.

They saw her car before they saw the registration, it was pink! Kevin flashed Vanessa and then pulled out to follow her. They drove for fifteen minutes and onto a country road before arriving at a huge gated entrance.

Once they'd parked Vanessa got out of her bright pink Range Rover and walked towards them. What immediately surprised Kevin was she wasn't a sixty something widow type. She had ginger blond hair, large breasts on a slim frame and was late thirties to early forties. Pete looked at Kevin and said 'Kev, she's hot!'

They both got out of the car and Kevin said 'Hi Vanessa, Kevin.' 'Hi Kevin, nice to meet you, who's your friend?' 'Oh, Pete, sorry Vanessa but your estate is so impressive I forgot my manners.' 'No worries Kevin, God two hot hunks in my home for the night, how lucky am I?'

She showed them to their rooms first and then made a point of telling and showing Kevin where her room was. Vanessa then showed them the grounds and where Kevin could pitch the marquees and where the cars could park. She showed him how they could get power to the marquees and said she'd pop in on the party as she was really interested in what he was doing.

On the way back into the house Kevin got the case of champagne out of his car and presented it to Vanessa. 'A little thank you.' He said with a smile. She kissed him on the lips and a little bit too full on before saying 'Kevin, Claire said how nice you were.'

Kevin thought about one of his trade mark comments but decided against it. In, cook, sleep, home was his agenda today and tonight. She took them to the Kitchen. 'Kevin, what I'd really like to eat is shell fish to start and then a big piece of meat and a spicy sauce for my mains. I'd like smooth and creamy for dessert.' He nodded at her and said if she had the ingredients he could do it all. 'Don't you worry Kevin, I have all the ingredients.' She said before adding 'I'm retiring for a nap now. I'll be down at seven for drinks?' Kevin managed a 'No problem Vanessa' as she disappeared up to her room. 'Kevin, she wants you with a capital W mate!' Pete said giggling at Kevin. 'Well she isn't getting me Pete. I'm not on the menu.'

At seven he was ready, he hadn't had chance for a shower but Vanessa was back down in a very short red dress. She grabbed a couple of the bottles of champagne he'd brought and filled them all up with larger than normal flutes. She asked Kevin if he minded if she took Pete away to dance whilst he cooked. Kevin nodded not letting her see the relief on his face.

He had the food ready on time. Shell food starter with white wine, cream and saffron sauce, Fillet steak in a red wine and chili sauce with roasted garlic and thyme potatoes with buttered caramelized carrots and courgettes. Then finally sticky toffee and apple nut pudding with a warm vanilla cream.

By the time they'd eaten and polished off two more bottles of champagne, three bottles of a very nice and what must have been a very expensive red wine it was eleven-thirty. Vanessa then got cognac and Cuban cigars out and joined the boys in both. By midnight Kevin said he was tired. Pete said he was happy to stay up with Vanessa but she said she was tired too. They all went to bed just after twelve-thirty.

Kevin fell asleep almost instantly. He did have a dream quite quickly though. He was aroused by the dream and woke up. He had a naked body next to him. The naked body also had hold of his surprised rise. He turned around and put the bedside light on. Vanessa was naked and coaxing his rise to somewhere he didn't want it to go. He jumped up out of bed. 'Impressive.' She said as she looked at his still risen rise. 'Vanessa what the hell are you doing?' 'Kevin, I came for you, I thought you'd be up for a bit of fun now you're single.' 'Vanessa, just because I'm single doesn't mean I'm game for anything.'

'No worries Kev, I'll go and disturb Pete.' Locking the door he went back to bed and tried to sleep but still had a rise he needed to deal with before it came.

12th December 1999

He was back at eleven and his mother asked him for a chicken dinner. 'No problem mum, it'll take my mind off last night.' 'You were good weren't you Kevin?' 'Me mum cock in pants all night.' Felicity was badgering him to tell her what went on. 'Later mum, I promise.' He kept repeating each time she asked him.

He cooked chicken, stuffing, roast vegetables and a home-made gravy and served it at seven o' clock. As they sat Kevin poured them a glass of red each and started to eat before his mother demanded 'And Kevin . . . ?'

Kevin told her the whole story during dinner. 'And you definitely didn't do anything Kevin?' 'No mum, absolutely nothing, well other than a five finger shuffle.' 'Kevin!' 'Sorry mum, you did ask.'

13th December 1999

Felicity was still amazed at breakfast, 'God Kevin, Claire told me what she was like but even she, I don't think, actually realizes.' 'Mum, even at my lowest ebb, that's one you run from.' Felicity agreed to cook tonight, Kevin wanted to ring Claire and thank her and ask her how much she really knew about Vanessa Giles-Gilmour.

'Claire.' 'Kevin how are you?' 'A little miffed actually.' 'Why?' 'Your friend Miss high and mighty Giles-Gilmour.' 'Oh I know she's a bit heavy Kevin but her hearts in the right place.' 'I don't know about her heart but her breasts weren't in the right place Saturday night.' 'What do you mean?' 'Well she came on nonstop as you told me but once I was asleep on my own in the bedroom she climbed into bed with me naked.' 'Oh Kevin, I didn't think she'd do that!' 'Well I only realized as she aroused my sleeping rise Claire!' 'Kevin, she didn't, you know, I mean, she didn't go further did she?' 'She didn't get the chance I jumped out and told her to get out.' 'You did?' 'Yes Claire, I did!' Then she went to Pete's room and I locked my bedroom door.' 'Kevin who's Pete?' 'He's a new friend of mine. I took him because after I'd spoken to Vanessa I thought I needed some company.' 'You did?' Yes Claire I did.' 'Kevin don't you think Vanessa is gorgeous though?' 'Yes

Claire I do, she told me as much herself but I told her I loved you.' 'You did?' 'Yes Claire I did' 'Oh Kevin, I didn't think she'd go that far, I thought she was all talk.' 'Claire she's talk, walk and stalk, let me tell you. Claire, please can I see you?' 'Not yet Kevin, I'm sorry about Vanessa but no, sorry.'

He finished the call, lit a Benson and shouted to his mother that he wasn't hungry and went to bed. Sleep didn't come easily but he drifted off some time he couldn't remember.

16th December 1999

The last two days had been a blur. His disappointment of Claire's response had knocked him a bit. He'd thrown himself into the projects in a big way. Today he felt differently, one big knock back from Claire wasn't enough to put him off. He did decide though that he'd leave it a while before ringing her again.

He had to sit and plan the restaurant project tonight with his mother, telling her he needed half an hour to update the Party Blog Page. They sat down at seven and wrote a list. When they crossed referenced all Felicity had on her list was food and drink suppliers.

'What about the rest mum?' 'Well my darling son, I've been busy again. Staff, we have two Sous chefs, Michael and James, two trainees, Anthony and Heston and a dish washer, Brian. Our Matrdee is Judy, she's also the Manager. Her deputy is Jason who runs the bar. We have four bar staff working part time, Ros, Vanessa, Nemash and Steve. We have four waiters and waitresses working the shifts, Lisa, Michelle, Carl and Paul. Our Cleaning Company is Albany and oh yes, the gardener is Mike I think that covers the staffing arrangements, doesn't it?'

Kevin looked dumfounded. 'Kevin, I've been speaking to Oliver and Richard for advice and recruiting for weeks. I know you've had other things on your mind but if we're opening Boxing Day I had to get on with it.' 'Mum, we're opening Boxing Day?' 'Yes Kevin, I know you've got the party to plan but you'll need to work Boxing day, you'll have trained Michael and James by then but I want them to cook under your supervision on the first night.'

'Mum, just so I'm not missing anything here what about furniture and decoration?' 'Already arranged Kevin, the decorators start Tuesday, it's going to be like being in a volcano setting, an appearance of being in a fire. The furniture is all black. Wooden tables and leather and wood high back chairs. The table decoration is all red, any questions so far?'

'Doesn't it take time to order the furniture mum?' 'It's being delivered Friday, when the decorators have finished.' 'Mum, I need vodka.' 'Me too Kevin and make it a bloody strong one, my heads hurting remembering all this.' He got back with two very orange scared vodkas and they took a time out.

> My dearest Party Planning Peeps
>
> Kevster here and yes I know I've not been good. Let me tell yous lot though that it stops now. I have twenty one days left to sort this party out and let me tell yous lot it is happening Dudesters. I've been to the place we are staying and arranged all the marquees and caterers. Don't forget though yous lot need your own sleeping bags. Dudes and Dudesses this place is the dog's cahooners, the lamb's wool, the cows milk Peeps and were going to party, let me here you say P.A.R.T.Y . . .
>
> The Kevster is drawing directions and will post these on this page next week Peeps. As I've already told yous lot, all the cash is in, I can't believe how committed yous lot have been to me.
>
> For now though, sleep tight, keep bright and keep remembering were going to Party like Its Nineteen Ninety Nine!

18th December 1999

The previous day was another one to forget, up and five and in bed by eight. Still he'd sorted all the suppliers out and arranged his house furniture. He bathed Sooty after this morning's wet walk and had another shower himself. He joined his mother for breakfast at eleven. 'God mum, this is a real ride, it's picked up and there's no stopping it.' 'I know darling, exciting isn't it?' 'God mum super exciting.'

'Kevin, what are you up to this evening?' 'Dunno yet, I said I'd ring Tesh and Pete, maybe go out for a beer. Why you fancy coming?' 'Bloody right I do Kevin. This last week I haven't stopped. Look two things though. I'm wearing trousers and if you Pete or Tesh mention my G String or snatch I'm going to squeeze all of your balls until you squeal.'

They got to the Wine Press before Pete and Tesh and Felicity ordered two bottles of tequila, four bottles of champagne and picked a large table for them. She also ordered her and Kevin a large glass of red each. 'Mum, what are you doing?' 'Watch and learn Kevin, watch and learn.'

Pete and Tesh arrived just after seven. Pete saw the tequila and said to Felicity, 'at least you've got trousers on tonight Felicity.' 'Watch it Pete, didn't Kevin warn you?' 'He did but I didn't mention silky G Strings or snatch Felicity, all as instructed.' She smiled at him adding 'Ok fair point, tequila and champagne slammer Pete?'

By twelve Pete and Tesh were in a right state and Felicity said they'd play a game. Kevin thought he knew what was coming. His mother had a photographic memory and could also do sums in her head quicker than a calculator.

She continued to explain they would play a numbers game and whoever got it wrong had to take an item of clothing off. The game started at twelve-fifteen. By one o' clock she had Tesh completely naked and ordered him to the bar for a bottle of red wine with only a beer mat for company. By one-thirty Pete had to do an impression of a dog completely stark naked, Felicity made him sit, give a paw and roll over, much to the pub's delight.

By two she handed them back their clothes and asked the whole place what they'd remember most, her falling off the chair the other week, the naked wine buyer or the naked dog? 'Right all of you, no mention of my silky's again no? And Tesh your back needs shaving.' They all agreed and Kevin, despite being off his face felt huge admiration for his mother. The night had really been a super laugh.

....

20th December 1999

Felicity had left a note to say she was out so he looked in the fridge for food. He chose a tuna salad and sat and ate it with a cool glass of Chablis.

Right Peeps

Serious Kevster here, directions attached. What I need now from yous lot is the number of cars. Please advise by Friday how yous lot are getting here and I'll allocate numbers. Once they go Dudesters, they go. There's only so much space.

On another front the Kevster has arranged for a band to play before we head to Cardiff Peeps it's a huge surprise Dudesters. Suffice to say yous lot will be more than well impressed. Guys and Gals, my last note is to tell you my, let me here yous say my . . . Restaurant opens Boxing Day. The name's Julie's and it's Devilishly Good Food. That's my marketing all you Dudes and Dudesses but I expect you all to come soon. There's a fifty percent discount for all the Party Peeps yous lot so be neat, be sweet, and dance your feet to Julie's devilishly good place to eat.

....

22nd December 1999

The previous day was all about meeting and greeting the new restaurant team, he didn't finish until eleven. Today was about tonight's dress rehearsal. Kevin and the chefs had worked from four in the morning until three in the afternoon. He took a quiet hour in the seating area with a Benson and reflected. So much had gone on, was he ready? Was his head ready? Was this what he wanted?

Kevin went into the kitchen and told the team to get ready. They all took high fives and stood on guard. Judy had the waiting staff to perfection, she had orders in groups. Heston's job was to coordinate the timing by table and he set the chefs off and controlled the pass. Kevin took control in the kitchen but didn't cook.

They were evidently nervous as four of the first five dishes Kevin rejected. He held a rallying call and jumped in to help get the first eight ready, two tables worth. The guy's did more than rally after that they hit every dish to his expectation.

Judy came into the kitchen when everyone was eating and held two big thumbs up. 'Right guys, get on the mains' Heston boomed out. Kevin stayed with Michael and James and mucked in. Between the three of them they served all the mains to perfection and on time. By the end of service Kevin was really proud and opened a couple of bottles of champagne for the kitchen and held a toast to them.

As they drank Kevin said softly 'Look guys, that was great but we all know guests normally arrive at different times so we won't be able to be so arranged next time. Starters and mains will have to be cooked the same time as desserts, depending on the table. We'll all be back for eight in the morning ok?'

....

24th December 1999

The previous day was a seventeen hour slog. Kevin had sent them home at three in the morning but stayed until they returned at six this morning. 'Guys and Gals, you've all worked like Trojans. We have a day left today to get it right if we all want Christmas day off. I want everything off all of you today this will map out our futures.'

Kevin called fifty covers in different orders for the team to deliver to fifty tables. Judy led all the Soup Kitchen attendees in for their free Christmas meal. By two-thirty Kevin called a halt.

'You guys have surpassed my expectations. We're finishing now and we have Boxing Day to nail people. Take the rest of today off but be ready for me for the day after tomorrow. Succeed or fail, each of you will get a thousand pounds bonus for your efforts this week as a little thank you from me.'

He grabbed a wine and pondered on ringing Claire. Despite all he'd said to himself about waiting he dialed the number. 'Claire.' 'Hi Kevin, you ok?' 'Yeah, pretty good actually, just finished all the trials on the restaurant.' 'How did they go?' 'Perfect actually, I think this will work and expand massively.' 'Good Kevin, I'm pleased for you.' 'Thanks Claire. Look I don't want to get too heavy but I wanted to ring to say Happy Christmas.' 'Kevin that's so nice.' 'I haven't quite finished, I don't want you to scream or shout or say anything really but I needed to tell you I love you with all my heart,' 'Kevin!' 'Claire, I didn't ask for comment I just wanted you to know before Christmas came in, bye.' His birthday had passed by with no interest but Kevin didn't care, there was too much other stuff going on at the moment.

25th December 1999

Kevin arrived downstairs at seven. Jane and Alexis were like children and bouncing around like idiots. Sooty thought it was a game and joined in whilst Snowy turned her nose up. Kevin made a pot of tea and as it was brewing went to wake his mother. He knocked the door but she didn't answer. After waiting a minute he knocked again, still no answer. Trying the third time Kevin banged on the door and still no answer. Now he burst through the door and looked not at his ill mother as he thought but an empty bed. Her bed hadn't been slept in and there was a note along with five presents. He picked the note up first.

> Dear Kevin
> Sorry I've had to revert to a note, especially on Christmas Day, Happy Christmas darling. Please pass on the same to Jane and Alexis and of course Snowy and Sooty. I wouldn't have gone if it wasn't so urgent but it was. Darling I know you can cope with tomorrow and then your party. I will be back for New Years Eve but won't have time to catch up with you before you depart for your party.
> I can't believe I've had to do this but one day I'm sure you'll understand. There are presents on the bed for you, Jane, Alexis, Snowy and Sooty. Please just tell them I'm ok and will be back soon.
> All my Love
> Mum xxxx

He served at four o' clock and had a few wines but was in bed by eight o' clock. Tomorrow was a big day and he needed to be ready. Sooty and Snowy joined him.

26th December 1999

He opened the place up at four and was pleased to see Michael, James, Anthony, Heston and even Brian in five minutes after him. Judy and the bar and waitress team were in ten minutes later. Kevin held a team briefing and delivered what he thought was the required level of communication to his team.

'Right Guys, no one got any objections to the Male phrase? Good it's easier in the pressured environment we've put ourselves in to keep things simple. This is the real deal all of you and the first of many successful nights at Julie's. You and I will always be known as the original team. If this brand goes where I think it will that will only be good for all of us.

Tonight isn't going to be a walk in the park, one hundred covers coming in between seven and nine. This is the start and will be bloody tough. Once we've mastered this though we challenge ourselves for two covers an evening, that's two hundred, or six hundred dishes over an evening. This isn't for the faint hearted. What I will say though is the group we have become in such a short space of time is probably the only group I could imagine that can deliver it. Go to it guys!'

Preparation was completed by twelve and Kevin sent everyone home for a few hours break but asked that they be back at five o' clock. He was back at the restaurant at three. He decided tonight he would help Judy at the head of house but be on standby if he was needed in the kitchen.

The whole team arrived back in at four. 'Guys, we said five!' Kevin said but smiled and hugged each one of them. He split himself and Judy to do pre start briefings. He took the kitchen she took the front of house.

By six o' clock they were all ready and Kevin opened the doors. Julie's official opening night! By ten-past six there were already twenty guests there, all seeming to want to have a look around. Kevin had a small pad and told Judy he would tell her who was free and who wasn't. 'Will you remember Kevin?' 'You bet Judy, it's our profits now.' 'Then I'll remember too Kevin.' 'I thought you might say that.'

Oliver and Jude arrived with Richard, Barry, Jane and Alexis. They were followed in by Jack and Katie and Kevin couldn't quite believe it had Lewis and Bruno with them. Next up Kevin saw Mary, Suzanne, a male companion of hers he didn't know, then Steve, Deb and Jamie and couldn't resist hugging them all as they came in. The rest of his invited guests weren't far behind either.

He checked in the kitchen and told the guys everyone was in so this was it, orders could be coming faster than they'd practiced. 'Do you need me to pitch in?' He asked aloud to the group. Michael answered 'No boss, we've got it.'

Smiling he went back into the restaurant and started to socialize. He made sure he spent more time with the non famous guests to make them feel important. Judy gave him a wink and thumbs up. He still managed to check above every other dish that hit the pass.

By the time ten o' clock came everyone had eaten and most were staying behind drinking and chatting. He wasn't sure how much he'd drunk but the red wines had been flowing all night. He spent a good twenty minutes with Pete and Tesh and thanked them for all their help. Pete said he wanted another go at Jack. 'Ok mate, just not tonight yeah?' Pete laughed and said 'Ok, but the big fella's going down Kev, big time down.' Kevin nodded and laughed, then realized he'd have to cook for the gannets again.

He spent half an hour with Mary and the guys, they couldn't believe the place or the food, this made Kevin's night. 'Remember your first cooking attempt Kevin?' Mary asked. 'Do I ever, and you and your pants down darling.' They shared a laugh the rest of the table didn't get.

His last but one table was Oliver, Richard, Alexis and Jane's. He sat down, hugged everyone but looked at Oliver first 'And?' 'Kevin me old mucker, we're going to be rich, and the sign is inspirational, especially the way it's lit up.' He hugged Kevin and then Kevin looked right into Richard's eyes. 'Richard?' 'Well put it this way Kevin, Barry wants' to bloody well marry you, he'll have to beat me though, God it was that good!' Kevin hugged Richard and then Barry, Jude and then his best friends, Jane and Alexis. They looked at him and blew kisses as he moved on.

Next and finally he went to Jack and Katie who were sat with Lewis and Bruno. He kissed Katie and hugged Jack. 'Hi Bruno hi Lewis' he said as he joined them at their table. Jack threw him a Cuban and said 'Deserved mate that was top stuff. I had to eat two mains but apart from that . . . !' At twelve most of the guests had gone. The guys had cleaned down. Katie, Jack, Alexis, Jane, Pete, Tesh, Richard, Barry and Oliver and Jude were left. Kevin opened more champagne and called all the staff together in the kitchen for a drink. He handed all of them envelopes with cheques with their bonuses in.

'Guys to say that was a success is vastly understated. It was nailed on fucking brilliance! Every single one of you was fantastic. Well done, give each other a huge round of applause. Guys, that's the standard we meet here, anything short and we'll fail. Enjoy tonight though and be ready for tomorrow. I can't be here for a week or so, so Judy is not only in charge but has my backing for anything she wants to do. Come out into the restaurant with me and meet some of my very best friends. Stay as long or as short as you like but remember we are open again tomorrow.'

Kevin left with Jane, Richard and Barry. Alexis took Jack, Katie, Oliver and Jude. Pete and Tesh grabbed a taxi back to his mums by two o' clock. They all sat up talking and drinking silly strong vodka's until five. Kevin managed to get into his bed with Snowy and Sooty and sleep hit him like a truncheon blow over the head had knocked him out.

....

27th December 1999

Oliver and Jude left at two-thirty, Richard and Barry at three and Pete and Tesh at five. The rest of them sat down at five-thirty and Katie dared Kevin and Jack to have hair of the dog. Kevin bit, much to Alexis's delight and downed a strong orange juice scared vodka. Jack followed suit and Katie eventually joined the boys.

Jane and Alexis served a stir fry at eight, Jack having three plates of it. Jane took Alexis to bed. Katie went at eight-thirty and Jack fell asleep on the sofa. Kevin though had other things to do. He dialed his mum's mobile first, bloody answer phone. He left a message telling her he missed her and wanted to know if she was ok.

> Well hello Peeps
> Please tell me what day it is? No. Well I'll tell yous lot. It's the twenty seventh of December Nineteen Ninety Nine Dudesters, that's how many days to go? Yous not getting it Peeps, it's only bloody well three, count them yous lot, three days to go.
> Guys and Gals, this is it, we're nearly there and I promise and I mean promise this is going to rock Dudesters. I will say

hello before we party but need to be planning now Peeps. The final details! Happy Christmas and very happy times with yous and your loved ones but remember folks this is the party we're going to party like it's Nineteen Ninety Nine!

Hitting some more strong vodka Kevin sat for an hour and a half with three Bensons as Jack snored away and rang Judy at ten-thirty. She told them they'd done one hundred and ten covers and there was nothing but compliments from the guests. Putting the phone down he realized he'd done it, somehow, with all the help he'd bloody well done it. Now though all he could think of was sleep and he fell asleep where he sat.

···

28th December 1999

Kevin woke and went into town. He'd promised Pete another crack at Jack and tonight was the only real option. It had to be a mixed grill. He could please the girls and give Pete and Jack an un-finishable plate. Popping into the Bluebell for a quick pint with the lads he got home at four. He asked Jane, Alexis and Katie to meet him in the kitchen at five. Jack gave him a suspicious look but Kevin waved him away. 'Right ladies, tonight is an eating competition, sorry Katie but Jack stuffed Pete last time so it's a rematch. Pete's demands, don't blame me.'

Pete arrived looking bullish at eight. Jack told Pete he was going down but Pete shrugged and said 'Bring it on big guy.' Kevin had snacked so was happy with his Chablis. Kevin delivered each of them a twelve ounce T bone, an eight ounce lamb rump, three pork belly slices, two chicken thighs, a duck breast, a six ounce gammon steak, veal steak, four sausages and two fried black puddings. He served it with chips, three eggs and a really spicy chili sauce.

It didn't fit on one plate so each of them had two plates each. Kevin and the rest of them watched as the two mad idiots started to eat. An hour later they'd both finished all of the food on their two plates. Pete looked at Jack and said 'Draw?' 'Not unless you're giving up Pete, Kevin is there any more?'

29ᵗʰ December 1999

Kevin said he needed to go to work and would be as quick as he could. He arrived at Julie's at four, Judy hugged him as he went in. 'Kevin last night was brilliant, it's such a shame you couldn't be here.' 'I know, a couple more days and I'll be around a bit more, trust me.'

'Guys, look, you have tonight and tomorrow to keep it going but we are not opening New Years Eve, you're all welcome to the party I've planned for the last twelve months. We reopen Friday the seventh of January. You'll all be paid your full shifts and no holidays taken from your entitlement. It's a little extra present from me for all of your efforts. We will all need to be in on the sixth as we will go for two covers from the seventh onwards.'

He got back home and sat with Jack and Katie and lit a Benson. 'God this has been a busy few days.' He said drawing his first pull. Jack looked at him and said 'Kevin, you've nailed it, like you've nailed everything since I've known you.' 'Thanks mate I appreciate it, how are you feeling anyway?' 'Hungry mate, what's for dinner?' Katie shrugged and said 'this is what I live with all the time Kevin.'

Kevin went into the kitchen and prepared for a chicken balti. He knew he could do this quickly enough, he needed an early night tonight. He served food at eight o' clock. Curry, sticky rice and homemade chutney and onion bhaji. Jack loved it, Jane and Alexis seemed to be fighting with him over extra portions and Katie was in stitches but said she loved it too. Despite feeling tired Kevin had to post a last but one message on his blog.

Hi Nearly Party Peeps

Kevster here and on the crest of a wave, riding the tide, living the life and rocking and rolling yous lot. Tomorrow is the day before the Party of Nineteen Ninety Nine. One day to go Dudesters. Can yous all believe we are nearly there, nearly together, nearly having the time of our lives? Well if yous lot can I can't quite get it into my dull head but you Guys and Gals its happening. Let me here you say. P.A.R.T.Y . . .

I will of course post a note to yous all tomorrow and then see yous lot less than twenty four hours later. Don't forget Peeps, this will and I mean will be the party of the Millennium. Nothing can stop us now, ain't no mountain high enough, if yous catch my drift. Night Peeps, sleep well and be ready, oh so ready.

....

30th December 1999

Kevin and Katie took Snowy and Sooty out. 'Kevin. You know Jack now considers you one of his best friends don't you?' 'The feeling's mutual, for him, you and the kids.' 'I know that, it's easy to see, there's something I'd like to tell you though.'

Kevin looked at her expectantly and a little worriedly. 'Katie, come on don't leave it there, you're making me panic.' 'Sorry Kevin, look Jack had a brother just like you who died when he was thirty.' 'Katie, he never said.' 'I know, he doesn't and won't but he connected with you like you couldn't believe Kevin. If he lost you as a friend he'd go backwards.' 'Katie, God now, more than ever I have the opportunity to move more, I'd like to think of you lot as family as well. Jack, perhaps the brother I never had.' Katie hugged him for over five minutes. They agreed a pact to see each other four times a year and wiped the tears from each other's eyes.

Before he got too smashed he told everyone he had to make the final update on his blog page for the party people.

Good Evening Party Peeps

The last update of the year is here! Can yous lot believe we've got here? Well the Kevster can, the Kevster knew this was possible but yous lot have made it real. Remember you Dudesters this has to be the biggest party we've all been to so I need all of yous to have your drinking shoes on tomorrow Guys and Gals. We will be the best this Island can offer, that I promise yous all. Peeps we are at the eve of something we will all remember for the rest of our lives. Please, please come with yous biggest party heads yous ever had. If the world does blow up at least you can say I was there! Biggest Julie lovin hugs ever.

31ˢᵗ December 1999

They were up and at Vanessa's by ten. Kevin yawned but Jack told him he needed his business head for the next few hours. After slapping himself Kevin got to it. The caterers arrived at eleven, Richard's security team at eleven-thirty and by twelve they were ready.

By two the guests started to not just arrive but pour in, in droves and droves. Kevin tried to greet all of them as they came in but wasn't as successful as he'd hoped. By four the place was jumping.

'My party Peeps, welcome, welcome all of yous, well Peeps, we've got food next, all courtesy of the Kevster and before the buses come to take us at eight-thirty Peeps, only the Gramophonic's.'

Chants of Kevster, Kevster, Kevster echoed on for a few minutes. 'Thank yous, all of yous but we've got the next and best part of the next part of the night Peeps. Ok Peeps here they are, all for yous and no one else tonight, all courtesy of the Kevster, let me here you give it to Gramophonic's . . . !'

Kevin jumped back on the mike after the applause had settled down and announced. 'The coaches have arrived. We're on our way to Cardiff. Let me here you say P.A.R.T.Y . . . Everyone the coaches leave Cardiff at two in the morning. Not on the coach, no lift back, well no free lift anyway!'

They were all off by nine ten and in the centre of Cardiff by ten o' clock. Kevin got out of his bus with Pete, Tesh, Jack and Katie. He grabbed Richie the head of security and said 'Five bottles, no make it ten of champagne.'

Kevin handed each of them two bottles apiece and said 'Come on guys lets party.' There were shows and people galore but it was cold and it was raining. They met a gang of Kiwi's. Flossy, Craig and Big Marty were the names Kevin remembered and stood chatting and sharing drinks with them. Big Marty had a bottle of something from the Caribbean that was seventy percent alcohol and enjoyed daring anyone to try it.

The main party crowd was watching Big Marty, Craig and Flossy do the New Zealand Hakka. A crowd of about three hundred gathered to watch and the guys absolutely got it bang on.

Craig challenged Pete to a competition. Pete accepted without knowing what it was. Craig said real men didn't feel the cold so if they took their tops off the first one to give in and put his top back on wasn't a man as much as the one who kept it off the longest.

Pete said he was having a bit of that, Jack then jumped in. 'If Pete's in. I'm in.' The three of them took off their tops just before midnight. The Auld Lang Syne tradition took over at the bell for the year two thousand in Cardiff. The world hadn't blown up and Kevin was relieved, perhaps he could do it all again next year? The boys celebrated but Kevin could see the effects of the cold kicking in.

By one o' clock Jack and Craig were shivering, Pete was laughing and calling them Canadian and Kiwi Pussy's. At half-one Craig was shaking violently but Pete and Jack, Jack seeming to get a second lease of life still stood strong. Craig relented at quarter to two and Pete and Jack just looked at each other. 'I won't give in Pete.' 'Me neither Jack.' At two o' clock Katie jumped in. 'Right that's it the two of you. You draw and if you argue I'll pinch your freezing nipples until you squeal like baby pigs.' They didn't argue to that!

Following hugs and good-byes Kevin grabbed who was with him back to the buses. He had said two and he'd meant it.

To his huge surprise Kevin reckoned ninety nine percent of his guests were there to get on the coaches. He didn't count now but told the drivers to depart at ten past. The coaches pulled into Vanessa's at around three, the bar Marquees were still open, something Kevin had pre arranged.

Kevin got into his sleeping bag at four and alongside him were Jack, Katie, Pete and Tesh. Jack said 'Kevin that was the party of Nineteen Ninety Nine. And my opinion the best one of the Millennium' 'Thanks Jack' Kevin said as his eyelids gave way.

....

01st January 2000

Everyone was having breakfast. Kevin joined them and had a full fry up breakfast but by seven o'clock was back in his sleeping bag. Jack woke him at eleven and said they needed to get going.

They spent another couple of hours greeting whoever was left before finding Pete and Tesh.

They left Vanessa's at three after Kevin had said goodbye to everyone and checked with Vanessa that she was happy no damage had been caused. He drove but felt empty. It was all over, all gone, no more party planning and he felt a sense of loss. They parked and got out of the car. Sooty came running to Kevin and was doing a jig Kevin hadn't seen him do since he was a puppy.

He hugged his dog and gave him a huge kiss on the cheek, Snowy came running out soon after and again seemed more excited than Kevin could ever remember. He was still tired and wanted to go back to bed but as he walked into the hall something hit him like a bolt out of the blue and saw something that couldn't be real! Claire was walking towards him but Claire wasn't Claire as he remembered, Claire was pretty well fucking pregnant!

'Claire, you're here,' 'Yes Kevin.' 'But how, why, I mean wow, but Claire you, I mean, you're pregnant!' 'Yes Kevin, it will be our son. I'd like to call him Clarke, you know like a Super Hero that no one knows.' He looked at her dumfounded 'Claire, you want me, I would drop everything I own to be with you, I love you with all my heart and will do for eternity.' Can you prove it Kevin?' 'How Claire, whatever it takes.' 'Kevin, will you marry me?' 'Yes Claire but what about your house, what about Paul?' 'Well Paul's the easy part the divorce came through before Christmas. He didn't get anything, he thought you might go after him again and was frightened off. The house, well it's on the market Kevin. I don't need it anymore.'

Kevin looked at her 'Claire but it's a mansion.' 'Yes Kevin and one I'll get quite a few million for.' 'Oh Claire I can't believe this, two thousand is going to be the best year ever. Claire can we go and buy you a ring? You need to have a ring.' 'Calm down Kevin, yes we can have a look but when the guests have gone.' 'Oh God yeah, come on we need to go and tell them.' He said with the biggest smile that had ever crossed his face.

They walked into the lounge and Felicity, Jane, Alexis, Jack and Katie all had congratulations banners and Jane shouted 'P.A.R.T.Y ... !'

Lightning Source UK Ltd.
Milton Keynes UK
UKOW050852020212

186518UK00001B/15/P